From the Author of
THE THORN BIRDS
The 8½-Million-Copy International Bestseller

NOW COMES HER UNFORGETTABLE STORY OF SACRIFICE AND LOVE
Over 5 months on National Bestseller Lists

"AN INDECENT OBSESSION IS TAUT AND REALISTIC . . .
A story about strength and weakness and the difficulty of balancing the two when you are in love."
Glamour

"A THOUGHTFUL, INTELLIGENT TALE OF LOVE AND HUMAN RESPONSIBILITY"
Chicago Sun-Times

"MISS McCULLOUGH IS A NATURAL STORYTELLER,
more than merely clever at getting up a head of emotional steam . . . Her characters are immediately present."
The New York Times

"COLLEEN McCULLOUGH IS ABLE TO MAKE THE READER CARE."
The New York Times Book Review

Other Avon Books by
Colleen McCullough

THE THORN BIRDS

Avon Books are available at special quantity discounts for bulk purchases for sales promotions, premiums, fund raising or educational use. Special books, or book excerpts, can also be created to fit specific needs.

For details write or telephone the office of the Director of Special Markets, Avon Books, 959 8th Avenue, New York, New York 10019, 212-262-3361.

AN INDECENT OBSESSION

COLLEEN McCULLOUGH

 AVON
PUBLISHERS OF BARD, CAMELOT, DISCUS AND FLARE BOOKS

AVON BOOKS
A division of
The Hearst Corporation
959 Eighth Avenue
New York, New York, 10019

The Harper & Row Publishers, Inc. edition contains the
following Library of Congress Cataloging in Publication Data:

McCullough, Colleen
  An indecent obsession.
  1. Title.
PR9619.3.M3215   1981   823   81-47547
                                                   AACR2

First Avon Printing, October, 1982

for
"baby sister"
Mary Nargi Bolk

I am grateful to Colonel R. G. Reeves, Austrailian Staff Corps (Ret.), Mrs. Alma Critchely, and Sister Nora Spalding for their generous technical help.

—CMcC

PART 1

1

The young soldier stood looking doubtfully up at the unlabelled entrance to ward X, his kit bag lowered to the ground while he assessed the possibility that this was indeed his ultimate destination. The last ward in the compound, they had said, pointing him gratefully off down a path because they were busy and he had indicated he could find his own way. Everything save the armaments his battalion gunsmith had taken from him only yesterday was disposed about his person, a burden with which he was so familiar he didn't notice it. Well, this was the last building, all right, but if it was a ward it was much smaller than the ones he had passed along his way. Much quieter, too. A troppo ward. What a way to end the war! Not that it mattered how it ended. Only that it did end.

Watching him undetected through her office window, Sister Honour Langtry gazed down neatly divided between irritation and fascination. Irritation because he had been foisted on her at a stage when she had confidently expected no further admissions, and because she knew his advent would upset the delicate balance within ward X, however minutely; fascination because he represented an unknown whom she would have to learn to know. *Wilson, M. E. J.*

He was a sergeant from an illustrious battalion of an illustrious division; above the line of the pocket over his left breast he wore the red-blue-red ribbon of the Distinguished Conduct Medal, most prestigious and infrequently awarded, together with the ribbons of the 1939–1945 Star, the Africa Star without an 8, and the Pacific Star; the almost white-looking puggaree around his hat was a relic of the Middle East and bore a

3

grey-bordered divisional color patch. He was wearing faded greens neatly laundered and pressed, his slouch hat was at the regulation angle, chin strap in place, and the brass of his buckles shone. Not very tall, but hard-looking, the skin of his throat and arms burned dark as teak. He'd had a long war, this one, and looking at him, Sister Langtry couldn't begin to guess why he was scheduled for ward X. There was a subtle aimlessness about him, perhaps, as of a man normally well accustomed to knowing his direction suddenly finding his feet pointing down an utterly unfamiliar path. But that any man coming to any new place might feel. Of the more usual signs—confusion, disorientation, disturbances of comportment or behavior—there were none. In fact, she concluded, he looked absolutely normal, and that in itself was abnormal for ward X.

Suddenly he decided it was time to act, swung his kit bag off the ground and set foot on the long ramp which led up to the front door. At precisely the same moment Sister Langtry walked round her desk and out of her office into the corridor. They met just inside the fly-curtain, almost perfectly synchronized. Some wag long since recovered and gone back to his battalion had made the fly-curtain out of beer bottle caps knotted on endless yards of fishing line, so that instead of tinkling musically like Chinese glass beads, it clashed tinnily. They met therefore amid a discord.

"Hello, Sergeant, I'm Sister Langtry," she said, her smile welcoming him into the world of ward X, which was her world. But the apprehensive irritation still simmered beneath the surface of her smile, and showed in the quick peremptory demanding of her hand for his papers, which she had seen were unsealed. Those fools in admissions! He'd probably stopped somewhere and read them.

Without fuss he had managed to shed sufficient of his gear to salute her, then removed his hat and gave her the envelope containing his papers without demur. "I'm sorry, Sister," he said. "I didn't have to read them to know what's in them."

4

Turning a little, she flicked the papers expertly through her office door to land on her desk. There; that should inform him she wasn't going to expect him to stand like a block of wood in front of her while she delved into his privacy. Time enough to read the official story later; now was the time to put him at his ease.

"Wilson, M. E. J.?" she asked, liking his calmness.

"Wilson, Michael Edward John," he said, a tiny smile of answered liking in his eyes.

"Are you called Michael?"

"Michael or Mike, it doesn't matter which."

He owned himself, or so it seemed; certainly there was no obvious erosion of self-confidence. Dear God, she thought, let the others accept him easily!

"Where did you spring from?" she asked.

"Oh, further up," he answered vaguely.

"Come on, Sergeant, the war's over! There's no need for secrecy now. Borneo, I presume, but which bit? Brunei? Balikpapan? Tarakan?"

"Balikpapan."

"You couldn't have timed the hour of your arrival better," she said cheerfully, and walked ahead of him down the short corridor which opened into the main ward. "The evening meal's due shortly, and the kai's not bad here."

Ward X had been thrown together from the bits left over, parked like an afterthought down on the perimeter of the compound, never intended as housing for patients requiring complex medical care. When full it could hold ten beds comfortably, twelve or fourteen at a pinch, besides what beds could be fitted on the verandah. Rectangular in shape, it was built of unlined ship-lapped timber painted a shade of pale brown the men called baby-cack, and it had a hardwood plank floor. The windows might more accurately have been termed large apertures, unglazed, with wooden louvers to shut out the weather. The roof was unlined palm thatch.

There were only five beds in the main ward room at

5

the moment, four down one wall in proper hospital rank, the fifth oddly out of place, for it lay on its own against the opposite wall and along it rather than at right angles to it, in contravention of hospital regulations.

They were drab low cots, each neatly made up, no blankets or counterpanes in this steamy latitude, just a bottom and a top sheet of unbleached calico long gone whiter than old bones from hard use in the laundry. Six feet above the head of each bed was a ring rather like a basketball hoop, yards of jungle-green mosquito netting attached to it and draped with a style and a complication worthy of Jacques Fath at his best. Beside each bed sat an old tin locker.

"You can dump your kit on that bed there," said Sister Langtry, pointing to the end bed in the row of four, the one nearest to the far wall, and so with louvered openings along one side of it as well as behind. A good bed for catching the breeze. "Stow everything away later," she added. "There are five other men in X, and I'd like you them before dinner arrives."

Michael placed his hat on the pillow, the various components of his kit on the bed, then turned toward her. Opposite his bed was an area of ward completely fenced off by a series of screens, as if behind it lay some mysterious dying; but calmly beckoning him to follow, Sister Langtry slipped with the ease of long practice between two of the screens. No mystery, no dying. Just a long narrow refectory table with a bench drawn up along either side, and at its head one fairly comfortable-looking chair.

Beyond was a door leading out onto the verandah, which was tacked like a showy petticoat down one side of the ward building, ten feet wide and thirty-six feet long. There were bamboo blinds below the eaves to keep out the weather when it rained, but at the moment they were all rolled up out of the way. A post-and-rail fence formed a balustrade, slightly less than waist high. The floor was hardwood like the ward, and rolled with

6

a hollow drum sound at the beat of Michael's booted steps. Four beds were lined up against the ward wall, rather close together, but the rest of the verandah was furnished with a motley collection of chairs. A longer twin of the refectory table within the ward was standing near the door, benches down either side; quite a few of the chairs were scattered nearby, as if this part of the verandah was a favorite spot to sit. The ward wall consisted mostly of louvered apertures, wooden slats fully opened to permit whatever breeze there was full entry to the interior, for though the verandah was on the monsoon lee of the hut, it also happened to be the side of the southeast trades.

The day was dying, but not yet spent of its last breath; pools of soft gold and indigo shadows dappled the compound beyond the verandah railing. A great black thunderhead swimming in bruised light sat down on the tops of the coconut palms, stiffening and gilding them to the panoply of Balinese dancers. The air glittered and moved with a languid drifting of dust motes, so that it seemed a world sunk to the bottom of a sun-struck sea. The bright banded rib cage of a rainbow soared upward, a crutch for the vault of the sky, but was cruelly smeared out of existence in mid-arch. The butterflies were going, the night moths coming, and met, and passed each other without acknowledgment, no more than silent flickering ghosts. A chiming and a clear joyous trilling of many birds came from the cages of the palm fronds.

Oh, God, here goes, thought Sister Langtry, preceding Sergeant Michael Wilson out onto the verandah. I never know what they're going to be like, because whatever rationale they obey is beyond all save my instincts, and how galling that is. Somewhere inside me is a sense or a gift that understands them, yet my thinking mind can never manage to grasp what it is.

She had informed them half an hour ago there was a new patient coming, and felt their uneasiness. Though she had expected it; they always regarded a newcomer

7

as a threat, and until they got used to him, readjusted the balance of their world, they usually resented him. And this reaction was in direct proportion to the newcomer's state when he arrived; the more of her time he took away from them, the deeper their resentment. Eventually things righted themselves, for he would slide from new hand to old hand, but until he did her life was bound to be hard.

Four men sat around or near the refectory table, all save one shirtless; a fifth man lay full-length on the nearest of the beds, reading a book.

Only one of them rose at the intrusion: a tall, thin fellow in his middle to late thirties, fair and bleached fairer by the sun, blue-eyed, dressed in a faded khaki bush jacket with a cloth belt, long straight trousers and desert boots. His epaulettes carried the three bronze pips of a captain. The courtesy he manifested in rising seemed natural to him, but it extended only to Sister Langtry, at whom he smiled in a way that excluded the man at her side, the newcomer.

The first thing Michael noticed about them was the way in which they looked at Sister Langtry; not lovingly as much as possessively. What he found most fascinating was their refusal to look at him, though Sister Langtry had placed her hand on his arm and drawn him out of the doorway until he stood alongside her, so that not to look at him was difficult. However, they managed it, even the slight sickly lad reclining on the bed.

"Michael, I'd like you to meet Neil Parkinson," said Sister Langtry, blandly ignoring the atmosphere.

Michael's reaction was perfectly instinctive; because of the captain's pips he stiffened to rigid attention, precise as a guardsman.

The effect of his respect was more in keeping with a slap across the face.

"Oh, for Christ's sake, stuff it!" Neil Parkinson hissed. "We're all tarred with the same brush in X—there's no rank to barmy yet!"

Training stood Michael in good stead; his face showed no reaction to this gross rudeness as his pose relaxed from attention to an informal at ease. He could feel Sister Langtry tensing, for though she had dropped her hand from his arm, she stood close enough to him for her sleeve to brush against his; as if she wished in some way to support him, he thought, and deliberately moved a little away from her. This was his initiation, and he had to pass it on his own.

"Speak for yourself, Captain," said another voice. "We are not *all* tarred with the troppo brush. You can call yourself barmy if you like, but there's nothing wrong with me. They shut me in here to shut me up, for no other reason. I'm a danger to them."

Captain Parkinson moved aside to turn on the speaker, a young man lolling half naked in a chair: fluid, insolent, striking.

"And you can get stuffed too, you slimy bastard!" he said, the sudden hatred in his voice unnerving.

Time to take over, before it got out of hand, thought Sister Langtry, more annoyed than she showed. It seemed this was going to be one of their more intolerable welcomes, if any could be called a welcome. They were going to play it in a meanly minor key, the sort of behavior she found hardest to take always, for she loved them and wanted to be proud of them.

So when she spoke her tone was cool, detachedly amused, and threw, she hoped, the small clash into its tight perspective for the newcomer. "I do apologize, Michael," she said. "To repeat myself, this is Neil Parkinson. The gentleman in the chair who contributed his mite is Luce Daggett. And on the bench next to Neil is Matt Sawyer. Matt's blind, and prefers me to tell people straight away. It saves embarrassment later. In the far chair is Benedict Maynard, on the bed Nugget Jones. Gentlemen, this is our lastest recruit, Michael Wilson."

Well, that was it. He was launched. Frail human ship, frailer than most or he wouldn't be here, setting his sails into the storms and swells and calms of ward X. God help him, she thought. There doesn't look to be a thing the matter with him, but there must be. He's quiet, yes, but that seems natural to him. And there is a strength, a core of resilience quite undamaged. Which in my duration on ward X is unique.

She looked sternly from one man to another. "Don't be so touchy," she said. "Give poor Michael half a chance."

Subsiding onto the bench, Neil Parkinson laughed, and slewed himself sideways so he could keep one eye on Luce while he addressed his remarks to the latest recruit.

"Chance?" he asked. "Oh, Sis, come off it! What sort of chance do you call it to wind up in here? Ward X, this salubrious establishment in which you find yourself, Sergeant Wilson, is really limbo. Milton defined limbo as a paradise of fools, which fits us to a tee. And we wander our limbo about as much use to the world and the war as tits on a bull."

He paused to check the effect of his oratory on Michael, who still stood beside Sister Langtry: a fine young man in his full tropical uniform, his expression interested but undismayed. Normally Neil was kinder than this, and would have served as buffer between the newcomer and the other men. But Michael Wilson didn't fit the X mold. He was not uncertain, emotionally impoverished, dazed, any of the multitude of things he might have been and still fitted. Indeed, Michael Wilson looked like a hard, fit, young but veteran soldier in full possession of his wits and in no need of the concern Sister Langtry was plainly suffering on his behalf.

Ever since the news had come several days ago of the cessation of hostilities with Japan, Neil had felt the anguish of time outstripping him, of decisions not yet satisfactorily made, of strengths returning but untested. What time was left to Base Fifteen and ward X he needed, every second of it, without the disruption a new man was bound to cause.

"You don't look troppo me," he said to Michael.

"Nor to me," said Luce with a chuckle, and leaned to poke the blind man in the ribs a little too hard and viciously. "Does he look troppo to you, Matt?" he asked.

"Cut that out!" snapped Neil, his attention diverted.

Luce's chuckle became a laugh; he threw back his head and roared, a barrage of sound without amusement.

"That's *enough!*" said Sister Langtry sharply. She looked down at Neil, found nothing to help her, and then looked at each of the others in turn. But their resistance was complete, they were determined to show themselves to the new patient in prickly, squabbling disorder. At such times her impotence tormented her, yet experience had taught her never to push them too hard. Moods like this never lasted, and the worse the mood, the stronger the swing in an opposite direction was likely to be when it was over.

She finished her scansion of the group with Michael, and discovered his eyes on her intently, which was a little disquieting too, for unlike most new patients, his eyes had erected no walls to hide behind, held no rudderless plea for help; he was simply staring at her as a man might regard a charming novelty, or a pup, or some other article of great sentimental appeal but little practical value.

"Do sit down," she said to him, smiling, concealing the irritation she felt at being so dismissed. "You're probably weak at the knees by now."

He picked up immediately the fact that her comment about being weak at the knees was more a reprimand to the other men than sympathy directed at himself, which surprised her. But she got him settled in a chair facing Neil and the others, then seated herself where she could see Neil, Michael, Luce and Benedict, and leaned forward, unconsciously smoothing the grey cesarine of her uniform.

Used to focussing her attention on those among them who seemed to warrant it at any particular time, she made a mental note that Ben was beginning to look restless and distraught. Matt and Nugget had the happy knack of ignoring the bickering which was a permanent

11

thing between Neil and Luce, where Ben flinched from the discord, and if it was allowed to go on would become very distressed.

Luce's eyes, half shut, were dwelling on her with the kind of chilling sexual familiarity her whole character, upbringing and training found offensive, though since being in ward X she had learned to suppress her disgust, had become more interested in discovering just what made a man stare at her so. However, Luce was a special case of it; she had never managed to make any headway with him at all, and sometimes felt a little guilty for not trying harder. That she did not try harder she readily admitted was a consequence of the fact that during his first week in ward X he had fooled her gloriously. That she came to her senses quickly and with no harm done either to him or to herself could not mitigate her original lack of judgment. Luce had a power, and he stirred a timorousness in her which she hated to feel but had perforce to endure.

With an effort she turned her gaze away from Luce and back to Ben; what she saw in his long dark drawn face caused her to glance casually down at her watch, which she wore pinned to the breast of her uniform. "Ben, would you mind seeing what's become of the kitchen orderly, please?" she asked. "Dinner's late."

He got jerkily to his feet, nodded to her solemnly, and stalked inside.

As if the movement had triggered some other train of thought in him, Luce sat up straighter, opened his yellowish eyes fully, and let them drift to Michael. From Michael they wandered to Neil, then back to Sister Langtry, where they rested very thoughtfully, no sexuality in them now.

Sister Langtry cleared her throat. "You're wearing a lot of spaghetti, Michael. When did you join up? In the first batch?" she asked.

His hair was cut very short and glittered like pale metal; his skull was beautiful, and he had the sort of face which made an onlooker think of bones rather

12

than flesh, yet it didn't have the death's-head look of Benedict's face. There were fine lines in the skin around the eyes, and two deep lines furrowing between cheeks and nose. A man, not a boy, but the lines were premature. Single-minded sort of chap, probably. His eyes were grey, not the changeful camouflaging color of Luce's eyes, which could turn green or yellow; an ageless and remorseless grey, very still, very self-controlled, very intelligent. Sister Langtry absorbed all that in the fraction of a second it took him to draw breath to reply, unaware that every eye was fixed on her and her interest in the newcomer, even the eyes of blind Matt.

"Yes, I was in the first batch," said Michael.

Nugget completely abandoned the dog-eared nursing dictionary he had been pretending on and off to read, and turned his head sideways to stare fixedly at Michael; Neil's flexible brows rose.

"You've had a long war," said Sister Langtry. "Six years of it. How do you feel about it now?"

"I'll be glad to get out," he said, matter-of-fact.

"But you were anxious to go in the beginning."

"Yes."

"When did your feelings about it change?"

He looked at her as if he thought her question incredibly naive, but he answered courteously enough, shrugging. "It's one's duty, isn't it?"

"Oh, duty!" sneered Neil. "That most indecent of all obsessions! Ignorance got us in, and duty kept us in. I would love to see a world that raised its children to believe the first duty is to oneself."

"Well, I'm darned if I'd raise my children to believe that!" said Michael sharply.

"I'm not preaching hedonism nor advocating the total abandonment of ethics!" said Neil impatiently. "I'd just like to see the establishment of a world less prone to slaughter the flower of its manhood, that's all."

"All right, I'll grant you that and agree with you,"

13

said Michael, relaxing. "I'm sorry, I misunderstood you."

"I'm not surprised," said Luce, who never missed an opportunity to irritate Neil. "Words, words, words! Is that how you scored all your kills, Neil, by talking them to death?"

"What would you know about kills, you sideshow freak? It's not a duck shoot! They had to drag you into the army squealing like a stuck pig all the way, and then you dug yourself into a nice cushy job well behind the lines, didn't you? You make me sick!"

"Not as sick as you make me, you stuck-up bastard," snarled Luce. "One of these days I'm going to have your balls for breakfast!"

Neil's mood altered magically; his anger fell away, his eyes began to dance. "My dear old chap, it really wouldn't be worth the effort," he drawled. "You see, they're such *little* ones."

Nugget sniggered, Matt whooped, Michael laughed aloud, and Sister Langtry dipped her head suddenly downward to look desperately at her lap.

Then, composure recovered, she terminated the exchange. "Gentlemen, your language tonight is offensive," she said, cool and crisp. "Five years in the army may have improved my education, but my feelings are as fine as they ever were. When I am within earshot, you will kindly refrain from bad language." She turned to glare fiercely at Michael. "That goes for you too, Sergeant."

Michael looked at her, quite unintimidated. "Yes, Sister," he said obediently, and grinned.

The grin was so infectiously likable, so . . . *sane,* that she sparkled.

Luce got to his feet in a movement which was both naturally and artificially graceful, slid between Neil and Benedict's vacant chair, and leaned over to ruffle Michael's hair impudently. Michael made no attempt to jerk away, nor indeed showed anger, but suddenly there was a quick, guarded watchfulness about him—a

14

hint perhaps that here was someone not to be played with? wondered Sister Langtry, fascinated.

"Oh, you'll get on!" Luce said, and turned to look derisively at Neil. "I do believe you've got yourself a bit of competition, Captain Oxford University! Good! He's a late starter, but the winning post's not in sight yet, is it?"

"Push off!" said Neil violently, hands closing into fists. "Go on, damn you, push off!"

Luce got himself past Michael and Sister Langtry with a boneless sideways twist and headed for the door, where he collided with Benedict and stepped back with a gasp, as if he had been burned. He recovered quickly, lifting his lip contemptuously, but standing to one side with a bow and a flourish.

"How does it feel to be a killer of old men and little children, Ben?" he asked, then disappeared inside.

Benedict stood so starkly alone, so devastated, that for the first time since entering ward X Michael experienced a stirring of deep feeling; the look in those quenched black eyes moved him profoundly. Maybe that's because this is the first honest emotion I've seen, he thought. The poor bastard! He looks the way I feel, as if someone has switched off all the light inside.

As Benedict moved to his chair with a monklike shuffle, hands folded one on top of the other across his midriff, Michael's gaze followed, studying the dark face intently. It was so eaten away, so consumed by what went on behind it, so very pitiable. And though they were not alike, Michael found himself suddenly reminded of Colin, and he wanted so badly to help that he willed the withdrawing eyes to look back at him; when they did, he smiled.

"Don't let Luce get your goat, Ben," said Neil. "He's nothing more than a very lightweight twerp."

"He's *evil*," said Benedict, bringing the word out as if it chewed its way into utterance.

"So are we all, depending how you look at us," said Neil tranquilly.

15

Sister Langtry got up; Neil was good with Matt and Nugget, but somehow with Ben he never managed to hit the right note. "Did you find out what's happened to dinner, Ben?" she asked.

For a moment the monk became a boy; Benedict's eyes warmed and widened as they looked at Sister Langtry with unshadowed affection. "It's coming, Sis, it's coming!" he said, and grinned, grateful for the consideration which had prompted her to send him on the errand.

Her eyes on Ben were soft; then she turned away. "I'll help you get your stuff sorted out, Michael," she said, stepping inside. However, she wasn't quite finished with the group on the verandah yet. "Gentlemen, since dinner's late, I think you had better have it inside, shirts on and sleeves rolled down. Otherwise you won't beat the mossies."

Though he would rather have remained on the verandah to see what the group was like when she wasn't present, Michael took her request as an order and followed her into the ward.

His webbing, his pack and his kit bag lay on the bed. Arms folded, standing to watch him, Sister Langtry noticed the methodical ease with which he proceeded to dispose of his possessions; he commenced with the small haversack attached to his webbing and unearthed toothbrush, a grimy but precious morsel of soap, tobacco, shaving tackle, all of which he stowed neatly in the drawer of his locker.

"Did you have any idea what you were getting into?" she asked.

"Well, I've seen plenty of blokes go troppo, but it isn't the same thing as this. This is a troppo ward?"

"Yes," she said gently.

He undid the roll of his blanket and groundsheet from the top of his pack, then began to remove socks, underwear, a towel, clean shirts, trousers and shorts from the pack's interior. As he worked he spoke again. "Funny, the desert never sent a tenth as many men

16

around the bend as the jungle. Though it stands to reason, I suppose. The desert doesn't hem you in; it's a lot easier to live with."

"That's why they call it troppo . . . tropical . . . jungle." She continued to watch him. "Fill your locker with what you'll need. There's a cupboard over there the rest can go in. I've got the key, so if you need anything, just yell. . . .They're not as bad as they must seem."

"They're all right." A faint smile turned one corner of his nice mouth up. "I've been in a lot loonier places and predicaments."

"Don't you resent this?"

He straightened, holding his spare pair of boots, and looked directly at her. "The war's over, Sister. I'll be going home soon anyway, and at this stage I'm so fed up I don't much care where I wait it out." He gazed around the room. "It's better housing than camp by a long shot, and the climate's better than Borneo. I haven't slept in a decent bed in ages." One hand went up, flicked the folds of mosquito netting. "All the comforts of home, and a mum too! No, I don't resent it."

The reference to a mum stung; how dared he! Still, time would disabuse him of that impression. She went on probing. "Why don't you resent it? You should, because I'll swear you're not troppo!"

He shrugged, turned back to his kit bag, which seemed to contain as many books as items of spare clothing; he was, she had noted, a superb packer. "I suppose I've been acting under pretty senseless orders for a long time, Sister. Believe me, being sent here isn't nearly as senseless as some of the orders I've had to follow."

"Are you declaring *yourself* insane?"

He laughed soundlessly. "No, there's nothing wrong with my mind."

She felt flummoxed; for the first time in a long nursing career she really didn't know what to say next.

Then, as he reached into his kit bag again, she found a logical thing to say. "Oh, good, you've got a decent pair of sandshoes! I can't abide the sound of boots on this board floor." Her hand went out, turned over some of the books lying on the bed. Modern Americans mostly: Steinbeck, Faulkner, Hemingway. "No English writers?" she asked.

"I can't get into them," he said, and gathered the books together to stack in his locker.

That faint rebuff again; she fought an annoyance she told herself was quite natural. "Why?" she asked.

"It's a world I don't know. Besides, I haven't met any Poms to trade books with since the Middle East. We've got more in common with the Yanks."

Since her own reading background was thoroughly English and she had never opened a book by a modern American, she let the subject drop, returned to the main theme. "You said you were so fed up it didn't matter where you waited it out. Fed up with what?"

He tied the cords around his kit bag again, and picked up the emptied pack and webbing. "The whole thing," he said. "It's an indecent life."

She unfolded her arms. "You're not frightened of going home?" she asked, leading the way across to the cupboard.

"Why should I be?"

Unlocking the cupboard, she stood back to allow him to place his clobber inside. "One of the things I've noticed increasingly over the last few months in most of my men—and in my nursing colleagues too, for that matter—is a fear of going home. As if it's been so long all sense of familiarity and belonging has been lost," she said.

Finished, he straightened and turned to look at her. "In here, it probably has. This is a home of sorts, it's got some permanence to it. Are you frightened of going home too?"

She blinked. "I don't think so," she said slowly, and smiled. "You're an awkward beggar, aren't you?"

18

His answering smile was generous and bone deep. "It has been said of me before," he said.

"Let me know if there's anything you want. I go off duty in a few minutes, but I'll be back about seven."

"Thanks, Sister, but I'll be all right."

Her eyes searched his face; she nodded. "Yes, I think you will be all right," she said.

2 The orderly had arrived with dinner and was making a racket in the dayroom; instead of going straight to her office, Sister Langtry entered the dayroom, nodding to the orderly.

"What is it tonight?" she asked, removing plates from the cupboard.

The orderly sighed. "I think it's supposed to be bubble-and-squeak, Sister."

"More squeak than bubble, eh?"

"More flop than either, I'd say. But the pud's not bad, sort of dumplings in golden syrup."

"Any pud's better than none, Private. It's remarkable how much the rations have improved in the last six months."

"My word, Sister!" the orderly agreed fervently.

As she turned toward the Primus stove on which it was her habit to reheat the meal before serving it, a small movement in her office caught Sister Langtry's eyes; she put the plates down and stepped soundlessly across the corridor outside the dayroom.

Luce was standing by her desk, head bent, the unsealed envelope containing Michael's papers in his hand.

"Put that down!"

He obeyed quite causally, as if he had simply picked the envelope up in passing; if he had read them, the deed was already done, for she could see that the papers resided safely inside the envelope. But looking at Luce she could not be sure. That was the trouble with Luce: he existed on so many levels he had difficulty himself knowing which end was up; of course, that meant he was always able to assure himself he had done nothing wrong. And to look at, he was the epitome of a man who could have no need to spy or have recourse to underhand dealings. But such was not his history.

"What do you want in here, Luce?"

"A late pass," he said promptly.

"Sorry, Sergeant, you've had more than your share of late passes this month," she said coldly. "Did you read those papers?"

"Sister Langtry! As if I'd do such a thing!"

"One of these days you'll slip, and I'll be there to catch you," she said. "For the moment you can help me get the dinner on, since you're down this end of the ward."

But before she left the office she took Michael's papers and locked them away in the top drawer, cursing herself for a degree of carelessness she could not remember ever committing before, not in her entire career. She ought to have made sure the papers were under lock and key before taking Michael into the ward. Perhaps he was right; the war had gone on too long, which was why she was starting to make mistakes.

3 "For the food we are about to receive, may the good Lord make us truly thankful," said Benedict into a partial silence, and then lifted his head.

Only Luce had ignored the call to grace, eating all the way through it as if he were deaf.

The others waited until Benedict finished before picking up knives and forks to dissect the dubious messes on their plates, neither embarrassed by Benedict's prayer nor thrown off balance by Luce's irreverence. The whole ritual had long lost any novelty it might once have had, Michael concluded, finding his palate titillated by an unfamiliar cook, even if the cooking was army yet. Besides, there were luxuries here. Pudding.

To form conclusions about any new group of men had come to be a routine with him, a part of survival—and a game, too. He would bet himself imaginary sums of money on the correctness of his conclusions, preferring to do this than to acknowledge that for the last six years what he was usually actually betting was his life.

The men of ward X were a rum lot, all right, but no rummer than some other men he had known. Just men trying to get on with the other men, and succeeding about as well as most. If they were like himself, they were tired past endurance with the war, and with men, men, men. .

"Why on earth are you here in X, Mike?" asked Benedict suddenly, eyes bright.

Michael laid his spoon down, for he had finished the pudding anyway, and pulled out his tin of tobacco. "I nearly killed a bloke," he said, working a sheet of rice paper out of its folder. "I would have killed him, too, if there hadn't been enough other blokes around to stop me."

"Not one of the enemy, then, I presume?" asked Neil.

"No. The RSM in my own company."

"And that's *all?*" asked Nugget, making the most peculiar faces as he swallowed a mouthful of food.

Michael looked at him, concerned. "Here, are you all right?"

"It's just me hiatus hernia," said Nugget in a tone of fatal acceptance. "Hits me every time I swallow."

This was announced with great solemnity and the same kind of reverence Benedict had given to his little prayer; Michael noticed that the others, even Luce, simply grinned. They were fond of the little ferret-faced lad, then.

His cigarette rolled and lit, Michael leaned back, his arms behind his head because the bench offered no spinal support, and groped after what sort of men they were. It was very pleasant to be in a strange place, surrounded by strange faces; after six years in the same battalion, you knew from the smell which one of your fellow soldiers had farted.

The blind one was probably well into his thirties, didn't say much, didn't demand much. The opposite of Nugget, who was their mascot, he decided. Every company had its good luck talisman; why should ward X be different?

He wasn't going to like Luce, but then probably no one ever did like Luce. As with Nugget, there was nothing about him which suggested he had ever seen battle action. On no one would Michael have wished battle action, but the men who had seen it were different, and not in terms of courage, resolution, strength. Action couldn't manufacture these qualities if they weren't there, couldn't destroy them if they were. Its horror went far deeper than that, was far more complex. Looking death in the eye, weighing up the importance of living. Showing a man the randomness of his own death. Making a man realize how selfish he was, to thank his lucky stars the bullet had every name on it save his own. The dependence on superstition. The anguish and self-torment after each action was over because at the time a man became an animal to himself, a statistic to those in control of his military destiny. . . .

Neil was talking; Michael forced himself to listen, for Neil was a person to respect. He'd had a very long war. His garb was desert, and he bore himself like a real soldier.

". . . so as far as I can gather, we've got about eight more weeks," Neil was saying; Michael had been half listening, and understood that Neil was referring to the duration of ward X.

Fascinated, he directed his eyes from one face to another, his mind assimilating the discovery that the news of an imminent return home dismayed them. Blind Matt actually shivered in dread! They're a rum lot, all right, he thought, remembering Sister Langtry's saying they were frightened to go home.

Sister Langtry . . . It was a very long time since he had had anything to do with women, so he wasn't quite sure how he felt about her. The war had turned things topsy-turvy; he found it hard to conceive of women in authority, women with a kind of confidence he never remembered their owning before the war. For all her kindness and her interest, she was used to being the boss, and she felt no discomfort in exercising her authority over men. Nor, to give her credit, did she appear to relish that authority. No dragon, Langtry, even a young one. But he found it awkward to deal with a woman who calmly assumed they spoke the same language, thought the same thoughts; he couldn't even reassure himself he had seen more of the war than she, for it was likely that she had spent a considerable part of it under fire herself. She wore the silver pips of a captain in the nursing corps, which was a fairly high rank.

The men of ward X adored her; when she had first

led him out onto the verandah he was immediately aware of the resentment in them, the wary bristling assessment of committed owners for a potential shareholder. That reaction of theirs, he decided, was the reason for their display of crotchety lunacy. Well, they needn't worry. If Neil was right, it seemed none of them would be here long enough to be obliged to readjust the pecking order on his behalf. All he wanted was to be rid of the war, the army, every last memory of the six years coming to a close.

And though he had welcomed the idea of a transfer to Base Fifteen, he didn't relish the idea of spending the next couple of months lying idle around a ward; too much time to think, too much time to remember. He was well, he had full command of his mental faculties; he knew it, and so did the blokes who had been responsible for sending him here. But as for these poor bastards in ward X, they suffered; he could see it in their faces, hear it in their voices. In time he could come to learn why, how. In the interim it was enough to understand they were all troppo, or had been troppo. The least he could do was to make himself useful.

So when the last man had finished with his pudding, Michael rose to his feet and collected the dirty enamel dishes, then made himself familiar with the lay of the land in the dayroom.

4

At least six times a day Sister Langtry crossed the compound between the nurses' quarters and ward X, the last two of her trips being after nightfall. During the day she enjoyed the opportunity to stretch her legs, but she had never felt at ease in the dark; in childhood she had actively feared it and refused to sleep in a room without a night light, though of course she had long since cultivated sufficient self-control to be able to cope with such an idiotic, groundless terror. Still, while she walked the compound after dark she used the time to think about some concrete idea, and lit her way with an electric torch. Otherwise the shadows menaced too tangibly.

On the day of Michael Wilson's admission to X, she had left the ward when the men sat down to dinner, to walk back to the mess for her own dinner. Now, the beam of her torch projecting a steady dot of light onto the path in front of her, she was returning to X for what she regarded as the most pleasant tenure of each day, that slice of time between her own evening meal break and lights out in the ward. Tonight she particularly looked forward to it; a new patient always added interest, and sharpened her wits.

She was thinking about different kinds of pain. It seemed very long ago that she had railed at Matron because of her posting to ward X, protested angrily to that adamant lady that she had no experience with mental patients and indeed felt antagonistic toward them. At the time it had appeared as a punishment, a slap in the face from the army as all the thanks she got for those years in casualty clearing stations. That had been another life—tents, earthen floors, dust in the dry and mud in the wet, trying to keep healthy and fit for nursing duty when the

26

climate and the conditions ground one down remorse-lessly. It had been a battering ram of horror and pain, it had lasted for weeks on end and stretched across years. But the pain had been different then. Funny, you could weep your heart out over an armless man, a sticky mass of entrails spilling everywhere, a heart suddenly as cold and still as a piece of meat in an ice chest; yet they were physical *faits accomplis*. Over and done with. You patched up what you could, mourned what you could not, and proceeded to forget while you moved always onward.

Whereas the X pain was a suffering of the spirit and the mind, not understood, often derided or dismissed. She herself had regarded her posting to X as an insult to her nursing ability and her years of loyal service. She knew now why she had felt so insulted. Bodily pain, physical maiming in the course of duty, had a tendency to bring out the best in those who suffered it. It had been the heroism, the downright nobility, which had come close to breaking her during those years in casualty clearing stations. But there was nothing noble about a nervous breakdown; it was a flaw, evidence of a weakness in character.

In that frame of mind had she come to ward X, tight-lipped with resentment, almost wishing she could hate her patients. Only the completeness of her nursing ethic and the scrupulousness of her attention to duty had saved her from closing her mind against any change in her own attitude. A patient was a patient after all, a mind in need as much a reality as a body in need. Determined no one would be able to accuse her of dereliction, she got herself through the first few days on ward X.

But what turned Honour Langtry from a caring custodian into someone who cared far too much to limit her role to mere custodian was the realization that at Base Fifteen no one was interested the men in ward X. There were never very many X-type patients in a hospital like Base Fifteen, which had started off its existence much too close to the actual fighting to gear itself toward tropponess. Most of the men who wound up in ward X were transferred there from one of the other wards, like Nugget, Matt and Benedict. Severe cases of psychic disturbance were mostly shipped straight back to Australia; those who came to ward X were less disturbed, more stealthy in their symptoms. The army had few psychiatrists, none of whom were attached to places like Base Fifteen, at least in Sister Langtry's experience.

Since there was little or no real nursing for her to do, she began to apply her considerable intelligence and that boundless energy which had made her such a good medical nurse to the problem of what she called the X pain. And told herself that to recognize what the men of X suffered as a genuine pain was the beginning of a whole new nursing experience.

The X pain was travail of the mind as distinct from the brain; amorphous and insidious, it was based in abstractions. But it was no less an entity, no less the ruin of an otherwise sound organism than any physical pain or handicap. It was futile, ominous, uneasy and empty; its malaise was enormous, its effect far longer-lasting than physical hurt. And less was known about it than almost all other branches of medicine.

She discovered in herself a passionate, partisan interest in the patients who passed through ward X, was fascinated by their endless variety, and discovered, too, a talent in herself for actively helping them through the worst of their pain. Of course she had failures; being a good nurse meant one accepted that, provided one knew one had tried everything one could think of. But unschooled and ignorant though she knew herself to be, she also knew that her presence in ward X had made a great deal of difference to the well-being of most of her patients.

She had learned that the expenditure of nervous energy could be more draining by far than the most gruelling of physical work; she had learned to pace herself differently, to cultivate huge reserves of patience. And understanding. Even after she got over her mild prejudices against those "character weaknesses," she had to cope with what seemed a total self-centeredness in her patients. To someone whose adult life to date had been devoted to a busy, happy and largely altruistic selflessness, it came hard to realize that the apparent self-orientation of her patients was only evidence of lack of self. Most of what she learned was through personal experience, for there was no one to teach her, and little to read. But Honour Langtry was truly a born nurse; she battled on, stimulated, absorbed, quite in love with this different kind of nursing.

Often for far longer than she hoped or expected, there was no tangible evidence that she had reached a patient. Often the breakthrough when it came made her wonder if anything she had done personally had actually contributed. Yet she *knew* she helped. Had she doubted that for one moment, she would have wangled herself a transfer months ago.

X is a trap, she thought, and I'm in it. What's more, I enjoy being in it.

When the beam of the torch slid onto the beginning of the ramp, she turned it off and walked up its wooden length as quietly as her booted feet would permit.

Her office was the first door on the left down the corridor, a six-by-six cubbyhole which two louvered exterior walls saved from a submarine-like horror. It barely held the small table she used as a desk, her chair on one side, a visitor's chair on the other, and a small L-shaped area of plank shelving plus two lockable wooden drawers which she referred to as her filing cabinet. In the top drawer resided the paper shells of all the men who had been inmates of ward X since its inception, not very many files altogether; she had kept carbon copies of the men who had been discharged from the ward. In the second drawer she kept the few drugs Matron and Colonel Chinstrap deemed necessary for her to have on hand—oral paraldehyde and paraldehyde for injection, phenobarb, morphine, mist

APC, pot cit, milk of magnesia, mist creta et opii, castor oil, chloral hydrate, sterile water, placebos, and a large bottle of Chateau Tanunda three-star hospital brandy.

Sister Langtry took off her slouch hat, her gaiters and her army boots, and stacked them very neatly behind the door, then tucked the little wicker basket in which she carried her few personal requirements while on duty beneath her desk and put on her sandshoes. Since Base Fifteen was in an officially designated malarial zone, all personnel were obliged after dark to clothe themselves from wrists to neck to toes, which in a miserable heat made life just that bit more miserable. In actual fact, copious spraying with DDT for miles around had rendered the anopheles threat almost non-existent, but the rule about after-dark apparel still held. Some of the more emancipated nurses wore their grey bush jackets and long trousers during the day as well as after nightfall, vowing that skirts had never been so comfortable. But those like Honour Langtry who had spent most of the war in casualty clearing stations where trousers were mandatory preferred amid the relative luxury of Base Fifteen to wear a more feminine uniform when they could.

Besides, Sister Langtry had a theory. That it did her patients good to see a woman in a dress rather than in a uniform akin to their own. She also had a theory about noise, removed her own boots when she entered the ward after dark, and forbade the men to wear boots indoors.

On the wall behind the visitor's chair a collection of pencil portraits was pinned, about fifteen in all: Neil's record of the men who had passed through ward X in his time, or were still residents of ward X. When she looked up from her work she stared straight at that most revealing pictorial record; as a man moved on elsewhere his sketch was removed from the central row and placed more peripherally on the wall. At the moment there were five faces in the central row, but there was more than enough room for a sixth. The trouble was she hadn't counted on a sixth face appearing, not with time for Base Fifteen rapidly dwindling, the war over, the sound of the guns stilled. Yet today Michael had arrived, a fresh subject for Neil's piercing eye. She wondered what Neil would see in Michael, found herself looking forward to the day when the result of that eye would be pinned up opposite her.

She sat down in her chair and put her chin on her hand, staring at the central row of drawings.

They're mine, she caught herself thinking complacently, and pulled herself sharply away from that most dangerous concept. Self, she had discovered since being in X, was an unwelcome intruder, of no help to the patients. After all, she was, if not the arbiter of their final destinies, at least the fulcrum of their sojourns in X. In that lay considerable power, for the balance of X was a very delicate thing, and she was the one who stood at the point where it could tip either way, ready to shift her weight as needed. She tried always to respect her power by not using it and not dwelling upon it. But just occasionally, as now, awareness that she did possess it popped into consciousness and stared her a little too smugly in the eye. Dangerous! A good nurse should never develop a sense of mission, nor delude herself that she was the direct cause of her patients' recovery. Mental or physical, recovery came from within the patients.

Activity was what she needed. She got up, unearthed the tape which pinned her keys to the inside of her trouser pocket and pulled it through her hands until she came at the key for the top drawer, unlocked it and took out Michael's case history.

5 When Neil Parkinson came in on the echo of his knock she was getting herself settled back in her chair, the papers still unopened on the desk in front of her. He sat down in the visitor's chair and looked at her gravely. She, taking his look for granted, merely smiled and waited.

But the eyes she took for granted never gazed on her with the blinded ease of a friendly liking; they took her apart and put her back together again at each meeting, not in any lascivious sense, but as a delighted small boy might dissect the mystery of his most treasured toy. The novelty in discovering her had never left him, and he took fresh pleasure in it every evening when he came to her office to sit with her and chat in private.

Not that she was any raving beauty, or could substitute sensuality for beauty. She did have youth and the advantage of a particularly lovely skin, so clear the veins showed under it smokily, though atabrine yellow marred it now. Her features were regular, a little on the small side save for her eyes, which were the same soft brown as her hair, large and tranquil unless she was angry, when they snapped fiercely. She had a born nurse's figure, neat but sadly flat-chested, with very good legs, long, slender yet well-muscled, fine in the feet and ankles; all this the result of constant movement and much hard work. During daylight hours when she wore a dress, the white crisp folds of her nurse's veil formed a charming frame for her face; at night when trousered, she wore a slouch hat to and from duty, but went bareheaded within the ward. Her short, wavy hair she kept that way by trading off a part of her generous nurses' liquor allowance in return for a cut, shampoo and set from a QM corporal who had been a hairdresser in civilian life and did the nurses' hair upon request.

That was her surface. Underneath she was as tough as annealed metal, intelligent, very well read in a posh girls' school way, and shrewd. She had decision, she was crisp, and for all her kindness and understanding she was clinically detached in some core of her. She belonged to them, she had committed herself to them, these patients of hers, yet whatever it was that lay at the center of her being she always held back from them. Maddening, but probably a part of the secret of her attraction for Neil.

It couldn't have been easy, finding the lightest and deftest touch in dealing with soldiers to whom she was a restatement of that almot forgotten race, women. Yet she had managed it beautifully, never given one of them the slightest indication of sexual interest, romantic interest, call it what you would. Her title was Sister, they called her Sis, and that was how she always presented herself—as a sister to them, someone who was extremely fond while not willing to share all of her private self.

However, between Neil Parkinson and Honour Langtry there existed an understanding. It had never been discussed nor indeed even so much as openly mentioned, but they both knew that when the war was over and they were back on Civvy Street he would pursue his relationship with her, and she would welcome that pursuit.

They were both from the very best homes, had been brought up with an exquisite appreciation of the nuances duty scarcely began to define, so that to each of them it was inconceivable that personal matters should claim precedence over what was owed to duty. At the time they met, the war had dictated a strictly professional kind of relationship, to which they would adhere strictly; but after the war circumspection could be abandoned.

To that prospect Neil clung, looking forward to it with something more painful than eagerness; what he dreamed of was virtually the rounding out of his life, for he loved her very much. He was not as strong as she, or perhaps it was simply that his passions were more involved than hers, for he found it difficult to keep their relationship within the bounds she laid down. His minor infringements were never more than glances or remarks; the idea of touching her intimately or kissing her appalled him, for he knew were he to do so, she would send him packing on the spot, patient or no. The admission of women to wartime front conditions had been reluctant, and was largely limited to nurses; to Honour Langtry, the army had placed her in a position of trust which could not permit an emotionally draining intimate relationship with a man who was patient as well as soldier.

Yet he never doubted the existence of the unspoken understanding between them; had she not shared it, and acquiesced to it, she would have disabused him immediately, feeling it to be her duty to do so.

The only child of wealthy, socially prominent Melbourne parents, Neil Longland Parkinson had undergone the peculiar genesis of that time in that country, Australia: he had been molded into a young man more English than the English. His accent held no single trace of his Australian lineage, it was as pear-shaped and upper-crust as any accent that ever belonged to an English noble. He had gone straight from Geelong Grammar School to Oxford University in England, taken a double first in history, and since his Oxford days he had spent no more than months back in the land of his birth. It was his ambition to be a painter, so from Oxford he gravitated to Paris, and then to the Greek Peloponnese, where he settled to an interesting but undemanding life enlivened only by stormy visits from the Italian actress who functioned as his mistress but would have preferred to be his wife. Between these exhausting bouts of emotional stress he learned to speak Greek as fluently as he spoke English, French and Italian, painted frantically and thought of himself far more as an expatriate Englishman than as an Australian.

Marriage had not entered his plans, though he was aware that sooner or later it must; just as he was aware that he was postponing all decisions about the future course of his life. But to a young man not yet into his thirties there had seemed all the time in the world.

Then everything changed, suddenly, catastrophically. Even in the Greek Peloponnese murmurs of war had been sounding for some time when a letter had come from his father: a stiff, unsympathetic letter to the effect that his days of sowing wild oats were over, that he owed it to his family and his position to come home immediately, while he still could.

So he had sailed for Australia in the latter part of 1938, arriving back in a country he scarcely knew to greet parents who seemed as remote and devoid of love for him as Victorian gentry, which happened to be exactly what they were—not Queen Victoria, but the State of Victoria.

His return to Australia coincided with his thirtieth birthday, milestones which even now, over seven years later, he found hard to remember without a fresh upsurge of the awful terrors which had plagued him since last May. *His father!* That ruthless, charming, crafty, incredibly energetic old man! Why hadn't he sired a whole quiverful of sons? It didn't seem believable that he had produced only one, and late at that. Such a burden, to be Longland Parkinson's only son. To want to match, even to surpass, Longland Parkinson himself.

It was not possible, of course. Had the old man only realized it, he was himself the cause of Neil's failure to measure up. Deprived of the old man's working-class background with all its attendant bitterness and challenge, saddled with his mother's refined preciousness into the bargain, Neil knew himself defeated from the time when he became old enough to form opinions about his world.

He was into his teens before he realized that he cared

for his father a great deal more than he cared for his mother. And that in spite of his father's indifference to him, his mother's cloyingly brainless protectiveness. It had been an enormous relief to go away to boarding school, and set a pattern which he was to follow from that first term at Geelong Grammar until the day of his thirtieth birthday. Why try to struggle with a situation that was manifestly impossible? Avoid it, ignore it. His mother's money had been settled on him at the time of his majority, and was more than enough for his needs. He would live his own life, then, far from Melbourne and parents, carve his own kind of niche.

But the imminence of war had destroyed all that. Some things could not be avoided or ignored, after all.

His birthday dinner had been a splendid affair, very formal, the guest list liberally sprinkled with ladylike young debutantes his mother considered eligible contenders for marriage to her son. There were two archbishops at the board, Church of England and Roman Catholic, one minister from the state legislature and one from the federal, a fashionable medical practitioner, the British High Commissioner and the French ambassador. Naturally his mother had been responsible for all the invitations. During the meal he scarcely noticed young ladies or important personages, indeed was hardly conscious of his mother. All his attention was focussed on his father, sitting at the far end of the table, wicked blue eyes forming irreverent conclusions about most of the guests. How he could divine so accurately what was going on in his father's head Neil didn't know, but it warmed him deliciously and made him long for an opportunity to talk with the little old man who had contributed nothing to his son's appearance save the color and shape of his eyes.

Later Neil had understood the magnitude of his own immaturity at that relatively late stage in his life, but when his father had linked an arm through his as the men finally rose to join the ladies in the drawing room, he was simply absurdly pleased at the gesture.

"They can do without us," said the old man, and snorted derisively. "It'll give your mother something to complain about if we disappear."

In the library full of leather-bound books he had never opened, let alone read, Longland Parkinson settled himself into a wing chair, while his son chose to subside onto an ottoman at his feet. The room was dimly lit, but nothing could disguise the signs of hard living in the old man's seamed face, nor diminish the laceration of a gaze that was fierce, stone hard, predatory. Behind the gaze one could see an intelligence which lived quite independent of people, emotional weakness, moral shibboleths. It was then Neil translated what he felt for his father in terms of love, and wondered at his own contrariness; why choose to love someone who did not need to be loved?

"You haven't been much of a son," the old man said without rancor.

"I know."

"If I'd thought a letter would bring you home, I'd have sent it a long time ago."

Neil spread out his hands and looked at them; long, thin-fingered, smooth as a girl's, having the kind of childishness which only comes from never putting them to work that had soul-deep meaning and importance to the brain controlling them; for his painting had not meant that to him. "It wasn't your letter which brought me home," he said slowly. ·

"What was it, then? War?"

"No."

The wall sconce shining behind his father's head lit up its pink hairless dome, threw all the shadows forward onto his face, in which the eyes burned but the hard gash of a mouth remained resolutely closed.

"I'm no good," said Neil.

"No good at what?" Typical of his father, to interpret the statement dynamically rather than morally.

"I'm a rotten painter."

"How do you know?"

37

"I was told so, by someone who does know." The words began to come more easily. "I'd accumulated enough work for a major showing—somehow I always wanted to start with a bang, no single work hanging here, a couple there. Anyway, I wrote to a friend in Paris who owns the gallery I wanted for my debut, and since he rather fancied the idea of a holiday in Greece, he came down to see what I'd done. And he wasn't impressed, that's all. Very pretty, he said. Quite, quite charming, really. But no originality, no strength, no instinctive feeling for the medium. He then suggested I turn my talents to commercial art."

If the old man was moved by his son's pain he didn't show it, just sat there watching intently.

"The army," he said finally, "will do you the world of good."

"Make a man out of me, you mean."

"To do that, it would have to start on the outside and work in. I mean that what's on the inside has to have a chance to work its way out."

Neil shivered. "What if there's nothing there?"

And the old man had shrugged, smiled a small indifferent smile. "Then isn't it better to know that there's nothing there?" he asked.

Not one word had been said about his learning the family businesses; Neil had known any such discussion to be superfluous. In a way he felt his father wasn't worried about the businesses; what happened to them after his own hands relinquished control did not concern him. Longland Parkinson was as detached from generational empire building as he was from wife and son. He didn't demand that his son prove himself, felt no animosity toward a son who didn't measure up; it wasn't necessary for him to fuel his ego by demanding that his son be what he was himself, or achieve what he had achieved. No doubt when he married Neil's mother he had known what sort of progeny she was likely to throw, and not cared; in marrying her he was thumbing his nose at the very society he aspired to enter by marrying her. In this as in everything, Longland Parkinson acted to please himself, fulfill himself.

Yet as he sat watching his father, Neil had seen a fondness there, and a pity which had wounded to the heart. The old man simply didn't think Neil had it in him, and the old man was a very good judge of character.

So Neil had gone into the army, commissioned rank of course. On the outbreak of war he had been posted to an A.I.F. battalion and shipped out to North Africa, which he enjoyed immensely, feeling more at home than he had in his native country, picking up Arabic with extreme ease and generally making himself useful. He became a very capable and conscientious soldier, and turned out to have a streak of extraordinary braveness; his men liked him, his superiors liked him, and for the first time in his life he began to like himself. There *is* a bit of the old man in me after all, he told himself exultantly, looking forward to the end of the war, seeing himself returned home seasoned, honed by his experiences to a fine sharp ruthlessness which he felt his father would instantly recognize and admire. More than anything else in life, he wanted those bird-of-prey eyes to look on him as an equal.

Then came New Guinea, and after that the Islands, a kind of war far less to his taste than North Africa. It taught him that even while he had assumed his maturing process to be complete, he had really only been playing games. The jungle closed in on his soul the way the desert had freed it, drained him of exhilaration. But it strengthened him too, brought out a stubborn endurance he had not known he owned. He ceased finally to act a part, to care how he looked to others, too busy reaching into himself for the resources which would ensure survival for himself and his men.

In a fruitless, extremely bloody minor campaign early in 1945 it had all come to an end. He made a mistake, and his men paid for it. All the precious hoard of confidence crumbled immediately, disastrously. If they had only held it against him, only reviled him for it, he could have borne it better, he told himself; but everyone from the surviving men in his company to his superior officers *forgave* him! The more they told him it wasn't his fault, that no one was perfect, everyone made a blue sometimes, the more depressed he became. Having nothing to fight against, he faltered, broke down, and stopped.

In May of 1945 he was admitted to ward X. On his arrival he was weeping, so immersed in his despair that he neither knew nor cared where they put him. For several days he had been permitted to do as he pleased, and all he pleased to do was huddle inside himself, shake, weep, grieve. Then the person who had hovered greyly in the background began to intrude upon his misery, make an irritating nuisance of herself. She stuck herself onto him, bullied and even forced him to eat, refused to admit there was anything different or special about his plight, made him sit with the other patients when all he wanted to do was to shut himself inside his cubicle, gave him jobs to do, needled and poked him into talking, first about anything, then about himself, which he infinitely preferred.

Returning awareness stirred sluggishly at first, then seemed to leap. Things not directly concerning himself impinged upon him; he began to see his fellow patients, and to notice his surroundings. He started to be interested in the phenomenon of ward X, and in Sister Honour Langtry.

She had acquired a name and an identity within his mind. Not that he always liked her at first; she was too matter-of-fact and unimpressed by his uniqueness. But just as he had decided she was a typical army nurse, she began to thaw, to reveal a softness and a tenderness so alien to most of the experiences of the last few years that he would have drowned in it had she let him. She never, never did. Only when he deemed himself cured did he begin to understand how subtly she had chivvied him along.

He had not needed to be shipped to Australia for further treatment. But he wasn't shipped back to his unit, either. Apparently his CO preferred that he remain where he was; the division had been laid off active duty for the moment, so he wasn't needed.

In many ways his continued enforced rest in ward X delighted him, since it kept him near Sister Langtry, who these days treated him more as colleague than as patient, and with whom he was establishing the foundations of a relationship having nothing to do with ward X. But from the time when he considered himself cured and ready to resume duty, doubt had begun to gnaw at him. Why didn't they want him back? He found the answer for himself—because he couldn't be trusted any more, because if for some reason the war flared up again, he would not prove equal to command, more men would die.

Though everyone denied it, Neil knew that was the real reason why after almost five months he still remained a prisoner of ward X. What he couldn't yet understand was that his neurosis lingered on, showing itself chiefly as an extreme self-doubt. Had the war flared up again, he would probably have been returned on probation to duty, and would probably have done very well. Neil's tragedy was that the war really had ended, and there was no more active duty.

He leaned across to read the name on the papers lying on Sister Langtry's desk, and grimaced. "A bit of a slap in the eye, isn't it, getting him at this late date?"

"A shock, yes. A slap in the eye remains to be seen. Though he doesn't strike me as the troublesome type."

"There we agree. Very bland. He reminds me a bit of a cliché-ridden parrot."

Startled, she turned from the window to look at him; Neil wasn't usually so obtuse about men, nor so critical.

"*I* think he's quite a man," she said.

An unexpected and inexplicable irritation rushed up and out, surprising him as much as it did her. "Why,

Sister Langtry!" he exclaimed. "Are you attracted, then? I wouldn't have said he was your type at all!"

Her frown became a laugh. "Not on me, Neil! It's unworthy of you, my dear friend. You sound exactly like Luce, and that isn't a compliment. Why be so hard on the poor chap?"

"I'm just jealous," he said flippantly, and drew his cigarette case out of his pocket. It was plain heavy gold, expensive-looking, and bore his initials in one corner. No one else in the ward smoked tailor-mades, but at the moment no one else in the ward was an officer.

He flipped the case open and offered its contents to her, lighter ready in his other hand.

She sighed, but took a cigarette and held it while he lit it. "I should never, never have let you talk me into sneaking a smoke with you while I'm on duty," she said. "Matron would hang, draw and quarter me. Besides, I'm going to have to throw you out in a tick. I've got to plough through Michael's papers before Colonel Chinstrap arrives."

"Oh, God! Don't tell me we've got to put up with him tonight!"

She looked amused. "Well, actually it's me has to do any putting up with, not you."

"And what brings our stalwart chief so far down the compound after dark?"

"Michael, of course. I rang and asked him to come, because I have no instructions about Michael. I don't know why he's here in Base Fifteen or why he's been slotted into X. Personally, I'm mystified." She sighed suddenly, and stretched minutely. "Somehow it hasn't been a very nice day today."

"As far as I'm concerned, no day in X is ever a very nice one," Neil said somberly, leaning to tap his cigarette into the spent shell case she used as an ashtray. "I've been moldering in X for nearly five months, Sis. Others seem to come and go, but here I sit like a lily on a dirt tin, a permanent fixture."

And there it was, the X pain, in him and in her. So

galling to have to watch them suffer, to know she was incapable of removing the cause of their suffering, since it was rooted in their own inadequacies. She had learned painfully that the good she did them during the more acute stage of illness rarely extended to this long-drawn-out period of almost-recovery.

"You did have a bit of a breakdown, you know," she said gently, understanding how futile a comfort that must sound. And recognizing the beginning of an oft-repeated cycle of conversation, in which he would castigate himself for his weaknesses, and she would try, usually vainly, to point out that they were not necessarily weaknesses.

He snorted. "I got over my breakdown ages ago, and you know it." Extending his arms in front of him, he clenched his fists until the sinews knotted, the muscles shaped themselves into ridges, unaware that it was when she watched a small display of physical power like this that she felt a sharp jerk of attraction to him. Had he known it, he might have nerved himself to make a positive move toward cementing his relationship with her, kissed her, made love to her; but in almost all circumstances Sister Langtry's face never betrayed her thoughts.

"I may not be any good as a soldier any more," he said, "but surely there's *something* useful I could be doing somewhere! Oh, Sis, I am so terribly, terribly tired of ward X! I am not a mental patient!"

The cry moved her; their cries always did, but this man's especially. She had to lower her head and blink. "It can't be too much longer. The war is over, we'll be going home soon. I know home's not the solution you want, and I understand why you rather dread it. But try to believe me when I say you'll find your feet in seconds once the scenery changes, once you've got lots to do."

"How can I go home? There are widows and orphans at home because of me! What if I meet the widow of one of those men? I killed those men! What could I possibly say to her? What could I do?"

"You'd say and do exactly the right thing. Come on, Neil! These are just phantoms you're exploiting to torment yourself because you haven't enough to do with your time in ward X. I hate to say stop pitying yourself, but that is what you're doing."

He wasn't disposed to listen, settling into his mood with a kind of inverted pleasure. "My incompetence was directly responsible for the deaths of over twenty of my men, Sister Langtry! There's nothing phantom about their widows and orphans, I assure you," he said stiffly.

It was many weeks since she had seen him so passionately down; Michael's advent, probably. She knew better than to interpret his behavior tonight as entirely related to herself; the arrival of a new man always upset the old hands. And Michael was a special case—he wasn't leadable, wasn't the sort who would knuckle under to Neil's brand of domination. For Neil did tend to dominate the ward, to dictate its patient policy.

"You have to lose this, Neil," she said curtly. "You're a fine, good man, and you were a fine, good officer. For five years no officer did a better job. Now listen to me! It isn't even established that your mistake was what actually caused the loss of life. You're a soldier, you know how complicated any action is. And it's *done!* Your men are dead. Surely the least you owe them is to live with all your heart. What good are you doing those widows and orphans, sitting here in my office stewing, pitying not them but yourself? There's no written guarantee that life is always going to go the way we want it to. We just have to deal with it, bad as well as good. You know that! Enough's enough."

Mood visibly soaring, he grinned, reached out to take her hand, and leaned his cheek upon it. "All right, Sis, message received. I'll try to be a better boy. I don't know how you manage to do it, but I think it's more your face than what you say. You always manage to take away the pain. And if you only knew how much difference you've made to my sojourn in X. Without you—" He shrugged. "Oh, I can't imagine what X might have been like."

He said she always managed to take away the pain. But how, why? It wasn't enough to do good; her intelligence needed to know what the magic formula was, and it always eluded her.

Frowning, she sat staring across the little desk at his face, wondering whether it was prudent of her to give him the few small encouragements she had. Oh, to be able to divorce personal feelings entirely from duty! Was she in fact doing Neil more harm than good by becoming involved with him? For instance, how much of this performance had been a ploy to gain her attention? Feeling more for the man than for the patient destroyed true perspective; she would find herself running along lines of thought having more to do with the future than the present situation, when the present situation should have had her whole energy bent upon it. Admittedly there were delicious possibilities in a peacetime relationship with Neil, from experiencing his first kiss to making up her mind whether she would actually marry him, but it was wrong to dwell on that now, here. Wrong, wrong!

As a man she found him attractive, exciting, interesting. His world was much like her world, which had made their friendship logical. She liked the way he looked, his manners, his education, his family background. And she more than liked the kind of man he was—except for this perpetual, unfortunate obsession of his. When he persisted in hearkening back to that day of slaughter as if it would permanently color the rest of his life to mourning, she doubted the viability of a peacetime relationship very much. For she didn't want to spend her own emotional coin on an emotional cripple, no matter how understandable that crippling was. She wanted, *needed,* someone able to meet her as an equal, not someone who leaned on her while simultaneously he worshipped her as a goddess.

"That's what I'm here for, to take away the pain," she said lightly, and removed her hand in a way which could not hurt his feelings. Michael's papers still lay under her other hand; she picked them up. "Sorry to have to cut it short, Neil, but I do have work to do."

He got to his feet, looking down at her anxiously. "You will be down to see us later, won't you? This new admission business won't prevent that, will it?"

She glanced up, surprised. "Nothing can prevent that! Have you ever known me to miss my late cuppa in the ward?" she asked, smiling at him, then bent her head back to Michael's papers.

6 Colonel Wallace Donaldson picked his way down to the far end of the compound by the light of a torch, feeling hard done by. It really was disgraceful! In these peacetime days, with the blackout at an end, and yet the super couldn't even arrange for a little exterior lighting! In fact the bulk of the hospital lay in utter darkness, for it was uninhabited, and did not give off so much as a reflection from inside lights.

Over the last six months Base Fifteen military general hospital had shrunk pitifully in people, though not in area; like a fat man gone thin yet doomed still to go on wearing his fat man's clothes. The Americans had built it a little more than twelve months previously, but had moved on immediately, leaving it, partially unfinished and only partially furnished, to the Australians who were driving in a more westerly direction through the East Indies.

During its heyday it had managed to squeeze five hundred patients within its compound, and had kept thirty MOs plus one hundred and fifty nurses so busy that off duty was a distant dream. Now there were only half a dozen inhabited wards left. And ward X, of course, right down on the margin of the palm forest that had once yielded a small fortune in copra for its Dutch owner. Of those thirty MOs, only five general or specialist surgeons and five general or specialist physicians were left, along with a single pathologist. Barely thirty nurses flitted through the huge nurses' quarters.

As the neurologist, Colonel Donaldson had been assigned ward X when Base Fifteen passed into Australian hands; he always did inherit the handful of emotionally disturbed men who came

47

bobbing to the top of the brew, there to be skimmed off, placed in a ward X.

Before the war Colonel Donaldson had been busy setting himself up in a Macquarie Street practice, struggling to become one of the entrenched on that most prestigious but capricious of Sydney specialist medical scenes. A lucky share speculation in 1937 as the world tried to haul itself out of the Depression had given him the money to buy into a Macquarie Street address, and the big honorariums at the major hospitals were just beginning to come his way when Hitler invaded Poland. At which point everything changed; sometimes he caught himself wondering fearfully whether things could ever go back to what they were before 1939. From the vantage point of this hellhole called Base Fifteen, the last in a succession of hellholes, it didn't seem possible that anything could ever be the same again. Even he himself.

Socially his background was excellent, though during the Depression the family money reserves had dwindled alarmingly. Fortunately he had a stockbroker brother who was largely responsible for the family's recovery. Like Neil Parkinson, he spoke without a trace of an Australian accent; his school was Newington, his university Sydney, but all his postgraduate medical qualifications had been secured in England and Scotland, and he liked to think of himself as more English than Australian. Not that he was precisely *ashamed* of being Australian; more that it was better to be English.

If he had a pet hate, the woman he was on his way to see now was most certainly that pet hate. Sister Honour Langtry. A snippet, barely thirty years old if that, a professional nurse but not army trained, though he was aware she had been in the army since early 1940. The woman was an enigma; she spoke very well, was obviously very well educated and finished, and had trained as a nurse at P.A., a very good training hospital indeed. Yet she had no spit and polish, no exquisite deference, no awareness of her basically servant status. Could he have been so honest with himself, he would have admitted that she frightened him to death. He had to gird himself up mentally and spiritually to all his encounters with her, for what good it did him. She always ended in wringing his balls so brutally it would be hours before he felt himself again.

Even the fly-curtain made of beer bottle caps irritated him. Nowhere but ward X would have been permitted to keep it, but Matron, foul underbred besom though she was, trod always very carefully in X. During its early days a patient had grown tired of listening to Matron harangue Sister Langtry, and had dealt with her in a stunningly simple and effective way; he just reached out and ripped her uniform apart from collar to hem. Mad as a March hare, of course, and shipped off forthwith to Austrailia, but after that incident Matron made sure she did nothing to offend the men of ward X.

The light in the corridor revealed Colonel Wallace Donaldson to be tall, a dapper man of about fifty, with the high petechial complexion of a spirits-lover. He had a carefully tended iron-grey moustache of military proportions, though the rest of his face was perfectly shaven. His hair now that his cap was off displayed a deep groove in its oiled greyness where the edge of his cap had rested and cut into the scalp, for it was not thick hair, not springy hair. His eyes were pale blue and a little protuberant, but he still showed the lingering vestiges of a youthful handsomeness, and his figure was good, broad-shouldered, almost flat-bellied. In an impeccably tailored conservative suit he had been an imposing man; in an equally impeccably tailored uniform he looked more like a field marshal than any of the real ones did.

Sister Langtry came to receive him at once, ushered him into her office and saw him comfortably seated in the visitor's chair, though she did not sit down herself—one of her little tricks, he thought resentfully. It was the only way she could tower over him.

"I apologize for having to drag you all the way down

here, sir, but this chap"—she lifted the papers she was holding slightly—"came in today, and not having heard from you, I presumed you were unaware of his arrival."

"Sit, Sister, *sit!*" he said to her in exactly the same tone he would have used to a disobedient dog.

She dipped down into her chair without demur or change of expression, looking like a schoolboy cadet officer in her grey trousers and jacket. Round one to Sister Langtry; she had provoked him into being rude first.

She extended the papers to him silently.

"No, I don't want to look at his papers now!" he said testily. "Just tell me briefly what it's all about."

Sister Langtry gazed at him without resentment. After his first meeting with the colonel, Luce had given him a nickname—Colonel Chinstrap—and because it suited him so perfectly, it had stuck. She wondered if he knew that the entire human complement of Base Fifteen now called him Colonel Chinstrap behind his back, and decided he did not. He couldn't have ignored a derogatory nickname.

"Sergeant Michael Edward John Wilson," she said levelly, "whom I will call Michael from now on. Aged twenty-nine, in the army since the very beginning of the war, North Africa, Syria, New Guinea, the Islands. He's seen a great deal of action, but there's no evidence of mental instability due to seeing action. In fact, he's an excellent and a very brave soldier, and has been awarded the DCM. Three months ago his only close friend was killed in a rather nasty engagement with the enemy, after which he kept very much to himself."

Colonel Chinstrap heaved a huge, long-suffering sigh. "Oh, do get on with it, Sister!"

She continued without a tremor. "Michael is suspected of unsound mind following an unsavory incident in camp one week ago. A fight broke out between him and a noncommissioned officer, highly unusual behavior for both of them. Had others not been present to drag Michael away from the RSM, it appears the RSM would now be dead. Michael's only comment since the incident was that he wanted to kill the man, and would have killed him. He has repeated this often, though he won't enlarge upon it.

"When the CO tried to find out what was at the bottom of it, Michael refused to answer. However, the RSM was very vociferous. He accused Michael of making homosexual advances to him, and insisted there be a court-martial. It appears Michael's dead friend had definite homosexual leanings, but as to whether Michael himself was activly involved, opinion was strongly divided. The RSM and his followers maintained the two had been lovers, where the vast majority of men in the company maintained just as firmly that Michael's attitude toward his dead friend was that of protector and friend only.

"That battalion CO knew all three men very well, as they'd all been with the battalion a long time—Michael and the dead man since its inception, the RSM since New Guinea. And it was the CO's opinion that under no circumstances should Michael come to court-martial. He preferred to believe that Michael had suffered a temporary derangement, and ordered Michael to submit to a medical examination, the results of which indicated he was definitely of unsound mind, whatever that might mean." Her voice was noticeably sadder, sterner. "So they bunged him on a plane and sent him here. The admitting officer automatically slotted him into X."

Colonel Chinstrap pursed his lips together and watched Sister Langtry carefully. She was choosing sides again, a most regrettable habit of hers. "I'll see Sergeant Wilson in my clinic in the morning. You can walk him down there yourself, Sister." He glanced up at the meager wattage of the light bulb in a naked socket over the desk. "I'll look at his papers then. I don't know how you can read anything in this light—I certainly could not." The chair became too hard, too uncomfortable; he rolled his buttocks on it, hemmed a little, frowned fiercely. "I loathe cases with a sexual connotation!" he said suddenly.

Sister Langtry was idly holding a pencil, and her hands closed around it convulsively.

"My heart bleeds for you, sir," she said without any attempt to disguise the sarcasm. "Sergeant Wilson does not belong in X—in face, he does not belong in any hospital ward of any kind." Her voice shook, she shoved an impatient hand into the front of her hair and slightly dislocated the set of its neat brown waves. "I think it's a pretty poor show when a fight and a highly suspect accusation can break up a young man's life, already greyed because his friend had died. I keep thinking of how he must feel at this moment. As if, I'm sure, he's groping through some appalling fog he's never going to manage to find his way out of. I've talked to him, you haven't. And there is absolutely nothing wrong with him, mentally or sexually or any other way you care to think of. The medical officer responsible for his being sent here ought to be the one facing a court-martial! To deny Sergeant Wilson the opportunity to clear himself by whisking him off instead to a place like ward X is a disgrace to the army!"

As always, the colonel found himself unable to deal with this kind of adamant insolence, for normally men in the hospital positions as high as his did not encounter it. Dammit, she talked to him as if she regarded herself as his educated and intellectual equal! Perhaps their officer status was what was wrong with these army nurses, that and the high degree of autonomy they enjoyed in places like Base Fifteen. And those stupid bloody veils nurses wore didn't help, either. Only nuns ought to wear veils, only nuns ought to be addressed as sister.

"Oh, come now, Sister!" he said, holding onto his temper and trying to be reasonable. "I do agree that the circumstances are somewhat unusual, but the war's over. The young man's stay here cannot possibly be any longer than a few weeks. And he could be in worse predicaments than ward X, you know."

The pencil flipped through the air, bounced onto the corner of the desk and fell with a hollow clatter just to one side of the colonel, who sat wondering whether her aim was good or bad. Strictly speaking, she ought to be reported to Matron; as head of nursing, Matron was the only officer permitted to discipline the nursing staff. But the trouble was that since the incident of the ravished uniform, Matron held Sister Langtry in considerable awe. Lord, what a fuss there would be if he complained!

"Ward X is a limbo!" cried Sister Langtry, more angry than he had ever seen her. His curiosity began to stir; Sergeant Michael Wilson's plight had certainly had an extraordinary effect on her. It might be interesting to see him in the morning after all.

She continued, fuelling her anger on her own words. "Ward X is a limbo! The patients no one knows what else to do with are just filed under X and forgotten! You're a neurologist. I'm a general-trained nurse. Not a whisker of experience or qualification between us. Do *you* know what to do with these men? I don't, sir! I grope! I try my best, but I'm miserably aware that it's nowhere near good enough. I come on duty every single morning praying—praying that I'll manage to get through the day without crushing one of these frail and difficult people. My men in ward X deserve better than you or I can give, sir."

"That is quite enought, Sister!" he said, a purplish tinge creeping under his skin.

"Oh, but I'm not finished yet," she said, unimpressed, unswerving. "Shall we leave Sergeant Wilson entirely out of it, for example? Let's look at the other five current inmates of ward X. Matt Sawyer was transferred here from neuro when they couldn't find an organic lesion to account for his blindness. Diagnosis hysteria. You cosigned that one yourself. Nugget Jones was transferred from abdominothoracic after two NAD laparotomies and a history of driving the entire ward mad with his complaining. Diagnosis hypochondria. Neil—Captain Parkinson, that is—had a simple breakdown which one might better call grief. But his CO thinks he's protecting him, so here Neil continues to sit, month after month. Diagnosis involutional melancholia. Benedict Maynard went quite mad after his company opened fire on a village in which it turned out there were no Japanese at all, just a lot of native women and children and old men. Because he sustained a mild scalp wound at the time his mental problems began, he was admitted to neuro as a concussion, and then transferred here. Diagnosis dementia praecox. I agree with that diagnosis, as a matter of fact. But it means Ben ought to be among the experts in Australia, receiving proper care and attention. And Luce Daggett, why exactly is he here? There's no diagnosis of any kind on his papers! But we both know why he's here. Because he was living the life of Riley, blackmailing his commanding officer into letting him do precisely whatever he wanted. But they couldn't make the charge stick, and they didn't know what else to do with him except to send him to a place like X until the shooting was all over."

The colonel stumbled to his feet, crimson with suppressed rage. "You are impertinent, Sister!"

"Do I sound impertinent? I beg your pardon, sir," she said, reverting to that unruffled calm which was usually her trademark.

His hand on the door, Colonel Chinstrap paused to look at her. "Ten in the morning in my clinic for Sergeant Wilson, and don't forget to bring him yourself." His eyes glittered, he searched for something hurtful to say, a mot capable of penetrating that impregnable facade. "I do find it peculiar that Sergeant Wilson, an apparently exemplary soldier, highly decorated, consistently in the front line for six years, has managed to rise no higher in rank than sergeant."

Sister Langtry smiled sweetly. "But, sir, we can't *all* be great white chiefs! Someone has to do the dirty work."

7 After the colonel had gone, Sister Langtry sat at her desk without moving, the slightly nauseating aftermath of her anger filming her brow and upper lip with a chill perspiration. Stupid, to rail at the man like that. It did no good, it simply revealed her inner feelings to him, when she preferred he remain ignorant of them. And where was the self-control which usually carried her victorious through her encounters with Colonel Chinstrap? A waste of time to talk to that man about ward X and its victims. She couldn't ever remember being quite so angry with him. That pathetic history had started it, of course. If he had arrived a little later, given her time to get her emotions under control, she would not have lost her temper. But he had arrived scant seconds after she put Michael's papers down.

Whoever the MO was who had written up Michael's case—and she didn't connect the signature with a face in memory—was no mean stylist. As she read his notes, the people involved had come alive. Especially Michael, alive for her already. The brief encounter in the ward had triggered lots of speculations, but none had rivalled the real story. How awful for the poor chap, and how unfair! How unhappy he must be. Without realizing what she was doing, as she read the history she wove her own emotions into the story it unfolded; she grieved so for Michael in the loss of his friend that she could hardly swallow for the lump in her throat, the pain in her chest. And then enter Colonel Chinstrap, who got the lot.

Ward X is getting to me, she thought; I've committed every sin in the nursing book these last few minutes, from unwarranted emotional involvement to gross insubordination.

But it was the memory of Michael's face. He could cope, he was coping, even with the fact of his admission to ward X. Usually her griefs were for the inadequacies in her patients, yet here she was, quite overcome by the plight of a man who patently had no need of her support. There was a warning in that. One of her chief defenses against personal involvement with her patients was always to think of them as unwell, sad, frail, any condition which paled them as men. Not that she was frightened of men, or of personal involvement. Only that to give of her best, a good nurse had to remain detached. Not steeled against feeling emotion; steeled against an all-out woman-with-man relationship. It was bad enough when that happened in medical nursing, but with mentally disturbed patients it was disastrous. Neil had cost her much thought, and she still wasn't sure she had done the right thing in allowing herself to contemplate seeing him when they returned home. She had told herself it was all right because he was so very nearly well now, because the existence of ward X was finite now, and because she could still command enough control of the situation to be able to think of him as poor, sad, frail, when it became necessary.

I am only human, she thought. I have never forgotten that, never! And it is so hard.

She sighed, stretched, pushed her thoughts away from Neil, and away from Michael. It was too soon to appear in the ward; her respiration and her color hadn't returned to normal. The pencil—where had the pencil gone when she threw it at the colonel? How unbelievably dense that man could be! He didn't know how close he came to bombardment by the rear end of a six-pounder shell when he came out with that remark about Michael's lack of promotion. Where had the man been hiding for the last six years? Sister Langtry's knowledge of other armies was sketchy, but after six years of nursing Australians, she was well aware that her country at least produced quite a few very special men—men who had intelligence, the gift of command, and all the other qualities associated with army officers, but who steadfastly refused promotion above the rank of sergeant. It probably had something to do with class consciousness, though by no means in a negative sense. As if they were content where they were, couldn't see any point in acquiring additional rank. And if Michael Wilson didn't belong to that special group of men, then her experience with soldiers had led to many more than this wrong conclusion.

Hadn't anyone ever told the colonel about men like Michael? Hadn't he managed to see it for himself? Very obviously not, unless he had simply seized at a straw in order to get under her skin. Colonel bloody Chinstrap. Those vowels of his were unbelievable, even more plummily rounded than Neil's. Stupid to be so angry with him. Pity him instead. Base Fifteen was a long way from Macquarie Street after all, he was nowhere near his dotage. He wasn't bad-looking, and presumably under his pukka uniform he suffered from the same urgencies and importunities as other men. Rumor had it that he had been having an affair with Sister Heather Connolly from theatres for months. Well, most of the MOs had their little flutters, and who else was there to flutter with except the nurses? Good luck to him.

The pencil was under the far edge of the desk; she crawled under to retrieve it, put it where it belonged, and sat down again. What on earth would Heather Connolly talk to him about? Presumably they did talk. No one spent every moment with a lover in loving. As a peacetime practicing neurologist, Wallace Donaldson's great interest had been an obscure set of spinal diseases with utterly unpronounceable hyphenated names; perhaps they talked about these, and mourned the lack of obscure spinal diseases in a hospital where when spines were treated it was for the gross, final, ghastly indignities inflicted by a bullet or shrapnel. Perhaps they talked about his wife, keeping the home fires burning in Vaucluse or Bellevue Hill. Men did tend to talk about their wives to their mistresses, like discussing the merits of one friend with another while simultaneously mourning the lack of opportunity to make them known to each other. Men were always so positive their wives and mistresses would be great friends could the social rules permit it. Well, that stood to reason. To think otherwise might reflect badly on their judgment and choice of women.

Her man had done that, she remembered all too painfully. Talked to her incessantly about his wife, deplored the fact that the conventions did not permit their meeting, sure they would adore each other. After his first three descriptive sentences about his wife, Honour Langtry had known she would loathe the woman. But she had far too much good sense to say so, naturally.

What a long, long time ago that was! Time, which could not be measured in the ticking away of hours and minutes and seconds, but grew in fits and starts like a gargantuan insect shrugging itself free of successive shells, always emerging looking and feeling different into a different-looking and different-feeling world.

He had been a consulting specialist, too, at her first hospital in Sydney. Her only hospital in Sydney. A skin specialist—a very new breed of doctor. Tall, dark and handsome, in his middle thirties. Married, of course. If you didn't manage to catch a doctor while he still wore the full whites of a resident, you never caught one at all. And she had never appealed to the residents, who preferred something prettier, more vivacious, fluffier, more empty-headed. It was only in their middle thirties that they got bored with the choice of their twenties.

Honour Langtry had been a serious young woman, at the top of her nursing class. The sort there was always a bit of specualtion about as to why she chose nursing instead of medicine, even if medicine was notoriously hard going for a woman. Her background was a wealthy farming one, and her education had been acquired at one of Sydney's very best girls' boarding schools. The truth was she chose to nurse because she wanted to nurse, not understanding entirely why before she began, but understanding enough to know it was physical and emotional closeness to people that she wanted, and that in nursing she would find this. Since nursing happened to be the most admirable and lady-like of all female occupations, her parents had been pleased and relieved when she declined their offer to put her through medicine if she really wanted it.

Even as a new trainee nurse—probationers they were called—she didn't wear spectacles and she wasn't gawky or aggressive about her intelligence. Both at boarding school and at home she had pursued an active social life without any real attachment to any one young man, and during the four years of her nursing training she did much the same kind of thing—went to all the dances, was never a wallflower, met various young men for coffee in Repins or an evening at the pictures. But never with a view to serious involvement. Nursing fascinated her more.

After she graduated she was appointed to one of the female medical wards at P.A., and there she met her skin specialist, newly appointed to his honorarium. They hit it off together from the beginning, and he liked the quick way she came back at him; she realized that early on. It took her much longer to realize that she attracted him deeply as a woman. By the time she did, she was in love with him.

He borrowed the flat belonging to a bachelor lawyer friend of his in one of the tall buildings down toward the end of Elizabeth Street, and asked her to meet him there. And she had agreed knowing exactly what she was getting herself into. For he had gone to great pains to tell her, with a directness and frankness she thought wonderful. There was no possibility he would ever divorce his wife to marry her, he said, but he loved her, and he wanted an affair with her desperately.

Founded honestly, the affair foundered honestly about twelve months later. They met whenever he could manufacture an excuse, which sometimes wasn't easy; skin specialists didn't have important emergencies like general surgeons or obstetricians. As he had put it humorously, whoever heard of a skin specialist being pulled out of bed at three in the morning to minister to a critical case of acne? It was not easy for her to find the time either, for she was a mere junior sister, still in an apron, and not able to demand any preferential treatment in the rostering of time off. During the course of the affair they managed to meet as often as once a week, sometimes as little as once every three or four weeks.

It had rather tickled Honour Langtry to think of herself, not as a wife, but as a mistress. Wifehood was tame and safe. But to all mistresses clung an indefinable aura of glamour and mystery. The reality just didn't measure up, however. Their meetings were furtive and too short; it was disconcerting to discover that too much of them had to be given over to lovemaking rather than to a more intelligent form of communication. Not that she disliked the lovemaking, or deemed it an activity beneath her dignity. She learned from him quickly, was intelligent enough to modify and adapt her new knowledge so that she could continue to please him sexually, and thereby also please herself. But the little clues he offered her to the central core of himself could never be followed up satisfactorily, for there just wasn't sufficient time.

And then one day he got tired of her. He told her immediately, offering no excuses for his conduct. With quiet good manners she accepted her congé in the same spirit, put on her hat and gloves and walked out of his life. Someone who looked and felt different.

It had hurt; it had hurt very badly. And the worst hurt of all was in not really knowing why. Why it had begun for him, why he felt compelled to terminate it. In her more optimistic moments she told herself it ended because he was getting out of his depth, caring for her too deeply to be able to bear the transience of their relationship. In her more honest moments she knew that the real reason was a combination of inconvenience and the hideously trapped feeling of sameness the affair had begun to assume. In all likelihood the identical reason why he had originally embarked on the affair. And she knew there was one more reason: her own changing attitude toward him, the resentment she found it harder and harder to hide, that she meant very little more to him than someone different in his bed. To hold him enthralled forever she would have had to devote all her time and energy to him alone, as very possibly his wife did.

Well, that degree of feminine acrobatics just wasn't worth it. She had more to do with her life than devote it exclusively to pleasing a rather egotistical and selfish man. Though the great majority of women seemed to want to live that way, Honour Langtry knew it never would be her way. She didn't dislike men; she just felt it would be a mistake for her to marry one.

So she had continued to nurse, and found in it a pleasure and a satisfaction she had not genuinely found in love. In fact, she adored to nurse. She loved the fussing, the busyness, the constantly changing parade of faces, the really absorbing problems life on the ward threw at her constantly. Her good friends, and she had several, looked at each other and shook their heads. Poor Honour was badly bitten with the nursing bug, no doubt about it.

There would probably have been other love affairs, and perhaps one profound enough to cause her to change her mind about marriage. But the war intervened. Twenty-five years old, she was one of the first nurses to volunteer, and from that moment of entering army life there had been no time for thinking of herself. She had served in a succession of casualty clearing stations in North Africa, New Guinea and the Islands, which had effectively destroyed all vestiges of normality. Oh, what a life that had been! A treadmill so demanding, so fascinating, so alien that in many respects she knew nothing thereafter would ever measure up to it. They were a pretty exclusive band, the nurses on active service, and Honour Langtry belonged heart and soul to that band.

However, those years had taken their toll. Physically

she had survived better than most, for she was both tough and sensible. Mentally she had also survived better than most, but when Base Fifteen appeared in her life she greeted it with a sigh of relief. They had wanted to send her back to Australia, but she had fought that successfully, feeling that her experience and her basically sound health would be of more service to her country in a place like Base Fifteen than back in Sydney or Melbourne.

When the pressure had begun to ease about six months ago, she had time to think a little, to reassess her feelings about what she wanted to do with the remainder of her life. And began to wonder if indeed nursing back in some civilian hospital would ever satisfy her again. She also found herself thinking of a more personal, concentrated, intimate emotional life than nursing offered.

Had it not been for Luce Daggett, she might not have been in a state of readiness to respond to Neil Parkinson. When Luce was admitted, Neil was still in the worst throes of his breakdown; she thought of him in no other way than as a patient. Luce did something to her, she was still not quite sure what. But when he strolled into ward X looking so *complete,* so in command of himself and the situation in which he found himself, he took her breath away. For two days he fascinated her, attracted her, made her feel as she had not felt in years. Womanly, desirable, lovely. Being Luce, he destroyed her feeling himself, by tormenting a pathetic little private they had had at the time following a suicide attempt in camp. The discovery that he was lead rather than gold had almost caused her to resign from her nursing commission, which was a foolish overreaction, she told herself later. At the time it had seemed that big. Luckily Luce had never realized the effect he had on her; one of the few times in his life, no doubt, when he had failed to follow up an advantage. But ward X was new to him, all the faces were new, and he left his move to cement a relationship with Sister Langtry just one day too late. When he turned the full power of his

62

charm upon her, she rebuffed him stingingly, and without caring about frailty.

However, that very minor aberration in her conduct marked the commencement of a change. It may have been awareness that the war was all but won, and this bizarre life she had led for so long was going to come to an end; it may have been that Luce performed the office of a Prince Charming, and wakened Honour Langtry from a self-imposed personal sleep. But ever since, she had been unconsciously moving herself and her thoughts away from utter dedication to her duty.

So when Neil Parkinson popped out of his depression and manifested interest in her, and she saw how attractive a person he was, how attractive a man, that hitherto sturdy adherence to proper nursing detachment began to erode. She had begun in liking Neil enormously, and only now was starting to love him. He wasn't selfish, he wasn't egotistical, he admired and trusted her. And he loved her. To look forward to a life with him after the war was bliss, and the faster that life approached, the more eagerly she welcomed it.

With iron self-discipline she had never permitted herself to dwell upon Neil as a man, to look constantly at his mouth or his hands, to imagine kissing him, making love with him. She couldn't, or it would already have happened. And that would have been disastrous. Base Fifteen was no place to commence an affair one hoped would last a whole lifetime. She knew he felt the same way, or it would already have happened. And it was rather fun to walk an emotional tightrope above the rigidly suppressed wants, desires, appetites, to pretend she didn't see the passion in him at all. . . .

Startled, she saw that her watch said a quarter past nine. If she didn't get into the ward soon they would all be thinking she wasn't coming.

8 As Sister Langtry walked out of her office, down the short corridor and into the ward, she had no presentiment that the subtly poised balance of ward X was already beginning to wobble.

There was a quiet drone of conversation from behind the screens arranged opposite Michael's bed; she slipped between two of them and emerged at the refectory table. Neil was sitting on one bench at the end nearest to her chair, with Matt beside him. Benedict and Nugget sat on the opposite bench, but had left the section next to her chair vacant. She assumed her usual position at the head of the table unobtrusively, and looked at the four men.

"Where's Michael?" she asked, a tiny spurt of panic bubbling into her chest—fool, was her judgment already so distorted that she could have decided he lay in no mental peril? The war wasn't over yet, nor was ward X defunct. Normally she would never have left a new admission unobserved for so long during his first few hours in X. Was Michael going to mean bad luck? To leave his papers lying around while she talked to him—now she couldn't even guard the man himself.

She must have lost color; all four men were looking at her curiously, which meant her voice had betrayed her concern, too. Otherwise Matt could not have noticed.

"Mike's in the dayroom making tea," said Neil, producing his cigarette case and offering it to each of the other men. He would not, she knew, commit the indiscretion of offering her a cigarette outside the four walls of her office.

"It seems our latest recruit likes to make himself useful," he went on, lighting all the cigarettes from his lighter. "Cleared away the dirty plates after dinner, and helped the orderly wash them. Now he's making tea."

Her mouth felt dry, but she didn't dare add to the oddity of her reaction by trying to moisten it. "And where is Luce?" she asked.

Matt laughed silently. "He's on the prowl, just like a tomcat."

"I hope he stays out all night," said Benedict, lips twisting.

"I hope he doesn't, or he's in trouble," said Sister Langtry, and dared to swallow.

Michael brought the tea in a big old pot that had seen better days, rusting where the enamel had chipped off, and badly dented. He put it down in front of Sister Langtry, then returned to the dayroom to fetch a piece of board which functioned as a tray. On it were six chipped enamel mugs, a single bent teaspoon, an old powdered milk tin containing sugar, and a battered tin jug containing condensed milk in solution. Also on the board was a beautiful Aynsley china cup and saucer, hand-painted and gold washed, with a chased silver spoon beside it.

It amused her to note that Michael sat himself down opposite Neil at her end of the table, as if it never occurred to him that perhaps the place was being saved for Luce. Good! It would do Luce good to discover he wasn't going to have an easy mark in the new patient. But then why should Michael be bluffed or intimidated by Luce? There was nothing the matter with Michael, he didn't have the apprehensions and distorted perceptions the men of X were usually suffering on admission. No doubt to him Luce was more ridiculous than terrifying. In which case, she thought, if I am as it seems using Michael as my standard of normality, I too am a little queer, for Luce bothers me. He's bothered me ever since I came out of that early daze to discover he's some sort of moral imbecile, a psychopath. I'm frightened of him because he fooled me; I almost fell in love with him. I welcomed what seemed his normality. As I'm welcoming what seems to be Michael's normality. Am I wrong, too, in my first judgment of Michael?

"I imagine the mugs are ours and the cup and saucer belong to you, Sister," said Michael, looking at her.

She smiled. "They do indeed belong to me. They were my birthday present."

"When's your birthday?" he asked immediately.

"November."

"Then you'll be at home to celebrate the next one. How old will you be?"

Neil stiffened dangerously, so did Matt; Nugget merely looked awed, Benedict disinterested. Sister Langtry looked more caught off guard than offended, but Neil got in first, before she could answer.

"It's none of your business how old she is!" he said.

Michael blinked. "Isn't that for her to say, mate? She doesn't look old enough to make it a state secret."

"*She* is the cat's mother," said Matt. "*This* is Sister Langtry." His voice trembled with anger.

"How old will you be in November, Sister Langtry?" Michael asked, not in a spirit of defiance, but as if he thought everyone was far too touchy, and he intended to demonstrate his independence.

"I'll be thirty-one," she said easily.

"And you're not married? Not widowed?"

"No. I'm an old maid."

He laughed, shaking his head emphatically. "No, you don't have the old-maidy look," he said.

The atmosphere was darkening; they were very angry at his presumption, and at her tolerance of it. "There's a tin of bikkies in my office," she said without haste. "Any volunteers to get it?"

Michael rose immediately. "If you tell me where it is, Sister, I'd be glad to."

"Look on the shelf below the books. It's a glucose tin, but it has a label on the lid marked Biscuits. How do you take you tea?"

"Black, two sugars, thank you."

While he was gone there was absolute silence at the

table, Sister Langtry pouring the tea placidly, the men producing smoke from their cigarettes as if it were an organic offshoot of fury.

He came back bearing the tin, but instead of sitting down went around the table, offering the biscuits to each man. Four seemed to be the number each man picked out, so when he came to Matt he took four from the tin himself and placed them gently beneath one of the loose unseeking hands folded quietly on the table. Then he moved the mug of tea close enough to them for Matt to be able to locate it by the warmth it gave off. After which he sat down again next to Sister Langtry, smiling at her with an unshadowed liking and confidence she found very touching and not at all a reminder of Luce.

The other men were still silent, watchful and withdrawn, but for once she didn't notice; she was too busy smiling back at Michael and thinking how nice he was, how refreshingly devoid of the usual rich assortment of self-inflicted horrors and insecurities. She couldn't imagine he would ever use her to further his own emotional ends the way the others did.

Nugget emitted a loud groan and clutched at his belly, pushing his tea away pettishly. "Oh, God, I'm crook again! Ohhhhhhhhh, Sis, it feels like me intussusception or me diverticulitis!"

"All the more for us," said Neil unsympathetically, grabbing Nugget's tea and emptying it into his own drained mug. Then he nipped Nugget's four biscuits away and dealt them out deftly, as if he handled playing cards.

"But, Sis, I do feel crook!" Nugget mewed piteously.

"If you didn't lie on a bed all day reading medical dictionaries you'd feel a lot better," said Benedict with dour disapproval. "It's unhealthy." He grimaced, gazed around the table as if something present at it offended him deeply. "The air in here is unhealthy," he said, then got to his feet and stalked out onto the verandah.

Nugget began to groan again, doubling up.

"Poor old Nugget!" said Sister Langtry soothingly. "Look, why don't you pop down to my office and wait there for me? I'll be with you as soon as I can. If you like, you can take your pulse and count your respirations while you wait, all right?"

He got up with alacrity, clutching his belly as if its contents were about to fall out, and beaming triumphantly at the others. "See? Sis knows! She knows I'm not having you all on! It's me ulcerative colitis playing up again, I reckon." And he sped away down the ward.

"I hope it isn't serious, Sister," said Michael, concerned. "He does look sick."

"Huh!" said Neil.

"He's all right," said Sister Langtry, apparently unperturbed.

"It's only his soul that's sick," said Matt unexpectedly. "The poor little coot misses his mother. He's here because here is the only place that can put up with him, and we put up with him because of Sis. If they had any sense, they would have packed him off home to Mum two years ago. Instead, he gets backaches, headaches, gutaches and heartaches. And rots like the rest of us."

"Rot is right," said Neil moodily.

There was a tempest blowing up; they were like the winds and the clouds at this same latitude, thought Sister Langtry, eyes travelling from one face to another. All set for fair weather one moment, swirling and seething the next. What had provoked it this time? A reference to rotting?

"Well, at least we've got Sister Langtry, so it can't be all bad," said Michael cheerfully.

Neil's laughter sounded more spontaneous; maybe the storm would abort. "Bravo!" he said. "A gallant soul has arrived in our midst at last! Over to you, Sis. Refute the compliment if you can."

"Why should I want to refute it? I don't get too many compliments."

That cut Neil, but he leaned back on the bench as if perfectly relaxed. "What a plumping lie!" he said gently. "You know very well we shower you with compliments. But for that plumper, you can tell us why you're rotting in X. You must have done something."

"Yes, as a matter of fact I have. I've committed the terrible sin of liking ward X. If I didn't, nothing compels me to stay, you know."

Matt got up abruptly, as if he found something at the table suddenly unbearable, moved to its head as surely as if he could see, and rested his hand lightly on Sister Langtry's shoulder. "I'm tired, Sis, so I'll say good night. Isn't it funny? Tonight's one of those nights I almost believe that when I wake tomorrow, I'm going to be able to see again."

Michael half rose to help him through the barrier of the screens, but Neil put out a hand across the table to restrain him.

"He knows the way, lad. None better."

"More tea, Michael?" asked Sister Langtry.

He nodded, was about to say something when the screens jiggled afresh. Luce slid onto the bench beside Neil, in the place where Matt had been sitting.

"Beaut-oh! I'm in time for some tea."

"Speak of the devil," sighed Neil.

"In person," Luce agreed. He put his hands behind his head and leaned back a little, looking at the three of them through half-shut eyes. "Well, what a cozy little group this is! I see we've lost the riffraff, only the big guns are left. It's not ten o'clock yet, Sis, so there's no need to look at your watch. Are you sorry I'm not back late?"

"Not at all," said Sister Langtry calmly. "I knew you'd be back. I've never yet known you to stay out one minute past ten without a pass, or commit any other breach of regulations, for that matter."

"Well, don't sound so sad about it! It makes me think nothing would give you greater pleasure than to be able to report me to Colonel Chinstrap."

"It wouldn't give me any pleasure at all, Luce. *That* is your whole trouble, my friend. You work so darned hard at making people believe the worst of you that you literally force them to believe the worst, just to have a little peace and quiet."

Luce sighed, leaned forward to put his elbows on the table and prop his chin on his hands. Thick and waving and a little too long to meet the strict definition of short-back-and-sides, his reddish-gold hair fell forward across his brow. How absolutely perfect he is, thought Sister Langtry with a shiver of real repulsion. Perhaps he's too perfect, or the coloring is impossible to absorb. She suspected he darkened his brows and lashes, maybe plucked the one and encouraged the growth of the other, but not because of sexual inversion; purely out of overweening vanity. His eyes had a golden sheen, were very large and set well apart below the arch of those too-dark-to-be-true brows. Nose like a blade, straight, thin, flaring proudly at the nostrils. The kind of cheekbones which looked like high, purely structural supports, the flesh beneath them hollowed. Though it was far too determined to be called generous, his mouth was not thin, and had the exquisitely defined edges one usually saw only on statues.

Little wonder that he knocked me sideways when I first saw him. . . . Yet I'm no longer attracted by that face, or the height of the man, or his splendid body. Not the way I am to Neil—or to Michael, come to think of it. There's something wrong with Luce, inside; not a weakness, nor merely a flaw, but something that is *all* of him, innate and therefore ineradicable.

She turned her head slightly to look at Neil, who in any company save Luce's would pass for a handsome man. Much the same sort of features as Luce's, though far less spectacular coloring. Most handsome men looked better with the sort of lines graven into the flesh of the face Neil had; yet when those lines appeared on Luce he would change from beauty to beast. They would be the wrong lines, perhaps. Would indicate dissipation rather than experience, petulance rather than suffering. And Luce would run to fat, which Neil never would. She particularly liked Neil's eyes, a vivid blue and fringed with fairish lashes. He had the sort of brows a woman might like to stroke with one fingertip, over and over and over again, just for the sheer pleasure of it. . . .

Now Michael was quite different. He might pass for the very best of ancient Roman. Character rather than beauty, strength rather than self-indulgence. Caesarish. There was a contained singularity about him which said, I've been looking after others as well as myself for a long time now, I've been through heaven and hell, but I'm still a whole man, I still own myself. Yes, she decided; Michael was enormously attractive.

Luce was watching her. She felt it, and brought her eyes back to him, making their expression cool and aloof. She defeated him, and she knew it. Luce had never been able to discover why his charm hadn't worked on her, and she was not about to enlighten him, either about his initial impact on her, or the reasons why it had been shattered.

Tonight for a change his guard was down a bit; not that he was vulnerable, exactly, more that perhaps he would have liked to be vulnerable.

"I met a girl from home tonight," Luce announced, his chin still propped on his hands. "All the way from Woop-Woop to Base Fifteen, no less! She remembers me, too. Just as well. I didn't remember her at all. She'd changed too much." His hands fell; he assumed a high and breathlessly girlish voice, conjuring for them an image so strong Sister Langtry felt physically thrust into the middle of that encounter. "My mother did her mother's washing, she said, and I used to have to carry the basket, she said. Her father was the bank manager, she said." His voice changed, dropped to become Luce at his most superior, most sophisticated. "That must have won him a lot of friends with the Depression on, I said. Foreclosing right, left and center, I said. Just as well my mother didn't have anything worth foreclosing on, I said. You're cruel, she said, and looked as if she was going to cry. Not at all, I said, just being truthful. Don't hold it against me, she said, big black eyes all wet with tears. How could I ever hold anything against anyone as pretty as you, I said." He grinned, quick and wicked as a razor slash. "Though that wasn't being at all truthful. I've got one thing I'd *love* to hold against her!"

Sister Langtry had adopted his earlier pose, elbows on table, chin on hands, watching fascinated as he mimicked and postured his way through the story.

"So much bitterness, Luce," she said gently. "It must have hurt a great deal to have to carry the bank manager's laundry."

Luce shrugged, tried unsuccessfully to assume his normal devil-may-care insouciance. "Yah! Everything hurts, doesn't it?" His eyes widened, glittered. "Though in actual fact carrying the bank manager's laundry—and the doctor's, and the headmaster's, and the Church of England minister's, and the dentist's— didn't hurt half so much as having no shoes to wear to school. *She* used to be in the same school; I remembered her when she said who she was, and I even remember the kind of shoes she used to wear. Little black patent-leather Shirley Temples with straps and black silk bows. My sisters were much prettier than any of the other girls, and prettier than her, too, but they had no shoes of any kind."

"Didn't it occur to you that those with shoes probably envied you your freedom?" asked Sister Langtry tenderly, trying to find something to say which would help him see his childhood in better perspective. "I know I always did, when I went to the local public school before I was old enough to be sent away to boarding school. I had shoes a bit like the bank manager's daughter. And every day I'd have to watch some wonderfully carefree little urchin dance his way across a paddock full of bindy-eye burrs without so much as a wince. Oh, I used to long to throw my shoes away!"

"Bindy-eyes!" exclaimed Luce, smiling. "Funny, I'd forgotten all about them! In Woop-Woop the bindy-eyes had spines half an inch long. I could pull them out of my feet without feeling a thing." He sat up straighter, glaring at her fiercely. "But in the winter, dear well-educated and well-fed and well-clothed Sister Langtry, the backs of my heels and all around the edges of my feet and up my shins used to *crack!*"—the word came out like a rifle shot—"and bleeeeeeed"—the word oozed out of him—"with the cold. Cold, Sister Langtry! Have you ever been cold?"

"Yes," she said, mortified, but a little angry too at being so rebuffed. "In the desert I was cold. I was hungry and I thirsted. In the jungle I've been hot. And sick, too sick to keep down food or drink. But I did my duty. I am not an ornament! Nor am I insensitive to your plight when you were a child. If my words were wrong, I apologize. But the spirit in which they were intended was *right!*"

"You're pitying me, and I don't want your pity!" cried Luce painfully, hating her.

"You haven't got it. I don't pity you. Why on earth should I? Whatever you came from doesn't matter. It's where you're going that does."

But he abandoned the mood of wistfulness and self-revelation, turned bright, metallic, chatty. "Well, anyway, before the army grabbed me I was wearing the best shoes money could buy. That was after I went off to Sydney and became an actor. Laurence Olivier, stand aside!"

"What was your stage name, Luce?"

"Lucius Sherringham." He rolled it out impressively. "Until I realized it was too long for the marquees, that is. Then I changed it to Lucius Ingham. Lucius is a good name for the stage, not bad for radio, either. But when I get to Hollywood I'll change the Lucius to something more swashbuckling. Rhett or Tony. Or if my image turns out more Colman than Flynn, plain John would sound good."

"Why not Luce? That has a swashbuckling air to it."

"It doesn't fit with Ingham," he said positively. "If I stay Luce, the Ingham has to go. But it's an idea. Luce, eh? Luce Diablo would thrill the girls, wouldn't it?"

"Daggett wouldn't do?"

"Daggett! What a name! It sounds like a sheep's bum." His face twisted as if at some half-remembered pain the years since had dulled. "Oh, Sis, but I was so good! Too young, though. I didn't have enough time to make a big enough dent before King and Country called me up. And when I get back, I'll be too old. . . . Some smarmy little bastard with high blood pressure or a rich father to buy him a discharge will be out there in *my* lights. It just isn't fair!"

"If you were good, it can't make any difference," she said. "You'll get there. Someone will see how good you are. Why didn't you try for one of the entertainment units after they were formed?"

He looked revolted. "I'm a serious actor, not an old music-hall comedian! The men in charge of recruiting for those units were old vaudeville types themselves; they only wanted jugglers and tappers. Young men need not apply."

"Never mind, Luce, you will get there. I know you will. Anything anyone wants as badly as you want to be a famous actor has to happen."

Sister Langtry became aware that someone in the far distance was groaning; she came reluctantly out of the insidious spell Luce had woven, almost loving him.

Nugget was making a terrific racket somewhere up near her office, and probably waking up Matt.

"Sis, I feel so crook!" came the wail of his voice.

She got to her feet, looking down at Luce with genuine regret. "I'm terribly sorry, Luce, I really am, but if I don't go, you'll all pay for it later tonight."

She was already halfway down the ward when Luce said, "It's not important. After all, *I* don't feel crook!"

His face was twisted again, bitter and frustrated, the glorious little moment of approbation and limelight snatched away by a child's peevish howl for Mummy. And Mummy, as all mummies must, had gone immediately to minister where ministry was really needed. Luce looked down at his mug of tea, which had cooled off enough to smear a thick ugly scum of congealing milk across its surface. Disgusted, he lifted the mug in his hand, and very slowly and deliberately turned it upside down on the table.

The tea went everywhere. Neil leaped to his feet away from the main stream of it, dabbing at his trousers. Michael moved just as quickly the other way. Luce remained where he was sitting, indifferent to the fate of his clothes, watching the slimy liquid course over the edge of the board and drip steadily onto the floor.

"Clean it up, you ignorant bastard!" said Neil through his teeth.

Luce looked up, laughed. "Make me!" he said, biting off each of the two words and giving them an intolerable edge of insult.

Neil was shaking. He drew himself up stiffly and curled his lip, face white. "If I were not your superior in rank, Sergeant, it would give me the greatest of pleasure to make you—and to rub your nose in it." He turned on his heel and found the opening between the screens as if more by chance than design, not floundering, but blinded.

"Sez you!" Luce called after him, shrill and mocking. "Go on, *Captain,* run away and hide behind your pips! You don't have the guts!"

The muscles in Luce's hands unlocked, went limp. Slowly he turned his face back to the table and discovered Michael busy with a rag, mopping up the mess. Luce stared in pure amazement.

"You stupid drongo!" he cried.

Michael didn't reply. He picked up the dripping rag and the empty mug, piled them among the other things on the makeshift tray, lifted it easily and carried it away toward the dayroom. Alone at the table, Luce sat with the light and the fire in him dying, willing himself fiercely and successfully not to weep.

9 Of her own choice entirely, Sister Langtry worked a split shift. When ward X was founded shortly after Base Fifteen, about a year earlier, there were two sisters on Matron's roster to care for its patients. A frail and antipathetic woman, the second sister was not the right temperament to cope with the kind of patients ward X contained. She lasted a month, and was replaced by a big, bouncingly brisk sister whose mentality was still in the jolly-hockey-stick schoolgirl stage. She lasted a week, and demanded a transfer not because of anything done to her personally, but after watching Sister Langtry deal with a terrifying episode of patient violence. The third sister was hot-tempered and unforgiving. She lasted a week and a half, and was removed at Sister Langtry's heated request. Full of apologies, Matron promised to send someone else as soon as she could find someone suitable. But she never did send anyone, whether because she couldn't or just forgot, Sister Langtry had no way of knowing.

It suited Sister Langtry beautifully to work ward X on her own, in spite of the toll it took in strength and sleep, so she had never agitated for a second sister. After all, what could one do with days off in a place like Base Fifteen? There was absolutely nowhere to go. Since she was not the partying or the sunbathing type, the only two diversions Base Fifteen had to offer were less enticing to Sister Langtry than the company of her men. So she worked alone, tranquilly convinced after three samples that it was better for the well-being of her men to have to cope with one female only, one set of orders and one routine rather than two. Her duty seemed clear: she wasn't a part of the war effort to serve her own interests, or to pamper herself unduly; as the servant of her country with her country in peril, she had to give of her very best, do her job as well as it could possibly be done.

It never occurred to her that in electing to run ward X on her own she cemented her power; not the shadow of a doubt ever crossed her mind that she might be perpetrating a wrong upon her patients. Just as her own very comfortable upbringing made it impossible for her to understand with heart as well as mind what poverty could do to a man like Luce Daggett, so a lack of experience prevented her from seeing all the ramifications of ward X, her tenure in it, and her true relationship with her patients. Conscious that she was freeing up a trained nurse for service in some other area than ward X, Sister Langtry merely carried on. When she was ordered away on a month's leave, she handed the ward over to her substitute without too much heartache; but when she returned to find mostly new faces, she simply picked up where she had left off.

Her normal day began at dawn, or shortly before it; at this latitude the length of the days varied little between winter and summer, which was nice. By sunup she was in the ward, well ahead of the kitchen orderly who would attend to breakfast. When a kitchen orderly turned up at all, that is. If none of her men were up, she made them a pot of early morning tea accompanied by a plate of bread and butter, and roused them. She partook of this early morning tea herself, then attended to the sluice room and the dayroom while the men went off to the bathhouse to shower and shave. Should an orderly still not have turned up, she also prepared the breakfast. About eight o'clock she ate breakfast with her men, after which she set them firmly on the road of the day: made beds with them, supervised one of the taller ones like Neil or Luce in the task of producing that complicated Jacques Fath drape to the mosquito nets. Matron had invented the style of daytime disposal of the nets herself, and it was a well-known fact that provided when she arrived to inspect a ward she found its nets properly arranged, she noticed little else.

In a ward full of ambulant men, housekeeping presented no problem, and did not require the services of an orderly. They managed cleanliness for themselves, under Sister Langtry's trained and meticulous eye. Let the orderlies go where they were most needed, they were a nuisance anyway.

The minor irritations of ward X's afterthought construction had long since been ironed out satisfactorily. Neil, an officer, had been given as his private quarters the old treatment room, a cubicle six feet wide and eight feet long, adjoining Sister Langtry's tiny office. No one in X needed medical treatment, and there was no psychiatrist to administer a more metaphysical kind of treatment. So the treatment room had always been available to house the rare officer patients. When Sister Langtry needed to attend to minor but ever-present ailments like tinea, boils, skin ulcers and dermatitis, she used her office. Malarial recurrences and the gamut of tropical enteric fevers were treated from the patient's bed, though occasionally if the illness was severe enough, the patient would be transferred to a ward more geared to physical illness.

There was no indoor toilet for the men, or for the staff. In the interests of hygiene, Base Fifteen's ambulant patients and all its staff used deep-trench latrines built at intervals through the compound; these were disinfected once a day and periodically fired with petrol or kerosene to prevent bacterial proliferation. Ambulant patients performed their ablutions in concrete structures called bathhouses; the bathhouse for ward X lay behind it and about two hundred feet away, and had once been patronized by six other wards as well. The other wards had been closed for six months now, so the bathhouse belonged solely to the men of X, as did the nearby latrine. The sluice room inside ward X, which held urine bottles, bedpans and bowls, covers for same, a meager supply of linen and a disinfectant-reeking can for bodily wastes, was rarely if ever needed. Water for the ward was stored in a corrugated iron tank on a stand which raised it to roof level and permitted a gravity feed of water to dayroom, sluice room and treatment room.

After the ward was straight, Sister Langtry retired to her office to deal with the paper work, everything from forms, requisitions and laundry lists to daily entries in the case histories. If it was X's morning for visiting the stores hut, an iron structure under lock and key and ruled from the quartermaster's office, she and one of her men walked across to fetch back whatever they managed to get. She had found Nugget to be her best escort to stores; he always looked so insignificant and shrunken, yet when they got back to X he would blithely produce from around his scraggy person everything from bars of chocolate to tinned puddings or cakes, saline powder, talcum powder, tobacco and cigarette papers and matches.

Visits from the brass—Matron, Colonel Chinstrap and the red-hat colonel who was the superintendent, and others—always occurred during the later part of the morning. But if it was a quiet morning undisturbed by brass, as most were, she would sit on the verandah with her men and talk, or perhaps even just be silent in their company.

After the men's lunch arrived somewhere around half-past twelve, depending upon the kitchen, she left the ward and headed for her own mess to eat her own lunch. The afternoon she spent quietly, usually in her room; she might read a book, darn a pile of her men's socks, shirts and underwear, or sometimes if it was cool and dry enough she might nap on her bed. Around four she would head for the sisters' sitting room to drink a cup of tea and chat for an hour with whoever might appear; this represented her only truly social contact with her fellow nurses, for meals in the mess were always snatched, hurried affairs.

At five she went back to ward X to supervise her

men's dinner, then returned to the sisters' mess for her own dinner about six-fifteen. By seven she was on her way back to X for the segment of the day she enjoyed most. A visit and a smoke with Neil in her office, visits and talks with the other men if they felt the need or she felt they needed it. After which she made the last and most major entry of the day in the case histories. And a little after nine someone made a final cup of tea, which she drank with her patients at the refectory table behind its screens inside the ward. By ten her patients were readying themselves for bed, and by half past she would have left the ward for the night.

Of course, these days things were quiet, it was an easy life for her. During ward X's heyday she had spent far more time in the ward, and would dole out sedation before she left. If she had a patient prone to violence, an orderly or a relief sister would have remained on duty all night, but those so ill did not stay long unless a definite improvement was noted. By and large ward X was a team effort, with the patients a most valuable part of the team; she had never known the ward not to contain at least one patient who could be relied upon to hold a watching brief in her absence, and she had found such patients more of a help than additional staff would have been.

This ward team effort she deemed vital, for the chief worry she had about men of X was the emptiness of their days. Once through the acute phase of his illness, a man faced weeks of inertia before discharge was possible. There was nothing to do! Men like Neil Parkinson fared better because they possessed a talent which was easy to cater to, but painters were rare. Unfortunately Sister Langtry herself had no gift for handicraft teaching, even had it been possible to obtain the materials. Occasionally a man evinced a desire to whittle, or to knit, or to sew, and this she did what she could to encourage. But whichever way one looked at it, ward X was a dull place to be. So the more the men could be persuaded to participate in the everyday routine of the ward, the better.

On that night of Michael's arrival in X, as on every other night, Sister Langtry came out of her office at a quarter past ten, a torch in her right hand. The lights in the ward were all extinguished save for one still burning at the far end above the refectory table. That she put out herself by flicking a switch at the junction of the short corridor and the main ward. At the same time she switched on her torch and directed its beam toward the floor.

Everything was quiet, except for a slight susurration of breathing around her in the semidarkness. Curiously, none of this present group of men snored; she sometimes wondered if this was one of the chief reasons why they had managed to put up with each other in spite of the rawnesses and the oddities. At least in sleep they did not encroach upon each other's privacy, could get away from each other. Did Michael snore? For his sake, she hoped not. If he did, they would probably end in disliking him.

The ward was never fully dark since the lifting of the blackout. The light in the corridor behind her remained on all night, as did a light at the top of the steps which led eventually to the bathhouse and the latrine; its wan rays penetrated through the windows in the wall alongside Michael's bed, for the door to the steps stood just beyond the foot of the bed.

All the mosquito nets were pulled down, draped in easy curves across and over each bed like ambitious catafalques. Indeed, there was something tomblike about the effect, a series of unknown warriors sleeping that longest and most perfect of sleeps lapped in dark clouds like smoke from funeral pyres.

Automatically after so many years as a nurse, Sister Langtry changed her hold on the torch; her hand slid across its front to mask the brightness, reduce it to a ruby glow and small white sparkles between the black bars of her embracing fingers.

She walked first to Nugget's bed and directed the dimmed light through the mosquito netting. Such a baby! Asleep of course, though in the morning he would inform her he had not so much as closed his eyes. His pajamas were neatly buttoned up to his neck in spite of the heat, the sheet drawn tidily up under his arms. If he wasn't constipated he had diarrhoea; if his head let him alone, his back played up; if his dermo wasn't flared to weeping bloody patches like raw meat, his boils had risen like beehives on his backside. Never happy unless tortured by some pain, real or imagined. His constant companion was a battered, dog-eared nursing dictionary he had filched from somewhere before arriving in X, and he knew it by heart, understood it too. Tonight she had dealt with him as she always did, kindly, full of commiseration, willing to engage in an interested discussion of whatever set of symptoms was currently uppermost, willing to purgate, analgize, anoint, follow obediently down the path of treatment he selected for himself. If he ever did suspect that most of the pills, mixtures and injections she fed him were placebotic, he never said so. Such a baby!

Matt's bed was next. He too was asleep. The gentle reddened glow from the torch probed at his lowered eyelids, softly illuminated the spare dignity of his man's features. He saddened her, for there was nothing she could do for him or with him. The shutter between his brain and his eyes remained fast closed and permitted no communications between. She had tried to persuade him to badger Colonel Chinstrap into weekly neurological examinations, but Matt refused; if it was real, he said, it would kill him anyway, and if as they thought it was imagined, why bother? A picture sat on top of his locker, of a woman in her early thirties, hair carefully rolled over wadding in best Hollywood style, a neat little white Peter Pan collar over the dark stuff of her dress. Three small girls wearing the same white Peter Pan collars were arranged around her like ornaments, and on her lap sat a fourth child, also a girl, half infant, half toddler. How strange, that he who could not or would not see was the only one who kept and treasured a picture of his loved ones. Though during her service in X she had noticed that a lack either of loved ones or of pictures of loved ones was commoner in X than in other kinds of ward.

Benedict asleep was not like Benedict awake. Awake he was still, quiet, contained, withdrawn. Asleep he thrashed and rolled and whimpered without true rest. Of all of them, he worried her the most: that eating away inside she could not seem to arrest or control. She couldn't reach him, not because he was hostile, for he never was, but because he didn't seem to listen, or if he listened, he didn't seem to understand. That his sexual instincts were a great torment to him she had suspected strongly enough to tax him with it one day. When she had asked him if he had ever had a girl friend, he had said a curt no. Why not? she had inquired, explaining she didn't mean a girl to sleep with, only someone to know and to be friends with, perhaps think of marrying. Benedict had simply looked at her, his face screwed up into an expression of complete revulsion. "Girls are dirty," he said, and would not say more. Yes, he worried her, for that and many other reasons.

Before she went to check on Michael she attended to the screens around the refectory table, for they came a little too close to the end of Michael's bed if he should need to get up during the night. Pleating them up into the economy of a closed fan, she pushed them away against the wall. It had been some time since anyone slept in that bed; it was not popular because of the light shining in the windows alongside it.

But she was pleased to see that Michael slept without a pajama jacket. So sensible in this climate! She worried far more for the welfare of those like Matt and Nugget who persisted in wearing confining nightclothes. Nothing she had managed to find to say could persuade Matt or Nugget to give up properly buttoned pajama jackets. She wondered if that was because both men lay enthralled by women who represented the decencies and modesties of the civilized world, a world far from ward X: wife, mother.

Michael was turned away from the ward, apparently not disturbed by the light shining on his face. That was good; he mustn't mind the bed, then. Unless she walked around to the other side his features were hidden from her, but she was loath to look upon his sleeping face, so stayed where she was. The soft light played upon the skin of back and shoulder, caught a glitter of silver from the chain on which he wore his meat-tickets, two dull-colored pieces of some pressed board material which sprawled one below, the other across the pillow behind him. That was how they would identify him if they found enough of him still intact enough to wear meat-tickets; they would chop off the lower one to send home with his effects, bury him with the other still around his neck. . . . That can't happen now, she told herself. The war's over. That can't possibly happen.

He had looked at her as if he found it difficult to take her seriously, as if she had somehow stepped out of a natural role and into an inappropriate one. Not exactly Run away and play, little girl; more Run away and deal with the poor coots who do need you, because I don't, and I never will. He was like suddenly running into a brick wall. Or encountering an alien force. The men felt it too, recognizing that Michael did not belong in ward X.

She continued standing beside him for longer than she realized, the torch fixed without deviation on the back of his head, her left hand extended, unconsciously smoothing and stroking the mosquito net.

A soft movement from the other side of the ward intruded. She looked up, able to see Luce's bed where it lay along the far wall because she had moved the screens back from the refectory table. Luce was sitting on the edge of his bed, naked, one leg propped up, both arms around it, watching her watch Michael. She felt suddenly as if she had been caught in the middle of some undignified and furtively sexual act, and was glad the ward was too dark to betray her blush.

For a long moment she and Luce stared at each other across the distance, like duelists coolly measuring the quality of the opposition. Then Luce broke his pose, lowering the leg as his arms fell away, and raised one hand to her in a mocking little wave. He twisted sideways under the edge of the net and disappeared. Moving quite naturally, she crossed the ward softly and bent to tuck in his net securely. But she made sure she didn't look anywhere near his face.

It was not her habit to check on Neil; unless he called for her, which he never did, once he was inside his own sanctum his life was absolutely his own. It was as much as she could do for him, poor Neil.

All was well; Sister Langtry paused at her office to change from sandshoes back into boots and gaiters, and clapped her hat on her head. She bent to pick up her basket, dropping two pairs of socks into it which she had culled from Michael's kit because they needed darning badly. At the front door she slipped absolutely without a sound through the fly-curtain, and let herself out. Her torch beam unshielded now, she set off across the compound toward her quarters. Half-past ten. By eleven she would have bathed and prepared herself for bed; by half past she would be enjoying the beginning of six uninterrupted hours of sleep.

The men of ward X were not entirely unprotected during her absence; if the inner alarm bell which was intrinsic to every good nurse sounded in her, she would visit the ward during the night herself, and tip off Night Sister to keep a special eye on X as she patrolled from ward to ward. Even without prior warning from Sister Langtry, the Night Sister would always look in once as a matter of course. And if the worst came to the worst, there was a telephone. It was three months since any sort of crisis had occurred during the night, so her dreams were easy.

PART 2

1 The visit to Colonel Chinstrap's clinic accomplished nothing, as Sister Langtry had expected. The colonel concentrated fiercely upon Michael's body, preferring to ignore soul and mind. He palpated, auscultated, poked, prodded, pinched, tapped, pricked, tickled, struck, all of which Michael bore with unruffled patience. On command Michael closed his eyes and touched the tip of his nose with the tip of his finger, used his eyes without moving his head to follow the erratic course of a pencil back and forth and up and down. He stood with feet together and eyes closed, walked a straight line, hopped first on one leg and then on the other, read off all the letters on a chart, had his visual fields plotted, played a little word association game. Even when the colonel's bloodshot eye loomed down on his own, ophthalmoscope at the ready, he endured that most intense and oppressive of close-quarters scrutiny with equanimity; Sister Langtry, sitting on a chair watching, was amused to see that he didn't even flinch at first contact with the colonel's halitosis.

After all this Michael was dismissed to wait outside, while Sister Langtry sat observing the colonel prodding at the inside of his own upper lip with the ball of his thumb; it always reminded her of nose-picking, though it was only the technique whereby the colonel stimulated his thinking processes.

"I'll do a lumbar puncture first thing this afternoon," he said at last, slowly.

"What on earth for?" asked Sister Langtry before she could restrain herself.

"I beg your pardon, Sister!"

"I said, what on earth for?" Well, in for a

penny, in for a pound. She had started and she owed it to her patient to finish. "There's absolutely nothing neurologically wrong with Sergeant Wilson, and you know it, sir. Why subject the poor chap to a rotten headache and bed rest when he's in the pink of health considering the sort of life and climate he's been enduring?"

It was too early in the morning to fight with her. Last night's tiny excess with the whisky bottle and Sister Connolly had largely been due to his run-in with Langtry yesterday evening, and made the very idea of renewing battle insupportable. One of these days there would be a final reckoning, he promised himself dourly, but today was not going to be the day.

"Very well, Sister," he said stiffly, putting down his fountain pen and closing Sergeant Wilson's file. "I will not perform a lumbar puncture this afternoon." He handed her the notes as if they were contaminated. "Good morning to you."

She rose at once. "Good morning, sir," she said, then turned and walked out.

Michael was waiting, and fell in beside her as she strode a little too quickly from the clinic hut into the welcome fresh air.

"Is that that?" he asked.

"That is most definitely that! Unless you develop an obscure disease of the spinal cord with an unpronounceable name, I can safely predict that you have seen the last of Colonel Chinstrap except on ward inspections and his weekly general round."

"Colonel who?"

She laughed. "Chinstrap. Luce nicknamed him that, and it's stuck. His real name is Donaldson. I only hope that Chinstrap doesn't follow him all the way back to Macquarie Street."

"I must say this place and the people in it are full of surprises, Sister."

"No more than camp and your own battalion, surely?"

"The trouble with camp and my own battalion," said

Michael, "was that I knew all the faces far too well, some of them for years and years. Not all of us who originally belonged were killed or invalided out. On the move or going into action, you don't notice the monotony. But I've spent almost all of the last six years in some sort of camp. Camps in desert dust storms, camps in monsoon rains, even camp in the Showground. Always hot camps. I keep thinking of the Russian front, wondering what a really cold camp would be like, and I find myself actually dreaming about it. Isn't it queer that a man's life can become so monotonous he dreams of a different camp rather than of home or women? Camp is just about all I know."

"Yes, I agree, the chief trouble with war is the monotony. It's the chief trouble with ward X, too. For me and for the men. I prefer to work long hours and run X on my own because if I didn't, I'd be troppo myself. As for the men, they're physically well, quite capable of doing a hard day's work at something. But they can't. There isn't any work to do. If there were, they'd be the better for it mentally." She smiled. "Still, it can't be for too much longer now. We'll all be going home soon."

Going home didn't appeal to them, Michael knew, but he said nothing, just marched shoulder to shoulder with her across the compound.

It occurred to her that he was nice to walk with. He didn't bend his head down to her deferentially as Neil did, nor posture like Luce, nor skulk like Nugget. In fact, he took it quite naturally and companionably, almost one man to another. Which sounded odd, perhaps, but felt *right*.

"Do you have a civilian occupation, Michael?" she asked, turning away from the direction of ward X to take a path which led between two deserted wards.

"Yes. Dairy farmer. I've got three hundred acres of river flat on the Hunter near Maitland. My sister and her husband are working it for the duration, but they'd rather be back in Sydney, so when I get home I'll take over. My brother-in-law's a real city bloke, but when it

91

came to the pinch he decided he'd rather milk cows and get woken up by roosters than wear a uniform and get shot at." Michael's face was faintly contemptuous.

"Another bush bunny for X! We're in the majority, then. Neil, Matt and Nugget are city, but now you're here, that makes four bush bunnies."

"Where are you from?"

"My father's got a property near Yass."

"Yet you ended up in Sydney, like Luce."

"In Sydney, yes. But not like Luce."

He grinned, gave her a quick sideways glance. "I beg your pardon, Sister."

"You'd better start calling me Sis the way the rest of them do. Sooner or later you will anyway."

"All right, Sis, I will."

They climbed a small undulating rise, sandy yet spidered with long rhizomes of coarse grass, dotted with the slim neat boles of coconut palms, and arrived at the edge of a beach. There they stopped, the breeze tugging at Sister Langtry's veil.

Michael pulled out his tobacco makings and squatted down on his heels the way all country men do, so Sister Langtry knelt beside him, careful not to get her duty shoes full of sand.

"It's when I see something like this I don't mind the Islands so much," he said, rolling a cigarette. "Isn't it amazing? Just when you think you can't take another day of mossies, mud, sweat, dysentery and triple dye, you wake up and it's the most perfect day God ever put upon the earth, or you see something like this, or something else happens that makes you think it isn't really so bad after all."

It was lovely, a short straight stretch of salt-and-peppery sand darkened near the water where it was wet from the retreating tide, and absolutely deserted. It seemed to be one side of a long promontory, for it ended against sky and water to the left, and to the right petered out in a mangrove flat reeking of decay. The water was like a thin wash of color laid on top of white: glassy, palest green, profoundly still. Far out was a reef, and the sea's horizon was hidden by the white spume fans of surf breaking.

"This is the patients' beach," she said, sitting back on her heels. "In the morning it's out of bounds, which is why there's no one here. But between one and five each afternoon it's all yours. I couldn't have brought you here then, because between one and five it's out of bounds to all females. Saves the army having to issue you with swimming costumes. The orderlies and the other noncom staff use it too, the same hours. For me it's been a godsend. Without the beach to divert them, my men would never get well."

"Do you have a beach, Sis?"

"The other side of the point is ours, though we're not as lucky as you. Matron's down on nude bathing."

"Old killjoy."

"The MOs and officers have their own beach too, on our side of the point, but cut off from us by a little headland. The officer patients can swim there or here."

"Do the MOs wear costumes?"

She smiled. "I really haven't thought to inquire." Her position was uncomfortable, so she used a glance to her watch as an excuse to get to her feet. "We'd better head back. It's not Matron's morning for rounds, but I haven't taught you yet how to drape your mosquito net. We've got time for an hour's practice before your lunch comes."

"It won't take an hour. I'm a quick learner," he said, reluctant to move, reluctant to break the pleasantness of this truly social contact with a woman.

But she shook her head and turned away from the beach, obliging him to follow. "Believe me, it's going to take you much longer than an hour. You haven't tried anything until you've tried to drape your net the right way. If I knew exactly what it portends, I'd suggest to Colonel Chinstrap that he use the Matron Drape as a test of mental aptitude."

"How do you mean?" He caught up with her, brushing a little sand from his trousers.

"Certain X patients can't do it. Benedict can't, for

instance. We've all tried to teach him, and he's very willing to learn, but he just can't get the hang of it, though he's intelligent enough. He produces the most weird and wonderful variations on Matron's theme, but do it her way he can't."

"You're very honest about everyone, aren't you?"

She stopped to look at him seriously. "There's no point in being anything else, Michael. Whether you like it or not, whether you think you fit in or not, whether you belong or not, you're a part of X now until we all go home. And you'll find that in X we can't afford the luxury of euphemisms."

He nodded, but said nothing, simply stared at her as if her novelty value was increasing, yet with more respect than he had admitted yesterday.

After a moment she dropped her eyes and continued to walk, but strolling along rather than striding out at her customary brisk pace. She was enjoying the break from routine, and enjoying his rather unforthcoming company. With him she didn't have to worry about how he was feeling; she could relax and pretend he was just someone she had met socially somewhere.

However, all too soon ward X came into sight around the corner of a deserted building. Neil was standing outside waiting for them. Which vaguely irritated Sister Langtry; he looked like an overanxious parent who had allowed his child to come home alone from school for the first time.

2 In the afternoon Michael went back to the beach with Neil, Matt and Benedict. Nugget had refused to come, and Luce was nowhere to be found.

The sureness with which Matt moved had Michael quite fascinated, discovering that a small touch on elbow or arm or hand from Neil was all Matt needed to navigate; Michael watched and learned, so that in Neil's absence he could substitute competently. Nugget had informed him in the bathhouse with much technical detail that Matt was not really blind, that there was nothing at all wrong with his eyes, but to Michael his inability to see seemed absolutely genuine. A man feigning blindness would surely have groped, stumbled, playacted the part. Where Matt did it with dignity and understatement, his inner self uncorrupted by it.

There were about fifty men scattered up and down the sand, which could have absorbed a thousand men without seeming crowded. All were naked; some were maimed, some scarred. Since there were noncom staff admixed with systemic convalescents after malaria or some other tropical disorder, the three whole healthy-looking men from ward X were not entirely out of place. However, Michael noticed that conviviality tended to confine itself within ward groups: neuros, plastics, bones, skins, abdominothoracics, general medicals; the staff element congregated together too.

The troppos from X shed their clothes far enough away from any other group not to be accused of deliberate eavesdropping, and swam for an hour, the water as warm and unstimulating as a tepid baby's bath. Then they spread themselves on the sand to dry off, skins powdered with rutile-bearing grains like tiny elegant sequins. Michael sat up to roll a cigarette, lit it and handed it to Matt. Neil smiled faintly but said nothing, merely watched the sure hands as Michael embarked upon making one for himself.

A nice change from camp, Michael was thinking, staring out across the water with eyes narrowed against the glare, watching the thin blue streaks of his smoke hover for a moment before being taken by a breath of wind and swirled into nothing. Nice to witness a different family than the battalion, though this was a much closer-knit family, gently ruled by a woman, as all families ought to be. Nice to have a woman around, too. Sister Langtry represented his first more than transient contact with a woman in six years. One forgot: how they walked, how they smelled, how different they were. The sensation of family he felt in X stemmed directly from her, the figurehead of whom no one in X, not even Luce, spoke lewdly or with disrespect. Well, she was a lady, that was true, but she was more than a lady. Ladies with nothing to back up a set of manners and attitudes than more of the same had never interested him; Sister Langtry, he was beginning to see, had qualities he felt he shared, most men shared. Not afraid to speak her mind, not afraid of men because they were men.

At first she had put his back up a little, but he was fair enough to admit the fault lay in him rather than in her; why shouldn't women have authority and rank if they could cope with it? She could, yet she was a womanly woman, and very, very nice. Without seeming to exert any obvious wiles, she held this motley collection of men together, no doubt about that. They loved her, really loved her. Which meant they all saw sex in her somewhere. At first he hadn't seen sex, but after only one day and two private talks with her, he was beginning to. Oh, not throwing her down and having her; something more pleasant and subtle than that, a slow and delicious discovery of her mouth, her neck and shoulders, her legs . . . A man switched off when he was unable to avail himself of anything save the guilty misery of masturbation, but having a woman around all day started the juices flowing again; his thoughts began to stir beyond the level of an unattainable dream. Sister Langtry wasn't a pinup poster, she was *real*. Though for Michael she did have a dreamlike quality—nothing to do with the war, or its scarcity of women. She was upper crust, a squatter's daughter, the kind of woman he would never have met in the ordinary sequence of civilian life.

Poor Colin, he would have hated her. Not the way Luce hated her, because Luce wanted her at the same time, and loved her to boot. Luce could pretend to himself that what he felt for her was hate because she didn't want him back, and he couldn't understand it. But Colin had been different. Which had always been Colin's trouble. They had been in it together since the beginning. He had gravitated toward Colin very soon after enlisting, for Colin was the sort of bloke other blokes picked on, not really understanding why he irritated them, just lashing out because the irritation was perpetually there; like horses pestered by flies. And Michael had a strong protective streak which had plagued him since early childhood, so that he had always accumulated lame ducks.

Colin had been girlishly skinny and a little too pretty and a demon soldier, as handicapped by the way he looked and how he felt as Benedict probably was. Burying the butt of his cigarette in the sand, Michael rested his eyes thoughtfully on Benedict. There was a lot of trouble packed down inside Ben's narrow frame, torment and soul-searching and a fierce rebellion, just as there had been inside Colin. He would have bet any sum an onlooker cared to name that Ben had been a demon soldier too, one of those unlikely men who were the picture of mildness until battle euphoria got into them, when they went mad and behaved like ancient heroes. Men with much to prove to themselves usually were demon soldiers, especially when spiritual conflicts gingered up the mixture of troubles.

Michael had started in pitying Colin, that protective instinct very much to the fore, but as the months went on and one country succeeded another, a curious affection and friendship had grown between them. They fought well together, they camped well together, and they discovered neither had a taste for whoring or getting blind drunk when on leave, so that to stick together at all times became natural, welcome.

However, proximity can blind, and it blinded Michael. It was not until they reached New Guinea that he fully came to understand the extent of Colin's troubles. The company had been saddled with a new noncommissioned officer, a big, confident, rather blustering regimental sergeant major who soon displayed a tendency to use Colin as his butt. It hadn't worried Michael too much; he knew things could only go so far while he was there to draw a line over which no one stepped. The RSM had got Michael's measure too, and wasn't about to step over the line. So the pinpricks directed at Colin were minor, confined to comments and looks. Michael waited placidly, knowing that as soon as they went into action again the RSM would see a different side to the flimsy, girlish Colin.

Therefore it came as a complete shock to Michael one day to discover Colin weeping bitterly, and it had taken much patient probing to learn what the problem was: a homosexual overture from the RSM which tormented Colin on many levels. His inclinations lay that way, he confessed. He knew it was wrong, he knew it was unnatural, he despised himself for it, but he couldn't help himself, either. Only it wasn't the RSM he wanted; he wanted Michael.

There had been no revulsion, no outraged propriety on Michael's part; only an enormous sorrow, the tenderness and pity long friendship and genuine love permitted. How could a man turn away from his best mate when they'd been through so very much together? They talked for a long time, and in the end Colin's confession had made no difference to their relationship, save perhaps to strengthen it. Michael's preferences didn't lie in that direction, but he could feel no differently toward Colin because his did. That was life, that was men, that was a fact. The war and the existence it had forced upon him had meant Michael had learned to live with many things he would have rejected outright when a civilian, for the alternative to living with them was literally to die. Choosing to live simply meant learning tolerance; so long as a man was let alone, he didn't inqure too closely into the private activities of his fellows.

But it was a burden to be loved as a lover; Michael's responsibilities toward Colin had suddenly multiplied. His very inability to return Colin's love the way Colin wanted it returned laid additional care upon Michael, increased his urge to protect. Together they had seen death, battle, hardship, hunger, loneliness, homesickness, illness; too much by far to abandon. Yet to be unable to return love fully was a burden of guilt only to be expiated in what help and service he could permit within the bounds of his own nature. And Colin, though the ultimate joy of a sexual relationship was always unattainable, bloomed and brightened immeasurably after that day in New Guinea.

When Colin died Michael hadn't been able to believe what his eyes were showing him, one of those fluke kills from a tiny splinter of metal driven faster than sound through the closecropped hair between neck and skull, so that he just lay down and died, so very quietly, without any blood, without disgust. Michael had sat beside him for a long time, sure that his clasp on the stiff cold hand would eventually be returned; in the end they had had to prise the two hands apart, living one and dead one, and persuade Michael to come away, that there was absolutely no hope of ever seeing life in that calmly sleeping face. It looked noble, at rest, sacred, inviolate. Death would have changed it in some way. It always did, for death was slack and emptied. He still found himself wondering whether in truth Colin's dead face had seemed to sleep, or whether his eyes had wrought a change in it that made it seem simply to sleep. Grief he had often known, but not grief like this.

Then after the first shock of Colin's death had evaporated Michael was horrified to discover in himself, living it appeared right alongside that intolerable grief, a wonderful sense of release. He was free! The incubus of duty toward one more helpless and less capable than himself was gone. As long as Colin had lived he would have been tied by that duty. Perhaps it would not have prevented his seeking love elsewhere, but it would certainly have hampered him, and Colin would not have been strong enough to resist trying to retain exclusive possession of him, he knew. So death after all came as a reprieve, and that tormented him.

For months afterward he kept to himself as much as he could given his peculiar status in the battalion; there were demon soldiers aplenty in a unit as illustrious as his, but Michael was more than a demon soldier. His CO called him the quintessential soldier, meaning by that a degree of military professionalism rarely found in any man. To Michael it was a job, and he never failed in it because he believed not only in himself but in the ultimate goodness of the cause. He conducted himself without passion, no matter what the provocation, which meant that he could be relied upon at all times to keep his head, do what had to be done without dwelling upon the consequences even in terms of his own life. He would dig a trench, a road, a dugout or a grave; he would take an untakable position or take it upon himself to retreat if he so judged; he never complained, he never made trouble, he never questioned an order even if he was already making up his mind to circumvent it. His effect on his fellow soldiers was calming, steadying, encouraging. They thought he bore a charmed life, and saw in him their luck.

After the landing on Borneo settled down, he was sent on a mission which appeared quite routine; since the battalion was short of officers, the RSM who had badgered Colin was put in charge of the sortie. It consisted of three barges of men. Their instructions were to proceed to such-and-such a beach, take possession of it, and infiltrate. Earlier reconnaissance had revealed no Japanese within the area. But when the exercise began the Japanese were there all right, and more than half the company died or was wounded. One barge had got clean away, its men not yet landed; one barge was sunk under fire; Michael, another sergeant and the RSM among them had managed to rally and collect the unwounded or lightly wounded men, and all together they had carried the seriously wounded on board the third barge, still afloat. Halfway home they were met by a relief party bearing medics, plasma, morphine; the unharmed barge had got home and sent them timely aid.

The RSM had taken the loss of so many good men hard, blamed it upon himself, for it had been his first independent command. And Michael, remembering New Guinea days and Colin, felt obliged to do what he could to comfort the man. It backfired spectacularly; the RSM had literally welcomed his attentions with open arms. For five hideous minutes Michael went mad; the quintessential soldier who never allowed his passions to become involved was consumed by passion. He saw the whole hideous cycle beginning again—an unwanted love, a painful servitude, himself the victim and the cause at one and the same time—and he suddenly hated the RSM as he had never in his entire life hated anyone. If this man had not made advances to Colin in the first place, none of it would ever have happened, for Colin would not have found the courage to unburden himself.

Luckily Michael's hands were all he had, but training, rage, and the advantage of surprise would have proven more than enough had the RSM not managed to scream for help, and had that help not been very near.

Once the madness lifted, Michael found himself destroyed. In all the years of his service in the army he had never hungered to kill, never got any satisfaction from it, never actually hated his adversaries. But with his hands around the RSM's throat he felt a pleasure akin only to sexual heights, and with his thumbs pressing down on the hyoid cartilage he had gloried in the sheer feeling of it, was driven on by the same sort of mindless carnality he had always despised in others.

Only he could know how he felt during those brief and violent seconds; and knowing, he elected not to fight the consequences. He refused to justify his actions, refused to say anything except that he had intended to kill.

The CO of the battalion, one of the best commanding officers men were ever lucky enough to have, collared Michael in a private interview. The only other man present was the RMO, an excellent doctor and a strong humanitarian. Together they informed Michael that the matter had been taken over their heads to divisional HQ; the RSM was determined on a court-martial, and was not prepared to be blocked at battalion level.

"The stupid bloody bugger," said the battalion CO dispassionately.

"He's not himself these days," said Michael, who was still occasionally shaken by a fit of something perilously close to tears.

"If you go on like this they'll convict you," said the RMO. "You'll lose everything you should come out of the war wearing proudly."

"Let them convict me," said Michael wearily.

"Oh, come off it, Mike!" said the CO. "You're worth ten of him, and you know it!"

"I just want to be out of this," said Michael, closing his eyes. "Oh, Johnno, I'm so bloody fed up with the war, men, the whole bloody lot!"

The two officers exchanged glances.

"What you obviously need is a good rest," said the RMO then, briskly. "It's all over bar the shouting anyway. How about a nice comfortable bed in a nice comfortable base hospital with a nice comfortable nurse to look after you?"

Michael had opened his eyes. "It sounds like heaven," he said. "What do I have to do to get there?"

"Just go on acting like a dill," said the RMO, grinning. "I'm sending you to Base Fifteen as suspected of unsound mind. It won't appear on your discharge papers, you have our word on that. But it will force our noncom friend to pull his horns in."

So the pact was sealed. Michael handed in his Owen gun and his ammunition, was loaded into a field ambulance and taken to the airfield, and thence to Base Fifteen.

A nice comfortable bed in a nice comfortable hospital with a nice comfortable nurse to look after him. But did Sister Langtry fit the definition of a nice comfortable nurse? He had rather imagined someone fortyish, stout, motherly in a no-nonsense sort of way. Not a whippy, fine-boned little thing scarcely older than he himself, with more aplomb than a brigadier and more brains than a field marshal. . . .

He came out of his reverie to find Benedict staring at him unwinkingly, and he had smiled back with unshadowed affection before the alarm bells could prevent him. No, never again! Not even for this poor, miserable bastard with the half-starved wistful look of a homeless mongrel cur. Never, never again. Still, forewarned was forearmed, and he could make sure this time that what friendship he offered remained limited. Not that Michael took Benedict for a homosexual. Ben just needed a friend badly, and none of the others were the slightest bit interested in him. No wonder. He had that disconcerting stoniness Michael had seen in other men from time to time, and it always rendered them friendless. They didn't so much rebuff overtures as react peculiarly, would start spouting religion or talk about things most men preferred to ignore. He probably frightened girls to death, and they probably frightened him to death, too. Ben struck him as the sort of man whose life had been an emotional desert, with the juicelessness starting inside. No wonder he loved Sister Langtry; she treated him so normally, where the rest of the men regarded him as a kind of freak. What they sensed without understanding it, though maybe Neil had had enough experience to see it, was the violence. God, what a soldier he must have been!

At which moment Benedict stirred; his face began to squeeze in on itself, nostrils pinched, eyes glassy. It turned to stone under Michael's eyes. Curious, Michael turned his head to see what Benedict had seen. And there was Luce in the distance, parading up the beach from its far end toward them, and parade he did. Stepping high in a mincing parody of a lifesaver's strut, superbly aware of his own superbness, the sun lighting up his golden body, the length and the thickness of his penis mocking every other man on the beach into sullen inadequacy and secret loathing envy.

"The bastard!" said Neil, long cobbled toes digging into the sand as if this were but the commencement of a mole process which would end in burying him. "God, if only I had the guts to take a Bengal razor to that load he's carrying!"

"Just once I wish I could see him," said Matt wistfully.

"A sight to behold," said Michael, looking amused.

Luce reached them and swung round gracefully to stand above them, one hand absently caressing his hairless chest. "Tennis, anyone?" he asked, the other hand swishing an imaginary racquet.

"Oh, is there a court here?" asked Michael, ingenuously surprised. "I'll have a game with you, then."

Luce stared at him suspiciously, the realization that the offer wasn't meant seriously dawning slowly. "You're pulling my leg, you sarcastic bastard!" he said, astonished.

"Why not?" asked Michael, grinning. "You've got three."

Matt and Neil laughed uproariously, and Benedict succumbed to a self-conscious titter, which the group nearest to them on the beach echoed, ears tuned guiltily. Luce stood for a moment flabbergasted, uncertain how to act. It was an infinitesimal pause; he shrugged and moved away toward the water as if such had been his intention all along.

"Very good, Mike," he said over his shoulder. "Very good indeed! I'm glad to see you noticed."

"How could a bloke not notice a donger like that? I thought at first it was a bit left over from the Sydney Harbor Bridge!" Michael called after him.

The next group down the beach abandoned all pretense at disinterest and burst out laughing; Luce's grand moment had become a farce. Neil picked up a handful of sand and threw it at Michael joyously. "Full marks, old son," he said, wiping his eyes. "God, how I wish I'd said that!"

When Sister Langtry came on duty a little after five, to discover that the rest of her charges had resoundingly decided to like Michael, she felt like cheering and waving flags. It mattered tremendously to her that they should like him, wished on them at the very last moment as he had been. Just why it should matter so much she had not quite worked out, but she suspected it was more on his behalf than for the sake of the others.

At first he had stirred her curiosity, then her sense of justice and fair play, then her frank interest. If she had doubted how he would settle into ward X, her doubt lay not so much with him as with Neil, the ringleader of X. For Neil had not been warm in his welcome; he might mock himself, but he was a leader, a naturally autocratic personality. The other men looked to him, even Luce, so it lay within his power to make ward X as much heaven or hell as limbo.

To discover Neil treating Michael as a full equal made her profoundly thankful. Michael would be all right from now on, therefore the rest of them would be too.

Then Benedict appeared and was delighted to learn that Michael played chess. Chess was apparently Ben's one fleshly weakness, but it bored Neil and frightened

Nugget; Matt had liked to play when he could see the board and the pieces, but said he found keeping a visual image in his mind all the time too much of a strain. Luce played well, but couldn't resist turning black against white into a metaphorical struggle between good and evil, which upset Ben more than Sister Langtry felt was good for him, so she had forbidden him to play with Luce.

Watching Benedict settle pleasurably on the bench opposite Michael after dinner, the chess set out, made Sister Langtry feel as if the ward was finally complete within itself. How nice to have an ally! she thought contentedly, too generous to resent the fact that apparently Michael was succeeding with a patient she had always known was not amenable to her own brand of help.

3 Luce had more than one quality in common with a cat: not only did he move like one, he could see in the dark like one. Thus he carried no torch as he moved surefooted through the spaces between deserted huts, making for a spot at the end of the nurses' beach where it was brought up short by a tall outcrop of rocks Sister Langtry had described erroneously to Michael as a headland.

The MPs were lax these days, as Luce well knew; the war was over, Base Fifteen was as quiet as the corpse it was soon to become, and there was no feeling of discord in the air. Sensitive to such things, MP antennae registered zero.

Tonight he was on his way to an important assignation, feeling powerful and light and almost painfully alive. Oh, yes, little Miss Woop-Woop, the bank manager's precious daughter! It hadn't been easy persuading her to meet him like this, and she had consented only when she realized there were no other ways of seeing him than illicitly or in the full public gaze of the verandah outside the nurses' mess. She was a nurse officer, he was a man from the ranks, and while innocent intercourse between old school chums was quite permissible, any intercourse more intimate would bring a sharp reprimand and disciplinary action from Matron, a real stickler for military conventions. But he had succeeded in persuading her to meet him on the beach after dark, and he had no doubts as to how matters would proceed from now on; the biggest hurdle was already behind him.

There was no moon to betray them, but in this place of dark peacefulness the sky shone with an unearthly brilliance, and the matted clouds of nebulae and star clusters along the axis of the galaxy breathed a still, cold light upon the world, faintly silvering it. Thus he had no trouble in picking out her form among the denser shadows around it, and moved very quietly until he stood alongside her.

She drew in her breath sharply. "I didn't hear you!" she said, shuddering a little.

"You can't possibly be cold on a night like this," he said, rubbing the goose bumps on the back of her hand with a friendly impersonal touch.

"It's nerves. I'm not used to sneaking out like this up here—it's different from sneaking out of a nice safe nurses' home in Sydney."

"Calm down, it's all right! We'll just sit ourselves over here where it's comfortable, and have a cigarette." With a hand under her elbow, he helped her down onto the sand, and sat far enough away from her to reassure her. "I hate to be a bludger, but do you happen to have any tailor-mades?" he said, teeth flashing in the dimness. "I can roll you one, but you mightn't like the taste."

She fumbled in one of the pockets of her bush jacket and produced a packet of Craven As, which he took without permitting his fingers to touch hers. Then he gave the act a certain intimacy by lighting the cigarette in his own mouth and passing it to her. For himself, he produced his makings and rolled one leisurely.

"Won't someone see our cigarettes?" she asked.

"Well, I suppose they might, but it isn't very likely," he said easily. "The nurses here are a pretty tame lot, so the MPs don't usually bother with places like this." He turned his head to watch her profile. "How's the old town these days?"

"A bit empty."

It came hard to say it, but he managed. "How's my mother? My sisters?"

"When did you hear from them last?"

"A couple of years ago."

"What? Don't they write?"

"Oh, all the time! I just don't read their letters."

"Then why feign interest in them by asking?"

The flash of spirit surprised him. "We have to talk about something, don't we?" he asked gently, and reached out to touch her hand. "You're nervous."

"You're just the way you were at school!"

"No, not a bit. There's been too much water under the bridge since then."

"Has it been very awful?" she asked, pitying him.

"The war, you mean? Sometimes." He thought of the office he had occupied, the pleasant safe job with the quivering jellyfish of a major who had been his titular boss, though in actual fact it had been the other way around. Luce sighed. "A man has to do his duty, you know."

"Oh, I know!"

"It's good to see a friendly face here," he said, after a slight silence.

"For me, too. I was so happy when Manpower released me to go into the army, but it hasn't been at all what I expected. Of course it would have been different if the war had still been on. But Base Fifteen's rather a dead place, isn't it?"

He laughed softly. "That's a good description of it."

The question she was burning to ask came out all of a sudden, before she could bite it back, or phrase it more tactfully. "What are you doing in ward X, Luce?"

His answer had been ready since the moment when he realized what he had in mind for little Miss Woop-Woop. "Battle fatigue, plain, pure and simple," he said, and heaved a huge sigh. "It happens to the best of us."

"Oh, Luce!"

This is the worst dialogue ever written, he thought to himself, but life's like that. No point in wasting Shakespeare where Daggett would do.

"Feeling warmer?" he asked.

"Much! It's hot up here, isn't it?"

"How about coming for a swim?"

"Now? I don't have my swimming costume!"

And pause to count four, then say: "It's dark, I can't see you. Even if I could, I wouldn't look."

Of course she knew as well as he that in consenting to meet him here she was also consenting to whatever liberties he planned to take; but the ritual moves had to be made, the ritual responses elicited. Otherwise conscience would not be satisfied, nor parents' ghosts propitiated. She was panting for him, and she meant to have him, but he mustn't ever think her cheap or easy.

"Well, all right then, but only if you go in first and promise to stay in until I'm out and dressed again," she said hesitantly.

"Done!" he exclaimed, and he sprang to his feet and twisted free of his clothes with the speedy dispatch of one who had been trained in quick-change techniques.

She didn't want to lose him in the water, so she followed him as quickly as she could, but things like boots and gaiters were new to her, slowed her down.

"Luce! Where are you?" she whispered, wading in until her knees were submerged, and frightened that he would grab her in a kind of sport she considered juvenile.

"I'm here," he said reassuringly, from somewhere fairly close at hand, and without attempting to grab her.

Breathing a sigh of relief, she waded further in and bobbed down until her shoulders were covered.

"It's nice, isn't it?" he asked. "Come on, swim out for a little bit with me."

She followed in the phosphorescent glitter of his wake, swimming strongly, and feeling for the first time in her life the voluptuous freedom of her unclothed body supported by the water. It excited her too much; she turned and began to swim in again, not looking to see whether he still swam out, or was accompanying her.

It was like some magic, enchanted dream, and her mind winged ahead of her flying body, already skin-deep in loving him. No tremulous virgin, she knew

110

what was going to happen, and knew because it was *him* that it was going to be better than it ever had been in her life.

Her conviction that she was caught up in a spell was heightened when out of the corner of her eye she saw him alongside her; she stopped, trod water, found her feet on the bottom and stood up, waiting for his kiss. But instead he lifted her bodily into his arms and walked from the water, up to the place where he had strewn his clothes, and laid her on them. She held up her hands to him, he sank down beside her and buried his face in her neck. When she first felt his teeth she arched her back and whimpered with pleasure, but the sound quickly became a suppressed groan of pain, for these were no gentle, nuzzling nips. He was biting her, really biting her, with a silent, savage, crushing ferocity that at first she bore, thinking it would stop, that he was starved for her. But the agony went on, became unbearable; she began to fight to get away, could not from his heavy, incredibly strong hold. Mercifully he moved from her neck, began biting less painfully at one breast, but with the pressure of his teeth increased again she could no longer keep the cry of terror in, for suddenly she was sure he intended to kill her where she lay.

"Oh, Luce, don't! Please, please, I beg of you! You're hurting me!"

The thin, wailing words seemed to penetrate, for he did stop, began to kiss the breast he had mauled so cruelly a moment before; but the kisses were perfunctory and soon ceased.

It was going to be all right. Her childhood love and her want came back, she sighed and murmured. He propped himself on his hands above her, nudged her knees apart imperatively, and fitted his legs between hers. Feeling the blind thing pushing at her, she reached down to guide it, found the right place with a shiver and took her fingers away to clasp his shoulders, draw him down onto her, welcome him, feel the weight

111

of him and the skin of him, his hands across her back. But he refused to lower himself, remaining propped away from her by the full length of his arms, supporting himself on his hands, touching her only where apparently he thought it mattered; as if to touch her elsewhere would channel precious energy away from the task at hand. The first great thrust made her gasp with pain, but she was young, wet, relaxed and desperately anxious for this; she let her legs rest fully on the ground to lessen the depth to which he could penetrate, and began to pickup his rhythm until she moved with him, not back when he moved forward, but forward to meet each thrust.

And it became beautiful, though she longed to feel him embrace her instead of holding himself aloof. His exasperating posture diminished the friction she found necessary, so it was a full ten minutes before she came to orgasm, which she did more hugely and wildly than ever in her life, feeling the spasms from her jaw to her feet like the clonic jerks of some ecstatic epilepsy.

Enormously grateful to him for controlling himself so long to please her, she expected him to follow immediately with his own orgasm; but he did not. That grim, steady, obsessive pounding continued and continued and continued. Exhaustion began to suffocate her; she went limp, dried up, endured it until she could endure no more.

"For God's sake, Luce! Enough! That's enough!"

He withdrew himself at once, still erect, not having achieved a climax. And it crushed her utterly. Never before had she felt so joyless, so devoid of any sweet victory. No use to whisper to him the timeless, inevitable "Was it all right?" It had clearly not been all right.

But it was not in her nature to remain cast down by the actions of others; if he wasn't satisfied, it was his problem, not hers. For a moment she lay where she was, hoping he would kiss her, hug her, but he did not; from the time when he picked her up until the end of it there had been no kiss; as if to touch her lips with his own would have destroyed his pleasure. Pleasure? Did he get any pleasure out of it at all? Surely he must! He had been as hard as a rock throughout.

She drew her legs to one side, rolled over on her elbow and began to grope for her cigarettes. The moment she found them Luce held out his hand for one for himself; she passed it over, and leaned to light it for him. The match revealed his face, expressionless, long dark lashes down to hide the eyes. He drew deeply on the cigarette, and the match went out, snuffed by the strength of his exhalation.

Well, that ought to keep the silly bitch happy, he thought, lying back with his hands behind his head, the cigarette held between lightly clenched lips. Thump them until they yelled for mercy, then they had no right to complain or criticize. How long that took didn't matter to him. He could keep it up all night if he had to. He despised the act, he despised them, he despised himself. The act was a tool, the tool of the tool between his legs, but he had vowed long ago never to be the tool of either. Always the operator. He was master, they were servants, and the only people he couldn't bend to his will were those like Langtry who felt no tug toward servants or master. God, what he wouldn't give to see Langtry down on her knees, begging and pleading for any and all of them, servants and master . . .

He glanced at his watch, saw that it was after half-past nine. Time to go or he would be late in, and he was not about to give Langtry the satisfaction of reporting him to Colonel Chinstrap. Reaching out, he gave the reclining figure near him a neat slap on her bottom.

"Come on, love, I've got to go. It's late."

He assisted her into her clothes with the scrupulous attention to detail of a ladies' maid, kneeling to lace up her boots, buckle her gaiters. He dusted her down, twitched the grey bush jacket into place, did up its belt and adjusted the set of her slouch hat to his satisfaction. His own clothes were wet in places from the sea, but he slid into them indifferently.

Then he walked with her to the boundary of the

113

sisters' blocks, his hand beneath her elbow to guide her through the darkness with an impersonal care she found infuriating.

"Will I see you again?" she asked when he stopped.

He smiled. "You certainly will, my love."

"When?"

"In a few days. We can't make the pace too fierce or we'll be nobbled. I'll come to pay my respects to you on the verandah outside your mess, and we'll arrange something then. All right?"

She stood on tiptoe to kiss his cheek self-consciously, then commenced the last lap home on her own.

He changed immediately into a cat, went slipping off into the gloom, skirting the patches of light, keeping well alongside buildings when he came to them.

And he thought about what he had been thinking about through most of the lovemaking: Sergeant Wilson, hero and shirt-lifting poofter. Shipped off to X by an embarrassed CO to escape the disgrace of a court-martial, he was willing to bet. Well, well! The admissions to X were certainly getting queerer and queerer all the time.

It had not escaped him that Langtry thought the new admission was a bit of all right. Perked her up no end, he had! Of course she didn't believe what she'd read in his papers, no woman ever did—especially when the bloke was as manly and strong as Sergeant Wilson, a proper answer to an old maid's prayers. The question: Was Sergeant Wilson the answer to Langtry's prayers? Luce had thought for a long time that privilege was going to be Neil's, but at the moment he was not so sure. He'd better do a bit of praying himself, that Langtry preferred a sergeant to a captain, a Wilson to a Parkinson. If she did, it would be a lot easier to do what he was planning to do. Make Langtry grovel.

He became aware that his balls ached all the way through to his teeth, and stopped in the lee of a deserted ward to urinate. But as usual the wretched stuff wouldn't come; it always took him ages to manage to pee. He dallied as long as he dared, willing the stream to start, holding his despised prize tool between his fingers, wrinkling its skin back and forth in a quiet frenzy of desperation. No use. Another look at his watch told him there wasn't any more time; he would have to endure the ache a few minutes more.

PART 3

1 Michael had been a patient in ward X for about two weeks when Sister Langtry first began to experience an odd feeling of premonition. Not a pleasant anticipation of pleasantness, but a morbid, crawling dread which had absolutely no basis in reality. The reality was the converse, a smooth new completeness. There were no undercurrents; everyone liked Michael, and Michael liked everyone. The men were relaxed, and certainly more comfortable, for Michael waited on them hand and foot, fetched and carried cheerfully. After all, he explained to her, he couldn't read endlessly, he had his indolent periods on the beach, and he needed to move around with some purpose. So he mended the plumbing such as it was, hammered in nails, fixed things. There was a cushion sewn to the back of her office chair, courtesy of Michael; the floors almost gleamed; the dayroom was tidier.

Yet still her disquiet persisted. He is a catalyst of some kind, she thought; in his own nature and essence harmless, but in ward X, who knows? Yes, everyone liked him and he liked everyone. And there were no undercurrents. But ward X was different since his advent, though she could not discover what the difference was. Just an atmosphere.

The heat became oppressive, very still, and the air brooded; the slowest, most leisurely of movements produced rivers of sweat, and the waters of the ocean beyond the reef turned a sullen green, horizon smudged. With the full moon came the rain, two days of awesome steady downpour which laid the dust but brought mud instead. Mildew popped out on everything: mosquito nets, sheets, screens, books, boots, clothes, woodwork, bread. But with the beach unavailable, it saved the men from complete idleness, for Sister Langtry kept them all hard at it cleaning off the mildew with spirit-dampened rags. She issued an order that all boots and shoes must come off just inside the front or back door, yet still by some osmotic process the mud infiltrated everywhere into the ward, and that kept the men busy too, with buckets and mops and floor cloths.

Luckily there was nothing depressing about the rain itself, as it didn't mourn the passing of the sun the way the tender, colder rains of higher latitudes did. As long as it didn't set in, such rain as this almost had the power to exalt, filling the human mind with a vast impression of might. If it set in, as it would when the real monsoons came, its effect was worse than any other rain, for the power became remorseless and overwhelming, human beings mere scurrying impotent ants.

But this rain was too early to be the beginning of the monsoon, and when the rain cleared, even that drab unlovely collection of buildings called Base Fifteen looked unexpectedly beautiful: scrubbed, rinsed, swept.

Well, that's that, thought Sister Langtry, feeling an enormous relief. All I was worrying about was rain! It always affects them this way. Affects me, too.

"How silly," she said to Michael, handing him a bucket of muddy water.

He was putting the finishing touches on the sluice room after the swabbing party had downed tools and was taking a well-earned rest on the verandah.

"What's silly?" he asked, tipping the water down the drain and wiping off the galvanized iron with a rag.

"I've had a feeling there was trouble brewing, but I think all it was was rain brewing. After all this time in the tropics you'd think I'd know better." She leaned her back against the doorjamb and watched him, the intent thoroughness with which every single task was done, the smooth roundedness of the whole.

After the rag was draped to dry over the edge of the bucket he straightened and turned, eyeing her with amusement. "I agree, you'd think so." He reached past her to pluck his shirt off a nail behind the door, and put it on. "It gets you down after a while, doesn't it? Never anything by halves up here. I never remember getting in a tizzy about a couple of days of rain back home, but up here I've seen it lead almost to murder."

"Did it in your own case?"

The smiling eyes looked arrested for a moment, then continued to smile. "No."

"If not rain, why?"

"That's my business," he said, quite pleasantly.

Her cheeks reddened. "It's also mine, considering the circumstances! Oh, why won't you see that it's better to talk about things? You're as standoffish as Ben!"

The shirt was buttoned and tucked in, all without any self-consciousness. "Don't get upset, Sis. And don't worry about me."

"I'm not worried about you in the least. But I've been in charge of X long enough to know that it's better for my patients to talk things out."

"I'm not your patient," he said, poised as if he expected to see her move out of his way.

She didn't. She continued to stand where she was, more exasperated than angry. "Michael, of course you're my patient! A pretty stable patient, admittedly, but you can't have been admitted to X for no good reason!"

"There was a very good reason. I tried to kill a bloke," he said dispassionately.

"Why?"

"The reason's there in my papers."

"It's not a good enough reason for me." Her mouth straightened, set hard. "I don't understand your papers. You're not a homosexual."

"How do you know?" he asked coolly.

She drew a breath, but met his eyes very directly. "I know," she said.

Whereupon he laughed, head thrown back. "Well, Sis, it doesn't matter to me why I'm here, so why

121

should it matter to you? I'm just glad I am here, that's all."

She moved away from the door, into the room. "You're fencing with me," she said slowly. "What are you trying to hide? What's so secret you can't bear to tell me?"

For a moment he was startled into dropping his ever-present guard, and she caught a glimpse of someone who was very tired, a little bewildered, and troubled within himself. And seeing these things, she was quite disarmed.

"No, don't even bother to answer that," she said, smiling at him in genuine friendship.

He responded by softening his expression into an affection purely for her, and said, "I'm just not a talker, Sis, when it comes to myself. I *can't* talk."

"Are you frightened I might sit in judgment?"

"No. But to talk, you have to find the right words, and I never seem to manage to find them. Or at least not at the right time. About three o'clock this morning they'll all be there, right where I want them."

"That's true of everyone. But all you have to do is start! I'll help you go on, because I want to help you."

His eyes closed, he sighed. "Sis, I do not need help!"

She gave up—for the moment. "Then tell me what you think of Benedict," she said.

"Why ask me about Ben?"

"Because you're succeeding with him, where I never have. Please don't think I'm resentful. I'm too glad to see it happen. But I am interested."

"Benedict." His head lowered while he thought. "I told you, I'm not good with words. What do I think of him? I like him. I pity him. He's not well."

"Dating only back to that incident in the village?"

Michael shook his head positively. "Oh, no! It goes back a long way further than that."

"Is it because he lost his parents at an early age? Or because of the grandmother who brought him up?"

"Maybe. It's hard to tell. Ben's not sure who he is, I think. Or if he is sure, then he doesn't know how to deal with what he is. I don't know. I'm not a mental specialist."

"Nor am I," she said ruefully.

"You do all right."

"If I'm honest with myself, Ben's the only one I fret about after Base Fifteen."

"When he gets out of the army, you mean?"

"Yes." She searched for the right words, not wanting to wound Michael's feelings; he was trying so hard with Ben. "You see, I'm not sure Ben's going to be capable of living independently of some kind of enclosed unit. Yet I don't feel it's fair to him to suggest that he be placed under detention."

"A mental asylum?" he asked incredulously.

"I suppose that's what I mean. They're all we've got for people like Ben. But I hesitate to do that."

"You're wrong!" he cried.

"I may well be. That's why I hesitate."

"It would kill him."

"Yes." Her face was sad. "As you see, my job's not all beer and skittles."

His hand came out to grip her shoulder hard, shake her. "Just don't do anything in a hurry, please! And don't do it without talking to me first!"

It was a heavy hand; she turned her head to look at it. "Ben's improving," she said. "Thanks to you. That's why I'm talking to you now. Don't worry!"

Neil spoke from the doorway. "We thought the pair of you must have gone down the drain," he said lightly.

Sister Langtry stepped back from Michael, whose hand had fallen away the moment he became aware of Neil. "Not quite down the drain," she said, and smiled at Neil a little apologetically; then she was annoyed with herself for feeling apology. And annoyed with Neil, for more obscure reasons.

Michael remained where he was, watching the slightly proprietary manner in which Neil ushered Sister Langtry from the sluice room. Then he sighed, shrugged, and followed them out onto the verandah. Ward X was about as private a place to conduct a private conversation as the middle of a parade ground. Everyone kept tabs on everyone else; and that was particularly true of Sister Langtry. If they didn't know where she was, who she was with, they couldn't rest until they found her. And sometimes they did a little mental arithmetic to make sure she was apportioning her time correctly among all of them. All of them? The ones who mattered. Neil was a master at mental arithmetic.

2 By dawn of the next day the weather had settled to an intoxicating balminess which caused everyone's mood to soar. The cleaning chores done, the men gathered on the verandah while Sister Langtry went into her office to catch up on her paper work. The beach would be open in the afternoon, and would be relatively crowded; only when it was closed did the patients of ward X realize how much it meant to be able to shrug off clothes and cares, switch off thought, swim and sun and doze themselves into pleasant stupor.

With half the morning still to get through, the usual fretting apathy was missing, everyone was so looking forward to the beach. Luce disposed himself to sleep on one of the verandah beds, Neil persuaded Nugget and Benedict to play cards at the table, and Michael took Matt up to the far end of the verandah, where some chairs sat beneath the back window of Sister Langtry's office, isolated enough to command peace.

Matt wanted to dictate a letter to his wife, and Michael had volunteered to act as his amanuensis. So far Mrs. Sawyer didn't know about Matt's blindness; he had insisted that it be kept from her, that he wanted to tell her himself, that no one had the right to deprive him of his request. Pitying him, Sister Langtry agreed to comply, knowing his real reason to be a despairing hope that before he met his wife again some miracle would have happened, and the blindness would have passed away.

When it was finished, Michael read the letter back to him slowly.

". . . and so because my hand has not yet healed properly, my friend Michael Wilson has volunteered to write this to you for me. However, you must not worry. All is going well. I think you are sensible enough to know that if the injury was a serious one they would have sent me back to Sydney a long time ago. Please do not worry about me. Give Margaret, Mary, Joan and little Pam a hug and a kiss from Daddy, and tell them it won't be long now. I miss you very much. Look after yourself and the girls. Your loving husband, Matthew."

All the letters home were stilted, the efforts mostly of men who had never expected to be far enough away from home and their loved ones to have to put pen to paper. And besides, the censors read everything, and you never knew who the censors were. So most men kept themselves polite and aloof, successfully resisting the temptation to pour out their miseries and their frustrations. And most men wrote home regularly, the way children do who are sentenced to a boarding school they loathe; where happiness and busyness are, the urge to communicate with loved ones far away diminishes very quickly.

"Will that do?" asked Matt anxiously.

"I think so. I'll put it straight into an envelope now and give it to Sis before lunch . . . Mrs. Ursula Sawyer . . . What's the address, Matt?"

"Ninety-seven Fingleton Street, Drummoyne."

Luce came strolling down the verandah and flopped into a nearby cane chair. "Well, if it isn't little Lord Fauntleroy about his good deeds!" he said provocatively.

"If you sit in that chair wearing nothing but shorts you'll be striped like a convict," said Michael, slipping Matt's letter into his pocket.

"Oh, bugger the stripes!"

"Keep it clean and keep it down, Luce," said Matt, gesturing accurately toward the open louvers of Sister Langtry's office.

"Hold on a tick, Mike! I've got a letter for Matt's wife you can post along with that one," Luce said, too softly for any but the three of them to hear. "Like me

126

to read it? Dear madam, did you know your husband's — as blind as a bat?"

Matt was out of the chair too quickly for restraint, but Michael placed himself between the frantic blind man and his tormentor, and held Matt firmly. "It's all right, mate! He's just being nasty. Calm down, now! It's all right, I tell you! He couldn't do that even if he wanted to. The censors would catch it."

Luce watched, enjoying the spectacle, and made no attempt to draw up his legs when he realized Michael had decided to put Matt with the others at the table. But rather than make an issue of it, Michael chose to guide Matt around the outflung legs, and so departed in peace.

After they were gone, Matt to the table and Michael into the ward, Luce got up and went to the verandah railing, leaning on it, his head cocked to hear the murmur of Michael's and Sister Langtry's voices through the open window; though his position and pose indicated that he was not listening should the inhabitants of the office look his way, he was still within earshot. Then the office door closed, all was silent again. Luce slipped past the cardplayers and went into the ward.

He found Michael in the dayroom buttering bread. Fresh crusty bread was the only culinary thrill, and a recent one at that, which Base Fifteen had to offer its inmates. Patients and staff alike consumed vast quantitites of the bread at every opportunity, for it was excellent. By nine o'clock in the evening and the last cup of tea of the day, there was never any of the fairly generous daily ration left.

The dayroom was not a kitchen, simply a food repository and utensil cleaning/storing area. It had a rough counter and cupboard unit running under one louvered opening and along the wall between it and the sluice room next door. There was a sink beneath the window, and a spirit stove on the counter some distance away from the sink. It lacked any sort of device to keep food cold, but there was a wire-mesh meat safe hanging on a rope from the roof joists and dangling in lazy turns like a Chinese lantern.

Tucked in the far corner of the bench was a small spirit-fired sterilizer in which Sister Langtry boiled up her hypodermic equipment and what few instruments she was ever likely to need, in the unlikely event of ever needing them at all. As a matter of good practice she kept two syringes, hypodermic needles, suture needles, a pair of suture needle holders, mosquito forceps and straight forceps permanently sterile in case a patient injured himself, required sedation by injection in a hurry, or was attacked, or attempted suicide. When ward X had first been opened there was heated debate as to whether its patients might be permitted to keep their razors, belts and other potential instruments of destruction, and whether kitchen knives should be kept under lock and key. But in the end it was admitted to be impractical, and only once had a patient availed himself of a suicide tool, luckily unsuccessfully. Violence of one patient toward others had never been sufficiently premeditated to review the decision, for patients who could not be managed under Base Fifteen's conditions did not remain there.

After dark the dayroom was alive with cockroaches; not all the hygiene in the world could eliminate them, for they flew in from outside, crawled up through the drain, dropped from the thatched roof, almost popped into existence out of nothing. If a man saw one he killed it, but there were always others to take its place. Neil was in the habit of organizing a full-scale hunt once a week, in which every man except Matt was expected to bag at least twenty cockroaches, and that probably kept the cockroach population down to something tolerable. However, the dreary little room was always very clean and tidy, so the pickings for scavengers of any kind were scant.

Luce stood in the doorway watching Michael for a few moments, then reached into the pocket of his shorts, withdrew his makings, and began rolling a cigarette. Though Michael was five inches shorter than Luce's six feet two, they looked well matched, each shirtless, broad in chest, wide in shoulders, and flat-bellied.

Turning his head toward the left, Luce saw that the door to Sister Langtry's office opposite the dayroom was firmly closed.

"I never manage to get under your skin, do I?" he asked Michael, tobacco tin back in his pocket and both hands lazily rolling a cylinder out of the shreds he had plucked from it; a little sheet of rice paper dangled from his bottom lip, and fluttered as he talked.

When Michael didn't bother to answer, he repeated it in a tone calculated to make anyone jump. *"I never manage to get under your skin, do I?"*

Michael didn't jump, but he did answer. "Why should you want to?" he asked.

"Because I like getting under people's skins! I like making people squirm. It breaks the God-awful monotony."

"You'd do better to occupy yourself being pleasant and useful." The way Michael said it, there was a vicious bite to it; he still felt Matt's distress.

The half-made cigarette fell unheeded to the floor, the rice paper flew away as he spat it out; Luce crossed the dayroom in one bound and grasped Michael hard about the upper arm, swinging him roughly around.

"Who do you think you are? Don't you *dare* patronize me!"

"That sounds like something you had to spout in a play," said Michael, looking steadily up into Luce's face.

For perhaps a minute they didn't move, simply stared at each other.

Then Luce's hand relaxed, but instead of falling away it cupped itself around Michael's biceps, its fingers caressing the angry marks which were beginning to flare up under the skin he had gripped so hard.

"There's something in you, our Michael, isn't

129

there?" Luce whispered. "Sister's darling little blue-eyed boy and all, there's something in you she wouldn't like one bit. But I know what it is, *and* I know what to do about it."

The voice was insidious, almost hypnotic, and the hand slipped down Michael's forearm, over his fist, gently forcing him to drop the butter knife. Neither man so much as took breath. Then as Luce's head came closer, Michael's lips parted, he hissed an intake of air between clenched teeth, and his eyes blazed into life.

They heard the noise simultaneously, and turned. Sister Langtry was standing in the doorway.

Luce's hand dropped from Michael's casually, not too quickly or guiltily, then with the action completed he moved naturally one pace away.

"Aren't you finished yet, Michael?" asked Sister Langtry, voice not quite normal, though the rest of her seemed so, even her eyes.

Michael picked up the butter knife. "Nearly, Sis."

Luce left his side, gave Sister Langtry a wickedly gleeful look as he passed her, and went out. The forgotten cigarette lay on the floor, tendrils and paper moving in a little wind.

Taking a deep breath, Sister Langtry walked into the room, not aware that she was wiping the palms of her hands against her dress, up and down, up and down. She stood where she could see Michael in profile as he began to cut the buttered bread into small segments and pile them on a plate.

"What was all that about?" she asked.

"Nothing." He sounded unconcerned.

"Are you sure?"

"Quite sure, Sis!"

"He wasn't . . . trying to get at you, was he?"

Michael turned away to make the tea; the kettle on the spirit stove was boiling fiercely, adding its steam to an atmosphere already laden. Oh, God, why wouldn't people leave him alone? "Trying to get at me?" he repeated, hoping simple obtuseness would deflect her.

She tried desperately to marshal her thoughts and

130

her emotions into some sort of disciplined order, aware that she had rarely been so upset, so thrown off balance. "Look, Michael," she said, speaking without a tremor, "I'm a big girl now, and I don't like being made to feel like a little girl again. Why do you persist in treating me as if what ever you've got on your mind is too much for me to cope with? I'll ask you again—was Luce making some sort of advance to you? *Was he?*"

Michael tipped a great bubbling stream of water between the kettle and the waiting empty teapot. "No, Sis, honestly he wasn't. He was just doing a Luce." A faint smile turned up the corner of his mouth; he put the kettle down on the stove, turned out the flame, and swung round to face her fully. "It's very simple. Luce was just trying to find a way to get under my skin. That's how he put it himself. But he can't. I've met men like Luce before. No matter how I'm provoked, I'm never going to lose control of myself again." One hand closed into a fist. "I can't! I'm afraid of what I might do."

There was something about him; funny, Luce had used those words, too. Her gaze fixed on his bare shoulder to one side of the fair hair on his chest, not sure if the skin was pearled with sweat or steam. Suddenly she was terrified to meet his eyes, felt light-headed and empty-bellied, as helpless and inadequate as a girl in the grip of her first crush on some remote adult figure.

The color drained from her face, and she swayed. He moved quickly, sure she was going to faint, and put his arm about her waist, supporting her with sufficient strength to remove all sensation of weight from her feet. Nothing else could she feel save his arm and side and shoulder, until, horrified, she felt something surge within herself that squeezed the flesh of her nipples into tight hard tingling ridges and swelled her breasts painfully.

"Oh, God, no!" she cried, wrenching herself away, and turning it like lightning into a protest against Luce by pounding her fist softly on the counter. "He's a menace!" she said through clenched teeth. "He would destroy anything just to watch it twitch."

She was not the only one so affected; Michael's hand when he lifted it to brush the sweat from his face shook and he half turned away from her, forcing himself to take easy breaths, not trusting himself to look at her.

"There's only one way to deal with Luce," he said, "and that's not to let him get under your skin."

"What he needs is six months on a pick and shovel!"

"I could do with that myself. All of us in X could," he said gently, and found the strength to pick up the tray. "Come on, Sis. You'll feel better after a cuppa."

She managed a travesty of a smile and looked at him, not knowing whether to be ashamed or exalted, and searching his face for something to reassure her. But save for the eyes it was quite impersonal, and the eyes gave nothing away except a high degree of emotional excitement, for the pupils were dilated. Which could as well have been because of Luce.

There was no sign of Luce in the ward, nor on the verandah. The cardplayers abandoned their game somewhat thankfully at sight of the teapot, for its advent had been expected for some time.

"The more I sweat, the more tea I drink," said Neil, draining his mug at a gulp, then holding it out for more.

"Salt tablet time for you, my friend," said Sister Langtry, trying to get the correct degree of cheerfulness and detachment back into her voice.

Neil glanced at her quickly; so did the others.

"Is anything wrong, Sis?" asked Nugget anxiously.

She smiled, shook her head. "A slight attack of the Luces. Where is he?"

"I have a feeling he took himself off in the direction of the beach."

"Before one o'clock? That doesn't sound like Luce."

Nugget grinned, his likeness to a small rodent enhanced by the appearance of two prominent upper incisors. "Did I say he was going swimming? And did I say which beach? He just went for a walk, and if he happens to meet a nice young lady—well, they stop and talk, that's all."

Michael sighed audibly, smiling at Sister Langtry as if to say, See, I told you there was nothing to worry about, and stretched back on the seat as he lifted his arms to put his hands behind his head, the heavily developed pectorals tightening, the hair in his armpits flattened and glistening darkly with sweat.

She felt her color going again, and managed with a huge effort to put her cup down in its saucer without spilling tea. This is ridiculous! she thought, fighting back stubbornly. I am not a schoolgirl! I'm a grown and an experienced woman!

Neil stiffened, reached out his hand to close it over hers reassuringly. "Here, steady on! What's the matter, Sis? A touch of fever?"

She stood up perfectly. "I think it must be. Can you manage if I go off early? Or would you rather I asked Matron for a relief until after lunch?"

Neil accompanied her into the ward while the others sat on at the table looking worried, Michael included.

"For God's sake don't inflict a relief on us!" Neil begged. "We'll go right round the bend if you do. Will you be all right by yourself? It might be better if I walk you to your quarters."

"No, Neil, truly. I doubt if it's anything more than that I just don't feel myself today. The weather, perhaps. It promised to be so cool and dry earlier, but now it feels like a soup tureen. An afternoon's rest should put me right." She parted the fly-curtain and smiled at him over her shoulder. "I'll see you this evening."

"Only if you feel better, Sis. If you don't, don't worry, and no relief, please. The place is as quiet as the grave."

3 Sister Langtry's room was one of a bank of ten similar rooms constructed in typical Base Fifteen style, side by side in a row and fronted by a wide verandah, the whole rickety structure standing ten feet above the ground on piles. For four months she had been the block's only inhabitant, an indication not of antisociality on her part, but of a mature woman's starvation for privacy. Since joining the army in 1940 she had shared accommodation, four to a small tent during her casualty clearing station days. When she had first come to Base Fifteen it had seemed like a paradise, though she had been obliged to share her room, the same she still occupied, and the block had vibrated shrilly with the sounds of women living far too close to each other. Little wonder then that as the nursing staff shrank those left on it put as much space between each other as they could, and wallowed in the luxury of being alone.

Sister Langtry let herself into her room and crossed immediately to the bureau, opened its top drawer and withdrew a bottle of Nembutal grains one and a half. There was a carafe of boiled water lidded with a cheap glass tumbler on top of the bureau; taking the glass off, she poured a little water into it, and swallowed the tablet before she could change her mind. The eyes looking back at her from the corroded depths of the little mirror on the wall above the bureau were dark-ringed and blank; she willed them to remain that way until the Nembutal took effect.

With practiced ease she found and removed the two long grips that fixed her veil in place and lifted the entire edifice off her sweat-lank hair, placing it empty and stiff on a hard chair, where it sat mutely mocking her. She subsided onto the edge of her bed to unlace her daytime duty shoes, put them neatly together far enough away to ensure that she wouldn't kick them getting in and out of bed, then stood up to remove her uniform and underclothes.

A cotton robe of vaguely Oriental design hung on a nail behind the door; she shrugged it on and went to take a shower in the clammy cheerless bathhouse. And finally, skin clean, decently clothed in limp cotton pajamas, she lay down on her bed and closed her eyes. The Nembutal was working, giving her a sensation not unlike that following too much gin, vertiginous and faintly nauseating. But at least it was working. She sighed and struggled to abandon her grasp on consciousness, thinking, Am I in love with him, or does it have a far different name than love? Have I simply been away too long from a normal life, been subjugating my physical feelings too harshly? It could be that. I hope it's that. Not love. Not here. Not with him. To me he doesn't seem the kind of man to esteem love. . . .

The images blurred, rocked, fused; she fell asleep so thankfully that she was able to tell herself it would be paradise never to have to wake up from sleep again, never, never. . . .

4 When she walked up the ramp of X about seven that evening she met Luce just outside the door; he would have nipped by her smartly, but she stepped across his path, looking grim.

"I'd like to see you for a moment, please."

He rolled his eyes. "Oh, Sis, fair go! I've got an appointment!"

"Then break it. Inside, Sergeant."

Luce stood watching her while she removed her slouch hat with its red-striped grey band, hung it where her red cape hung during the day; he liked her better in her night gear, a small soldier all in grey.

Settled behind her desk, she looked up at him to find he was lounging against the wall by the open door, arms folded, ready for a quick getaway.

"Come in, shut the door, and stand to attention, Sergeant," she said curtly, and waited until he complied. Then she continued. "I'd like you to explain to me exactly what was going on in the dayroom this morning between you and Sergeant Wilson."

He shrugged, shook his head. "Nothing, Sis."

"Nothing, *Sister*. It didn't look like nothing to me."

"Then what did it look like?" he asked, still smiling, still, it seemed, more amused at her than perturbed.

"As if you were making some sort of homosexual advance to Sergeant Wilson."

"I was," he said simply.

Taken aback, she had to pause for a moment to search for the next thing to say, which was, "Why?"

"Oh, it was just an experiment, that's all. He's a fairy. I wanted to see what he'd do."

136

"That's slander, Luce."

He laughed. "Then he can sue me! I tell you he's a great big fairy."

"Which doesn't explain why you were the one making the advance, does it? Leaving Sergeant Wilson out of it, you're not the slightest bit homosexual."

So suddenly the movement made her draw back involuntarily, he slid his hip onto the desk and sat side-on, leaning his face so close to hers that she could see the extraordinary structure of his irises, the multitude of differently colored streaks and flecks which gave them such a chameleon quality; his pupils were slightly enlarged and lustrous with reflections. And her heart took off at a gallop, remembering his effect on her during those first two days in the ward; she felt drowsy, hypnotized, almost bewitched. But what he said next jerked her out of the spell, away from the power.

"Sweetie, I'm *anything*," he said softly. "Anything you like to name! Young, old, male, female—it's all meat to me."

She couldn't prevent the gasp of revulsion. "Stop it! Don't say such things! You're damned!"

His face came even nearer, his clean and healthy smell curled around her. "Come on, Sis, try me! Do you know what your trouble is? You haven't tried anyone. Why don't you start with the best? I'm the best there is, I really am—oh, woman, I can make you shiver and yell your head off and beg for more! You couldn't imagine what I can do to you. Come on, Sis, try me! Just try me! Don't throw yourself away on a queen or a fake Pom who's too tired to get it up any more! Try *me!* I'm the best there is."

"Please go," she said, nostrils pinched.

"I don't usually like kissing people, but I am going to kiss you. Come on, Sis, kiss me!"

There was nowhere to go; the back of her chair was so close to the wall that it barely permitted her room to seat herself. But she pushed the chair back so sharply it whacked against the windowsill behind her, her body reared back in a convulsion of outrage even Luce could not mistake for anything but what it really was.

"Out, Luce! *Immediately!*" She clapped her hand across her mouth as if she was going to be sick, eyes fixed on that fascinating face as if she looked on the devil himself.

"All right, then, throw yourself away," he said, and stood up, plucking and rubbing at his trousers to ease his erection. "What a fool you are! You won't get any joy out of either of them. They're not men. I'm the only man here."

After he had gone she stared at the closed door with rigid attention to its construction until she felt the horror and the fright begin to ebb, and wanted so badly to weep that only a continued inspection of the door prevented the tears from coming. For she had felt the power in him, the will to have what he wanted at any cost. And wondered if that was how Michael had felt in the dayroom, impaled on those staring goatish eyes.

Neil knocked, entered and closed the door, one hand behind his back concealing something. Before he sat down in the visitor's chair he produced his cigarette case and offered it across the desk. It was a part of the ritual that she should make a token demur, but tonight she snatched the cigarette and leaned to have it lit as if she needed it far too badly to remember to demur.

Her boots scraped on the floor as she moved her feet; Neil raised one eyebrow.

"I've never known you to sit down without taking off your boots first, Sis. Are you sure you're fit to be here? Any fever? Headache?"

"No fever or headache, doctor, and I'm quite all right. The boots haven't come off because I caught Luce going out just as I was coming in, and I wanted a word with him. So the boots were rather forgotten."

He got up, came round the desk and knelt in the tiny space to one side of her chair, patting his thigh. "Come on, foot up."

The buckles on her webbing gaiter were stiff; he had

to work at them before they came undone, after which he peeled the gaiter off, loosened the laces of her boot enough to lever it off, and rolled her sock up over the trouser bottom. Then he performed the same service for her other foot, sat back on his heels and twisted to look for the pair of rubber-soled canvas shoes she wore in the ward after dark.

"Bottom shelf," she said.

"That's better," he said, the sandshoes laced to his satisfaction. "Comfortable?"

"Yes, thank you."

He returned to his chair. "You still look a bit washed out to me."

She glanced down at her hands, which trembled. "I've got the Joe Blakes!" she said, seeming surprised.

"Why don't you go on sick parade?"

"It's only nerves, Neil."

They smoked in silence, she looking purposely out the window, he looking intently at her. Then, as she turned to stub out her cigarette, he put the piece of paper he had been concealing down on the desk in front of her.

Michael! Just the way she herself saw him, fine and strong, eyes staring up at her so honestly and directly it seemed impossible to believe anything unmanly could ever lurk behind them.

"It's the best one you've done yet; even better than Luce, I think," she said, gazing down greedily at the drawing, and hoping she had not visibly jumped when she saw what he had brought her. Handling it carefully, she gave it back to him. "Would you pin it up for me, please?"

He obliged, fixing it at each corner with a thumbtack, positioning it at the right-hand end of the central row, next to himself. It outshone him, for in trying to depict himself his detachment had failed, and the face on the wall was weak, strained, attenuated.

"We're complete," he said, and sat down again. "Here, have another cigarette."

She took it almost as hastily as she had the first one,

drew a deep breath on the smoke, and while exhaling said to him rapidly and artificially, "Michael represents to me the enigma of men," pointing to the new drawing.

"You've got your signals crossed, Sis," Neil said easily, not betraying that he understood how difficult it was for her to broach the subject of Michael, nor betraying his own obsessive preoccupation with the subject of her and Michael. "It's women who are the enigma. Ask anyone from Shakespeare to Shaw."

"Only to men. Shakespeare and Shaw were men. It cuts both ways, you know. The opposite sex is the terra incognita. So every time I think I have men solved, you give some sort of complicated wriggle and you're off again. Swimming in the opposite direction from me." She tapped ash off her cigarette and smiled at him. "I suppose the chief reason why I like running this ward on my own is because it's such an excellent opportunity to study a group of men without other women interfering."

He laughed. "How very clinical! Say it to me, by all means, but don't ever say it to Nugget or he'll come down with a combined case of bubonic plague and anthrax." The expression in her eyes was a little indignant, as if she was about to protest that he misjudged her, but he continued smoothly before she could actually interrupt, wondering if she might yet be deflected by a mildly facetious response. "Men are basically the simplest of creatures. Not quite down to protozoa, perhaps, but certainly not up in the angels-on-a-pinhead class of conundrum." `

"Rot! You're a bigger mystery than any number of angels on a pinhead, and far more important! Take Michael—"

No, she couldn't do it. Couldn't bring herself to talk about what had happened between Michael and Luce in the dayroom, though walking from her quarters back to X she had decided Neil might be the only person who could help her. But she suddenly saw how telling him about them would expose herself, and she couldn't do that. And then there was her awful scene with Luce; she'd end in telling him about that as well, and there would be murder done. She closed her mouth, didn't finish the sentence.

"All right, then, let's take Mike," Neil said, as if she had produced a finished statement. "What's so special about our ministering angel Michael? How many of him could we fit on a pinhead?"

"Neil, if you say things that sound like Luce Daggett, I swear I will never speak to you again!"

He was so startled he dropped his cigarette, bent to pick it up and then sat staring at her with suspicion and consternation. "What on earth provoked that?" he asked.

"Oh, drat the wretched man! He rubs off," was all she would say.

"Sis, do you count me your friend? I mean someone really on your side, with you all the way?"

"Of course I do! You don't have to ask me that."

"Is it really Luce who's troubling you, or is it Mike? I've known and suffered Luce for over three months without feeling the way I do at the moment—ever since Michael arrived, as a matter of fact. In just two weeks this place seems to have turned into an unstable boiler. I keep waiting from minute to minute for it to explode, but so far it keeps seething up into the danger zone and flopping again. To wait for something to explode that you know must explode is a most unsettling feeling. Like being back under fire."

"I knew you were a bit down on Michael, but I didn't realize it went so deep," she said, tight-lipped.

"I am not down on Michael! He's a splendid chap. But Michael is the difference. Not Luce. Michael."

"That's ridiculous! How could Michael make everything different? He's so—so quiet!"

Well, here goes nothing, he thought, watching her carefully. Did she know what was happening to her, to him, to all of them?

"Perhaps because *you're* different. Since Michael came," he said steadily. "You must surely realize that

141

we tend to take our moods and attitudes from you, even Luce. And since Michael came you are a very different person—different moods, different attitudes."

Oh, God. Keep your face straight, Sister Langtry, don't let it give away a thing. It didn't; it looked at him with an almost polite interest, smooth and calm and impassive. Behind it her brain raced to cope with all the implications of this interview, and to formulate a behavior pattern which would if not pacify Neil, at least seem logical to him. Given what he knew of her, and he had just made her realize that he knew her better than she suspected. Everything he said was true, but she couldn't admit as much to him; she was too aware of his frailty, his dependence upon her. And damn him for trying to force an issue with her that she hadn't managed to sort out yet in her own mind!

"I'm tired, Neil," she said, her face suddenly showing all the strain of the long, difficult day. "It's just gone on too long. Or I'm proving too weak. I don't know. I wish I did know." She wet her lips. "Don't blame it all on Michael, please. It's far too complicated to deserve a simplification like that. If I'm different, it's because of things inside me. We're coming to an end, something else is about to begin. I think I'm preparing for that, and I think all of you are, too. And I'm so tired. Don't make it any harder, please. Just support me."

Something extraordinary was happening to Neil; he could actually physically feel it while he sat listening to an Honour Langtry who almost admitted defeat. As if in seeing her brought low his own inner resources were growing. As if he fed on her. And that was it, he thought exultantly; she was suddenly as human as he, a person with limits to her energies and endurance, and therefore fallible. To see her thus was to understand his own strengths instead of being forever paled by hers.

"When I first met you," he said slowly, "I thought you were made of solid iron. Everything I didn't have, you had. Lose a few men in a fight? You'd grieve for that, yes, but it wouldn't put you in a place like X. Nothing in the whole wide world could put you in a place like X. And I suppose at the time you were what I needed. If I hadn't needed that, you couldn't have helped, and you did help. Enormously. I don't want you to crack now. I'll do everything in my power to stop you cracking. But it's so nice to feel the balance tip a little bit my way for a change!"

"I understand that," she said, smiling. But then she sighed. "Oh, Neil . . . I am sorry. I really do feel a bit under the weather, you know. Not that I'm pleading it as an excuse. I'm not. You're quite right about my moods and attitudes. But I can deal with them."

"Just why is Michael in X?" he asked.

"You know better than to ask me that!" she said, astonished. "I can't discuss one patient with another!"

"Unless he's named Benedict or Luce." He shrugged. "Oh, well, it was worth a try. I didn't ask from idle curiosity. He's a dangerous man. He's got so much integrity!" The moment it was out he regretted saying it, not wishing to see her draw away when she had suddenly come so close to him.

However, she didn't recoil or become defensive, though she did get to her feet. "It's high time I put in an appearance on the ward. Which is not a dismissal, Neil. I have too much to thank you for." At the door she stopped to wait for him. "I agree with you, Michael is a dangerous man. But so are you, and so is Luce—and Ben, for that matter. In different ways, perhaps, but yes—you're all dangerous."

5 She left the ward a little earlier than usual that night, declining Neil's offer of an escort, and walked to her room slowly. Awful, not to have anyone to turn to. If she tried to talk to Colonel Chinstrap he'd mark her down for a mental examination herself, while as for Matron . . . There was no one she felt she could turn to, even among her nursing friends, for the dearest of them had gone when Base Fifteen partially closed down.

This had been the most disastrous day of her entire life, a shattering series of encounters which tormented, confused, worried and wearied her. Michael, Luce, Neil and herself, twisting and turning and popping in and out of focus like the images in those fun-parlor mirrors which reduced familiar forms to grotesqueries.

Probably there was a logical explanation for most of what she saw—or thought she saw—in the dayroom. Her instincts about Michael pointed her one way, his conduct in the dayroom and some of his statements to her another. Why hadn't he just shoved Luce away, even knocked him down? Why stand there like a ninny for what seemed like hours, letting that horrible physical presence dominate him? Because the last time he shoved someone away a lethal fight ensued and he wound up in X? That could very possibly be, though she didn't know for sure if that was the way the lethal fight had ensued. His papers weren't specific, and he said nothing. Why did he stand there letting Luce paw him? Surely he could simply have walked out! When he saw her standing watching there had been shame and disgust in his eyes, and after that he closed himself away from her completely. None of it made any sense at all.

144

The sound of Luce whispering. I'm anything, anything you like to name. . . . Young, old, male, female —it's all meat to me. . . . I'm the best there is. . . . I'm even a little bit of God. . . . Despite her personal and her nursing experience, it had never occurred to her that people like Luce existed, people who could gear themselves to permit sexual functioning on any level, purely as an expedient. *How* had Luce become what he was? Just to imagine the amount of pain necessary to create a Luce frightened her. He had so much, looks and brains and health and youth. And yet he had nothing at all. He was an emptiness.

Neil in the driver's seat, wringing admissions out of her she hadn't had time to understand fully herself. In her quite long and close acquaintance with Neil she had never thought of him as an innately strong man, but clearly he was. A hard man. Heaven help you if he didn't love you, or you did something to turn that love back in upon itself. Those gentle blue eyes had gleamed like two chips of lapis.

The shock of her own enormous, involuntary response to Michael, a weakness and a leaping that were there before she even knew. She had never felt like that in her life before, not in the wildest throes of what she had thought a complete love. If Michael had kissed her, she would have dragged him down onto the floor and had him then and there like a bitch on heat. . . .

Once in her room, she looked at the top drawer of the bureau longingly, but made herself leave the bottle of Nembutal untouched. Earlier in the day its employment had been absolutely necessary; she knew that if she spent the afternoon awake, nothing on earth would ever have forced her to go back to X. Shock treatment. But she was over the shock now, even if there had been plenty of fresh ones since. She had done her duty and gone back to X, back to the nightmare X had become.

Neil was right, of course. The change was in her, it was due to Michael, and it was affecting all of them badly. Fool, not to have realized that her presentiment of trouble had nothing to do with the ward or her patients per se; it started and it ended within herself. Therefore it had to stop. It *had* to stop! It had to, it had to, it had to, it had to. . . . Oh, God, I'm mad, I'm as insane as any man who ever passed through X, and where do I go from here? Where, God, where?

There was a stain on the floorboards in the corner where she had once spilled the only container of lighter fluid she owned. At the time it had upset her, she remembered. Now the stain sat there, an unsightly memento of clumsiness.

Sister Langtry fetched a bucket and a brush, got down on her hands and knees and scrubbed the patch until the wood began to look white. Then the rest of the floor seemed dirty by comparison, so she moved on, piece by piece, until all of the floor was wet, clean, bleached. But it had made her feel better. Better than the Nembutal. And she was tired enough to sleep.

6 "I tell you there is something wrong with her!" Nugget insisted, and shivered. "Christ, I feel crook!" He coughed from the bottom of his lungs, hawked, spat with stunning accuracy at a palm trunk over Matt's shoulder.

All six of them were squatting on the beach, naked, formed into a circle; from far enough away they looked like a ring of small standing stones, brown and quiet and put there intentionally at the bidding of some oracle or ritual. It was a perfect day, hovering between warmth and heat, and free from humidity. But in spite of the alluring weather their backs were turned on sea, sand and palms. They were looking inward at themselves.

Sister Langtry was the subject under discussion. Neil had called a council, and they were hard at it. Matt, Benedict and Luce felt that she was physically a bit under the weather but otherwise all right; Nugget and Neil thought something was radically wrong; and Michael, to Neil's fury, kept abstaining every time his opinion was asked.

How many of us are being honest? wondered Neil. We toss our theories back and forth about everything from dermo to malaria to women's troubles as if we really do believe it's only her body ailing. And I for one am not game to suggest a different cause than body. I wish I could crack Michael, but so far I haven't even opened up a cranny. He doesn't love her! I love her, he doesn't. Is that right or fair when she can't see me for him? Why doesn't he love her? I could kill him for what he's doing to her.

The discussion didn't rage, it jerked along punctuated by lengthy silences, for they were all afraid. She mattered so much, and they had never before had occasion to worry about her for any reason. The one unshakable rock in their uncertain sea, to which they had tethered themselves and ridden out their storms to eventual calm. The metaphors were endless: their beacon, their madonna, their rock, their hearth, their succor. For each of them had special memories and concepts of her, special only to himself, an absolutely individual reason for loving her.

To Nugget she was the only person other than his mother who had ever cared enough for him to worry about his precarious health. Transferred from abdominothoracic to ward X amid grateful cheers from the whole crew he was leaving, he was carried out of a busy, smelly, noisy world wherein no one ever had time to listen to him, and so had forced him to keep his voice insistently raised, demanding attention. He was sick, but they just wouldn't believe it. When he arrived in X he had a headache, admittedly not one of his migraines, but a thumping protest against muscular tension which at the time he had felt was just as bad as a migraine in a different way. And she had sat on the side of his bed and listened raptly while he described the exact nature of his pain, interested and concerned for him. The more lyrical he waxed about his pain, the more impressed and sympathetic she became. Cold towels were produced, a battery of little pills of different kinds displayed—and the *bliss* of being able to discuss sensibly with her the problems involved in choosing the most suitable medication for this particular headache as distinct from all the other headaches he had ever had . . . Of course he knew it was her technique; no fool, Nugget. The diagnosis on his history didn't change, either. But she really did care about him, for she devoted her precious time to him, and that to Nugget was the only criterion for caring. She was so pretty, so complete a person; and yet she always looked at him as if he mattered to her.

Benedict saw her as infinitely superior to all other women, distinguishing as always between women and girls. Females were born one or the other, they didn't change. Girls he found disgusting; they laughed at how he looked, they teased as cruelly and deliberately as cats. Women on the other hand were calm creatures, the guardians of the race, beloved of God. Men might kill and maim and fornicate, girls might tear the world apart, but women were life and light. And Sister Langtry was the most perfect of all women; he never saw her without wanting to wash her feet, die for her if necessary. And he tried never to think of her dirtily, feeling this as a betrayal, but sometimes in his unruly dreams she walked unbidden amid breasts and hairy places, and that alone was more than enough to convince him that he was unworthy to look upon her. He could atone only if he found the answer, and somehow he always felt that God had put Sister Langtry into his life to show him the answer. It still eluded him, but with her he lost his differences, he felt as if he belonged. Michael gave him the same sort of feeling; since Michael's arrival he had come to think of Sister Langtry and Michael as one person, indivisible, surpassingly good and kind.

Whereas the rest of ward X was like the rest of the world, a series of things. Nugget was a weasel, a stoat, a ferret, a rat. He knew it was silly to imagine that were Nugget to grow a beard he would grow rodent whiskers, but he did imagine it, and whenever he saw Nugget in the bathhouse shaving he worried, longed to urge him to borrow a Bengal and shave even closer, because those whiskers were lurking just beneath his skin. Matt was a lump, worry bead, a dull stone, an eyeball, a currant, an octopus turned inside out with all its tentacles chopped off, a single tear, all those round smooth opaque things, for tears were opaque too, they led from nowhere to nowhere. Neil was an old mountainside gouged deep by rain, a fluted column, two boards that fitted tongue in groove, the marks of anguished fingers down a pillar of clay, a sleeping seed pod that could not open, because God had stuck its edges together with celestial glue and was laughing at Neil, laughing! Luce was Benedict, the Benedict God would have fashionned had Benedict been more pleasing to Him; light and life and song. And yet Luce was evil, a treason to God, an insult to God, an inversion of intent. Luce being so, what did that make Benedict?

Neil was very worried. She was slipping away, and that could not be borne. Not at any price. Not now that he was finally beginning to understand himself, to see how like he was after all to the old man in Melbourne. He was growing in his power and enjoying the process. How odd, that it had taken a Michael to hold up the mirror in which he saw himself properly for the first time. Life could be cruel. To come to know himself through the offices of one who simultaneously was removing the reason why he was so anxious to know all about himself . . . Honour Langtry belonged to Neil Parkinson, and he was not going to let her go. There had to be a way to bring her back. There had to be!

To Matt she was a link with home, a voice in the darkness more dear to him than all other voices. He knew he would never physically see his home again, and at night he lay trying to remember what his wife's voice sounded like, the thin bells of his daughters' voices, but he could not. Where Sister Langtry's voice was cemented within the cells of the brain he knew was dying, the only echo which came to him of other times and other places, as if in her they had crystallized. Though his love for her was quite devoid of desire for her body. To him who had never seen her, she had no body. Somehow he didn't have the strength for bodies any longer, not even in his imagination. Meeting Ursula again was a terrifying thought, for he knew she would expect him to summon up a desire he did not have any more. The very idea of groping across and through and down his wife revolted him; like a snail or a python or a drift of seaweed, wrapping himself aimlessly around a chance obstacle. For Ursula belonged to a world he had seen, where Sister Langtry was the light in his darkness. No face, no body. Just the purity of pure light.

Luce was trying not to think of her at all. He could not bear to think of her, because every time she popped into his brain she had that look of nauseated rejection on her face. What on earth was the matter with the woman? Couldn't she just take one look at him and see what he would be like? All he wanted from her was the chance to prove to her what she was missing in ignoring him, and for once he just didn't know how to go about persuading a woman to try. It was usually so easy! He didn't understand. But he hated her. He wanted to pay her back for that look, that disgust, that adamant rejection. So instead of thinking about Langtry he thought about the details of the exquisite revenge he was going to take; and somehow every idea ended in a vision of Langtry kneeling at his feet, admitting she was wrong, begging for another chance with him.

Michael didn't know her yet, but the beginnings of a pleasure in learning to know her were stirring in him, which brought him no pleasure at all. Sex apart, his knowledge of women was extremely limited; the only one he had ever really known well was his mother, and she had died when he was sixteen. Died because apparently she had suddenly decided there was nothing worth living for, and it had been a great blow. He and his father somehow had both felt responsible, yet they genuinely didn't know what they had done to tire her of life. His sister was twelve years older than he, so he didn't know her at all. While he had still been at school it had awed and fascinated him to learn that girls thought him interesting and attractive, but his explorations as a result of discovering this had never been very satisfactory. His girls were always jealous of his lame ducks, and of his tendency to think of his lame ducks first. There had been one fairly long affair with a girl from Maitland, a bodily affair which had consisted only of constant and varied sex. It had pleased him to have it so, for she limited her demands to this, and he felt free of her. The war had broken it up, and very soon after he went to the Middle East she married someone else. When he found out it had not hurt much; he was too busy keeping alive to have time to dwell upon it. The oddest thing was that he didn't seem to miss the sex, felt stronger and more whole without it. Or perhaps he was just lucky enough to be one of those people who could turn sex off. He didn't know, wasn't concerned about, the reason.

His chief feeling for Sister Langtry was liking, nor was he sure just when something more personal and intimate had begun to color his liking. But that morning in the dayroom had come as a shock. Luce playing silly buggers, himself riding an absolute control on anger until the right moment to vent it, a moment in which he knew it could not proceed to that awful hunger to kill. And the moment had come; his mouth was literally open to tell Luce what he could do with himself when she made some sort of noise from the doorway. At first his shame had almost overwhelmed him—what must he and Luce have looked like? How could he possibly explain? So he hadn't even tried to explain. And then he touched her, and something had happened to both of them, something deeper than body yet all wrapped up in body. He knew it had affected her as strongly as it had himself; there were some things which didn't need words or even glances. Oh, God, why couldn't the sister in charge of ward X have been that comfortable middle-aged dragon he imagined before his admission? There was no point to a personal relationship with Sister Langtry, for where could it go? And yet . . . Oh, yes, the thought of it was wonderful. It carried a promise of excitement that had little to do with bodies; he had never, he realized, been enchanted by a woman before.

"Look," said Neil, "I think we've got to face one thing. Sis has been on X for a year now, and it seems logical to me that she's tired of Base Fifteen, tired of X, and tired of us. We're all she ever sees. Mike, you're the newest, what do you think?"

"That of all of you, I'm the least qualified to judge, so instead I'll ask Nugget. What do you think?"

"I won't have it!" said Nugget vehemently. "If Sis was fed up with us, I'd be the first to know."

"Not fed up, just tired! There's a difference," said Neil patiently. "Aren't we all tired? Why should it be any different for her? Do you really think when she wakes up in the mornings she jumps out of bed singing a song of joy because in a few minutes she's going to be back in X, back with us? Come on, Mike, I want an opinion from you, not from Nugget or any of the others. You're the newcomer, you're not in so deep you can't see straight any more. Do you reckon she wants to be with us?"

"I don't know, I tell you! Ask Ben," said Michael, and stared at Neil very directly. "You're barking up the wrong tree, mate."

"Sister Langtry is far too good a woman to grow tired of us," said Benedict.

"She's frustrated," said Luce.

Matt chuckled. "Well, X is a frustrating place," he said.

"Not that way, you blinkered dill! I mean she's a woman, and she's not getting any, is she?"

The revulsion stabbed at Luce from all sides, but he endured it as if he enjoyed it, grinning.

"You know, Luce, you're so low you'd have to climb a ladder to reach a snake's belly," said Nugget. "You make me want to puke!"

"Name something that doesn't make you want to puke," said Luce scornfully.

"Be humble, Luce," said Benedict softly. "Be very humble. All men should learn humility before they die, and none of us know when we'll die. It could as easily be tomorrow as fifty years from now."

"Don't you preach at me, spindleshanks!" snarled Luce. "If you go on the way you're going, you'll be in Callan Park a week after you're on Civvy Street."

"You'll never see that," said Benedict.

"My oath I won't! I'll be too busy being famous."

"Not on my money you won't," said Matt. "I wouldn't pay a farthing to watch you pee."

Luce guffawed. "If you can watch me pee, Matt, I'll *give* you the bloody farthing!"

"Neil is right!" said Michael suddenly, very loudly.

The bickering stopped; they all turned their heads to look at him curiously, for the tone of his voice was one they had never heard from him before—full of passion, full of anger, full of authority.

"Of course she's tired, and can you blame her? The same sort of thing day after day, Luce picking on everyone, and everyone picking on Luce. Why the hell can't you lay off each other, and lay off her? Whatever's wrong with her is her business, not yours! If she wanted to make it yours, she'd talk to you about it. Lay off her! You're enough to drive a man to drink!" He got to his feet. "Come one, Ben, into the water. Wash yourself clean. I'm going to try to, but with the amount of crap that's been flying around here, it may take a week."

A tiny chink in his armor at last, thought Neil, but with no exultation, watching Michael and Benedict walk toward the sea. Michael's back was very straight. Dammit, he does care for her! But the thing is, does she know it? I don't think she does, and if I can, I'm going to keep it that way.

"That's the first time I've ever seen you lose your temper," said Benedict to Michael, wading into the water.

Michael stopped, waist deep, and looked at the thin dark worried face with worry written on his own face. "It was a stupid thing to do," he said. "It always is stupid to go off half-cocked. I don't have a hot temper, so I hate it when people drive me to that sort of behavior. It's so useless! That's why I left them. If I'd stayed, I would have made a worse fool of myself."

"You're strong enough to resist temptation," said Benedict wistfully. "I wish I was!"

"Go on, mate, you're the best of the lot of us," said Michael affectionately.

"Do you really think so, Mike? I try so hard, but there's no easy way. I've lost too much."

"You've lost yourself, Ben, nothing else. It's all there, waiting for you to find your way back."

"It's the war. It's made me a murderer. But then I know that's only an excuse. It's not really the war, it's me. I just wasn't strong enough to pass the test God set me."

"No, it's the war," said Michael, hands floating on the water. "It does something to all of us, Ben, not only to you. We're all in X because of what the war's done to us. If it hadn't happened along we'd be all right. They say war's a natural thing, but I can't see it. Maybe it's natural for the race, natural for the old men to start it, but for the men who have to fight it—no, it's the most unnatural life a man can live."

"But God's in there," said Benedict, sinking down until his shoulders were submerged, then bobbing up again. "It must be natural. God sent me to the war. I didn't volunteer to go, because I prayed about it and God told me to wait. If He felt I needed testing, He'd send me. And He did. So it must be natural."

"As natural as birth and marriage," said Michael wryly.

"Are you going to get married?" asked Benedict, his head cocked as if he didn't want to miss the reply.

Michael thought about it; thought of Sister Langtry, well educated, well born, an officer and a gentle-woman. A member of a class he'd had little to do with before the war, and had elected not to join during the war. "No," he said soberly, "I don't think I've got enough to offer any more. I'm just not the way I used to be. Maybe I know too much about myself. To live with a woman and raise children I think you've got to have some illusions about yourself, and I don't have any these days. I've been there and I've come all the way back again, but where I am now isn't where I would have been if there'd been no war. Does that make sense?"

"Oh, yes!" agreed Benedict fervently, to please his friend; for he didn't understand at all.

"I've killed men. I've even tried to kill a compatriot. The old Shalt Nots don't apply the way they did before the war. How could they? I've hosed chunks of men out of bomber turrets because there wasn't enough of them left to pick up for decent burial. I've hunted for meat tickets in blood and offal inches deep, worse messes than any civilian slaughterhouse. I've been so afraid I thought I'd never again be able to move. I've cried a lot. And I think to myself, raise a son of mine to go through that? Not if I was the last man left to repopulate the earth."

"It's the guilt," said Benedict.

"No, it's the grief," said Michael.

7 Since it was well after four o'clock, the sisters'
sitting room was very nearly deserted when
Sister Langtry walked in. It was a large and airy
room, for it had great French doors on either
side opening out onto verandahs, and it was
screened with mesh, an unbelievable luxury, as
was the mess next door. Whatever obscure
military planner was responsible for its furnishing must have loved nurses; there were cushions
on the cane settees and a brave attempt at
cheerfulness through chintz. If the mildew had
long since marred the patterns on the chintz and
the laundry had managed to reduce color to
noncolor, it really didn't matter. In spirit it was a
big, cheerful room, and had a corresponding
effect on the nurses who used it.

When Sister Langtry came in she saw that its
only occupant was Sister Sally Dawkin from
neuro, a crusty middle-aged major who was no
more a professional army nurse than Sister
Langtry was, fat and jolly and chronically over-
worked, poor soul; neuro was a notoriously hard
ward for any nurse to run. In fact, Sister Langtry
could think of no more depressing branch of
medicine to be in than wartime neuro, with its
dismal prognoses and the incredible way its
cases sometimes lingered in defiance of all the
natural laws governing survival. An arm didn't
grow back, but the organism did function without it, mourned its loss yet coped with life in
much the same way. Brains and spines never
grew back either, but what was missing was not
the tool; it was the operator of the tool. Neuro
was a place where no matter how religious you
might be, you sometimes yearned to be able to
reconcile euthanasia with humanitarian ethics.

Sister Langtry knew that she could survive the

very worst ward X could ever offer her, where she would never have survived neuro. Sister Dawkin felt the opposite. Which was just as well. Their values and skills were alike excellent, but their preferences were quite different.

"Tea's fresh—well, not bad," said Sister Dawkin, looking up and beaming. "Good to see you, Honour."

Sister Langtry sat down at the small cane table and reached for a clean cup and saucer. She added milk to the cup first, poured in a dark and aromatic stream of tea not quite to the revoltingly stewed stage, then sat back and lit a cigarette.

"You're late, Sally," she said.

Sister Dawkin grunted. "I'm like Moses, always late. You know what the Lord said: Come forth, and Moses came fifth and lost his job."

"You'd have to have half a brain missing to appreciate that joke fully," said Sister Langtry, smiling.

"I know. What can you expect? It's the company I keep." Sister Dawkin bent to unlace her shoes, then hauled her uniform dress up and unhitched her suspenders from her stocking tops. Sister Langtry got a good glimpse of the army-issue bloomers everyone called "passion-killers" before the stockings were peeled off and thrown onto a vacant chair.

"Most of the time, Honour my pet, when I think of you stuck right down at the end of the compound with half a dozen loonies for company and no help, I don't envy you one bit. I much prefer my thirty-odd neuros and a few female cohorts. But today is one of the days when I'd gladly change places with you."

There was an ugly galvanized iron bucket full of water on the floor between Sister Dawkin's feet, which were bare now and revealing as being short, broad, bunioned and minus anything in the way of an instep arch. While Sister Langtry watched, amused and touched, Sister Dawkin plonked both feet into the bucket and slopped and splashed luxuriously.

"Ohhhhhhhhhh, that's so beeeeeee-yew-tiful! Truly, I could not have gone another flipping step on them."

"You've got heat oedema, Sally. Better take some pot cit before it gets any worse," observed Sister Langtry.

"What I need is about eighteen hours flat out in bed with my legs elevated," said the sufferer, and chuckled. "Sounds good when you put it that way, doesn't it?" She withdrew a foot from the bucket and probed with merciless fingers at the puffy red ankle above it. "You're right, they're up like a bishop at a girlie show. I'm not getting any younger, that's my real trouble." The chuckle came again. "Oh, well, it was the bishop's trouble, too."

A solid, well-known tread sounded at the door; in sailed Matron, her starched white veil perfectly formed into a lozenge down her back, her impossibly starched uniform not showing a crease, the glitter from her shoes quite blinding. When she saw the two at the table she smiled frostily and decided to come over.

"Sisters, good afternoon," she boomed.

"Good afternoon, Matron!" they chorused like obedient schoolgirls, Sister Langtry not rising to her feet out of consideration for Sister Dawkin, who could not.

Matron spotted the bucket, and recoiled. "Do you think, Sister Dawkin, that soaking your feet in a public room is quite seemly?"

"I think it all depends on the room and the feet, ma'am. You'll have to forgive me, I came from Moresby to Base Fifteen, and we didn't have many niceties at Moresby." Sister Dawkin hauled one foot out of the bucket and regarded it clinically. "I must agree, it's not a very *seemly* foot. Got bent out of shape in the service of good old Florence Nightingale. But then again," Sister Dawkin went on in exactly the same tone of voice, foot back in the water and splashing merrily, "nor is a grossly understaffed neuro ward quite *seemly.*"

Matron stiffened alarmingly, thought better of what she had been about to say because Sister Langtry was there as a witness; she turned sharply on her heel and marched out of the room.

"Old bitch!" said Sister Dawkin. "I'll give her *seemly!* She's been down on me like a ton of bricks all week because I had the temerity to ask her for extra staff in front of a visiting American surgeon general. Well, I'd been asking her in private for days without getting anywhere, so what did I have to lose? I've got four quads, six paras, nine hemis and three comas as well as the rest of the rabble. I tell you, Honour, if it wasn't for the three or four blokes who are compos enough and fit enough to lend us a hand, my ship would have sunk to the bottom a fortnight ago." She blew a very rude-sounding raspberry. "Flipping mosquito nets! I'm just waiting for her to tell me D ward's nets aren't quite *seemly,* because the minute she does, I'm going to wrap one of her precious nets around her neck and strangle her with it!"

"I agree she deserves a lot of things, but strangling? Really, Sally!" said Sister Langtry, enjoying the sparks.

"The old cow! She couldn't hit a bull on the bum with a handful of wheat!"

But the very promising display of Dawkin fireworks fizzled damply the moment Sister Sue Pedder walked through the door. Any further eruptions became impossible. It was one thing to blow one's top comfortably to Honour Langtry, who was if not in the same age group at least a topflight nurse of many years' experience; to Sister Dawkin they were peers. Besides, they had served together from New Guinea to Morotai, and they were friends. Where Sister Pedder was a kid, no older than the AAMWAs who had worked for something like forty-eight hours at a stretch in Moresby. And that was the rub, perhaps. No one could imagine Sister Pedder working for forty-eight hours at a stretch anywhere.

Barely twenty-two, extremely pretty and extremely vivacious, she was in theatres, and had not been on the Base Fifteen staff for very long. It was a current joke that even old Carstairs the urinary surgeon had whinnied and pawed the ground when Sister Pedder waltzed through his theatre door. Several nurses and patients had lost money at that moment, having laid bets that Major Carstairs was really dead but didn't have the grace to lie down.

The nurses left to man Base Fifteen until its extinction were all senior in age and experience, all veterans of jungle warfare and jungle nursing. Except for Sister Pedder, who was not generally regarded as part of the group, and was eyed by some with a great deal of resentment.

"Hello, girls!" said Sister Pedder brightly, coming over. "I must say I don't see much of the ward stars these days. How is life on the wards?"

"A darned sight harder than life in theatres making goo-goo eyes at the surgeons," said Sister Dawkin. "But enjoy it while you can. If I have anything to say about it, you'll be off theatres and on neuro."

"Oh, no!" squeaked Sister Pedder, looking utterly terrified. "I can't stand neuro!"

"Too bloody bad," said Sister Dawkin unsympathetically.

"I can't stand neuro either," said Sister Langtry, trying to make the poor girl feel more at ease. "It takes a strong back, a strong stomach, and a strong mind. I dip out on all three counts myself."

"So do I!" agreed Sister Pedder fervently. She gulped a mouthful of tea, discovered it was tepid and horribly stewed, but swallowed it because there was nothing else to do save swallow it. A rather awkward silence fell, which frightened her almost as much as the thought of being transferred from theatres to neuro.

In desperation she turned to Sister Langtry, who was always very pleasant but standoffish, she thought. "By the way, Honour, I met a patient of yours from X a couple of weeks ago, and discovered I went to school with him. Isn't that amazing?"

Sister Langtry sat up straight and bent a far more searching gaze on Sister Pedder than Sister Pedder considered her statement warranted.

"The bank manager's daughter from Woop-Woop!" she said slowly. "Saints be praised! I've been wondering for days which one of us he could possibly mean, but I forgot all about you."

"Woop-Woop?" asked Sister Pedder, affronted. "Well! I know it's not Sydney, but it's not quite Woop-Woop either, you know!"

"Don't get shirty, young Sue; Woop-Woop is just Luce's nickname for his home town," soothed Sister Langtry.

"Oh, Luce Daggett!" said Sister Dawkin, comprehending. She bent a fierce eye on Sister Pedder. "If you're seeing him on the sly, ducky, you'd better wear your tin pants—and don't let him reach for his tincutters."

Sister Pedder reddened and bridled; fancy being stuck on neuro with this old dragon! "I assure you that there's no need to be concerned about me," she said haughtily. "I knew Luce when we were both children."

"What was he like, Sue?" asked Sister Langtry.

"Oh, not much different." Sister Pedder began to lose her defensiveness, liking the fact that Sister Langtry was interested in her. "All the girls were crazy about him, he was so handsome. But his mother took in washing, which made it a bit difficult. My parents would have killed me if I'd looked sideways at him, but luckily I was a couple of years younger than Luce, so by the time I got out of the primary school he had already gone to Sydney. We all followed his career, though. I never missed one play he did on radio because our local station used to rebroadcast them. But I missed seeing him when he was in that play at the Royal. Some of the girls went down to Sydney, but my father wouldn't let me."

"What was *his* father like?"

"I really don't remember. He was the stationmaster, but he died not long after the start of the Depression. Luce's mother was very proud, she wouldn't go on the dole. That's why she took in washing."

"Does he have any brothers? Any sisters?"

"No brothers. Two older sisters, very pretty girls.

They were the handsomest family in the district, but the girls came to no good. One drinks and the less said about her morals the better, and the other got herself in the family way and still lives with her mother. She kept her baby, a little girl."

"Was he good at school?"

"Awfully clever. They all were."

"Did he get on with his teachers?"

Sister Pedder laughed a little shrilly. "Good lord, no! The teachers all detested him. He was so sarcastic, and yet so slippery they could never manage to pin him down hard enough to have much excuse to punish him. Besides, he had a habit of always getting back at the teachers who did punish him."

"Well, he hasn't changed much," said Sister Langtry.

"He's much handsomer now! I don't think in all my life I've ever seen anyone so handsome," said Sister Pedder, lapsing into a reverie and smiling.

"Oooops! Someone's riding for a fall!" Sister Dawkin chuckled, eyes twinkling, but not unkindly.

"Don't take any notice of her, Sue," Sister Langtry said, trying to keep her source of information in a receptive frame of mind. "Matron's on her back and she's got heat oedema."

Sister Dawkin removed her feet from the bucket and rubbed them sketchily with a towel, then picked up her shoes and stockings.

"There's no need to talk about me as if I wasn't even here," she said. "I am here, all thirteen and a half stone of me. Oh, my feet do feel better! Don't drink the water in the bucket, girls, it's full of Epsom salts. I'm off; I've got time for a quick nap." She pulled a face. "It's those darned boots we have to wear after dark do my feet in."

"Have you elevated the foot of your bed?" called Sister Langtry after her.

"Years ago, love!" came the faint reply. "It's a lot easier to look for the pair of boots that are never there, and I don't mean my own, either!"

This raised a laugh, of course, but after their spurt of amusement died the two sisters left at the table could do no better than an uncomfortable silence.

Sister Langtry sat wondering whether it was advisable to warn Sister Pedder about Luce, or at least make the attempt. In the end she decided that was where her duty lay, and reflected how unpalatable duty often was. She was well aware of the special difficulties young Sister Pedder faced at Base Fifteen, how friendless and isolated she must feel in this nest of senior sisters. There weren't even any AAMWAs for her to mix with. Still, Luce was a definite menace, and Sister Pedder looked ripe, nubile and ready for mischief. And since Luce represented childhood and home town, her guard would be down.

"I do hope Luce isn't giving you any trouble, Sue," she said at last. "He can be difficult."

"No!" said Sister Pedder, coming out of her daze with a start.

Sister Langtry picked up her cigarettes and matches and dropped them into the basket at her feet. "Well, I'm sure you've been a nurse long enough to be able to look after yourself. Just remember that Luce is a patient in X because he's a little disturbed. We can handle that, but we can't handle you if it rubs off."

"You make him sound as if he was a leper!" said Sister Pedder indignantly. "After all, there's no disgrace in battle fatigue; it happens to a lot of fine men!"

"Is that what he told you?" asked Sister Langtry.

"Well, it's the truth," said Sister Pedder, with just enough doubt in her voice to make Sister Langtry think something had happened which had given Sister Pedder pause to wonder already. Which was interesting.

"No, it is not the truth. Luce has never been any closer to the front lines than the orderly room of a base ordnance unit."

"Then why is he in X?"

"I don't think I'm at liberty to tell you more than that he displayed some rather disagreeable characteristics which made his COs feel he might be better off in a place like X."

"He *is* strange sometimes," said Sister Pedder, thinking of that hideously passionless, automatic, merciless ramming, and of those savage bites. Her neck had been so deeply bruised, the skin broken in places, that she had thanked her lucky stars for the precious little container of pancake makeup she had bought at the American PX in Port Moresby on her way up here.

"Then take my advice, and don't see Luce any more," said Sister Langtry, picking up her basket and rising to her feet. "Truly, Sue, I'm not coming a matron act at you, and I'm not preaching. I have absolutely no wish to pry into your personal business, but Luce happens to be my business in every way. Steer clear of him."

But that was too much for Sister Pedder to take; she puffed up with indignation, feeling chastised and belittled. "Is that an order?" she asked, white-faced.

Sister Langtry looked surprised, even a little amused. "No. Orders come from Matron."

"Then you can stick your damned advice up your jumper!" said Sister Pedder recklessly, then gasped. The precepts and disciplines of her training were too fresh still for her to be able to say things like that without immediately becoming devastated by her own temerity.

However, her retort fell sadly flat, for Sister Langtry had gone from the room without appearing to hear it.

She sat on for a few moments longer, chewing at her lip until the skin shredded, torn between the huge attraction she had for Luce and the feeling that Luce didn't really care two hoots about her.

PART 4

1 It took almost a week for Sister Langtry's rigidly suppressed feelings of confusion and embarrassment over her weakness in the dayroom to evaporate. Thank God Michael didn't seem to suspect anything, for he was his normal courteous, friendly self at all times. A great salve for her pride, perhaps, but not much help with the pain she suffered in other areas of her being. Still, every day she continued to survive was one day less ward X had to go, one day closer to freedom.

When she walked into the ward one late afternoon about two weeks after the incident in the dayroom, she almost collided with Michael coming out of the sluice room in a hurry, a worn and dented metal bowl in one hand.

"Put a cover over that, please, Michael," she said automatically.

He stopped, torn between the urgency of his mission and her seniority.

"It's for Nugget," he explained. "He's got a terrible headache and he feels sick."

Sister Langtry stepped around him and reached one hand into the sluice room, where some drab but clean cloths sat on the shelf just inside the door. She took the bowl from Michael and draped a cloth over it.

"Then Nugget's got a migraine," she said calmly. "He doesn't get them very often, but when he does he's quite prostrated, the poor little chap."

She walked into the ward, took one look at Nugget lying very still on his bed, a cool damp cloth over his eyes, and drew up a hard chair noiselessly to the side of his bed.

"Is there anything I can do, Nugget?" she

169

asked him softly, putting the bowl down very quietly on his locker.

His lips barely moved. "No, Sis."

"How long to go?"

"Hours yet," he whispered, two tears trickling from under the cloth. "It's just come on."

She didn't touch him. "Don't worry, just lie quiet. I'll be here to keep an eye on you."

She remained sitting beside him for perhaps another minute, then got up and went into her office.

Michael was waiting there, looking anxious. "Are you sure he's all right, Sis? I've never seen Nugget lie so still! He hasn't even squeaked."

She laughed. "He's all right! It's just an honest-to-goodness migraine, that's all. The pain is so acute he doesn't dare move or make a noise."

"Isn't there something you could give him?" Michael demanded, impatient at her callousness. "How about some morphine? That always does the trick."

"Not for migraine," she said positively.

"So there's nothing you're prepared to do."

His tone annoyed her. "Nugget is in no danger whatsoever. He's simply feeling ghastly. In about six hours he'll vomit, and that will relieve the worst of his pain immediately. Believe me, I'm very sorry for what he's going through, but I do not intend to run the risk of making him dependent upon drugs like morphine! You've been here quite long enough to understand what Nugget's real trouble is, so why are you making me out to be the villain of the piece? I'm not infallible by any means, but I do not appreciate being told my business by patients!"

He laughed heartily, putting his hand out to grip her arm and giving it a friendly little shake. "Good for you, Sis!" he said, grey eyes alight with more than warmth.

Her own eyes lit up; she was consumed by an enormous rush of gratitude. There could be no mistaking the way he was now looking at her. In that moment all her doubts were resolved; she knew she loved him.

170

No more misery, no more self-examination. She loved him, and it felt like the end of a journey she had not wanted to make.

He searched her face, then his lips parted to speak; dumb with longing, she waited. But he didn't speak. She could literally see his mind working, watched the love driven out by . . . fright? Caution? The grip on her arm changed its quality, from a caress to a merely friendly touch again.

"I'll see you later," he said, and walked out the door.

Luce didn't even give her the time to think about it; she was still standing numbed when he walked in.

"I want a word with you, Sis, and I want it now," he said, white-faced.

She moistened her lips. "Certainly," she managed to say, and put Michael out of her mind.

Luce advanced until he stood before her desk; she went to her chair and sat down.

"I've got a bone to pick with you."

"Sit down, then," she said calmly.

"It's not going to take long enough, pet," he said, lips lifted back from his teeth. "Why did you queer my pitch with little Miss Woop-Woop?"

Sister Langtry's eyes opened wide. *"Did* I?"

"You know bloody well you did! Everything was coming along beautifully, and now suddenly out of the blue she starts telling me that it isn't proper for her to associate with the likes of Sergeant Luce Daggett, because your talk with her made her see a lot of things she didn't see before."

"Nor is it proper for the two of you to associate in a clandestine manner," said Sister Langtry. "Officers do not engage in intimate relationships with men from the ranks."

"Oh, come off it, Sis! You know as well as I do that those rules are broken every night in this bloody place! Who else is there except men from the ranks? The MOs? There's not an MO in Base Fifteen who could get it up for Betty Grable! The officer patients? The only ones left are crocks who couldn't get it up for the Virgin Mary!"

"If you must be cheap and vulgar, Luce, you might at least refrain from blasphemy!" she snapped, her fact set, her eyes hard.

"But it's a cheap and vulgar subject, sweetie, and I feel like doing a lot worse than blaspheming. What a prissy old maid you are! No gossip in the mess about Sister Langtry, is there?"

He leaned forward across the desk, hands on its edge, his face looming within inches of her own, as it had loomed once before, but with a far different expression now.

"Let me tell you something! Don't you ever dare to interfere with me, or I'll make you wish you'd never been born! Do you hear? I was enjoying little Miss Woop-Woop in more ways than you'll ever know, you dried-up scrubber!"

The epithet penetrated where he could not be sure that anything else he said did; he saw her flare of pain and outrage, and pressed home this unexpected advantage with all the venom he could summon.

"You really are dried up, aren't you?" he drawled. "You're not a woman, you're just an apology for one. There you are, dying to go to bed with Mike, yet you can't even treat the poor coot like a man! Anyone would think he was your pet dog. Here, Mike, heel, Mike! Do you really think you'll get him to sit and beg for it? He's not interested enough, sweetie."

"You can't make me lose my temper, Luce," she said, coldly and slowly. "I prefer to treat your personal aspersions as not made at all. No exercise in the world is as futile as a post-mortem, and that's what this is, a post-mortem. If Sister Pedder has thought better of her association with you, I'm glad for both your sakes, but especially for hers. Ranting at me is not going to change how Sister Pedder feels."

"You're not an iceberg, Sister Langtry, because ice melts. You're stone! But I'm going to find a way to pay you back. Oh, yes I am! *I* am going to make you weep tears of blood!"

"What idiotic melodrama!" she said contemptuously. "I'm not frightened of you, Luce. Disgusted and sickened by you, yes. But not frightened. Nor can you bluff me the way you do the others. I see through you; I always have seen through you. You're nothing but a petty little confidence trickster!"

"But I'm not bluffing," he said airily, straightening. "You'll see! I've found something you think belongs to you, and I'm going to take great pleasure in destroying it."

Michael. Her and Michael. But Luce couldn't even begin to destroy that. Only Michael could. Or she could.

"Oh, go away, Luce!" she said. "Just go away! You're wasting my time."

"The dirty bitch!" Luce said, looking at his curled hands as if they astonished him, looking at the bed where Benedict sat hunched apathetically, looking at the ward crowding in around him. "The dirty bitch!" he said again more loudly, straight at Ben. "Do you know who I'm talking about, you barmy fucker—do you? Your precious Langtry, the dirty bitch!" He was beside himself, too obsessed by his own hatred to remember that Ben was not a man he usually provoked. He just wanted to lash out at anyone, and Ben was the only one around. "You think she cares about you, don't you?" he asked. "Well, she doesn't! She doesn't care about anyone except Sergeant bloody hero Wilson! Isn't that a laugh? Langtry in love with a shirt-lifting pansy!"

Ben came slowly to his feet. "Don't say it, Luce. Keep your filthy tongue off her and Mike." His tone was gentle.

"Oh, come off it, you stupid drongo! What do I need to do to show you? Langtry's nothing but a silly old maid in love with the biggest queen in the A.I.F.!" He moved across the space between his own bed and Benedict's with a slow, sideways gait that made him look immense and powerful. "A queen, Ben! That's Mike I'm talking about!"

The rage was gathering in Benedict, and in rage he grew too, his dark dour face sloughing its layers of dejection and apology off until something deeper and more appalling began to show like bones at the bottom of a wound. "Lay off them, Luce," he said calmly. "You don't even know what you're talking about."

"Oh, but I do, Ben! I do! I read it in his papers! Your darling Mike's a queen!"

Two small bubbles puffed out at the corners of Ben's mouth, thick and glistening. He began to tremble, a quick, minute shaking. "You're a liar."

"Why should I lie? It's all there in his papers—he buggered the arses off half his battalion!" Luce stepped back a pace hastily, deciding that he didn't want to be too close to Ben. "If Mike's a queen," he taunted, unable to stop himself, "what does that make you?"

A thin, wailing scream came ripping out of Benedict, a very quiet scream, but before his tensed muscles could react in the violence that leaped ahead of his body like a great shadow, Luce began to emit a staccato series of noises which sounded eerily like the chattering of a submachine gun. Benedict jerked and recoiled, his whole body jumping in time to the volley.

"Ah-ah-ah-ah-ah-ah-ah-ah-ah! Remember that, old son? Of course you do! That's the sound of your gun killing all those innocent people! Think of them, Ben! Dozens of them, women and children and old men, all dead! You murdered them in cold blood just so you could come to X and crawl to scum like Mike Wilson!"

His rage drowned in another, greater torment, Benedict subsided onto the bed, head back, eyes closed, tears flooding down his face, a human vacuum of despair.

"Get out of here, Luce!" said Matt's voice from behind Luce's shoulder.

Luce jumped, but as he remembered that Matt couldn't see, he turned, wiping the sweat from his face. "Go to hell!" he said, as he pushed roughly past Matt and plucked his hat off his bed. He put the hat on his head with a nonchalant air and walked away down the ward to the front door.

Matt had heard most of it, but until he judged the imminence of physical violence to be past he hadn't had the courage to interfere, thinking that he could well make matters worse by floundering between them, and knowing Ben would be more than a match for Luce— hoping for it, too.

He groped for the end of Benedict's bed, found it, sat down and slid up until his questing hands encountered an arm. He sighed. "It's all right, Ben," he said gently, feeling the tears and through them the face. "Come on now, it's all right. The bastard's gone, and he won't worry you again. Poor old bloke!"

But Benedict didn't seem to hear; his tears were drying, his arms were wrapped about his body, and he rocked back and forth on the bed.

The scene in the ward had gone undetected by all save Matt because Nugget was beyond caring, Michael had slipped across to the nearest inhabited ward to borrow some powdered milk, and Neil had invaded Sister Langtry's office almost as Luce slammed out of it. He discovered Sister Langtry sitting with her face buried in her hands.

"What is it? What's the bastard done to you?"

She removed her hands immediately, to reveal neither tears nor ravages. Just a very calm, composed countenance.

"He didn't do anything," she said.

"He must have! I could hear him all the way down into the ward."

"Histrionics, that's all. He is an actor. No, he was letting off steam because I put the kybosh on a little romance he was having with one of the sisters. The girl from Woop-Woop, the bank manager's daughter, remember?"

"I remember vividly," he said, sitting down and breathing easier. "That remains the only occasion on

175

which I have ever found myself in danger of liking Luce."

Out came his cigarettes; she took one greedily, drew in the smoke greedily.

"His interest in the girl is vindictive, of course," she said, exhaling. "I realized that the moment I found out what was going on. I don't suppose she ever figured personally in his fantasies, but when she popped up here in the flesh, he soon saw how he could use her."

"Oh, yes," said Neil, shutting his eyes. "Lucius Ingham the famous stage actor and Rhett Ingham the famous Hollywood film star, thumbing his nose at the inhabitants of Woop-Woop."

"I gather Sister Woop-Woop fancied Luce when they were children, but I'll bet she was far too stuck-up to let the washer-woman's son know she fancied him. And a bit too young to take his fancy then. So to compromise her now is doing wonderful things for him."

"Naturally." Neil opened his eyes to look at her intently. "I take it he wasn't pleased at being foiled?"

She laughed shortly. "That's a fair assessment."

"I thought it might be. I couldn't hear what he was saying, but I did hear the tone of his voice." He studied the tip of his cigarette. "I would venture to say that our Luce is pretty angry about it. Did he threaten you?"

"Not specifically. He was far more concerned with telling me all about my shortcomings as a woman." Her face screwed up in disgust. "Pah! Anyway, I simply let him see that I thought he was talking nonsense."

"No threats, though?" Neil persisted.

She sounded tired of being quizzed as she said impatiently, "What could Luce do to me, Neil? Assault me? Kill me? Come off it! That sort of thing happens in fiction, not in life. There's no sort of opportunity. Besides, you know nothing's more important to Luce than the safety of his own skin. He won't do anything he might be punished for. He just spreads those dark wings of his over our heads and lets our own imaginations do his dirty work for him. Only I don't fall for his tricks."

"I hope you're right, Sis."

"Neil, while ever I sit in this chair I *cannot* let any patient frighten me," she said very seriously.

He shrugged, prepared to let it go. "I shall now change the subject with typical Parkinsonian lightness, and inform you that I heard a rumor today. Well, more fact than a rumor, I suppose."

"Thank you so much," she said sincerely. "What rumor?"

"The place is on the skids at last."

"Now where did you hear that? It hasn't reached any of the nurses yet."

"From dear old Colonel Chinstrap himself." He grinned. "I happened to be passing his quarters this afternoon, and there he was on his balcony like Juliet after a visit from Romeo, ecstatic at the thought of going back to Macquarie Street. He invited me up for a drink, and told me, one officer and gentleman to another, that we have probably less than a month to go. The CO heard from Div HQ this morning."

Her face showed a dismay Luce had not been able to bring to it. "Oh, God! Only a month?"

"Give or take a week. We'll just squeak out ahead of the Wet as it is." He frowned at her, perplexed. "You stump me, you really do. The last time we had a serious heart-to-heart, you sat there looking like death warmed up wondering how you were going to get through to the end. Now you look like death warmed up because the end's definitely in sight."

"I wasn't well then," she said stiffly.

"If you ask me, I don't think you're well now."

"You don't understand. I shall miss ward X."

"Even Luce?"

"Even Luce. If it were not for Luce, I wouldn't know the rest of you half so well." She smiled wryly. "Or know myself for that matter."

Michael knocked on the door and poked his head around it. "I hope I'm not interrupting, Sis—tea's made."

"Did you manage to get milk?"

"No trouble."

She got to her feet immediately, relieved to be able to break off her conversation with Neil so naturally. "Come on, then, Neil. Grab the bikkies, would you? You're closer to them than I am."

Waiting until Neil found the biscuit tin, she stood back to let him precede her out the door, then followed the two men into the ward.

2 By Nugget's bed she signalled Neil and Michael to go on without her, and slipped behind the screen someone had put around his bed. He lay without moving and did not acknowledge her presence, so she merely changed the cloth over his eyes for a fresh one before leaving him in peace.

At the refectory table she discovered Luce was missing, looked at her watch and was surprised to find it much later than she had thought.

"If Luce isn't careful he's going to blot his copybook at last. Does anyone know where he is?" she asked.

"He went out," said Matt brusquely.

"He lied," said Benedict, rocking back and forth.

Sister Langtry looked at him closely; he seemed odder, more enclosed, and the rocking was something new.

"Are you all right, Ben?"

"All right. No, all wrong. It's all wrong. He lied. There's an adder in his tongue."

Sister Langtry's eyes met Michael's; she lifted one eyebrow in a mute query, but he, as puzzled as she, shook his head quickly. Neil was frowning, mystified too.

"What's all wrong, Ben?" she asked.

"All of it. Lies. He sold his soul a long time ago."

Neil leaned across to pat the thin bowed shoulder near him reassuringly. "Don't let Luce worry you, Ben!"

"He's *evil!*"

"Have you been crying, Ben?" asked Michael, sitting down next to him.

"He was talking about you, Mike. Dirty talk."

"There's nothing dirty about me, Ben, so why let it bother you?" Michael got up to fetch the chess set, and began to lay it out on the table.

"I'll be black tonight," he said.

"*I* am black."

"All right, then, I'll be white and you can be black. My advantage," said Michael cheerfully.

Benedict's face twisted, his eyes closed, his head reared back and tears began to catch the light between his lashes. "Oh, Mike, I didn't know there were any children there!" he cried.

Michael paid no attention. Instead, he moved his king's pawn two squares forward, and simply sat waiting. After a moment Benedict's eyes opened, saw the move through a wall of tears; he duplicated it quickly, snuffling like a child, wiping his nose on the side of his hand. Michael advanced his queen's pawn to stand alongside the king's pawn, and again Benedict duplicated the move, his tears beginning to dry. And when Michael lifted his king's knight over the pawn in front of it and set it down ahead of his king's bishop, Benedict chuckled, shaking his head.

"You never learn, do you?" he asked, toying tenderly with a bishop.

Sister Langtry heaved an enormous sigh of relief and got up, smiling a good night to everyone before leaving. Neil also got up, but walked around the table to where Matt was sitting, quite forgotten in the little crisis.

"Come and have a talk with me in my room," Neil said, touching him lightly on the arm. "Colonel Chinstrap gave me something this afternoon I'd like to share with you. It's got a black label, just like Luce, but inside—ah! It's pure, unadulterated gold."

Matt looked bewildered. "Isn't it lights out?"

"Officially I suppose it is, but we all seem to be a bit wound up tonight, which is probably why Sis has gone off duty without tucking us up. Besides, Ben and Mike look settled to chess. And don't forget Nugget—if we do get to sleep before he heaves up his guts, he'll only wake us."

Matt's movements as he got up seemed a little fumbling, but he was smiling with keen pleasure. "I'd love to come and talk. And solve your riddle. What's labelled black yet inside is pure gold?"

Neil's cubicle was just that, a space six feet wide by eight feet long, into which he had managed to jam a bed, a table and one hard chair, besides several shelves nailed rather precariously to the walls where he wasn't likely to stand up and hit his head on them. It was littered with painter's impedimenta, though someone in the know would have seen immediately that he had limited his techniques to less permanent and messy media than oil. Pencils, papers, charcoal, brushes, jars of dirty water, tins of children's watercolors, tubes of poster color, crayons and pastels. There was absolutely no order in the chaos; Sister Langtry had given up long ago trying to make him keep the cubicle tidy, and merely bore with fatalistic calm Matron's endless strictures about the state of Captain Parkinson's room. Luckily he could when he wanted charm the birds out of the trees, even, as he said most disrespectfully, a silly old chook like Matron.

The perfect host, he got Matt settled comfortably on the bed and swept various bits and pieces off the hard chair onto the floor before seating himself on it. There were two small tooth tumblers and two bottles of Johnnie Walker black label Scotch whisky sitting on the end of the table. Neil slit the seal and prized the cork carefully out of one bottle, then poured a generous measure into each glass.

"Cheers!" he said, and drank deeply.

"Mud in your eye," said Matt, and did the same.

They gasped rather like two swimmers coming up after a dive into unexpectedly frigid water.

"I've been a sober man too long," Neil said, his eyes watering. "God, this stuff packs a punch, doesn't it?"

"It tastes like heaven," said Matt, and drank again.

181

They paused to breathe deeply and savor the effect.

"Something must have happened tonight to push Ben off the deep end," said Neil. "Do you know anything?"

"It was Luce, chattering like a machine gun and taunting Ben with killing civilians. Poor old Ben burst out crying. Bloody Luce! He told me to go to hell and pushed off out somewhere. I think the man's possessed."

"Or else he really is the devil," said Neil.

"Oh, he's flesh and blood, all right."

"He wants to be mighty careful, then. Otherwise, one of us might put his mortality to the test."

Matt laughed, holding out his glass. "I'll volunteer."

Neil refilled the glass, then refilled his own. "God, how I needed this! Colonel Chinstrap must be a mind reader."

"Did he really give it to you? I thought you were joking."

"No, it came from him in person."

"What on earth for?"

"Oh, I expect it's a part of his ill-gotten hoard, and he worked out how much he can get through himself before Base Fifteen folds up. Then he decided to be Father Christmas and give the surplus away."

Matt's hand trembled. "We're going home?"

Cursing the loosening effect of the whisky on his tongue, Neil looked at Matt gently, but of course all the gentle looks in the world couldn't penetrate blindness, real or imagined. "About a month to go, old son."

"So soon? She'll know!"

"Sooner or later she has to know."

"I thought I'd have a bit more time than that."

"Oh, Matt . . . She'll understand."

"Will she? Neil, I don't want her any more! I can't even think of that any more! She's been waiting to have her husband back, and what's she going to get? Not a husband."

"You can't say that from where you're sitting now. Try not to cross your bridges—you don't know what's

182

going to happen. But the more you stew about it, the worse it will be."

Matt sighed, tipped up his glass. "I'm glad you had this stuff on hand. It's like an anaesthetic."

Neil changed the subject. "Luce must have been in the foul mood to end all foul moods tonight. He had a go at Sis before he had a go at Ben," he said.

"I know."

"Did you hear it too?"

"I heard what he said to Ben."

"You mean there was more to it than the machine gun?"

"A lot more. He came raving out of Sis's office and went for Ben because Ben objected to the things he was calling Sis. But what got Ben so upset was what he said about Mike."

Neil's head turned; he looked at Matt as if at something precious. "What exactly did he say about Mike?"

"Oh, that he was a queen. Did you ever hear anything so silly? He kept telling Ben he'd read it in Mike's papers."

"The bastard!" Oh, sometimes fate was kind! Handed all this, and by a blind man, a man who couldn't see how he looked, what effect the news had. . . . "Here, Matt, have some more."

The whisky went very quickly to Matt's head, or at least so Neil thought until he looked at his watch and saw it was well past eleven. He got up, draped Matt's arm about his shoulders and hoisted him to his feet, feeling none too steady on his own.

"Come on, old son, time you were in bed."

Benedict and Michael were putting the chess set away; Michael came quickly to help Neil, and together they stripped Matt of his trousers, shirt, singlet and underpants, then tipped him into bed, for once without his pajamas.

"Out to it," said Michael, smiling.

And looking at that calm, immensely strong face, knowing what he was going to do to blight it, Neil suddenly loved it clear through to his whisky-maudlined soul; he put his arms around Michael's neck and his head on Michael's shoulder, close to tears.

"Come and have a drink," he said sadly. "You and Ben come and have a drink with an old man. If you don't I'm going to cry, because I'm my old man's son. If I start thinking about you and him and her I'm going to cry. Come and have a drink."

"We can't have you crying," said Michael, disentangling himself. "Here, Ben, we've got an invitation."

Benedict had finished stowing the chess set in the ward cupboard, and came across. Neil reached out an arm and hung onto him.

"Come and have a drink," he said. "There's a bottle and a half left. I'm going to stop, but I can't leave all that lovely grog there undrunk, can I?"

Benedict drew back. "I don't drink," he said.

"It'll do you good tonight," said Michael firmly. "Come on now, none of that holier than thou crap."

So all together they walked across the ward, Michael and Benedict supporting Neil between them. At the corridor junction Michael reached up to switch off the light above the refectory table. There was a discordant rattle from the fly-curtain inside the front door as Luce came in, not stealthily but defiantly, as if he expected Sister Langtry to be lying in wait for him.

The three men stood looking at him, and he at them. Michael cursed Neil's dead weight between him and Benedict, worried that Luce's sudden appearance would start Ben off again. But at that moment Nugget managed to terminate his headache by vomiting.

"Oh, God, what a revolting noise!" said Neil, coming to life immediately.

He pushed Benedict and Michael through into his cubicle, went in after them, and shut the door firmly.

3 Luce continued toward his bed without another glance in the direction of the cubicle; he was alone in the ward in the soft dimness, with only a hideous retching sound for company.

So tired he could hardly move, he sat down on the edge of his bed; he had walked for hours up and down the paths of Base Fifteen, along the beaches, through the pallid groves of coconut palms. Thinking, thinking. . . . Wanting with a blind ferocity to lash out at Langtry until her head went rolling away as free as a football. The stuck-up bitch! Luce Daggett wasn't good enough, and then she'd had the hide to compound the insult by throwing herself away on a shirt-lifting pansy. She was mad. If she'd picked him she could have led the life of a princess, for he knew he was going to be rich and famous, a bigger star than Clark Gable and Gary Cooper combined. You couldn't want something as much as he wanted that and not get it. She'd said that, too. Every single minute of every single hour of every single day since before he left Woop-Woop had been directed toward hitting the big time as an actor.

On the day he arrived in Sydney, a half-grown lad of almost fifteen, he already knew that acting was his ticket to the big time. And he already hungered for the big time. He had never seen a play nor been to the moving pictures, but he had been listening for most of his school days to the adoring chatter of the girls about this actor and that actor, and fended off their suggestions that he should try to get into pictures when he grew up. Let them mind their own business; he'd do it his way and not have any idiot female walking around boasting that she'd pushed him into it, that it was all her brilliant idea.

He went to work as a storeman in a dry goods warehouse down on Day Street, filching the job right out from under the noses of several hundred men who had also applied. The manager had not been able to resist the lad with the beautiful hair and the amazing bright face, the quick mind to back them up. And the lad turned out to be a very good worker, too.

It hadn't taken Luce long to discover where and how to break into the acting profession, and he was working, therefore he was eating, so he grew quickly, filled out and soon looked older than his age. He sat around in Repins drinking innumerable cups of coffee, hung around Doris Fitton at the Independent Theatre, made his face known to the Genesians, and finally began to get small parts in radio plays at 2GB and the ABC, even a few one-liners at 2CH. He had a wonderful voice for radio, nonsibilant, the right timbre, and a quick ear for accents, so that by the time he had been six months moving in the right circles he had polished the Australian from his voice unless it was required.

Envying the people who could afford to finish high school and go on to university, he educated himself as best he could by reading everything people recommended, though his pride would not permit him to ask outright what he should read; he would winkle the information out of his friends very cleverly, then go to the library.

By the time he was eighteen he was earning enough from small radio jobs to be able to quit his warehouse employment. He found a little room for rent on Hunter Street, and did it up as artfully as he could by lining the walls with solid books, only he didn't tell anyone that the books were job lots purchased at Paddy's Markets for as little as threepence the dozen, as much as two and eightpence for a leather-bound set of Dickens.

As an escort he was a notorious nipfarthing—the girls soon learned that if Luce took them out, they paid. And after thinking it over, most of them decided to continue to pay quite cheerfully for the privilege of being seen out with a man who could literally turn all heads in a room. It was not long, of course, before he discovered the world of older women, women who liked nothing better than to foot his bills in return for the pleasure of his company in public, his penis in private.

At this time he began to train himself sexually, so that no matter how uninspiring, offputting or downright ugly the lady was who took him into her bed, he could rise to the occasion most satisfactorily. Simultaneously he developed a line of lover's small talk which charmed them into overestimating their desirability. And the presents flowed in, suits and shoes, hats and coats, cuff links and watches, ties and shirts and hand-made underwear. It worried him not at all to be the recipient of such largesse, for he knew he paid in full.

Nor did it worry him when he learned there were plenty of older men willing to indulge him financially in return for his sexual favors, and in time he came to prefer older men to older women; they were more honest about their needs and their monetary obligations, nor did he have to weary himself to distraction perpetually reassuring them that they were still beautiful, still desirable. Older men had better taste, too; from them he discovered how to dress superlatively well, how to conduct himself like an aristocrat at everything from a cocktail party to a ministerial banquet, and how to sniff out the best people.

After several small parts in small plays put on at small theatres, he auditioned for the Royal, and almost got the part. The second time he auditioned for the Royal he did get the part, a significant role in a straight drama. The critics treated him kindly, and he knew as he read the notices that he was really on his way at last.

But the year was 1942, he was twenty-one, and he was conscripted into the army. His life from then until now he regarded as useless, an utterly wasteful blank. Oh, it had been easy enough; it hadn't taken him long to learn how to get comfortable, nor to find the perfect fool to fool, an elderly career army officer who was more a spiritual than a practicing homosexual—until he met Luce, his new assistant. This man had fallen violently, pathetically in love, and Luce had used his love with total calculation. The affair lasted until the middle of 1945, when Luce, bored and restless because he knew the war was ending, ended the relationship in a diatribe of scathing, contemptuous repudiation. There was a suicide attempt, a scandal, and serious discrepancies in the accounting of moneys and equipment which had passed through their office. The investigation panel soon got Luce's measure, in particular his capacity for wreaking havoc, and dealt with him very simply. They sent him to ward X. And in ward X he remained.

But not for much longer, he told himself.

"Not for much longer!" he said to the darkness of the ward.

A friendly MP had stopped him on his peregrinations around Base Fifteen, and told him that the hospital would soon be no more. He had retired to the MP's doghouse and split a bottle of beer with him, toasting the news with light heart. But now that he was back inside ward X he knew postwar dreams could wait. First things first. And the first thing was fixing Langtry.

4 True to his word, Neil poured no more whisky for himself, but filled the two tumblers and gave one to Benedict, one to Michael.

"God, I'm turpsed to the eyeballs," he said, blinking. "My head's going round like a top. Stupid bloody thing to do. It's going to take me hours to get myself together."

Michael rolled his first sip around his tongue. "It is strong, all right. Funny, I never did like whisky."

Benedict seemed to have overcome his initial reluctance very well, for he polished off his first glass fairly quickly, and held it out for more. Neil obliged, feeling it would do the poor coot good.

Luce was a proper bastard. But wasn't it odd the way desired information arrived after one had despaired of ever getting it? In a round-about way, what he needed to know about Michael had come from Luce. He forced his eyes to focus on Michael's face, trying to see in it any trace of what Luce had maintained. Well, anything was possible, of course. For himself, that particular answer to the riddle would never have come. He didn't really believe it, no matter what Michael's papers said. They always, always gave themselves away; they had to give themselves away or they'd never get any, and Michael he was sure had nothing to give away. But Sis knew what was in those papers, and she wasn't nearly as experienced as men who had spent most of six long years almost exclusively in the company of other men. Did Sis have her doubts about Michael? Of course she did! She wouldn't be human if she didn't and of late she hadn't been very sure of anything within herself. Nothing

189

had happened between her and Michael—yet. So he still had time.

"Do you think," he said, speaking laboriously but quite distinctly, "that Sis knows we're all in love with her?"

Benedict looked up, glassy-eyed. "Not *in* love, Neil! Just love. Love and love and more love. . . ."

"Well, she's the first woman any of us have known as a part of our lives for a long time," said Michael. "It would be strange if we didn't all love her. She's very lovable."

"Do you think she's lovable, Mike? Really?"

"Yes."

"I don't know. Lovable seems the wrong word. I always think of lovable as . . . cuddly. Snub noses and freckles and a charming giggle. The sort of thing you see right off. But she's not like that at all. When you meet her she's all starch and steel, and she's got a tongue like an upper- crust fishwife. She's not pretty. Fantastically attractive, but not pretty. No, I wouldn't have said lovable was the right word at all."

Michael put his glass down and thought about it, then smiled and shook his head. "If that's how you saw her, Neil, you must have been a very sick man. I thought she was dinky. She made me want to laugh—not at her, because of her. No, I didn't see the starch and the steel at all, not at first. I do now. To me she was lovable."

"Is she still lovable?"

"I said so, didn't I?"

"Do you think she knows we're all in love with her?"

"Not the way you mean," Michael said steadily. "She's a dedicated person who hasn't lived her life dreaming about love. She hasn't got a schoolgirl mentality. I have a funny feeling about her, that when the chips are down she'll always love her nursing best."

"There's not a woman born who wouldn't opt for marriage given the right curcumstances," said Neil.

"Why?"

"They all live for love."

Michael's expression was actually pitying. "Oh,

come on, Neil, grow up! Do you mean men can't live for love? But love comes in all shapes and sizes—and both sexes!"

"What would you know about it?" Neil asked bitterly, feeling chastised, a little the way he sometimes felt in the presence of his father, and that wasn't right. Michael Wilson was no Longland Parkinson.

"I don't know how I know about it," said Michael. "It's an instinct. It can't be anything else, can it? I certainly can't claim to be an expert. But there are some things I know without ever remembering learning. People find their own levels, and every person is different." He stood up, stretched. "I'll be back in a tick. I'm just going to see how Nugget is."

When Michael returned a few minutes later Neil looked up at him rather derisively; he had created a third glass by the simple expedient of emptying the dirty water out of a watercolor jar, and had filled it with whisky for himself.

"Drink up, Mike," he said. "I decided I felt like another one after all. I'm celebrating."

5 Sister Langtry's alarm went off at one o'clock in the morning; she had set it because of Nugget, wanting to check on him at an hour when his headache should have eased off. And something about the men tonight had triggered a sharp attack of premonitory disquiet; it would not be a bad idea to check on everyone.

Since probationer days she had trained herself to rouse rapidly, so she got out of bed immediately, and took off her pajamas. She climbed into trousers and bush jacket without bothering to don underwear first, then pulled on thin socks and tied up her daytime duty shoes. At this time of night no one would be interested in whether she was in proper uniform or not. Her watch and keys were on the bureau along with her torch; she put them into one of the jacket's four patch pockets and belted it securely. Right. Ready. Just pray everything in X was nice and quiet.

When she slid around the fly-curtain and tiptoed into the corridor everything did seem to be quiet; too quiet, perhaps, as if the place brooded. There was something missing and something added which together gave the ward an alien lack of welcome. After a few seconds she realized what the differences were: no sounds of sleeping breathing, but a thin beam of light and a soft murmur of voices from under Neil's door. Only Matt's and Nugget's mosquito nets were tucked in.

At Nugget's bed she moved around the screen so softly he could not have heard her, but his eyes she saw were open, gleaming faintly.

"Have you managed to be sick yet?" she asked, after a check of the bowl's interior beneath its cloth showed nothing.

"Yes, Sis. A while ago. Mike gave me a new bowl." He sounded thin and lost and distant.

"Feeling better?"

"Much."

She was busy for a while taking pulse and temperature and blood pressure, entering them with the aid of her torch on the chart clipped to the bottom of his cot.

"Could you drink a cup of tea if I made you one?"

"Could I ever!" A little strength began to creep into his voice at the very thought. "Me mouth's like the bottom of a cocky's cage."

She smiled at him and went away, into the dayroom. No one prepared tea as she did, with the enormous ease and economy of an endless practice which stretched back through innumerable dayrooms to her weepy probationer days. If one of the men did it there was always some sort of tiny accident, tea leaves spilled or the freshness boiled out of the water or the pot insufficiently warmed, but when she did it, it was perfect. In less time than seemed possible she was back beside Nugget's bed with a steaming mug in her hand. She put it down on the locker and helped him to sit up, then drew a chair alongside and remained with him while he drank thirstily, blowing on the surface of the liquid impatiently to cool it, and taking quick, minute sips like a bird.

"You know, Sis," he said, pausing, "while the pain is there I think that as long as I live I'm never going to forget what it's like—you know, I could describe it with lots of words the way I can my ordinary headaches. Then the minute it goes away I can't for the life of me remember what it was like, and the only word I can find to describe it is 'awful.'"

She smiled. "That's a characteristic of our brains, Nugget. The more painful a memory is, the quicker we lose the key to unlock it. It's healthy and right to forget something so shattering. No matter how hard we try, we can never conjure up any kind of experience with its original sharpness. We ought not even want to try, though that's human nature. Just don't try too hard and too often—that's how you get yourself into a muddle. Forget the pain. It's gone! Isn't that the most important thing?"

"My oath it is!" said Nugget fervently.

"More tea?"

"No, thanks, Sis. That was the grouse."

"Then slide your legs off the bed and I'll help you up. You'll sleep like a baby if I change you and the bed."

While he sat shivering on the chair she stripped and remade his bed, then helped him clothe his skinny shanks in fresh pajamas. After which she tucked him in securely, gave him a last smile and shut him inside his mosquito net.

A quick check of Matt revealed him lying in a most unusual abandon, mouth slackly open and something suspiciously like a snore issuing from it. His chest was bare. But he slept she thought so deeply that there didn't seem to be any point in disturbing him. Her nose wrinkled, she stiffened in shock; there was a definite smell of liquor about him!

For a moment she stood regarding the empty beds with a frown between her brows, then in sudden decision turned and walked quickly to Neil's door. She didn't bother to tap on it, and she was speaking even as she entered.

"Look, chaps, I hate to have to act like Matron, but fair's fair, you know!"

Neil was sitting on the bed, Benedict on the chair, both slack-shouldered. Two bottles of Johnnie Walker, one empty and one just about full, stood on the table.

"You *idiots!*" she snapped. "Do you want to get us all court-martialled? Where did that come from?"

"The good colonel," said Neil, working hard at speaking distinctly.

Her lips thinned. "If he had no more sense than to give it to you, Neil, you ought to have had more sense than to take it! Where are Luce and Michael?"

Neil thought about that deeply, and finally said, with

many pauses, "Mike went for a shower. No fun at a party. Luce wasn't in here—went to bed. Huffy."

"Luce is not in bed, and he's not in the ward."

"Then I'll find him for you, Sis," Neil said, struggling to get off the bed. "I won't be long, Ben, I've got to find Luce for Sis. Sis wants Luce. I don't want Luce, but Sis does. Beats me why. I think I'm going to puke first, though."

"If you puke in here I'll rub your nose in it!" she said fiercely. "And stay where you are! The state you're in you couldn't even find yourself! Oh, I could murder the lot of you!" Her temper began to die, a trace of fondness crept into her exasperation. "Now will you be good chaps and clear the evidence of debauchery away? It's past one in the morning!"

6

After a thorough check of the verandah failed to locate either Luce or Michael, Sister Langtry marched across to the bathhouse like a soldier, chin up, shoulders back, still simmering. What on earth had possessed them to carry on like that? There wasn't even a full moon! Just as well X was down at the other end of the compound, right away from any of the other inhabited wards. She was so busy fuming that she ran into the clothesline the men had rigged up so they could do their own washing, and floundered amid towels, shirts, trousers, shorts. Damn them! It was a measure of the degree of her annoyance that she didn't even see the funny side of her collision with the clothesline, simply got it together again and marched on.

The squat bulk of the bathhouse loomed straight ahead. It had a wooden door which opened into one very large room, a barnlike place with showers along one wall and basins along the opposite wall, and a few laundry tubs at the back. There were no partitions or stalls, nowhere for a man to hide. The floor sloped to a drain in its middle, and was perpetually wet on the shower side of the room.

During the night a low-watt light bulb in the ceiling burned continually, but these days the bathhouse rarely saw visitors after dark, since the men of X showered and shaved in the morning and the latrine was in a separate, far less substantial building.

Coming in from the moonless night outside, Sister Langtry had no difficulty in seeing. The whole incredible scene was lit up for her like players on the stage for their audience. A shower, forgotten, still trickling its small curtain of water; Michael in the far corner, naked and wet, staring mesmerized at Luce; and Luce, naked, smiling, erect, standing some five feet away from Michael.

Neither of them noticed her in the doorway; she had a panicked sensation of déjà vu, and saw the scene as some sort of bizarre variation on that other scene in the dayroom. For a moment she stood paralyzed, then suddenly knew that this was something she couldn't handle on her own, didn't have the knowledge or the understanding to handle. So she turned and ran for the ward, running as she had never run in her life before, up the steps, in through the door near Michael's bed, up the ward.

When she burst into Neil's cubicle he and Benedict still seemed to be exactly as she had left them; had so little time passed? No, something had changed. The whisky bottles and the glasses had gone. God *damn* them, they were drunk! Everyone must be drunk!

"The bathhouse!" she managed to say. "Oh, quick!"

Neil seemed to sober, or at least he got to his feet and moving more quickly than she would have believed possible, and Benedict didn't seem too bad either. She herded them out like sheep and got them through the ward, down the steps, across the compound toward the bathhouse. Neil tangled himself in the clothesline and fell, but she didn't wait, just grabbed the hapless Benedict by the arm and hustled him along.

The scene in the bathhouse had changed. Luce and Michael were now crouched like wrestlers in a ring, arms half extended, circling each other; but Luce was still laughing.

"Come on, lover! You know you want it! What's the matter, afraid? Can't you take it that big? Oh, come on! It's no use playing hard to get, I know all about you!"

At first glance Michael's face looked very still, almost remote, but beneath that burned something vast and awful and terrifying, though Luce seemed not to be affected by it. Michael didn't speak, didn't evince a flicker of change as the flow of Luce's words went on; it was as if he hardly saw the real Luce, so intent was he upon the turmoil within himself.

"Break it up!" said Neil sharply.

The scene dissolved immediately. Luce swung round to face the three in the doorway, but for a moment Michael maintained his pose of defensive readiness. Then he collapsed back against the wall, leaning on it and drawing great gasping breaths as if his lungs were bellows. And suddenly he began to shake uncontrollably, his teeth chattering audibly, diaphragm still pumping beneath the skin of his upper abdomen.

Sister Langtry stepped past Luce, and Michael saw her for the first time, his face running sweat, his mouth open on the agony it was to breathe. At first he had to assimilate the simple fact of her presence, after which he looked at her with a passionate appeal that slowly faded into hopelessness; he turned his head away and closed his eyes as if it didn't matter, sagging but not falling, supported still by the wall behind him, something draining out of him so fast he seemed visibly to shrink. Sister Langtry turned away.

"We're none of us in a fit state to make this public tonight," she said, addressing Neil.

Then she turned to Luce, her eyes filled with a sick contempt. "Sergeant Daggett, I will see you in the morning. Kindly return to the ward immediately and don't leave it under any circumstances whatsoever."

Luce appeared triumphant, unrepentant, jubilant; he shrugged, bent to pick up his clothes where he had strewn them just inside the door, opened it and went out, the set of his naked shoulders indicating that he fully intended to make things as difficult as possible in the morning.

"Captain Parkinson, I am making you responsible for Sergeant Daggett's good conduct. When I come on duty I expect to see everything shipshape and normal, and heaven help the man who has a hangover. I am very, very angry! You've abused every trust I've put in you. Sergeant Wilson will not return to X tonight, nor will he return until after I have interviewed Sergeant Daggett. Now do you understand? Are you fit enough to cope?" This last was said with less stringency, and the look in her eyes had softened.

"I'm not as drunk as you appear to think I am," said Neil, gazing down at her with eyes that seemed nearly as dark as Benedict's. "You're the boss. Everything shall be exactly as you wish."

Benedict had neither moved nor spoken since coming into the bathhouse, but as Neil turned stiffly to leave he jumped convulsively, and his eyes flew from their unwinking contemplation of Sister Langtry's face to Michael, still leaning exhausted against the wall. "Is he all right?" he asked anxiously.

She nodded, managed a small, twisted smile. "Don't worry, Ben, I'll look after him. Just go back to the ward with Neil and try to get some sleep."

Alone in the bathhouse with Michael, Sister Langtry looked around for his clothes, but all she could find was a towel; he must have walked across to have his shower already stripped, the towel perhaps wound about his waist. Not allowed in the rules, of course, which stipulated that all personnel abroad at night be covered from neck to feet; still, he had probably never counted on being discovered.

She took the towel from its peg and walked across to him, pausing to turn the shower off.

"Come on," she said, sounding very tired. "Put this around you, please."

He opened his eyes but didn't look at her, took the towel and wrapped it about himself clumsily, his hands still shaking, then he moved away from the wall as if he doubted whether he could stand up unsupported; but he did.

"And how much have *you* had to drink?" she asked bitterly, grasping him ungently by the arm, urging him to walk.

"About four tablespoons," he said in a stiff, small, weary voice. "Where are you taking me?" And suddenly he shook himself free of her hand as if the peremptory and authoritative quality in it stung his pride.

"We're going to my quarters," she said curtly. "I'll put you in one of the vacant rooms there until the morning. You can't go back to the ward unless I call in the MPs, and I don't want to do that."

He followed her then without further protest, defeated. What could he possibly say to this woman that could make her refuse to believe the evidence of her own eyes? It must have looked like the dayroom all over again, only so much worse. And he was utterly exhausted, he didn't have an ounce of reserve strength left after that brief but superhuman struggle with himself. For he had known its outcome the moment Luce appeared; if he swung for it, he was going to have the deep and gloriously satisfying pleasure of killing the stupid, ignorant bastard.

Two things had prevented his leaping for Luce's throat immediately: the memory of the RSM and of the pain that had followed every day since, of the culminating pain which was ward X and Sister Langtry; and the drawn-out savoring of a moment which was going to be exquisite. So when Luce made his move, Michael hung grimly on and on to his shredding self-control.

Luce looked big and masculine and capable, but Michael knew he didn't have the hardness, the experience or the lust for killing. And he had always known that behind Luce's brash confidence, behind the insatiable appetite the man had to torment, there crouched a coward. Luce always thought he could get away with his antics forever, that men took one look at his size, felt his malice and lost their own courage. But Michael knew the moment his bluff was called he would crumble. And as he dropped into an attack position the whole of his future life was there, but it couldn't make any difference any more. He was going to call Luce's bluff, but when the big cocky bastard fell apart he was still going to kill him. Kill him just for the sheer pleasure of it.

Twice destroyed. Twice brought to face the knowledge that he was no better than anyone else exposed to killing; that he too could come to throw everything away for the gratification of a lust. It was a lust, he had always known that. There were many things he had learned about himself which he had also learned to live with; but this? Was having this inside him what closed his mouth on love in Sister Langtry's office? It had welled up, would have spilled out. And then he felt a shadow, something nameless and fearful. This. It had to be this. He had thought of it as his own unworthiness, but now for all time unworthiness had a name.

Thank God she had come! Only how could he ever explain?

7

As they mounted the steps outside her quarters, Sister Langtry realized the other rooms in the block were locked and barred. Not that it meant she was defeated; there were ways of getting into any locked room, and trained nurses who had undergone the convent-like incarceration of a nurses' home were always experts at getting in and out of supposedly secured premises. But it would take time. So she opened the door to her own room, flicked the light switch and stood back for Michael to enter in front of her.

How odd. Except for Matron on inspection rounds, he was the only person ever to see her private domain, for all the sisters preferred to congregate in the recreation area when they sought social contact; it was such a hike to go to a colleague's room. In spite of her weariness she looked at the place with new eyes, noting its drab bare impersonal quality. A cell rather than a lived-in space, though it was larger than a cell. It contained a narrow cot similar to the ones in X, a hard chair, a bureau, a screened-off area to hang her clothes, and two shelves nailed to the wall on which resided her books.

"You can wait in here," she said. "I'm going to find you something to wear, and open up one of the other rooms."

Scarcely waiting to see him seat himself on the hard chair by the bed, she closed the door and moved off, her torch beam going on before her. It was easier to raid one of the nearby wards for something for him to wear than to trek all the way back to X and disturb the men. Besides, she didn't feel up to seeing Luce before morning; she needed time to think first. A visit to B ward produced pajamas and a robe, upon solemn promise that tomorrow she would replace them.

The room right next door to her own was the obvious one in which to deposit Michael, so she set to work levering the wooden slats out of its louvered window. The locks were mortice and too strong to pick with a hairpin. There. Four panels ought to be plenty. She shone the torch through the gap to make sure there was still a bed inside, and discovered it in much the same position as her own, its mattress rolled up. He would have to make do without any sheets, that was all, and she couldn't summon up much pity for his plight anyway.

By the time she let herself back into her own room she had been absent for perhaps three-quarters of an hour. The night was close and humid, and she was soaked with sweat. There was a pain in her side; she stood for a moment massaging it with one hand, then looked toward the chair. He wasn't on it. He was on the bed, curled up on his side with his back to her, and he looked as if he was fast asleep. Asleep! How could he sleep after what he'd just been through?

But it softened her as nothing else could have. After all, what was she so angry about? Why did she feel like turning and rending the nearest object limb from limb? Because they'd all got drunk? Because Luce had merely acted true to form? Or because she wasn't sure any more about Michael, had not been since he turned away from her in the office? Yes, a little over the whisky, perhaps, but the poor beggars were only human, and none too strong at that. Luce? He didn't matter one iota. By far the largest part of her anger was rooted in her grief and uncertainty over Michael.

Quite suddenly she realized she was near to exhaustion herself. Her clothes were stuck to her, mottled with dark patches of sweat, and chafing because she had thought it would be a brief visit and so had not donned underwear. Well, as soon as she got him settled next door she could have a shower. She went across to the bed, not making a sound.

It was after half-past two by the clock on the bureau, and he was so absolutely relaxed that in the end she didn't have the heart to rouse him. Even when she tugged the upper sheet out from under him and spread it up over him, he didn't stir. Out to it.

Poor Michael, the victim of Luce's determination to pay her back for little Miss Woop-Woop. Tonight must have seemed like manna from heaven to Luce, all of them stupid with drink, Nugget incapacitated with a headache, the field clear when Michael went to the bathhouse. She wanted to believe that Michael had done nothing to invite Luce's advances, but surely if that was so he would simply have told Luce to get stuffed and walked out. He wasn't physically afraid of Luce, he never had been physically afraid of Luce. But had all that power made him afraid in a different way? If only she knew men better!

It looked as if she was going to have to be the one to sleep without sheets next door, unless she found the resolution to wake him. In the meantime, she could postpone that decision by going to have a shower. So she pulled her cotton robe off its hook behind the door and went to the bathhouse, shed her trousers and jacket and stood beneath the trickle of tepid water almost ecstatically. To be washed clean was a feeling that sometimes went far deeper than skin. The robe was a large, loose kimono-like affair which belted around the middle; rather than wait for a complete drying, which was debatable anyway on such a humid night, she dabbed herself with a towel and then pulled the robe on, folded it overlapping across the front, and belted it.

And, she thought, picking up her clothes, I'm darned if I see why it has to be me to sleep on a mattress full of crawlies. He can jolly well get himself together and transfer right now!

The clock said five past three. Sister Langtry dropped her sweat-soaked clothes onto the floor, moved to the bed and put the palm of her hand on Michael's shoulder. It was a hesitant, delicate touch, for she hated to have to wake him, and it remained delicate, for she decided after all not to wake him. Too tired even to be amused by her own lack of decision, she sank down onto the hard chair beside the bed and rested her whole hand on his bare skin, unable to resist the fulfillment of an impulse she had known all too often: to *feel* him. A sensation not to be resisted. She tried to remember what it had been like to feel the bare skin of a beloved man, but could not, perhaps because between him and that other man so long ago there stretched a life so different it obliterated sensuous memory; more than six years of burying her own needs beneath the more urgent needs of others. And, she realized with a shock, she hadn't really missed it! Not intolerably, not yearningly.

But Michael was real, and her feeling for him was real. For how long had she wanted to do this, touch the life in him as if she had every right to do so. This is the man I love, she thought; I don't care who he is, what he is. I love him.

Her hand moved on his shoulder, at first experimentally, then in small circles, the touch more and more like a caress. It was her moment, she didn't feel any sense of shame in knowing he had done nothing to indicate he wanted this; she touched him with love to please herself, for a memory. And utterly absorbed now in the perfect delight of feeling him, she leaned to put her cheek against his back, held it there, then turned it to taste his skin through her lips.

Yet when he moved toward her she stiffened in shock, her private paradise exposed; mortified, furious at her own weakness, she jumped away. He caught both her forearms, lifting her up from the chair so quickly and lightly that she had no sensation of force, moving herself at the same time. There was no aggression, no roughness; he seemed to shift himself and her so deftly she was scarcely aware of how he did it. She found herself sitting on the bed, one leg folded under her, his arms about her back, his head against her breast, and felt him trembling. Her own arms curved

205

about him possessively, and the two of them remained thus, almost still, until whatever it was that had made him tremble ceased to plague him.

The grip on her back relaxed, his hands fell away, passed lightly around her waist and began to tug at the knot in her belt. He undid it, then moved the material of the robe aside so that he could turn his face against her skin. One slight breast was curved within his hand, an almost reverent taking of it that moved her unbearably. His head came up, his body lifted away from hers, and her face turned of its own volition to seek his. She moved her shoulders to help him slide the robe off, then fitted her breasts against him, her hands around his shoulders, her mouth fascinated and entranced in his.

Only then did she permit the whole of her love to well up in her, closing her eyes which had been open and shining, feeling in every part of her surely some kind of love in him. He couldn't not love her yet be so much a joy in her, waking her to sensations now long forgotten, even unimportant, yet so familiar still, of a poignant sharpness quite new and wonderfully strange.

They rose to kneel; his hands drifted down her sides with hesitant slowness, as if he wanted to prolong everything to an agony point, and she didn't have the strength to help him or resist him any more, she was too intent on being one with a miracle.

PART 5

1 A little before seven the next morning Sister Langtry let herself quietly out of her room, clad in full daylight uniform—grey dress, white veil, red cape, celluloid cuffs and collar, the silver rising sun at her throat as polished as if it were new. She had taken special care in dressing, wanting to look how she felt, someone with the mark of love on her. And smiling, she lifted her face to greet the new day, and stretched her tired muscles luxuriously.

The way across to the ward had never been so long nor yet so short, but she wasn't sorry to be leaving him asleep behind her, wasn't sorry to be going to ward X. She had not slept herself at all, nor really had he until about six o'clock, when she left the bed and went outside. Before showering she did remember to replace the slats in the window of the next-door room, and so was away for half an hour, a little more. When she returned to her room he was sound asleep; she had left him with a kiss on unknowing lips. There would be time, years of it. They were going home soon, and she was a bush girl anyway; it wouldn't come to her as any shock to have to do without the conveniences of city living. Besides, Maitland wasn't so very far from Sydney, nor was dairy farming in the Hunter Valley anything like as harsh an existence as sheep and wheat out west.

Normally someone was up by half-past six, but then normally she would already have been in the ward for half an hour by that time, would have made the early morning tea and got them stirring. This morning everything was still and quiet, all the mosquito nets save Michael's fastened down.

She put her cape and basket in her office, then

went to the dayroom, where an orderly had already deposited the day's ration of fresh bread, a tin of butter and a new tin of jam—plum again. The spirit stove didn't want to go, and by the time she had managed to persuade it that its only function was the production of hot water she had lost all the advantages of her early shower; the warmth of the day and the ferocious blaze of the spirit stove combined to produce an out-pouring of sweat. The wet season was coming soon; humidity had increased twenty percent in the last week.

When the tea was made and the bread buttered she loaded everything except the teapot onto the board which served as a tray and carried it down the ward, out onto the verandah. A quick return for the teapot, and everything was ready for them. No, not quite! Though last night she had been so annoyed with them she had never thought to pity them in the morning, the later part of the night and Michael melted her resolve to be hard on them for once. After consuming so much of the colonel's whisky, they would be dreadfully hung over.

She went back to her office and unlocked the drug drawer, took out the bottle of mist APC. The aspirin and the phenacetin had sunk in coarse white granules to the bottom, the caffeine floated as a straw-colored syrup on top. It was an easy matter to decant off some of the liquid caffeine into a medicine glass. When she had them all assembled outside she would give each man a tablespoon of the caffeine; it was the oldest hospital trick in the world for treating a hangover, and it had saved many a young doctor's and young nurse's reputation.

At Neil's door she did no more than poke her head around it. "Neil, the tea's made! Rise and shine!" The air in the cubicle smelled foul; she withdrew her head quickly and went into the ward.

Nugget was awake, and gave her a sickly grin as she yanked the netting away from around him, twisted it swiftly into a bundle and threw it upward with an expert flick to rest higgledy-piggledy on the ring; time later to do battle with the Matron Drape.

210

"How's the headache?"

"All right, Sis."

"Good morning, Matt!" she said cheerfully, repeating her act with the mosquito net.

"Good morning, Ben!"

Of course Michael's bed was empty. She turned to go across to Luce, and something of her happiness died. What was she going to say to him? How would he behave during the interview she couldn't very well postpone much beyond breakfast? But Luce wasn't in his bed; the net was torn away from under the mattress, and the bed when she unveiled it had been slept in, but was quite cold.

She turned back toward Benedict and Matt, to find both of them sitting on the edges of their beds, their heads in their hands, shoulders hunched, looking as if every small movement provoked pain.

"Damn the Johnnie Walker!" she said under her breath as she caught sight of Neil weaving gagging from his cubicle to the sluice room opposite, his face grey-green.

Well, it seemed as usual as if she was the only one capable of locating Luce. So she opened the door next to Michael's bed, stepped onto the little landing outside, then headed down the plank steps toward the bathhouse.

But it was a beautiful, beautiful day, humidity and all, she thought, half blind with the dizziness of too little sleep and the glitter of the early sun on the grove of palms just beyond the compound perimeter. The light had never seemed so clear, so sparkling, so soft. When she found the clothesline in ruins she simply smiled and stepped over the tangled heaps of shorts, shirts, trousers and underclothes and socks, trying to picture her dear dignified Neil drunk and fighting free of laundry.

The bathhouse was very quiet. Too quiet. Luce was very quiet. Too quiet. He lay sprawled half against the wall, half on the rough concrete floor, a razor in his

211

spasmed hand. His glistening golden skin was strewn with stiffened, cracking rivers of blood, a congealing pool lay stagnant in the hollow of his belly amid other more hideous things, and the floor around him was awash with blood.

She came only as close to him as she needed to see properly what he had done to himself: the mutilated genitals, the hara-kiri slash which had opened up his abdomen from side to side. It was his own razor, the ebony-handled Bengal he preferred to a safety razor because of the closeness of its shave, and his fingers around it were unquestionably the only fingers which had ever been around it: there was nothing artificial about his grip on the handle, nor about the blood sticking razor and fingers inextricably together—thank God, thank God! His head was tilted unnaturally far back, and almost she fancied his eyes moved derisively at her beneath half-lowered lids; then she saw that it was the golden sheen of death in them, not the gold they had been in the gold of his so vital life.

Sister Langtry didn't scream. Once she had looked, her reaction was instinctive; she stepped quickly back through the door and slammed it shut, scrabbling frantically at the padlock which hung by its unsnapped handle through an eyelet on the doorjamb. With controlled desperation she managed to fling the hinge nailed to the door itself over the eyelet, to thread the padlock back through and press its handle home. Then she leaned against the door limply, her mouth opening and closing, yammering up and down with the nightmarish automatism of a shiny wooden ventriloquist's dummy.

It was perhaps as many as five minutes before the yammering stopped, before she could unglue her hands from their flattened stance against the door.

The insides of her thighs felt sticky, and for a horrid humiliating moment she thought she must have wet herself, then realized it was only sweat and the aftermath of Michael.

Michael, oh, Michael! She beat one fist against the door in a sudden frenzy of rage, of despair. God damn Luce to eternal hell for doing this! Oh, why hadn't those drunken fools in there kept better custody of him? Did she have to do everything herself? Luce, you bastard, you've won after all! You utter, foul, insane, maggoty bastard, to have carried your notions of revenge so far. . . .

Oh, Michael! There were tears on her face, tears of a terrible grief at a snatched imperfect brutally brief joy, with all the dear bright morning in ruins at her feet, drowned in blood. Oh, Michael! My Michael . . . It wasn't fair. They hadn't even talked yet. They hadn't begun to get together the unravelled knots of what had been their previous relationship, hadn't had the time to knit them into a common thread. And, straightening, moving away from the door, she knew then, knew irrevocably, that there could be no hope of happiness for her and Michael. No relationship of any kind. Luce had won after all.

The walk across the compound she did like a robot, moving quickly and jerkily and mechanically, heading at first she knew not where, then heading in the only possible direction. Remembering the feel of tears on her face, she lifted one hand to wipe her eyelids with its palm, tinkered with the set of her veil, smoothed down her brows. There. There, Sister Langtry, *Sister* Langtry, you're in charge of this mess, it's your damned duty! Duty, remember duty. Not only your duty to yourself, but to your patients. There are five of them who have to be protected at any cost from the consequences of Luce Daggett.

2 Colonel Chinstrap was sitting out on his little private verandah attached to his little private hut, stirring his tea reflectively and not thinking anything very much at all. It was that sort of a day, somehow. A nothing very much at all sort of day. After a night with Sister Heather Connolly it usually was, but last night had been hard in a different way; they had spent most of it talking about the coming disintegration of Base Fifteen and the possibility of continuing their affair when they returned to a civilian life.

As it was his habit to overstir his tea, he was still turning his spoon over and over in his cup when Sister Langtry, looking neat and precise as a pin, marched around the corner of his hut and stood on the grass below him, looking up.

"Sir, I have a suicide!" she announced loudly.

He half leaped off his chair, subsided onto it again, then slowly managed to lay the spoon down in the saucer and find his feet. He tottered across to the flimsy balustrade and leaned on it gingerly, looking down at her.

"Suicide? But this is dreadful! Dreadful!"

"Yes, sir," she said woodenly.

"Who?"

"Sergeant Daggett, sir. In the bathhouse. Very messy. Cut himself to ribbons with his razor."

"Oh, dear! Oh, dear!" he said feebly.

"Do you want to have a look for youself first, sir, or do you want me to go straight for the MPs?" she asked, dragging him inexorably on to decisions he felt he didn't have the energy to make.

He mopped his face with his handkerchief, the color so died out of his skin that the grog blossoms on his nose stood out in blue and crimson glory. His hand twitched, a betrayal; he thrust it defensively into his pocket and turned away from her toward the interior of his hut.

"I suppose I had better have a look for myself first," he said, and raised his voice peevishly. "My hat, where the devil is my damned hat?"

They looked quite normal as they moved together across the compound, but Sister Langtry set the pace and it kept the colonel puffing.

"Any . . . idea . . . why . . . Sister?" he panted, slowing down experimentally, but discovering that she continued to forge ahead without any sort of regard for his wind.

"Yes, sir, I do know why. I caught Sergeant Daggett last night in the bathhouse attempting to molest Sergeant Wilson. I imagine that at some time during the night Sergeant Daggett was seized by some sort of fit of guilt or remorse, and decided to end his life where the attack had occurred, in the bathhouse. There's a definite sexual motif—his genitals have been slashed about rather badly."

How could she speak so effortlessly when she was walking so damned quickly? "God spare me days, Sister, will you bloody slow down?" he shouted. Then what she had said about genitals penetrated, and the dismay crept over him as lankly as a jellyfish. "Oh, dear! Oh, dear!"

The colonel took but one brief look inside the bathhouse, which Sister Langtry had unlocked for him with rock-firm hands. He dodged out again barely hanging onto his gorge, but also determined that he was not going to lose it in front of this woman above all people in the world. After a period of deep breathing which he disguised by strutting about with his hands behind his back, looking as important and thoughtful as his gorge would let him, he harumphed and stopped in front of Sister Langtry, who had waited patiently, and now eyed him with faint derision. Damn the woman!

"Does anyone know about this?" he asked, bringing

out his handkerchief and mopping his face, which was gradually returning to its normal high color.

"The suicide, I don't think so," she said, voice coolly considering. "Unfortunately the attempt to molest Sergeant Wilson was witnessed by Captain Parkinson and Sergeant Maynard as well as by me personally, sir."

He clicked his tongue. "Most regrettable! At what time did the attempt to molest Sergeant Wilson occur?"

"Approximately half-past one in the morning, sir."

He stared at her in mingled suspicion and exasperation. "What on earth were you all doing buzzing around the bathhouse at that hour? And how did you permit any of this to happen, Sister? Why didn't you put an orderly in the ward overnight, if not a relief nurse?"

She stared back expressionlessly. "If you're referring to the attack on Sergeant Wilson, sir, I had no basis to suppose Sergeant Daggett's intentions lay in that direction. If you're referring to the suicide, I had absolutely no indication that such were Sergeant Daggett's intentions regarding himself."

"Then you have no doubt that it's suicide, Sister?"

"None at all. The razor was in his own hand when the injuries were inflicted. Didn't you see that for yourself? Holding a Bengal to cut down deeply instead of to scrape the surface of the skin is the same hold reinforced by strength."

He resented the inference that his gorge had not permitted his staying long enough to inspect the corpse as thoroughly as apparently she had done, so he switched tactics. "I repeat, why did you not have someone stand guard in the ward during the night, Sister? And why did you not report Sergeant Daggett's attack on Sergeant Wilson to me immediately?"

Her eyes opened guilelessly wide. "Sir! At two in the morning? I really didn't think you'd thank me for rousing you at such an hour for something which was not a true medical emergency. We broke it up before Sergeant Wilson sustained any physical harm, and when I left Sergeant Daggett he was in full possession of his wits and his self-control. Captain Parkinson and Sergeant Maynard agreed to keep an eye on Sergeant Daggett during the night, but provided Sergeant Wilson was removed from the ward, I did not see any necessity to restrain Sergeant Daggett forcibly, nor to have him placed under arrest and taken into custody, nor to start yelling for staff assistance. In fact, sir," she concluded calmly, "I was hoping not to have to draw your attention to the incident at all. I felt that after talking to Sergeant Daggett and to Sergeant Wilson when both of them had recovered somewhat, everything might be resolved without an official fuss. At the time I left the ward I was optimistic such would prove to be the case."

He seized upon a new item of information. "You say you removed Sergeant Wilson from the ward, Sister. Just what do you mean by that?"

"Sergeant Wilson was in severe emotional shock, sir, and considering the circumstances I thought it advisable to treat him in my own quarters rather than in the ward right under Sergeant Daggett's nose."

"So Sergeant Wilson was with you all night."

She looked at him fearlessly. "Yes, sir. All night."

"All night? You're sure it was all night?"

"Yes, sir. He's still in my quarters, as a matter of fact. I didn't want to bring him back to the ward until after I had talked to Sergeant Daggett."

"And were you with him all night, Sister?"

A tiny horror crept into her mind. The colonel was not busy thinking salacious thoughts about her and Michael; he probably didn't consider her the least capable of salacious activity. He was contemplating something far different than love—he was contemplating murder.

"I did not leave Sergeant Wilson's side until I came on duty half an hour ago, sir, and I discovered Sergeant Daggett only minutes after coming on duty. He had then been dead for several hours," she said, her tone brooking no argument.

"I see," said Colonel Chinstrap, tight-lipped. "This is a pretty mess, isn't it?"

"I disagree, sir. It isn't pretty at all."

He returned to the main theme like a worrisome dog. "And you're absolutely sure that Sergeant Daggett did or said nothing to indicate a suicidal state of mind?"

"Absolutely nothing, sir," she said firmly. "In fact, that he did commit suicide staggers me. Not that it's so inconceivable he'd take his own life. Only that he chose to do so with so much blood, so much . . . *ugliness*. As for the assault on his own masculinity—I can't even begin to grasp why. But then, that's the trouble with people. They never do what you expect them to do. I'm being quite open and honest with you, Colonel Donaldson. I could lie and say Sergeant Daggett's state of mind was definitely suicidal. But I choose to speak the truth. My incredulity over Sergeant Daggett's suicide doesn't alter my conviction that it is suicide. It can't be anything else."

He turned and began to walk toward X, setting a sober pace which she seemed content to follow at last. By the collapsed clothesline he paused to poke about in the heaps of laundry with his swagger stick, reminding Sister Langtry of the matron of a mixed-sex teenage camp looking for suspicious stains. "There seems to have been a bit of a fight here," he said, straightening.

Her lips twitched. "There was, sir. Between Captain Parkinson and some shirts."

He moved on. "I think I had better see Captain Parkinson and Sergeant Maynard before I send for the authorities, Sister."

"Of course, sir. I haven't been back to the ward since I discovered the body, so I imagine none of them know what's happened. Even if any of them have tried to get into the bathhouse, I locked it before I went to find you."

"That at least is something to be grateful for," he said austerely, and suddenly realized life was offering him the perfect opportunity to slap Sister Langtry down for good. A man in her quarters all night, an absolutely sordid sexual mess culminating in a killing—by the time he was finished with her, she'd be pilloried and out of the army in disgrace. Oh, God, the bliss! "Permit me to say, Sister, that I consider you have botched this entire affair from start to finish, and that I shall make it my personal business to see that you receive the censure you so richly deserve."

"Thank you, sir!" she exclaimed, apparently without irony. "However, I consider that the direct cause of this entire affair was two bottles of Johnnie Walker whisky which were consumed in full last night by the patients of ward X. And if I only knew the identity of the brainless fool who was responsible for giving Captain Parkinson, an emotionally unstable patient, those two bottles yesterday, I would take great pleasure in making it *my* personal business to see that *he* receives the censure *he* so richly deserves!"

He tripped going up the steps and had to grab at the rickety banister to save himself. Brainless fool? Blithering idiot! He had forgotten all about the whisky. And she knew. Oh, she knew, all right! He would have to forget revenge. He would have to backpedal very quickly indeed. Damn the woman! That smooth and oh, so fearless insolence was bone deep; if her nursing training had not eradicated it, bloody nothing ever would.

Matt, Nugget, Benedict and Neil were sitting at the table on the verandah, looking ghastly. Poor souls, she hadn't even given them the caffeine she had skimmed off the top of the mist APC, and she couldn't very well dole it out to them now, with Colonel Chinstrap looking on.

At sight of the colonel they all rose to attention; he sat down heavily on one end of a bench and was obliged to make a flying leap for its middle when it tipped dangerously.

"As you were, gentlemen," he said. "Captain Parkinson, I would greatly appreciate a cup of tea, please."

The teapot had already gone through several refills and one remake, so the tea Neil poured with a none-too-steady hand was fairly fresh. Colonel Chinstrap took the mug without seeming to notice its ugliness, and buried his nose in it gratefully. But eventually he had to put the mug down, at which time he glared sourly at the four men and Sister Langtry.

"I understand that Sergeants Wilson and Daggett were involved in an incident early this morning in the bathhouse?" he asked, his manner indicating that this was what had brought him all the way down the compound to ward X so early in the day.

"Yes, sir," said Neil easily. "Sergeant Daggett made an attempt to molest Sergeant Wilson sexually. Sister Langtry fetched us—Sergeant Maynard and myself, that is—to the bathhouse, and we broke it up."

"Having seen the actual incident with your own eyes, or only having heard of it from Sister Langtry?"

Neil eyed the colonel with a contempt he didn't even bother to conceal. "Why, having seen it with our own eyes, of course!" He packed his voice with the nuances of someone forced to pander to an inexplicably prurient interest. "Sergeant Wilson must have been surprised in the shower. He was naked, and quite wet. Sergeant Daggett was also naked, but not at all wet. He was, however, in a state of extreme sexual arousal. When Sister Langtry, Sergeant Maynard and myself entered the bathhouse, he was attempting to grapple with Sergeant Wilson, who had dropped into a defensive position to ward him off."

Neil cleared his throat, looked carefully past the colonel's shoulder. "Luckily Sergeant Wilson had not imbibed very freely of the whisky we just happened to have in our possession last night, otherwise things might have gone a lot harder for him."

"All right, all right, that's quite enough!" said the colonel sharply, feeling every nuance like a rapier, and the mention of the whisky like a club. "Sergeant Maynard, do you agree with Captain Parkinson's description?"

Benedict looked up for the first time. His face had the strung and drawn weariness of someone who had reached a point of no return, and his eyes were red-rimmed from the whisky. "Yes, sir, that's the way it happened," he said, dragging the words out as if he had been sitting there for days concentrating on nothing but those words. "Luce Daggett was a blot on the face of the earth. Dirty. Disgusting—"

Matt got up quickly and put his hand unerringly on Benedict's arm, the grip pulling Benedict to his feet. "Come on, Ben," he said urgently. "Hurry! Take me for a walk. After all that grog last night I don't feel well."

Colonel Chinstrap didn't argue, for a fresh reference to the whisky terrified him. He sat as quietly as a mouse while Benedict led Matt rapidly from the verandah, then turned to Neil again. "What happened after your arrival put an end to the incident, Captain?"

"Sergeant Wilson had a bit of a reaction, sir. You know, the sort of thing that can happen after you've been keyed up to fight. He got the shakes, couldn't breathe properly. It seemed to me better that he go with Sister Langtry, so I suggested to her that she remove Sergeant Wilson from the ward, somewhere like her quarters, right away from Sergeant Daggett. That left Sergeant Daggett without—ah—further temptation during the remainder of the night. It also left him in a state of considerable apprehension, which I freely confess I did rather encourage him to feel. Sergeant Daggett, sir, is not my favorite person."

At the beginning of this speech Sister Langtry merely watched Neil courteously, but when she heard him tell the colonel it had been his idea to remove Michael from the ward, her eyes widened in surprise, then softened in gratitude. The silly, noble, wonderful man! It would never occur to the colonel to doubt that it had been Neil's doing; he expected men to take charge and make the decisions. But it also seemed Neil knew very well where she had intended to put Michael for the night, and that gave her pause; had the latter part of the night been written even then on her face, or was it just an inspired guess?

"How was Sergeant Daggett after you returned to the ward, Captain?" asked the colonel.

"How was Sergeant Daggett?" Neil closed his eyes. "Oh, much the same as always. An acid-tongued bastard. Not a bit sorry, except for being caught. Full of his usual spite. And carrying on about getting even with us all, but especially with Sister Langtry. Luce detests her."

So much undisguised dislike of someone dead offended the colonel, until he remembered they didn't know Luce was dead. He pressed on toward his denouement.

"Where is Sergeant Daggett now?" he asked casually.

"I neither know nor care, sir," said Neil. "As far as I'm concerned, I would be delirious with joy if he were never to set foot in ward X again."

"I see. Well, Captain, you're honest."

Everyone could see the colonel trying to make allowances for the precarious emotional balance of the men of X, but when he turned to Nugget his exasperation was beginning to show. "Private Jones, you're sitting there very quietly. Have you anything to add?"

"Who, sir, me, sir? *I* had a migraine," said Nuggett importantly. "The classical pattern, sir, it really was— you would have been fascinated! A two-day prodroma of lethargy and some dysphasia, followed by an hour-long aura of scotomata in the right visual field, and then a left hemicranial headache. I was as flat as a tack, sir." He thought for a moment. "Well, flatter, really."

"Flashing lights are not called scotomata, Private," said the colonel.

"*Mine* were scotomata," said Nugget decisively. "They were fascinating, sir! I told you, it wasn't your minimal migraine by a long shot. If I looked at something big, I saw it all, no trouble. But if I looked at a small bit of the big thing, like a knob on a door or a knothole in the wall, I only saw the left half of the knob or knothole. The right half was—I don't know! Just not there! Scotomata, sir."

"Private Jones," said the colonel tiredly, "if your knowledge of military matters even remotely equalled your knowledge of your own symptomatology, you'd be a field marshal, and we would have been marching through Tokyo in 1943. When you go back to civilian life, I strongly suggest that you consider studying medicine."

"Can't, sir," said Nugget regretfully. "I've only got me Intermediate. But I am thinking about training as a male nurse, sir. At the Repat."

"Well, the world will have lost a Pasteur, perhaps, but it may gain Mister Nightingale instead. You'll do splendidly, Private Jones."

Out of the corner of his eye the colonel noticed that Matt had returned without Benedict, and was standing in the doorway listening intently.

"Corporal Sawyer, what have you to offer?"

"Never saw a thing, sir," said Matt blandly.

The colonel's lips disappeared; he was obliged to draw a deep breath. "Have any of you gentlemen visited the bathhouse since Sergeant Daggett's attack on Sergeant Wilson?"

"Afraid not, sir," said Neil, looking apologetic. "Sorry you've caught us unwashed and unshaved, but after our little lapse with the whisky last night what we all seemed to need first this morning was gallons of tea."

"I do think you might have issued them the top off the APC, Sister!" snapped the colonel, glaring at her.

Her brows lifted; she smiled slightly. "I have it all ready to go, sir."

The colonel finally reached his denouement. "I suppose none of you are aware that Sergeant Daggett has been found dead in the bathhouse, then," he said curtly.

As a climax it was dismally ineffective; no one evinced surprise, shock, sorrow or even interest. They

223

just sat or stood looking much as if the colonel had made a particularly banal remark about the weather.

"Now why on earth would Luce do a thing like that?" asked Neil, apparently feeling the colonel was waiting for some sort of comment. "I didn't think he'd be so considerate."

"Good riddance to bad rubbish," said Matt.

"All me Christmases have come at once," said Nugget.

"Why do you assume it is suicide, Captain?"

Neil looked astonished. "Well, isn't it? He's a bit on the young side to be popping off from natural causes, surely?"

"True, he did not die from natural causes. But why do you assume it was suicide?" the colonel persisted.

"If he didn't have a heart attack or a stroke or whatever, then he put the kybosh on himself. I'm not trying to say that we wouldn't have been delighted to assist him, but last night was not a night for murder, sir. It was a night for a wee drop of whisky."

"How did he die, sir?" asked Nugget eagerly. "Cut his throat? Stab himself? Hang himself, maybe?"

"You would be the one to want to know that, wouldn't you, you little ghoul?" exclaimed the colonel, looking fed up. "He committed what the Japanese call hara-kiri, I believe."

"Who found him, sir?" asked Matt, still in the doorway.

"Sister Langtry."

This time their reaction was all he might have hoped for when he had announced Luce's death; there was an appalled silence as every eye turned toward Sister Langtry. Nuggett looked as if he were about to weep, Matt stunned, Neil despairing.

"My dear, I am so sorry," Neil said eventually.

She shook her head, smiled at them lovingly. "It's all right, truly. As you can see, I've survived. Don't look so upset, please."

Colonel Chinstrap sighed and slapped his hands on his thighs in defeat; what could one do with men who felt no regret at the death of a fellow man, then flew into small pieces because their darling Sister Langtry had had a nasty experience? He rose to his feet. "Thank you for your time and the tea, gentlemen. Good morning to you."

"They knew," he said, walking down the ward with Sister Langtry. "Those smug devils *knew* he was dead!"

"Do you think so?" she asked coolly. "You're quite wrong, you know. They were just trying to get on your nerves, sir. You shouldn't let them succeed the way you do; it only makes them worse."

"When I need your advice, madam, I shall ask for it!" he snapped, fizzing with rage. Then recollection of his own very delicate position and the dictatory position of Sister Langtry occurred simultaneously, but he couldn't resist saying, rather maliciously, "There will have to be an inquiry."

"Naturally, sir," she said calmly.

It was all far too much, especially after the kind of night he had passed. "It would seem there was no foul play," he said wearily. "Luckily for him, perhaps, Sergeant Wilson has an ironclad alibi furnished by no less a person than your good self. However, I shall reserve my decision until after the military police have inspected the corpse. If they concur that there is no suspicion of foul play, I imagine the inquiry will be a mere matter of form. However, that's up to Colonel Seth. I shall notify him immediately." He sighed, cast her a quick sidelong glance. "Yes, indeed, how fortunate for young Sergeant Wilson! It would be wonderful if all the sisters on all my wards were so solicitous of patient welfare."

She stopped just inside the fly-curtain, wondering why there were some people one felt compelled to hurt, yet why one was amazed when they in their turn lashed back. That was she and Colonel Chinstrap; from their first moment of meeting and sizing each other up, it had been a competition to see who could strike hardest. And, by now dedicated to that course, she didn't feel charitable enough to let him get away with his taunts about Michael.

So she said like silk, "I shall request the men to refrain from this running on at the mouth about their alcoholic indiscretions, sir, don't you think? I really can't see why it has to be mentioned at all, provided the military police feel there is no doubt Sergeant Daggett committed suicide."

He writhed, would have given anything he owned to fling it back in her smiling face, shout at her to tell the whole bloody world he had given troppo patients whisky, but he knew he couldn't. So he merely nodded stiffly. "As you see fit, Sister. Certainly *I* shall not mention it."

"You haven't seen Sergeant Wilson yet, sir. I left him asleep, but he's quite all right. Fit for an interview, of that I'm sure. I'll walk over to my quarters with you now. I would have put him in one of the vacant rooms around my own if I could, but they're all locked up. Which as it turns out was just as well, wasn't it? I had to keep him in my own room, right under my eye. Very uncomfortable, as there's only one small bed."

The bitch, the *bloody* bitch! If Private Nugget Jones was a potential Pasteur, she was a potential Hitler. And, he was forced to admit, even on his best days he was never equal to Sister Langtry. He was so tired, and the affair had been a considerable shock.

"I'll see the sergeant later, Sister. Good morning."

3 Sister Langtry watched without moving until the colonel was well on his way back in the direction of his own hut, then she walked down the ramp and began the journey to her room.

If only when things happened there was time to think! It never seemed to turn out that way, unfortunately. The best she could do was to keep on the move and one jump ahead. She didn't trust Colonel Chinstrap an inch. It would be just like him to scuttle like a cockroach back to his hut and then to disptach Matron to do his dirty work by having Matron descend on her room. Michael had to be moved, and at once. But she would have liked more time before seeing him, a few precious hours in which to find the perfect way to say what had to be said. A few precious hours; days would not have been long enough for this.

There was ruin in the air. The cynics might have put it down to a gathering monsoon, but Sister Langtry knew better. Things built themselves up and then tumbled back to nothing again so fast one knew immediately there had been no proper foundations laid. Which was certainly true of Michael and herself. How could she ever have hoped for something enduring to come out of an utterly artificial situation? Hadn't she resolutely refused to develop her relationship with Neil Parkinson because of that? Usually a man went to bed, if not with someone he knew, at least with someone he thought he knew. But to Michael there. could have been nothing real about Honour Langtry; she was a figment, a phantasm. The only Langtry he knew was Sister Langtry. With Neil she had preserved enough sanity to understand this, to suppress her hopes until both of them were back in a more normal environment, until he had a chance to meet Honour Langtry rather than Sister Langtry. But with Michael there had been no thought, no sanity, nothing save a drive to find love with him here and now and hang the consequences. As if in some utterly unconscious part of her she had known how tenuous it was, how unviable.

Years ago a sister in the preliminary training school at P.A. had taken the probationers for a special lecture on the emotional hazards involved in nursing. Honour Langtry had been one of those probationers. Among the hazards, said the sister tutor, was that of falling in love with a patient. And if a nurse should insist upon falling in love with a patient, she said, let him be an acute patient. Never, never a chronic one. Love might grow and prove durable with an acute abdomen or a fractured femur. But love with spastic or paraplegic or tuberculotic was not, in the measured words of that measured voice, a viable proposition. A viable proposition. It was a phrase Honour Langtry never forgot.

Not that Michael was ill, and certainly he was not chronically ill. But she had met him in a long-term nursing situation, colored by all the darknesses of ward X. Even supposing he was not infected, she definitely was. Her first and her only duty should have been to see Michael as an inmate of ward X. With Neil Parkinson she had succeeded; but she didn't love Neil Parkinson, so duty had proceeded on its serene way.

Now here she was, trying to wear two hats at once, love and duty, both donned for the same man. The same patient. The job *said* he was a patient. It didn't matter that he didn't fit that description at all. For there was duty. There was always duty. It came first; not all the love in the world could change the ingrained habits of so very many years.

Which hat do I wear, love or duty? she asked herself, treading more heavily than usual up the steps onto the verandah outside her room. Shall I be his lover or his nurse-custodian? What is he? My lover or my patient? A sudden puff of wind caught under the edge of her veil and lifted it away from her neck. Questions all answered, she thought. I am wearing my duty hat.

When she opened the door she saw Michael dressed in the pajamas and robe she had borrowed from B ward, sitting waiting patiently on the hard chair. The chair he had relocated half the room away from the bed, now neatly made up and looking as if under no stretch of the wildest imagination could it ever have been the site of more pleasure and pain, more gloriously hard work than any oversized, pillow-strewn voluptuary's couch. In an odd way the bed's spartan chasteness came as a shock; she had already enacted the scene to come as she crossed the verandah, and in that scene she had pictured him still lying naked in her bed.

Had he been so she might have been able to be soft, might have sunk onto the mattress beside him, might in spite of her duty hat have summoned up the courage from somewhere to do what she most longed to do: put her arms about him, offer her mouth for one of those powerful and ardent kisses, reinforce with fresh experiences the memories of the night so horribly overshadowed by the dead thing still sprawled in the bathhouse.

She stood in the doorway, unsmiling, stripped of the capacity to move or speak, quite without resources. But the look on her face must have told him more than she realized, for he got up immediately and came across to her, standing close, but not close enough to touch her.

"What's happened?" he asked. "What is it? What's the matter?"

"Luce committed suicide," she said baldly, and stopped, run down again.

"Suicide?" At first he gaped, but the astonishment and revulsion faded more rapidly than they should have, and were replaced by a curious, horrified consternation, as if at some action of his own. "Oh, my God, my God!" he said slowly, and looked as if he was beginning to die. The guilt and distress on his face grew whitely; then he said, "What have I done?" and

repeated it, "What have I done?" in the voice of an old, enfeebled man.

Her heart came uppermost at once, and she moved close enough to him to clasp his arm in both her hands, looking into his face imploringly. "You've done nothing, Michael, nothing at all! Luce destroyed *himself,* do you hear? He was just using you to get back at me. You cannot blame yourself! It's not as if you led him on, encouraged him!"

"Isn't it?" he asked harshly.

"Stop it!" she cried, terrified.

"I should have been there with him, not here with you. I had no right to leave him."

Appalled, she stared at him as if she hardly knew him, but then somehow she managed to find a small mocking smile from somewhere in her grab bag of emergency expressions, and smeared it across her mouth. "My word!" she exclaimed. "That's quite a compliment to me!"

"Oh, Sis, I didn't mean it that way!" he cried wretchedly. "I wouldn't hurt you for the world!"

"Can't you remember to call me Honour even now?"

"I wish I could. It suits you—oh yes, it does suit you. Yet I always think of you as Sis, even now. I wouldn't hurt you for the world, Sis. But if I had stayed where I belonged, this could never have happened. He'd be safe, and I—I'd be free. It is my fault!"

His agony could mean nothing to her, for she didn't know its source. Who was he? What was he? A nauseated revulsion and a huge nameless sorrow welled up from some central part of her, spread insidiously through her from fingertips to wide incredulous eyes. Who was he, that after spending hours making the most passionate and loving of love to her, he could stand now bewailing it, dismissing it in favor of *Luce?* Horror, grief, pain, she might have dealt with those, but not when he was experiencing all of them for Luce. She had never in her life felt less a woman, less a human being. He had thrown her love right back in her face in favor of Luce Daggett.

"I see," she said tautly. "I've been terribly mistaken about a lot of things, haven't I? Oh, how stupid of me!" The bitter laugh came unbidden, and was so successful he flinched. "Hang on for a minute, would you?" she asked, turning away. "I must have a quick wash. Then I'll take you back to X. Colonel Chinstrap wants to ask you a few questions, and I'd much rather he didn't find you still here."

There was a tin dish on a little shelf below the back window, and it contained a small quantity of water. With face averted she hurried to it, the tears pouring down, and made a great show of splashing in the water, then stood with a towel pressed against her eyes and cheeks and nose, willing with will of iron those senseless, shaming tears to stop.

He was what he was; should that therefore automatically mean her love for him was worthless? Should that mean there was nothing in him worth loving, that he could prefer Luce to her? Oh, Michael, Michael! In all her life she had never felt so betrayed, so dishonored, Honour without honor indeed, and yet why should she feel so? He was what he was and it had to be beautiful or she would never have loved him. But the void between reason and her own feminine feelings was unbridgeable. No rival woman could ever have hurt like that. Luce. Weighed and found wanting in favor of *Luce*.

What an idiot Colonel Chinstrap was, to suspect Michael of killing Luce! A pity he couldn't have witnessed this little scene. It would have scotched his suspicions on the spot. If any man was ever sorry another man was dead, that man was Sergeant Michael Wilson. He could have done it, she supposed; during the night she had been absent from her room long enough for him to have made the journey, done the deed and returned. But he hadn't. Nothing would ever convince her he had. Poor Michael. He was probably right. If he had remained in ward X, Luce would not have needed to kill himself. His victory over her would have been complete—no, more complete.

231

Oh, God, the mess! What a tangle of desires, a confusion of motives. Why had she removed Michael from the ward? At the time it had seemed the right thing to do, the only thing to do. But had she planned all along to seize any opportunity to have Michael to herself? Ward X gave one no chance of that; they were all so jealous of time spent alone with any of them. And men, she supposed, were men. Since she had virtually thrown herself at a Michael suffering some sort of withdrawal from his encounter in the bathhouse, why should she blame him for picking her up and using her?

The tears dried. She put the towel down and walked to the mirror. Good, the tears hadn't lasted long enough to mar. Her veil was crooked, her duty hat that never, never betrayed her. Love might; duty never did. You knew where you stood with duty—what you gave to it, you got back. She slid open some deep dark drawer in her mind and dropped the love into it, straightening her veil in the mirror above eyes as cool and detached as that sister tutor so many years ago. Not a viable proposition. She turned away from herself.

"Come one," she said kindly. "I'll take you back where you belong now."

Stumbling occasionally, Michael plodded along beside her, so wrapped in his own misery he scarcely knew she was there. It was not merely beginning again; it had already begun, and it was a life sentence this time, a whole eternity of living. Why did it have to happen to him? What had he ever done? People kept dying. And all because of him, of something in him. A Jonah.

The temptation to lie on her bed, smell her sheets, press his body flat where hers had lain . . . She was regretting it now, but she hadn't then. All that love he had never known, and it was there. Like a dream. And it had come at the end of something hideous, was born in his shame at being caught naked and compromised by Luce Daggett. It was born in the destruction of his self-esteem, the total realization that he too hungered to kill.

Visions of Luce danced in his brain, Luce laughing, Luce mocking, Luce staring at him in amazement because he had been willing to clean up the mess Luce had made, Luce in the bathhouse unable to believe his overtures were unwelcome, Luce sublimely unaware that murder hung above him like a sword. *You stupid drongo!* As Luce had once said it to him, so now he said it to the ghost of Luce. You stupid, stupid drongo! Didn't you realize how you were asking for it? Didn't you realize that war blunts a man's objections to killing, accustoms him to it? Of course you didn't. You never got closer to war than a base ordnance unit.

There was no future left. No future for him. Perhaps there never had been. Ben would say a man always brought it upon himself. It wasn't fair. Oh, God, how angry he was! And she, whom he didn't know, he would never know now. She had looked at him just now as at a murderer. And he was a murderer; he had murdered hope.

4   The moment they arrived in the ward Michael hurried away; the one glance into his face that he permitted her tore afresh at her own ribboned feelings, for the grey eyes had gone beyond tears, so deeply troubled she would have been willing to put herself aside and offer him what comfort she could. But no; he hurried away as if he couldn't escape from her quickly enough. And yet the moment he saw Benedict sitting disconsolate on the side of his bed he swerved, and sat down.

Sister Langtry could bear it no longer, and turned to go into her office, as much angry now as anguished. Clearly everyone was more important to Michael than she was.

When Neil came in with a cup of tea and a small plate of bread and butter she was tempted to order him out, but something in his face prevented her. Not a vulnerability, exactly, more a simple anxiety to serve and to help that could not thus be so lightly dismissed.

"Drink and eat," he said. "You'll feel better."

She was very grateful for the tea, but didn't think she would be able to get any of the bread down; however, once her first cup was succeeded by her second she managed to eat about half of what was on the plate, and did indeed feel better.

Neil sat down in the visitor's chair and watched her intently, fretting at her grief, frustrated by his own impotence, chafing at the restrictions she had imposed upon his conduct toward her. What she was prepared to do and give for Michael did not apply to himself, and that was galling, for he knew he was the better man. Better for her in every way. He had more than an inkling that Michael knew it too, this morning if not yesterday. But how to convince her? She wouldn't even want to hear.

As she pushed the plate away he spoke. "I am so desperately sorry that you of all people had to be the one to find Luce. It can't have been pretty."

"No, it wasn't. But I can cope with that sort of thing. You mustn't let it worry you." She smiled at him, unaware that she looked as if she waded through the depths of a private hell. "I must thank you for taking the blame for my decision to remove Michael from X."

He shrugged. "Well, it helped, didn't it? Let the colonel cling to his stronger-sex convictions. If I had told him I was drunk and incapable where you were well in command, he would have found me far less believable."

She pulled a face. "That's true."

"Are you sure you're all right, Sis?"

"Yes, perfectly all right. If I feel anything, it's rather as if I've been cheated."

His brows twitched. "Cheated? That's an odd word!"

"Not to me. Did you know I had taken Michael to my quarters, or was it purely a shot in the dark?"

"Logic. Where else would you take him? I knew last night that when it came to the morning you wouldn't want to haul Luce up before the MOs or the MPs. So that meant you couldn't create speculation by putting Mike in another ward, for instance."

"You're very acute, Neil."

"I don't think you realize how acute I actually am."

Not being able to answer, she turned slightly away and looked out the window.

"Here, have a cigarette," he said, pitying her, but bitter too, because he knew there were some things of which she would not permit him to speak.

She turned back. "I daren't, Neil. Matron is bound to be along any tick of the clock. By now the colonel will have told her and the super and the MPs, and she at least will be champing at the bit. The seedier the sensation the better, as far as she's concerned, provided she's not an active part of the seediness. She's going to lap this little chapter of disasters up."

"How about if I light a cigarette for myself, and you sneak the odd puff from it? You need something more than tea."

"If you dare mention whisky to me, Neil Parkinson, I'll order you to stay in your room for a month! And I can do without the cigarette, truly. I have to salvage what respectability I can or Matron will drum me out of the corps. She'd smell the smoke on my breath."

"Well, at least as the donor of the grog the colonel's well and truly hoist with his own petard."

"Which reminds me of two things. First, I'd be grateful if none of you mentions the whisky to a soul. Second, take this glass to the ward with you and give yourself and the others a tablespoon each. It'll cure your hangovers."

He grinned. "For that I could kiss your hands and feet!"

At which point Matron bustled through the door, nostrils quivering like a bloodhound's. Neil disappeared with a sketchy obeisance to Matron en route, leaving Sister Langtry to face her superior officer alone.

5 Matron was the start of a different kind of wearing day. She was followed by the super, a mild little red-hat colonel who really only cared about hospitals in the abstract, and felt quite helpless when faced with patients in the flesh. As commanding officer of Base Fifteen, he bore the responsibility of determining the style of the inquiry. After a brief inspection of the bathhouse, he rang the DAPM at divisional headquarters, and requested the services of a Special Investigations sergeant. A bush man, the super had scant interest in what his eyes clearly told him was an open and shut case of suicide, albeit suicide of a particular unpleasant kind. So he handed the physical execution of the inquiry over to Base Fifteen's quartermaster, a tall, amiable and most intelligent young man named John Penniquick; then with mind relieved of a burden having considerable nuisance value, he went back to the complicated business of closing a whole hospital down.

Captain Penniquick was if anything even busier than the super, but he was also a very efficient and hardworking officer, so when the SI sergeant arrived from HQ he briefed him thoroughly.

"I'll see any of them myself whom you think I ought," he said, peering over his glasses at Sergeant Watkin, whom he found perceptive, sensible and likable. "However, it's your pigeon entirely, unless the pigeon turns out to be a hawk, in which case, yell your head off and I'll come running."

After ten minutes in the bathhouse with the major who was Base Fifteen's pathologist, Sergeant Watkin walked carefully across the distance between the bathhouse and the back steps of ward X, then skirted the ward and came in up the ramp at its front. Though Sister Langtry was not in her office, the telltale rattle of the fly-curtain alerted her, and she came speeding up the ward. A neat little thing, thought the sergeant with approval; real officer material, too. It cost him no pangs to salute her.

"Hello, Sergeant," she said, smiling.

"Sister Langtry?" he asked, removing his hat.

"Yes."

"I'm from the DAPM's office at divisional HQ, and I'm here to look into the death of Sergeant Lucius Daggett. My name's Watkin," he said, his voice slow, almost sleepy.

But he wasn't a bit sleepy. He declined her offer of tea once they were established in her office, and got straight down to business. "I'll need to see your patients, Sister, but I'd like to ask you a few questions first, if you don't mind."

"Please do," she said tranquilly.

"The razor. Was it his own?"

"Yes, I'm sure it was. Several of the men use Bengals, but I fancy Luce's was the only one with an ebony handle." She decided to be quite open, and thus establish the fact that she was in charge of things, too. "Though there's surely no doubt in your mind as to suicide, Sergeant? I saw the way Luce was holding the razor. The fingers had spasmed on it exactly the way the living hand would have held it, and the hand and arm were caked with an enormous amount of blood, as they would be while he made incisions like those I saw. How many cuts were there?"

"Three only, as a matter of fact. But they were two more than he needed to finish himself fast."

"What does the pathologist say? Have you brought in someone from outside, or are you using Major Menzies?"

He laughed. "How about I just take a little snooze on one of your spare beds and let you handle the inquiry?"

She looked mortified, demure, and somehow oddly girlish. "Oh, dear, I do sound bossy, don't I? I'm so sorry, Sergeant! It's just that I'm fascinated."

"It's all right, Sister, ask away. You tickle me to death. Seriously, there's very little doubt that it was suicide, and you're quite right about the way the razor was held. Major Menzies says there's no doubt in his mind that Sergeant Daggett inflicted the wounds on himself. I'll just ask around among the men about the razor, and if it all tallies I reckon the whole thing can be wound up pretty quickly."

She heaved a huge sigh of relief and smiled at him enchantingly. "Oh, I'm so glad! I know everyone thinks mentally unstable patients are capable of anything, but truly my men are a gentle lot. Sergeant Daggett was the only violent one."

He looked at her curiously. "They're all soldiers, aren't they, Sister?"

"Of course."

"And mostly front line, I'll bet, or they wouldn't be troppo. Sorry to contradict you, Sister, but your men can't be a gentle lot."

Which told her that the investigations he carried out would be as thorough as he felt necessary. So it all devolved upon whether he had spoken the truth when he said he believed Luce had committed suicide.

His inquiries about the razor revealed that indeed the only ebony-handled Bengal had belonged to Luce. Matt owned an ivory-handled Bengal, and Neil a set of three with mother-of-pearl handles which had been custom made for his father before the First World War. Michael used a safety razor; so did Benedict and Nugget.

The men of X made no attempt to hide their dislike of the dead man, nor did they hinder Sergeant Watkin's investigations by any of the means they had at their disposal, from assumed lunacy to assumed withdrawal. At first Sister Langtry had feared they would be recalcitrant, for loneliness, segregation and idleness sometimes did lead them to play childish games, as they had on the afternoon of Michael's admission. But they rallied to the call of good sense and cooperated splendidly. As to whether Sergeant Watkin found talking at length to them a pleasant task, he didn't say, though he paid rapt attention to everything, including Nugget's lyrical description of the scotomata which had prevented his seeing more than mere knobs and knotholes, and then only the left halves.

Michael was the only member of ward X the quartermaster asked to see personally, but it was a friendly talk rather than an interrogation. He held it in his own office simply because ward X was a difficult place in which to obtain any real privacy.

Though Michael didn't realize it, his own appearance was his best defense. He reported in full uniform save for his hat, and so did not salute when he came in, only stood to attention until bidden to sit down.

"There's no need to worry, Sergeant," said Captain John Penniquick, his desk clear except for the various papers pertaining to the death of Sergeant Lucius Daggett. The pathologist's report covered two handwritten pages, and indicated besides a detailed description of the wounds which had caused death that there had been no foreign substances in stomach or bloodstream such as barbiturates or opiates. Sergeant Watkin's report was longer, also handwritten, and included synopses of all the conversations he had had with the men of X and with Sister Langtry. Forensic investigations were extremely limited in a wartime army, and did not run to fingerprinting; had Sergeant Watkin seen anything suspicious he would heroically have done his duty in this respect, but a wartime army SI sergeant was not very conversant with fingerprints. As it was, he had seen nothing suspicious, and the pathologist had concurred.

"I really only wanted to ask you about the circumstances which led up to Sergeant Daggett's death," the quartermaster said, a little uncomfortably. "Had you any suspicion that Sergeant Daggett intended to proposition you? Had he made any sort of advance to you before?"

"Once," said Michael. "It didn't go anywhere, though. In all honesty I don't think Sergeant Daggett was a proper homosexual, sir. He was a mischief-maker, that's all."

"Are your own leanings homosexual, Sergeant?"

"No, sir."

"Do you dislike homosexuals?"

"No, sir."

"Why not?"

"I've fought alongside and under the command of them, sir. I've had friends who were inclined that way, one very good friend especially, and they were decent blokes. That's the only thing I ask of anyone, that he be a decent bloke. I reckon homosexuals are like any other group of men, some good, some bad, and some indifferent."

The QM smiled faintly. "Have you any idea why Sergeant Daggett had his eye on you?"

Michael sighed. "I think he got at my papers and read them, sir. I can't think why else he would have looked at me twice." He stared very directly at the QM. "If you've read my papers, sir, you'll know this isn't the first time I've been involved in trouble about homosexuals."

"Yes, I know. It's very unfortunate for you, Sergeant. Did you leave Sister Langtry's room at any time during the night?"

"No, sir."

"So after the incident in the bathhouse you never saw Sergeant Daggett again?"

"No, sir, I never did."

The QM nodded, looked brisk. "Thank you, Sergeant. That will be all."

241

"Thank you, sir."

After Michael had gone Captain Penniquick gathered all the papers concerning the death of Sergeant Lucius Daggett into one sheaf, pulled a fresh piece of paper into the middle of his desk, and began to write his report to the super.

6

Though Base Fifteen was still three or four weeks away from its appointment with extinction, for the five patients and one nursing sister of ward X all sense of belonging to any kind of community ceased upon the death of Sergeant Lucius Daggett. Until the result of the inquiry they walked on eggshells around each other, each so conscious of the huge unspoken undercurrents which sucked and thundered through the ward that anything more than a bland contact with the others could not be borne. The general misery was a palpable thing, the individual miseries touchy and secret and shaming. To speak of it was impossible, to generate a false gaiety equally so. Everyone simply prayed for an innocuous finding at the end of the inquiry.

Not so immersed in her own troubles as to lose sight of how fragile these her men were, Sister Langtry watched for the slightest sign of breakdown in any and all of them, including Michael. Strangely, it didn't appear. Withdrawn they were, but not from reality; they had withdrawn from her, flung her into a chilly outer orbit where she was merely called upon to do unimportant things, like get their early morning tea, get them out of bed, get them through the cleaning, get them down to the beach, get them into bed. Courteous and deferential they always were; truly warmly friendly, never.

She wanted to beat her fists against the wall, cry out that she didn't need punishing like this, that she too suffered, that she wanted, needed desperately, to be drawn into the circle of their regard, that they were killing her. Of course she couldn't do that, didn't do that. And since she could only interpret their reaction in the light of her own guilts, the path her own thoughts trod, she understood very well what they were too basically kind to tell her in so many words. That she had failed in her duty, and so failed them. Madness, it must have been madness! To have so lost all regard for what was the right thing to do for all her patients that she had spiritually abandoned them for the sake of her own physical gratification. The balance and insight which would normally have assured her this was far too simple an assumption had entirely deserted her.

Honour Langtry had known many different kinds of pain, but never a pain like this, all-persuasive, self-perpetuating, asphyxiating. It wasn't even that she dreaded walking into ward X; it was the bitter knowledge that there was no longer a ward X to walk into. The family unit was broken.

"Well, the verdict's in," she said to Neil on the evening three days after Luce's death.

"When did you hear?" he asked, but as if it didn't really interest him very much.

He still came for those private little chats with her, but a chat was all it could be. Banal observations about this and that and the other thing.

"This afternoon, from Colonel Chinstrap, who stole a march on Matron. Since she told me later, I got it twice. Suicide. The result of an acute depressive state following an acute burst of mania—claptrap, but convenient claptrap. They have to put something impressive down."

"Did they say anything else?" he asked, leaning forward to ash his cigarette.

"Oh, we're none of us too popular, as you can imagine, but no blame is attached to us officially."

He kept his voice light as he asked, "Did you get your knuckles rapped, Sis?"

"Not officially. However, Matron had a few words of her own to say on the subject of my taking Michael to my quarters. But luckily my blameless reputation stood me in good stead. When it came right down to it she just couldn't imagine *me* hauling poor Michael off with any but the purest of motives. As she said, it merely looked bad, and because it looked bad, I let the whole side down. I seem to have been letting whole sides down all over the place lately."

During the past three days his imagination had played indescribable tricks, visualizing her with Michael in any one of a thousand different ways, by no means all to do with sex. Her betrayal ate at him, try as he would to be dispassionate, and so understand. There wasn't the room for understanding when he had also to accommodate his own torment and jealousy, his own unshakable determination to have what he wanted, what he *needed*, in spite of her obvious preference for Michael. She had turned to Michael without thinking of any of the rest of them, and he couldn't seem to forgive her. Yet his feelings for her were as strong, as intense as ever. I am going to have her, he thought; I will not give her up! And I am my father's son. It has taken this to make me see how much I am my father's son. It's a strange sensation. But it's a good sensation.

She, poor lost soul, suffered so. He couldn't take any pleasure in witnessing that, nor did he wish it upon her, but he did feel hers was a case where to suffer would eventually lead her back to the place where she had once been, where he, Neil, belonged rather than Michael.

He said, "Don't take it so hard."

She thought he was referring to her rapped knuckles, and smiled wryly. "Well, it's over and done with now, thank God. It's a pity that life with Luce wasn't more pleasant. I never wished him dead, but I did wish we didn't have to put up with his living presence. Only now it's some kind of hell."

"Is that really to be laid at Luce's door?" he asked; perhaps now that the verdict was in they could both relax enough to begin communicating again.

"No," she said sadly. "It has to be laid at my door. At no one else's."

Michael tapped. "Tea's made, Sis."

She forgot where the conversation with Neil might have been leading, and looked straight past Neil to Michael. "Come in for a moment, would you? I'd like to talk to you. Neil, will you hold the fort? I'll be down shortly, but you might like to pass on the news to the others."

Michael shut the door behind Neil's back, his face a mixture of unhappiness and dread. And discomfort. And fear. As if he would rather be any place on earth than standing in front of her desk, *her* desk.

In that she was correct; he would rather have been anywhere else than there. But what she saw in his face was on his own behalf, not anything to do with her. And yet everything to do with her. He was terrified of breaking down in front of her, aching to spill all the reasons for his pain to her; but that would be to lift a floodgate which must remain closed. It was all gone, and perhaps it had never been, and certainly it could never be. A chaos. A confusion more desperate than any he had ever known, while he stood there and longed for things to be different, and knew things could not be different. Sorrowing for her because she didn't know, agreeing that she couldn't be permitted to know, fighting himself and what he wanted. Knowing that what she wanted could not make her happy. And continuing to learn as he watched her face that he had hurt her very cruelly.

Some of this showed on his face, too, while he stood in front of her desk, waiting.

And suddenly it literally blazed in her, that look of his, set fire to a store of wounded pride and pain she had scarcely known she possessed.

"Oh, for God's sake will you get that bloody look off your face?" she cried, her voice a quiet scream. "What on earth do you think I'm going to do to you, get down on my bended knees and beg for a repeat performance? Well, I'd rather be dead! Do you hear me? Dead!"

He flinched, whitened, set his mouth, said nothing.

"I can assure you, Sergeant Wilson, that the thought of any personal relationship with you is the farthest thing from my mind!" she went on feverishly, like a lemming to the killing sea. "I simply called you in here privately to inform you that the verdict on Luce's death is in, and it's suicide. Along with the rest of us, you've been completely exonerated. And now perhaps you'll be able to stop this nauseating display of self-recrimination. That's all."

It had never occurred to him that the largest part by far of the hurt he had inflicted upon her was due to what she saw as his rejection of her. Horrified, he tried to put himself in her place, to feel that rejection as she was feeling it, a purely personal thing all tied in with her womanhood. Had he valued himself more, he might have understood sooner, better. But to him, her reaction was almost inconceivable; she was interpreting the whole thing in a way he could not. Not because he wasn't sensitive, or perceptive, or involved with her. But because where his mind had been dwelling since Luce's death was so divorced from the personal aspects of what had happened in her room. There had been so many other considerations to torment him—and so much to do—that he hadn't stopped to think how his behavior looked to her. And it was too late now.

He seemed ill, grief-stricken, curiously defenseless. And yet, Michael as always, still his own man. "Thank you," he said, without irony.

"Don't *look* at me like that!"

"I'm sorry," he said. "I won't look at all."

She transferred her gaze to the papers on her desk. "So am I sorry, Sergeant, believe me," she said with cold finality. The papers might have been written in Japanese for all the sense she could make of them. And suddenly it was just too much to bear; she looked up, her heart in her eyes, and cried, "Oh, Michael!" in a very different tone of voice.

But he had already gone.

It took her five minutes to get moving, the reaction

was so devastating. She sat and shook, her teeth chattered, she wondered for a moment if she might truly be going mad. So much shame, so little self-control. It had not occurred to her that she could possess such a huge blind urge to hurt anyone she loved, or that the knowledge she had succeeded in hurting could be so comfortless and intolerable. Oh, God, dear God, she prayed, if this is love, heal me! Heal me or let me die, for I cannot live with this kind of agony one minute more. . . .

She went to the door of her office, reaching to unhook her hat, then remembered she had to change back into boots. Her hands were still trembling; it took time to lace the boots, do up the gaiters.

Neil appeared as she bent over in her chair to pick up her basket.

"You're going off now?" he asked, surprised and disappointed. After that promising final remark of hers before Michael had appeared he had been hoping to resume where they had been cut off. But as usual Michael took precedence over him.

"I'm awfully tired," she said. "Do you think you can manage without me for the rest of the evening?"

It was gallantly said, but he only had to look at her eyes to see that there was very little between gallantry and despair. In spite of himself he reached out, took her hand and held it between both his own, chafing the skin to instill in it a little warmth.

"No, my very dear Sister Langtry, we can't possibly do without you," he said, smiling. "But we will, just this once. Go to bed and sleep."

She smiled back at him, her comrade of so many months in X, and wondered where her burgeoning love for him had gone, why Michael's coming had so abruptly snuffed it out. The trouble was she had no key to the logic behind love, if key there was, if logic there was.

"You always take away the pain," she said.

It was his phrase he used of her; her saying it affected him so powerfully he had to remove his hands quickly.

Now was not the time for him to say what he longed to.

Taking her basket from her, he ushered her out of the ward as if he were the host and she a visitor, refusing to give the basket back until they reached the bottom of the ramp. And then he stood until long after her grey shape flickered and vanished into the darkness, looking up at the darkness, listening to the soft dripping of condensation on cooling eaves, the vast chorus of the frogs and the endless murmur of the surf far out on the reef. There was a downpour in the air; it would rain before very long. If Sis didn't hurry she'd be wet.

"Where's Sis?" asked Nugget when Neil sat down in her chair and reached for the teapot.

"She's got a headache," said Neil briefly, avoiding eye contact with Michael, who sat looking as if he too had a headache. Neil pulled a face. "God, I loathe being mother! Who is it has milk again?"

"Me," said Nugget. "Good news, eh? Luce is properly dead and buried at last. Phew! It's a relief, I must say."

"May God have mercy on his soul," said Benedict.

"On all our souls," said Matt.

Neil finished his chore with the teapot, and began pushing the various mugs down the table. Without Sis there was little joy in late tea, he reflected, staring at Michael because Michael's attention was on Matt and Benedict.

With a great show of importance, Nugget produced a very large book, spread it out where there was no danger of spilling tea on it, and began on page one.

Michael glanced at him, amused and touched. "What's that in aid of?" he asked.

"I've been thinking about what the colonel said," Nuggett explained, one hand extended across the open book with the reverence of a holy man for his bible. "There's no reason why I can't go to night school to get me matriculation, is there? Then I could go to university and do medicine."

"And do something with your life," Michael said. "Good on you and good luck to you, Nugget."

I wish I didn't like him through every moment of hating him, thought Neil; but that's the real lesson the old man wanted me to learn out of the war—not to let my heart stand in the way of what has to be done, and to learn to live with my heart after it's done. So Neil was able to say very calmly, "We've all got to do something with our lives when we're out of the jungle greens. I wonder how I'll look in a business suit. I've never worn one in my life." Then he sat back and waited for Matt to respond to the deliberate stimulus.

Matt did, quivering. "How am I going to earn a living?" he asked, the question bursting from him as if he had never meant to say it, yet had been thinking of nothing else. "I'm an accountant, I've got to see! The army won't give me a pension; they reckon there's nothing wrong with my eyes! Oh, God, Neil, what am I going to do?"

The others were very still, everyone looking at Neil. Well, here goes, he thought, as deeply moved by Matt's cry as the others, yet filled with a purpose that overruled his pity. Now isn't the right time and place to go into specifics, but there's been enough groundwork laid for me to see if Mike gets the message.

"That's my share, Matt," Neil said positively, his hand on Matt's arm firmly. "Don't worry about anything. I'll see you're all right."

"I've never taken charity in my life, and I'm not about to start now," said Matt, sitting straight and proud.

"It is not charity!" Neil insisted. "It is *my share*. You know what I mean. We made a pact, the lot of us, but I have yet to contribute my full share." And he said this looking not at Matt but at Michael.

"Yes, all right," said Michael, who knew immediately what was going to be demanded of him. In a way it came as an exquisite relief to have it asked of him rather than to have to offer it. He had known the only solution for some time, but he didn't want it, and so had not found the strength to offer it. "I agree with that, Neil. Your share." His eyes left Neil's stern unyielding face, rested on Matt with great affection. "It's not charity, Matt. It's a fair share," he said.

7 Sister Langtry beat the rain. It came cascading down just as she let herself in her door, and within minutes every kind of living small creature seemed to materialize out of it: mosquitoes, leeches, frogs, spiders reluctant to wet their feet, ants in syrupy black rivers, bedraggled moths, cockroaches. Because her two windows were screened she usually did not need to pull the net down around her bed, but the first thing she did tonight was to tug it free of its ring and drape it down.

She went to take a shower in the bathhouse, then wrapped herself in her robe, packed her two pathetically thin pillows against the wall at the head of her bed, and lay back against them with a book she hadn't even the strength to open, though sleep felt far away. So she put her head back and listened instead to the ceaseless hollow roar of rain on an iron roof. Once it had been the most thrilling and wonderful sound in the world, during her childhood days in country where rain was the harbinger of prosperity and life; but here, in this profligate climate of perpetual growth and decay, it meant only an external deadening to everything save what went on in her mind. You couldn't have heard anyone speak unless he shouted in your ear; the only voices you really heard were those which chattered on inside your head.

The sick horror of discovering she could lash out at someone beloved as she had lashed out at Michael had faded to an almost apathetic self-disgust. And right alongside it had crept a hunger for self-justification. Hadn't he done to her what no man should ever do to any woman? Hadn't he indicated a perverse preference for

Luce Daggett? Of all the men in the world, Luce Daggett!

This was fruitless. Round and round and round in every-diminishing circles, getting nowhere, achieving nothing. She was so tired of herself! How could she have allowed this to happen? And who was Michael Wilson? There were no answers, so why bother to ask the questions?

Mosquito nets suffocated. She threw hers back impatiently, not having heard the tiny dive-bomber sound of a mosquito, and forgetting that the rain would have drowned the noise of a real dive-bomber. There was never enough light within the confines of the net to read, and she felt better; she would read for a while and hope sleep came.

A leech dropped with a soundless plop from some crevice in the unlined roof, and landed wriggling obscenely on her bare leg. She tore at it in a frenzy, gagging at the feel of it, but could not dislodge it. So she leaped to light a cigarette, and without caring whether she burned herself, she applied the red-hot tip to the leech's slimy black stringlike body. It was a big tropical leech, four or five inches long, and she could not have borne to wait the process out, invaded by it, watch it grow bloated and congested on her blood, then finally roll off replete like a selfish man from a woman after sex.

When the thing was fried enough to shrivel away from her skin she ground it to smeared pulp beneath a boot, shivering uncontrollably, feeling as violated and besmirched as any Victorian heroine. Loathsome, repulsive, horrible thing! Oh, God, this climate! This rain! This awful, eternal dilemma. . . .

And then of course the place where the leech had fastened its blind seeking mouth kept bleeding, bleeding, the tissue impregnated with an anticlotting factor from its saliva, and it had to be attended to immediately or in this climate the wound would ulcerate. . . .

It was not very often that she found herself reminded

so physically of Base Fifteen, its difficulties, isolation, introspection. Of all the places she had ever been, she thought, dealing with iodine and sterile swabs, Base Fifteen had made less impression than any. In fact, almost no impression at all. As if it were a stage set, without substance or real meaning of its own, simply a claustrophobic backdrop for a complicated interplay of human emotions, wills, desires. Which was logical. Base Fifteen as anything more than an insubstantial backdrop didn't make sense. A more sterile, dreary institution had never been erected; even the wet canvas world of a casualty clearing station had more personality. Base Fifteen was there to serve a war, it had been dumped where the convenience of war dictated, without respect to the ideal site, staff contentment, or patient welfare. No wonder it was a painted cardboard world.

And, leg propped up on the wooden chair, the walls oozing sweat and speckled with great patches of mildew, the cockroaches waving their antennae from every dark cranny, itching for the light to go off, Sister Langtry looked around her like someone doubting the reality of a dream.

I shall be so glad to go home, she thought for the very first time. Oh, yes, I shall be so glad to go back to my home!

PART 6

1 Sister Langtry came into the sisters' sitting room about four the next afternoon feeling more like herself, and looking forward to a cup of tea. There were five sisters scattered in two groups about the room, and Sister Dawkin on her own, sitting in one chair with her feet propped up on another, her head nodding toward her ample chest in a series of jerks which culminated in one large enough to startle her into waking. Eyes about to close again, she saw who was standing in the doorway, waved and beckoned.

As Sister Langtry walked across to join her friend a strong wave of dizziness provoked a sudden panic; she wasn't sleeping and she wasn't eating properly, and if she wasn't careful she would become ill. Contact with the men of X and their problems had educated her sufficiently to understand that her present symptoms were escapist, a means whereby to manufacture an end demanding her removal from ward X without the humiliation of having to request Matron for a transfer. Therefore pride dictated that she sleep and eat. Tonight she would take a Nembutal, something she had not done since the day of the incident in the dayroom.

"Sit down, love, you look knocked up," said Sister Dawkin, tugging at a chair without getting up herself.

"You must be pretty knocked up yourself to snatch forty winks in here," said Sister Langtry, seating herself.

"I had to stay on the ward last night, that's all," said Sister Dawkin, disposing her feet in a new position. "We must look like Abbott and Costello to the rest of the room, me like the wreck of the *Hesperus* and you like a poster to recruit army nurses. That tomfool of a woman,

257

even daring to suggest there was any ulterior motive! As if you'd ever stoop to anything vulgar or underhand!"

Sister Langtry winced, wishing that Matron had had the good sense to hold her tongue. But the stupid woman had blabbed to her best friend, who had blabbed to her best friend, and so on, and so on. The whole nursing staff (which meant the MOs as well) knew that Sister Langtry—of all people!—had kept a soldier in her quarters all night. And of course the place was buzzing about the hara-kiri suicide; it was no use hoping such drama would not be talked about. Though luckily her own reputation was so good that few indeed believed there was anything more in her conduct with the soldier than an urgent and understandable desire to keep him out of harm's way. If they only knew, thought Sister Langtry, feeling the eyes on her from the two other tenanted tables, if they only knew what my real troubles are! Inversion, murder, rejection. Though murder has gone, thank God. I don't have to worry about that one.

The kind fading eyes that forthrightness saved from being commonplace were looking at her shrewdly; Sister Langtry sighed and moved a little, but did not say anything.

Sister Dawkin tried another gambit. "As of next week, me dear, it's back to dear old Aussie and Civvy Street," she said.

Sister Langtry's cup just missed making contact with it saucer, and slopped tea all over the table. "Oh, bother! Now look what I've done!" she exclaimed, reaching into her basket for a handkerchief.

"Are you sorry, Honour?" Sister Dawkin demanded.

"Just taken by surprise," Sister Langtry said, mopping up tea with her handkerchief and wringing it out into her cup. "When did you hear, Sally?"

"Matey told me herself a few minutes ago. Came sweeping into D ward like a battleship in full sail and let it drop with her mouth all pursed up as if she'd been eating alum for a week. She's devastated, of course. She'll have to go back to that poky little convalescent home she ran before the war. None of the big hospitals or even the district hospitals would touch her with a barge pole. It beats me how she ever got so high up in the army."

"It beats me too," said Sister Langtry, spreading her handkerchief out to dry on a corner of the table, then dispensing more tea into a fresh cup and saucer. "And you're right, none of the decent hospitals would touch her with a barge pole. Somehow she always reminds me of a night-shift forewoman in a big food factory. Still, if the army will keep her on she might remain in the army. She'd be better off. Better pension when she retires, too, and she can't be all that far off retirement."

"Hah! If the army keeps her it will be better luck than she deserves." Sister Dawkin reached for the teapot and replenished her own cup. "Well, I know I'm going to be sorry to go home," she said abruptly. "I hate this place, I've hated every place the army has sent me, but I've loved the work, and God, how I've loved the freedom!"

"Yes, freedom is the right word, isn't it? That's what I've loved too. . . . Do you remember that time in New Guinea when there was no one else fit to operate but you and me? I'll never forget that as long as I live."

"We did all right, too, didn't we?" Sister Dawkin smiled, swelling visibly with pride. "Patched those boys up as if we'd got our FRCSs, and the boss recommended us for decoration. Ah! I'll never wear any ribbon with more pride than my MBE."

"I am sorry it's over," said Sister Langtry. "I'm going to loathe Civvy Street. Bedpan alley again, women patients again. Bitch bitch, moan moan. . . . It would be just my luck to land on gynae or obstets. Men are so easy!"

"Aren't they? Catch women patients lending you a hand if the staff situation's desperate! They'd rather be dead. When women hit a hospital they expect to be waited on hand and foot. But men pop on their halos and do their best to convince you that their wives never treated them the way nurses do."

"What are you going to do on Civvy Street, Sally?"

"Oh, have a bit of a holiday first, I suppose," said Sister Dawkin unenthusiastically. "Look up a few friends, that sort of thing. Then back to North Shore. I did my general at Royal Newcastle and my midder at Crown Street, but I've spent most of my nursing career at North Shore, so it's more or less home by now. Matron ought to be glad to see me if no one else is. As a matter of fact, I'm in line for a deputy matronship, and that's about the only thing I am looking forward to."

"My matron will be glad to see me, too," said Sister Langtry thoughtfully.

"P.A., right?" asked Sister Dawkin, using the universal nursing slang for the Royal Prince Alfred Hospital.

"P.A. it is."

"Never fancied a hospital quite that big myself."

"Actually, though, I'm not sure I want to go back to P.A.," Sister Langtry remarked. "I'm toying with the idea of going to Callan Park."

Since Callan Park was a mental hospital, Sister Dawkin sat up very straight and subjected Sister Langtry to a hard stare. "Seriously, Honour?"

"Deadly earnest."

"There's no status to mental nursing! I don't even think there's a certificate to collect. I mean you must know that mental nurses are regarded as the dregs."

"I've got my general certificate and my midder, so I can always go back to proper nursing. But after X, I'd like to try a mental hospital."

"They're not the same as X, though, Honour! Troppo is a temporary thing, most men get over it. But when a patient walks through the gates of a mental hospital he's facing a life sentence."

"I know all that. But maybe it's going to change. I like to hope it will, anyway. If the war helps it as much as it's helped things like plastic surgery, lots of things are going to happen in psychiatry. And I'd like to be in on the ground floor of the changes."

Sister Dawkin patted Sister Langtry's hand. "Well, ducky, you know your own mind best, and I never was one to preach. Just remember what they always say about mental nurses—they wind up dottier than their patients."

Sister Pedder walked into the room, looking around to see which group would welcome her most cheerfully. On seeing Sister Dawkin and Sister Langtry she gave Sister Dawkin a wide smile and Sister Langtry a frosty nod.

"Have you heard the news, young Sue?" called Sister Dawkin, nettled by the girl's rudeness.

Common courtesy therefore compelled Sister Pedder to approach the table, looking as if there was a bad smell in the vicinity.

"No, what news?" she asked.

"We're almost a thing of the past, dearie."

The girl's face came alive. "You mean we're going home?" she squeaked.

"Jiggety-jig," said Sister Dawkin.

Tears sprang to Sister Pedder's eyes, and her mouth hovered between the twisted tremble of weeping and the softer curve of smiling. "Oh, thank God for that!"

"Well, well! A proper reaction at last! Easy to tell the old warhorses among us, isn't it?" asked Sister Dawkin of no one in particular.

The tears began to fall; Sister Pedder saw how she could rub it in. "How am I ever going to be able to face his poor mother?" she managed to articulate between sobs, so distinctly that all the heads in the room turned.

"Oh, dry up!" said Sister Dawkin, disgusted. "And grow up, for pity's sake! If there's one thing I can't stand, it's crocodile tears! What gives you the right to judge your seniors?"

Sister Langtry sprang to her feet, appalled. "Sally, please!" she cried. "It's all right, truly it's all right!"

Neither of the other two groups of nurses was making any pretense at disinterest any more; those with their backs to the Langtry table had frankly swung their chairs around so they could watch comfortably. It was not a malicious interest at all. They just wanted to see how Sally Dawkin handled that presumptuous young monster Pedder.

"In your quarters all night with Sergeant Wilson, t-t-t-t-t-treating him for shock!" said Sister Pedder, and brought out her handkerchief to cry in good earnest. "What luck for you there's no one else in your block these days! But I know what's been going on between you and Sergeant Wilson, because Luce told me!"

"Shut up, you silly little bitch!" shouted Sister Dawkin, too angry now to remember discretion.

"It's all right, Sally!" begged Sister Langtry, trying desperately to get away.

"No, dammit, it's not all right!" roared Sister Dawkin in the voice which made probationers shiver. "I won't have such talk! Don't you dare make insinuations like that, young woman! You ought to be ashamed of yourself! It wasn't Sister Langtry in over her head with a man from the ranks, it was you!"

"How dare you!" gasped Sister Pedder.

"I dare pretty bloody easy," said Sister Dawkin, who somehow still managed in spite of posture and stockinged misshapen feet to gather the awesome power of a senior sister about her. "Just you remember, my girl, that in a few weeks it's all going to be mighty different. You'll be just another pebble on that big civilian beach. And I'm warning you now, don't ever come looking for a job anywhere I am! I wouldn't have you on my staff as a wardsmaid! The trouble with all you young girls is that you climb into a smart officer's uniform and you think you're Lady Muck—"

The tirade came to a sudden halt, for Sister Langtry gave such a horrifyingly despairing cry that Sister Dawkin and Sister Pedder forgot their quarrel. Then she collapsed onto a settee and began to weep; not soft, fluttering sobs like Sister Pedder's, but great grinding tearless heaves which seemed to the worried eyes of Sister Dawkin almost like convulsions.

Oh, it was such a *relief!* Out of the angry atmosphere, out of the misguided affection of Sister Dawkin and the dislike of Sister Pedder, Honour Langtry finally managed to give birth to the terrible lump of suffering which had grown and chewed inside her for days.

"Now see what you've done!" snarled Sister Dawkin, lumbering out of her chair and sitting down beside Sister Langtry. "Go away!" she said to Sister Pedder. "Go on, skedaddle!"

Sister Pedder fled, terrified, as the other sisters began to gather around; for Sister Langtry was well liked.

Sister Dawkin looked up at the others, shaking her head, and began with infinite kindness to stroke the jerking, shuddering back. "There there, it's all right," she crooned. "Have a good cry then, it's more than time you did. My poor old girl! My poor old girl, so much trouble and pain. . . . I know, I know, I know. . . ."

Only vaguely conscious of Sister Dawkin beside her, talking so kindly, of the other sisters still gathered around and concerned for her too, Sister Langtry wept and wept.

2 A kitchen orderly brought the news of Base Fifteen's imminent demise to ward X, transmitting it to Michael in the dayroom, and grinning from ear to ear as he babbled incoherently about seeing home again, home for good.

Michael didn't move back to the verandah at once after the orderly had gone; he stood in the middle of the dayroom with one hand plucking at his face and the other pressed against his side, kneading it. So soon, he thought dully. So soon! I'm not ready because I'm frightened. Not depressed, and not unwilling, either. Just so frightened of what my future holds, what it's going to do to me, what it's going to make me. But it has to be done, and I am strong enough. It's the best way for all concerned. Including me. Including her.

"This time next week we're all going to be on our way back to Australia," he said when he returned to the verandah.

A leaden silence greeted his news. Reclining on the nearest bed with a Best & Taylor he had wheedled out of Colonel Chinstrap held up in front of him, no mean feat of strength, Nugget lowered the enormous book and stared. Matt's long hands closed into fists, and his face became still. Busy with a pencil and a piece of paper, Neil dropped the pencil onto the drawing, which happened to be of Matt's hands, and looked ten years older than his age. Only Benedict, rocking back and forth in a chair that had never been designed to rock, seemed uninterested.

A slow smile began to dawn on Nugget's mouth. "Home!" he said experimentally. "Home? I'm going to see Mum!"

But Matt's tension didn't lessen, and Michael

knew he was thinking of that first encounter with his wife.

"What a pisser!" said Neil, picking up his pencil again, and discovering that the repose of the beautiful hands was quite destroyed. He put the pencil down, got up, strolled to the edge of the verandah and stood with his back to everyone. "What a bloody pisser!" he said to the palms, voice bitter.

"Ben!" said Michael sharply. "Ben, do you hear that? It's time to go home; we're going back to Australia!"

But Benedict rocked on, back and forth, back and forth, the chair creaking dangerously, face and eyes shut away.

"I'm going to tell her about it," said Michael suddenly, strongly. He spoke to any and all of them, but it was at Neil he looked sternly.

Neil didn't turn, but his long slim neat back subtly altered; all at once it didn't appear slack or weary or without resource. The back looked as if it was the property of a powerful and an aggressive man.

"No, Mike, you're not going to tell her," he said.

"I have to," said Michael, not pleading, not looking at Matt or Nugget or Benedict, though both Matt and Nugget had tensed warily.

"You can't say one thing to her, Mike. Not one thing! You can't without all our consents, and we don't give them."

"I can tell her, and I will tell her. What does it matter now? If she knows, it can't change anything; we've all decided what to do in that situation." He reached out to put his hand on Benedict's shoulder, as if the rocking irritated him, and Benedict stopped rocking immediately. "I've taken the biggest share because I'm the only one who can, and because it was more my fault than anyone else's. But I'm not willing to suffer in silence! I'm just not that much of a hero. Yes, I know I'm not the only sufferer. But I *am* going to tell her."

"You can't tell her," said Neil, voice steely. "If you do, so help me I'll kill you. It's too dangerous."

Michael didn't mock, as Luce might have done, but the set of his face was unafraid. "There'd be no point in killing me, Neil, and you know it. There's been enough killing."

Sister Langtry's soft step sounded; the group froze. When she walked out onto the verandah she stood taking stock of them, a little puzzled, wondering just what she had interrupted. If someone had got ahead of her with the news about Base Fifteen, why should that provoke a quarrel? But they knew about Base Fifteen, and they had been quarreling.

"That footstep!" said Matt suddenly, breaking the silence. "That wonderful footstep! It's the only woman's step I know. When I had eyes I didn't listen. If my wife were to walk in now, I wouldn't be able to pick up the sound of her."

"No, mine is not the only woman's step you know. There's one other," said Sister Langtry, walking over to Matt and standing behind him, her hands on his shoulders.

He closed the eyes that couldn't see and leaned back a little against her, not enough to offend her.

"You hear Matron's step at least once a week," said Sister Langtry.

"Oh, her!" he exclaimed, smiling. "But Matron clomps like a GOPWO, Sis. There's no woman's sound to her feet."

"A GOPWO?" she asked, stumped.

"A Grossly Over-Promoted Warrant Officer," he said.

She burst out laughing, gripping his shoulders hard, laughing at some joke that was entirely her own, and laughing with real, happy abandon. "Oh, Matt, that's a truer description than you'll ever know!" she said when she could. "Wait until I tell Sally Dawkin that one! She'll love you forever."

"Sis! Sis! Isn't it good news, eh?" called Nugget from his bed, Best & Taylor forgotten. "I'm going home, I'm going to see my mum soon!"

"It certainly is good news, Nugget."

Neil remained standing with his back turned. Sister Langtry leaned over to study the drawing of Matt's hands, then she straightened and released Matt's shoulders, moving slightly away. And managed then finally to look at Michael, whose hand still rested on Benedict's shoulder, a parody of her own touching of Matt. Their eyes met, both armored against pain, both stern with some purpose; met like the eyes of strangers, politely, without personal interest.

She swung away and went back inside.

Neil appeared not long afterward, shutting the office door behind him with an air that said he wished he had a Do Not Disturb sign to hang outside it. When he saw her face, eyes swollen down to the cheekbones, he studied it grimly.

"You've been crying."

"Like a waterfall," she admitted readily. "I made an utter fool of myself right in the middle of the sisters' sitting room, as a matter of fact, and not while I had the place to myself, either. I had quite an audience. A delayed reaction, I suppose. The young sister from Woop-Woop—you know, the bank manager's daughter —came in at the wrong moment and accused me of victimizing Luce. That annoyed my friend Sister Dawkin from D ward, they began to squabble, and suddenly there I was, in floods of tears. Ridiculous, isn't it?"

"That's what really happened?"

"Now could I make up a story like that?" She sounded more like her old self, placid and calm.

"Do you feel better for it?" he asked, offering her one of his cigarettes.

She smiled slightly. "Deep down, yes. On the surface, quite the opposite. I feel ghastly. Like something the cat dragged in. My mainspring's all unwound."

"That's a very mixed metaphor," he said gently.

She considered it. "I'd say it all depended what the cat dragged in, wouldn't you? Perhaps it was a mechanical mouse. I feel mechanical."

He sighed "Oh, Sis! Have it your own way, then. I'll leave the subject—and you—severely alone."

"Thank you, I'd appreciate that," she said.

"And in a week it comes to an end," he said conversationally.

"Yes. I suspected they'd try to have us all out before the monsoons really begin."

"Going home to Australia—I mean when you're discharged?"

"Yes."

"To do what, may I ask?"

Even with the swollen relic of tears on her face, she looked very remote. "I'm going to nurse at Callan Park. Since you're from Melbourne, you may not know that Callan Park is a big mental hospital in Sydney."

He was shocked, then saw that she really meant it. "God, what a waste!"

"Not at all," she said crisply. "It's useful and necessary work. I badly need to continue doing something useful and necessary. I'm lucky, you see. My family has sufficient means to ensure that when I'm old and unable to work, I won't be on the breadline. So I can please myself what I do with my life." Her congested eyelids lifted, the cool eyes looked him over. "But you? What are you going to do, Neil?"

That was that, then. Exit Neil Parkinson. Her voice, her look, her manner all said that he would not be welcomed into her life after the war.

"Oh, I'll be off to Melbourne," he said easily. "What I would really like to do is return to the Greek Peloponnese—I have a cottage near Pylos. But my parents, particularly my father, aren't getting any younger—nor am I getting younger, for that matter. So I fancy it will be Melbourne rather than Greece for me. Besides, Greece would have meant painting, and I'm only a competent painter, nothing more. That used to hurt, oddly enough. But it doesn't now. It seems a minor consideration. I've learned so much during the last six years, and ward X has rounded off my education beautifully. I've got my priorities right these days, and I know now that I can be an active help to the old man—to my father. If I'm to follow in his steps, I'd better start finding out how the family businesses are run."

"You'll be busy."

"Yes, I will." He rose to his feet. "Will you excuse me? If we're really moving out of here soon I have a great deal of packing to do."

She watched the door shut behind him, and sighed. If Michael had done nothing else for her, he had at least shown her that there was a vast difference between affection and love. She was fond of Neil, but she certainly didn't love him. Steady, reliable, upright, courteous, well-bred Neil, willing to yield up everything he was to her. A very good marriage prospect. Handsome, too. Stuffed with all the social graces. To prefer Michael to him was not sensible. But what she prized in Michael was his self-containment, that air which said no one could ever turn him from his elected path. An enigma he might be, but not knowing him had not prevented her loving him. She loved his strength. She didn't love Neil's willingness to subjugate his own wishes before hers.

Odd that Neil should seem so much better in himself these days, though he must know she had decided there was no future in a relationship with him after the war. And it was a relief to find him not upset by that decision, not sounding as if he felt rejected. The knowledge that she was hurting him had been there ever since the incident in the dayroom, but so much else had happened she hadn't thought very much about how Neil must be feeling. Now was about the time her guilt would have turned in on itself to plague her, and it seemed not necessary after all. His fondness for her showed again today, but there was no sign of bitterness, of hurt. And that was such a relief! To have given expression to her grief at last, and now to find Neil was whole in spite of her conduct; today was the first good day in weeks.

3 It was an odd week which followed. Normally when the occupants at one place for months or years prepare to leave it, there is a distracted flurry of activity, worries about everything from pets to vehicles. The quick disintegration of Base Fifteen was not like that. Its inhabitants had been steadily whittled down for months anyway; all that remained was a nucleus which would be shelled out swiftly and competently. No one was encumbered by the kind of baggage which usually clutters up a life, for in essence Base Fifteen was minus clutter. The country around it did not abound in desirable handcrafts, handmade furniture or any of the other impedimenta collectors had accumulated in the war theatres of Europe, India, the Middle East, North Africa. A lot of the sisters found themselves the recipients of shy gifts from their men, mostly small things made in the ward, but on the whole the inmates of Base Fifteen would depart with no more to ship than what they had brought with them when they arrived.

A target time to be ready was posted, and adhered to with the easy discipline of trained personnel; it came and it went, but Base Fifteen remained. No one had expected it to be any different. The target date was actually a warning bell, at the sound of which everyone had to be prepared to evacuate at once.

Matron fussed and clucked, mosquito nets less important than the schedules and timetables she carried everywhere with her to consult during interminable briefings of her nurses, all of whom could cheerfully have strangled her. Now that Base Fifteen was ending, what the nurses really wanted to do was spend the maximum amount of time with their patients.

Ward X lay fairly much outside the main area of activity, down in its little afterthought building far away from the other inhabited wards, with its tiny complement of five patients and one lone nurse. And among its tiny complement there was more awkwardness than joy, sudden silences which were hard to break, forced cheerfulness when things became to unbearable, and a rather chilling loss of rapport. Sister Langtry was absent quite a lot, unwillingly pressed into service on various Matron-inspired subcommittees to handle the evacuation. And the five patients took to haunting the beach all day, for the old official times governing its use had gone by the board.

Sorrowfully Sister Langtry realized her patients had decided to do without her where possible, even had she more time to spend with them. Neil seemed to have forgiven her, the others had not. And she noticed that a certain polarization had come into being among them. Nugget had shifted himself away from the rest, filled with a new purpose and a happy optimism which seemed to be a combination of rejoining his mother and reorganizing his civilian life to encompass a career as a doctor. His aches and pains had quite vanished. Neil and Matt were inseparable; she knew Matt leaned on Neil heavily, unburdening himself about the many problems he would have to face. Which left Michael to concentrate on Benedict, as indeed he always had. They too were inseparable.

Benedict, she thought, was not well, but what she could do about it she didn't know. A talk to Colonel Chinstrap had got her predictably nowhere, yet he had been willing, even eager, to do what he could to procure a military pension for Matt in spite of the hysterical tag on his history. When she begged the colonel to consider shipping Ben straight into a proper psychiatric unit for further investigation, his attitude was unyielding. If she had no more to base her suspicions on than a vague disquiet, he said, what did she expect him to do? His examination of Sergeant Maynard had revealed no deterioration. How to explain to

271

a man who was a competent enough neurologist but had no interest in mental disorders without organic foundation that she wanted to call a man back who was slipping away? And how did one call him back? That was what nobody in the world knew how to do. Ben had never been an easy patient to contend with because of that very tendency to shut himself away; what worried her was that without the security of ward X about him, Benedict would accomplish the ultimate in disappearing acts, and swallow himself up. So Michael's attachment to him she viewed as a godsend, for he did have more success with Ben than anyone else, including herself.

Watching them all more or less doing without her, she began to understand better what was happening to them, and to herself. The overemotional interpretation she had put on everyone's conduct including her own since Luce's death was fading; that outburst in the sisters' sitting room, she realized, must have done her a great deal of good. Without consciously knowing it, the inhabitants of ward X were all relinquishing their ties to each other; the family unit that had been ward X was falling apart right along with Base Fifteen. And she, as its mother figure, was probably more sensitive and more hurt by what she saw than her men, her children. Odd, that as her strength waned theirs appeared to be growing. Was that what mothers did? Tried to hold a family unit together when the natural reasons for its existence had ceased?

They are going back to a different world, she thought, and I'm sending most of them back equipped to deal with it. Or I'm trying. So I mustn't cling, I mustn't let them cling. I must let them go with as much grace and dignity as I can possibly muster.

4 And then it began, with a roaring of trucks and a huge windlike stirring. Luckily the monsoon had not yet arrived in force, and it looked as if evacuation would be completed in plenty of time to avoid being rained out.

Apathy changed to euphoria, as if now that it was actually here, people could bring themselves to believe in it; suddenly home was not a dream, it was a coming reality. Cries rose and fell on the air, shrill whistles, cooees, snatches of song.

Iron-disciplined sisters found themselves caught up in a mood they could not control, were subjected to hugs, kisses, fabulously exotic Hollywoodish embraces, sometimes tears, and turned one and all into adorably confused women. For them it was a parting of great moment, the end of the high point in their lives; they were all unmarried women, most of them halfway at least toward retirement, and in this most difficult, isolated place they had put forth their very best, a vital part of a great cause. Life would never again hold quite so much of everything; these boys were the sons they never had, and they knew themselves worthy mothers of such sons. But now it was all over, and while they had to thank God for that, they knew nothing ever again could equal the pleasure and the pain and the heights of these last few years.

Down in X the men waited that final morning clad in full uniform instead of what was clean and came first to hand; their tin trunks, kit bags, packs and haversacks lay in mounds on the floor, and that same floor was assaulted for the first time in its memory by the heavy pounding of many pairs of boots. A warrant officer came, gave Sister Langtry last-minute instructions as to where she was to bring her enlisted men for embarkation, and supervised the removal of extra kit which the men would not normally be expected to carry.

As she turned away from the front door after the warrant officer left, Sister Langtry saw Michael alone in the dayroom, making tea. A quick glance down the ward assured her no one was watching; the rest of them apparently were out on the verandah waiting to be waited on.

"Michael," she said, standing in the dayroom doorway, "come for a walk with me, please. There's only half an hour left. I should very much like to spend ten minutes of it with you."

He considered her thoughtfully, looking much as he had that afternoon he had arrived, jungle-green trousers and shirt, American gaiters, webbing, tan boots polished until they shone, brass glittering, everything neat, pressed, and worn so well.

"I'd like that too," he said seriously. "Just let me drop this out on the verandah first. I'll meet you at the bottom of the ramp."

I wonder if he'll appear with Benedict in tow? she asked herself as she stood in the watery sun at the bottom of the ramp. See one and you saw the other.

But Michael was alone, and fell into step alongside her. They paced down the path which led to the beach, stopping just short of the sand.

"It came too quickly. I'm not ready after all," she said, looking at him a little guardedly.

"Nor am I," he said.

She began to babble. "This is the first opportunity I've had to see you alone since—since Luce died. No, since the verdict came in. That was awful. I said so many awful things to you. I want you to know I didn't mean them. Michael, I'm so sorry!"

He listened to her quietly, his face sad. "There's nothing to be sorry for. I'm the one who ought to be doing all the apologizing." Seeming to deliberate within himself, he went on slowly. "The others don't think so, but I feel I owe you some sort of explanation, now that it doesn't matter much any more."

All she heard was the last little bit. "Nothing matters much any more," she said. "I'd like to change the subject, ask you about home. Are you going back to your dairy farm right away? What about your sister and your brother-in-law? I'd like to know, and we don't have much time."

"We never did have much time," he said. "Well, I have to get my discharge first. Then Ben and I are going to head for my farm. I've just had a letter from my sister and they're counting the days until I can take over again. Harold—my brother-in-law—wants to get his old job back before too many soldiers are demobbed."

She gaped. "Ben and you? Together?"

"Yes."

"Ben and you."

"That's right."

"In God's name, *why?*"

"I owe it to him," said Michael.

Her face twisted. "Oh, come off it!" she snapped, rebuffed.

He set his shoulders. "Benedict is alone, Sis. He doesn't have anyone at all waiting for him. And he needs someone with him all the time. Me. It's my fault, I wish I could make you see that! I have to make sure it never happens again."

Her torment became bewilderment; she stared at him and wondered if she would ever begin to get to the bottom of the mystery that surrounded Michael. "What are you talking about? What never happens again?"

"I said it before," he said patiently. "I think I owe you an explanation. The others don't agree. They think you ought to be kept right out of it forever, but I want to tell you. I understand why Neil's so set against your knowing, but I still believe I owe you an explanation. Neil wasn't with you that night, I was. And it entitles you to an explanation."

"What explanation? What is all this?"

There was a big petrol drum lying on its side just

where the path petered out; he turned, put one foot up on it, gazed down at his boot. "It's not easy to find the right words. But I don't want you to look at me the way you've been looking at me ever since that morning, not understanding. I agree with Neil, telling you isn't going to change anything, but it might mean that the last time I ever see you, you won't be looking at me as if half of you hated me and the other half was wishing it could hate me too." He straightened, faced her. "This is hard," he said.

"I don't hate you, Michael. I couldn't ever hate you. What's done is done. I'm not fond of post-mortems. So tell me, please. I want to know. I have a right to know. But I don't hate you. I never have, I never could."

"Luce didn't kill himself," he said. "Benedict did the killing."

She was back in the midst of all that blood, all that ruined magnificence, Luce sprawled without consideration of grace, fluidity of line, theatrical effect—unless sheer horror was the effect he had aimed for, and Luce was not like that. Luce loved himself too much, visually anyway.

Her face went so pale the light striking down through the palms gave it a greenish hue; for the second time in their acquaintance Michael moved close to her, slipped an arm around her waist and supported her so strongly all she could feel was the feel of him.

"Here, love, don't pass out on me! Come on now, take a few deep breaths, that's the good girl!" He spoke tenderly, he held her tenderly.

"I knew it all the time," she said slowly, when at last she was able to speak. "There was something wrong. It just wasn't typical of Luce. But it's typical Benedict, all right." The color stole back beneath her skin, she clenched her fists in an impotent anger directed entirely against herself. "Oh, what a *fool* I am!"

Michael released her and stepped back a pace, looking more at ease with himself. "If I didn't think so much of you I wouldn't have told you, but I couldn't bear to see you hate me. It's been killing me. Neil knows that, too." Then, seeming to decide he was drifting from the subject, he turned back to it. "Benedict won't ever do anything like it again, Sis, you have my word. As long as I'm there to look after him, he can't do it again. You do understand that, don't you? I have to look after him. He's my responsibility. He did it for me, or he thought he did it for me, which amounts to the same thing. I told you in the morning, remember? I told you it was wrong of me to stay with you all night. I should have gone back to the ward to keep an eye on Ben. If I had been there where I belonged, it would never have happened. Funny, I've killed men, and for all I know they were better men by far than Luce. But Luce's death is my responsibility. The death of the others I've killed is the responsibility of the King; the King has to answer to God for them, not me. I could have stopped Ben. No one else could have, because no one else had any idea what was going on in Ben's mind." He closed his eyes. "I was weak, I gave in to myself. But oh, Honour, I wanted to stay with you! I couldn't believe it! A little bit of heaven, and I'd been in hell so long. . . . I loved you, but I never dreamed you loved me until then."

Huge reserves of strength, she had huge reserves of strength; she plundered them with the carelessness of a freebooter. "I should have known that," she said. "Of course you loved me."

"I was thinking of myself first," he said, apparently happy he could talk to her at last. "If you knew how much I blame myself! There was *no need* for Luce to die! All I had to do was be there in the ward to show Ben I was all right, that it wasn't in Luce's power to harm me." His chest heaved, more a shudder than a sigh. "While I was with you in your room, Ben was all alone, thinking Luce had somehow managed to destroy me. And once Ben came to that conclusion, the rest followed naturally. If Neil had known, it might have been different. But Neil had no idea. He had other things on his mind. And I wasn't even there to tidy up the mess, the rest had to do that too." His hand went out to her, fell back to his side. "I have a lot to answer for, Honour. The way I hurt you—there are no excuses for that, either. I can't make any, even to myself. But I'd like you to know that I . . . feel it, that I do understand what I've done to you. And that of everything I have to answer for, hurting you is the hardest to bear."

The tears were coursing down her face, more for his pain than her own. "Don't you love me now at all?" she asked. "Oh, Michael, I can stand anything but losing your love!"

"Yes, I love you. But there's no future in it—there couldn't be, there never was, Luce and Ben aside. If it hadn't been for the war, I would never have met anyone like you. You would have met men like Neil, not men like me. My friends, the sort of life I like to lead, even the house I live in—they don't fit with you."

"You don't love a life," she said, wiping the tears away. "You love a man, and then you *make* a life."

"You would never have made your life with a man like me," he said. "I'm just a dairy farmer."

"That's a ridiculous thing to say! I'm not a snob! And tell me the difference between one kind of cocky and another—my father's a cocky too. The scale's bigger, that's all. Nor am I dependent upon having money for my happiness."

"I know. But you are from a different class than me, and we don't have the same outlook on life."

She stared at him strangely. "Don't we, Michael? Now I find that an odd thing for you of all people to say! I think we do have the same outlook on life. We both like to look after those less capable than ourselves, and we both aim at the exact same thing—encouraging them to be self-sufficient."

"That's true. . . . Yes, that's very true," he said slowly, and then: "Honour, what does love mean to you?"

The apparent non sequitur took her back. "Mean?" she asked, hedging for more time to think.

"Mean. What does love mean to you?"

"My love for you, Michael? Or for others?"

"Your love for me." He seemed to enjoy saying it.

"Why—why, it means sharing my life with you!"

"Doing what?"

"Living with you! Keeping your home, having your babies, growing old together," she said.

He looked remote; her words affected him, she could see, but had no power to penetrate deeply enough to reach that calm determination which possessed no image of self.

"But you haven't served any sort of apprenticeship for that," he said. "You're thirty now, and your apprenticeship has been for something quite different. A different sort of life. Hasn't it?" He paused, not taking his eyes off her face, raised to his in a fearful bewilderment that yet showed the germ of a comprehension she was unwilling to acknowledge. "I think neither of us is suited for the life you're describing. When I started to talk to you I didn't think I'd mention this, but you're a good fighter, you won't be palmed off with anything but the real root of the matter."

"No, I won't," she said.

"The real root of the matter is just what I said— neither of us is suited for the sort of life you describe. It's too late to wonder what or why now. I'm the sort of man who mistrusts the wants that come out of a part of me I'm normally able to control. I don't want to cheapen it by calling it my bodily desires, and I don't want you to think I'm belittling my feelings for you." He gripped her arms near the shoulder. "Honour, listen to me! I'm the sort of bloke who mightn't come home one night because on a trip into town I found someone who in my mind needed me more than you do—I don't mean I'd desert you, and I don't necessarily mean another woman; I mean that I'd know you could get along without me until I could come home again. But I might be two days helping that person, or I might be two years. I'm like that. The war gave me a chance to see what I am. It's given you a chance to see what you are, too. I don't know how much you're

279

willing to admit to yourself about yourself, but I've learned that when I'm moved to pity, I'll always be moved to help. You are a complete person. You don't need my help. And not needing my help, I know you can get along without me. You see, love is beside the point."

"You're approaching a paradox," she said, throat aching from the effort to quell fresh tears.

"I suppose I am." He paused, searching for the next thing to say. "I don't think I have a very high opinion of myself. If I did, I wouldn't need to be needed. But I do need to be needed, Honour! I've got to be needed!"

"I need you!" she said. "My soul, my heart, my body—every bit of me needs you; it always will! Oh, Michael, there are all kinds of need, all kinds of loneliness! Don't confuse my strength with a lack of need! *Please* don't! I need you to fulfill my very life!"

But he shook his head, obdurate. "You don't. You never will. You're already fulfilled! If you weren't, you couldn't be the person I know you to be—warm, loving, interested, happy doing a job few women can do. Almost all women can make a home, have babies. But you're too different to be content in that sort of cage. Your apprenticeship's wrong for it. Because after a while that's how you'd see the life you described with me, devoted exclusively to me. As a cage! You're a stronger bird than that, Honour. You've got to stretch your wings in wider territory than a cage."

"I'm prepared to risk that happening," she said, white-faced, desolate, but still fighting.

"I'm not. If it was just you I was describing, maybe I would risk it. But I'm describing me as well."

"You're chaining yourself to Ben far more rigidly than you would to me."

"But I can't hurt Ben the way I'd end in hurting you."

"Looking after Ben is a full-time job. You won't be able to take off to help anyone else on a trip to town."

"Ben needs me," he said. "I'll live for that."

"What if I offered to share your charge of Ben?" she

asked. "Would you agree to a life with me that shared our need of being needed?"

"Are you offering that?" he asked, uncertain.

"No," she said. "I can't share you with the likes of Benedict Maynard."

"Then there's no more to be said."

"About us, no." She still stood between his hands, and made no move to escape them. "Do the others agree that you should look after Ben?"

"We made a pact," he said. "We all agreed. No lunatic asylum for Ben, no matter what happens. Nor will Matt's wife and children go hungry. We all agreed."

"*All* of you? Or you and Neil?"

He acknowledged the accuracy of this with a rueful twist of lips and head. "I'll say goodbye now," he said, hands sliding up across her shoulders to cradle the sides of her neck, thumbs moving against her skin.

He kissed her, a kiss of deep love and pain, a kiss of acceptance for what must be and hunger for what might have been. And a voluptuous, erotic kiss filled with the memories of that one night. But he took his mouth away abruptly, too soon; a lifetime would scarcely have been long enough.

Then he came stiffly to attention, a smile in his eyes, turned on his heel and walked away.

The petrol drum was there; she sank down onto it so that she wouldn't have to watch him until he disappeared, looking at her shoes, at the weak brown tendrils of grass, at the infinity of grains which made up the sand.

So that was that. How could she compete with the kind of need a Benedict had for a Michael? He was right thus far. And how lonely he must be, how driven. Wasn't that always the way it was? The strong abandoned in favor of the weak. The compulsion—or was it the guilt?—the strong felt to serve the weak. Who battened first? Did the weak demand, or did the strong offer themselves unsolicited? Did strength beget weakness, or reinforce it, or negate it? What was strength, what weakness, for that matter? He was right, she could get along without him. Was that therefore a lack of need for him? He loved her for her strength, yet he couldn't live with what he loved. In loving, he turned away from loving. Because it didn't, or it couldn't, satisfy him.

She had wanted to cry out to him, Forget the world, Michael, curl yourself up in me! With me you'll know a happiness you've never dreamed of! Only to cry that would have been to cry for the moon. Had she done it deliberately? Chosen to love a man who preferred to minister than to love! Since the day of his arrival in X she had admired him, and her love had grown out of that admiration, out of valuing what he was. Each of them had loved the other's strength, self-reliance, capacity to give. Yet it seemed these very qualities pushed them apart, not together. Two positives. My dearest, my most beloved Michael . . . I shall think of you, and pray for you, that you continue always to find the strength.

She looked out over the beach, a little battered after the wind and rain of a few days before. There were two beautiful white terns soaring, soaring, wingtip to wingtip as if tied; they wheeled suddenly, still tied, dipped, and were gone. That's what I wanted, Michael! No cage! Only to fly with you against a great blue sky.

Time to get going. Time to walk Matt, Benedict, Nugget and Michael to the assembly point. It was her duty to do so. Neil as an officer would leave separately, she didn't yet know when. They'd tell her in due time.

As she walked, other thoughts than Michael began to intrude. There had been a conspiracy among the patients of ward X. A conspiracy in which Michael had been a willing party. And Neil was its ringleader. It didn't make any sense. Oh, it made sense to keep her in ignorance of what had really happened in the bathhouse until the cause of death was officially established and any inquiry closed. But why was Neil so against Michael's wish to tell her now, when it couldn't possibly matter? Neil knew her well enough to understand it was not in her nature to go running off to Colonel Chinstrap with the true story. What use would there be in that? What could it change? It could ensure Benedict's permanent commitment to some civilian institution, perhaps, but it would also result in dishonorable discharges for the rest of them, if not prison. Probably too they had agreed to close ranks against her, and would have denied all she might have told Colonel Chinstrap. *Why* had Neil fought to retain her ignorance? Not only Neil. Matt and Nugget were in it too.

What had Michael said, right at the last? They made a pact. Matt's wife and children would not go hungry. No doubt Nugget would get through medicine without starving, either. Benedict would not go to a mental asylum. Michael and Neil . . . They had split up the responsibilities between them, Michael and Neil. But what did Neil get out of it, if he was furnishing the money for Matt's family and Nugget's education? Two weeks ago she would have said, nothing; but today she wasn't so sure.

That hurt Neil didn't seem to have, his apparent acceptance of her rejection with sufficient tranquillity and lack of concern to make her feel he couldn't possibly be hurt. And who had been talking to Michael, that he came out with all those antiquated class differences between them? She clutched at this prideful straw eagerly. Someone had been working on Michael, trying to convince him he had to give her up. Someone? Neil!

5 The evacuation was very well organized. When she reached the assembly point with her four men they were snatched from her very quickly, barely time for a hug and a pecking kiss from each. And afterward she couldn't even remember how Michael looked at her, or how she looked at him. It seemed futile to linger hoping for another sight of them, so she slipped through the knots of waiting men and shepherding sisters, and walked back to X.

Second nature to tidy and straighten up; she went down the length of the ward smoothing the sheets, adjusting the nets for the last time in the Matron Drape, opening lockers, folding up the screens which hid the refectory table.

Then she went into her office, kicked her shoes off without unlacing them and sat down in her chair with her feet tucked under her, something she had never done before in that official seat. It didn't matter. There was no one to see, ever again. Neil was gone too. A harassed sergeant with a clipboard informed her of Neil's departure. She didn't understand what or who had slipped up, but it was too late to do anything about it anyway. And perhaps it was better not to be obliged to confront the ringleader of the conspiracy. There would be too many uncomfortable questions to ask him.

Her head drooped, propped on her hand; she dozed, and dreamed not unpleasantly of Michael.

It was about two hours later than Neil came swinging across the compound behind ward X, whistling jauntily, looking neat and at home in his captain's uniform, swagger stick tucked into the crook of his arm. He leaped lightly up the steps at the back of X and came into the dim and lifeless interior. Shocked, he pulled up sharply. X was empty; its emptiness shouted at him from everywhere. After a moment he began to move again, but less surely, less lightheartedly; he opened the door to his cubicle and received another shock, for all his baggage was gone. There was not a trace of Neil Parkinson, troppo patient, left.

"Hello?" came Sister Langtry's voice through the thin wall. "Hello; who's there, please?"

She was sitting in a pose he had never seen before, not dignified, not professional, side-on to her desk, with her legs curled up under her on the chair, and her shoes empty on the floor. The room was full of smoke; her own cigarettes and matches lay in full view on the desk. And she looked as if she had been sitting so for a very long time.

"Neil!" she said, staring. "I thought you were gone! They told me you went hours ago."

"Tomorrow for me. What about you?"

"I'll be detailed to special one of the serious stretcher cases all the way to wherever we're going—Brisbane or Sydney, I suppose. Tomorrow or the day after." She stirred. "I'll find you something to eat."

"Don't bother, honestly. I'm not hungry. I'm just glad I didn't have to go today." He sighed luxuriously. "I've got you all to myself at last."

Her eyes gleamed. "Have you really?"

The way she said that gave him pause, but he sat back easily in the visitor's chair, and smiled. "Indeed I have. And not before time, too. It took some wangling, but the colonel's still a little sensitive about the whisky, so he managed to get my departure postponed. And he gave me a clean bill of health while he was about it. Which means I am no longer a patient in ward X. For tonight I'm merely a tenant."

She answered obliquely. "Do you know, Neil, I loathe the war and what it's done to us? I feel so personally responsible."

"Assuming the guilt of the whole world, Sis? Come now!" he chided gently.

"No, not the whole world, Neil. Only that share of the guilt which you and the rest withheld from me," she said harshly, and looked at him.

He drew a long, hissing breath. "So Michael couldn't keep his damned mouth shut after all."

"Michael was in the right of it. I was entitled to know. And I want to know. All of it, Neil. What *did* happen that night?"

Shrugging, mouth screwed up, he settled himself as if to embark upon a rather boring anecdote he secretly felt was not worth the telling. She watched him closely, thinking that the wall behind him, stripped now of its drawings because they resided in her baggage, threw his face into an intense relief it had always needed.

"Well, I had to have another drink, so I went back to the whisky," he said, lighting a cigarette and forgetting to offer her one. "The racket Luce was making woke up Matt and Nugget, so they decided to help me finish the second bottle. That only left Benedict to look after Luce, who had gone to bed. I'm afraid we did rather forget Luce. Or maybe we just didn't want to have to remember him."

As he talked the memory of that night began to move in him, to regenerate something of its original horror, and his face reflected this vividly. "Ben dug into his kit and found one of those illicit souvenirs we all have tucked away somewhere—a Japanese officer's pistol. He made Luce take his own razor, and he marched Luce to the bathhouse with the pistol right against his ribs."

"Was it Ben who told you about marching Luce to the bathhouse?" she asked.

"Yes. That much we got out of him, but as to what actually happened inside, I have only the sketchiest of ideas. Ben gets confused about it himself." He lapsed into silence.

"And?" she prompted.

"We heard Luce screaming like one damned, all the

way from the bathhouse, screaming, screaming. . . ."
He grimaced. "But by the time we got there it was far
too late for Luce. It's a miracle no one else heard,
except that the wind was blowing toward the palm
grove, and we are a long way from civilization. We
were too late—I said that, didn't I?"

"Yes. Can you give me any idea of how Ben did it?"

"I would guess Luce didn't have the guts to fight his
way out, and maybe didn't even believe what was going
to happen until it was too late. Those damned razors
are so sharp. . . .Having forced Luce at gunpoint to
hold the razor properly, I think Ben just reached out,
grabbed Luce's hand, and it was all over. I can see Luce
screaming and gibbering in fear, not even realizing
what Ben was doing to him until it was done. You don't
realize it, with something as sharp as a Bengal razor."

Frowning, she thought about it. "But his hand wasn't
bruised, Neil," she objected. "If it had been, Major
Menzies would have seen it. And Ben must have had to
grip Luce very hard indeed."

"Hands don't bruise all that easily, Sis. Not like
arms. The major wouldn't have been looking for
anything more than external bruising—this isn't Scotland Yard, thank God. And it was done, knowing Ben,
so quickly. He must have thought and thought about
how he was going to kill Luce. It wasn't spur of the
moment. And yet he could never have carried it
through without being found out, because the minute it
began to happen he went slightly mad—or mad in a
different way; I don't know. Besides, he wasn't worried
about getting caught. He just wanted to dispatch Luce
in a way he knew would ensure Luce retained consciousness until the end. Because I think what he really
wanted Luce to see was the maiming of his own
genitalia."

"Was Luce dead when you got there?"

"Not quite. That was what saved our bacon. We got
Ben away from him just before Luce went into some
sort of death convulsion, still hanging onto the razor,
and bleeding like a fountain. There were vital arteries

severed. So while Matt took Ben outside and kept watch, Nugget and I tidied up. It only took a few minutes. What took the time was waiting until we were absolutely sure Luce had breathed his last, because we didn't dare touch him."

"It *must* have occurred to you to fetch help, to try to save him," she said, tight-lipped.

"Oh, my dear, there was not the slightest chance of saving him! Give me more credit than that! Had we been able to save him, Ben wouldn't have been in such jeopardy. I'm not medically trained, no, but I am a soldier. I admit I never liked Luce, but it was hell to have to stand there and watch the man die!"

Grey-faced, he leaned to ash his cigarette, watching her absolutely absorbed, pain-filled eyes.

"Nugget was remarkably calm and competent, would you believe that? It just goes to show that you can live with a man for months without ever knowing what's inside him. And in all the days afterward, not once did I see him look as if he was going to lose his nerve."

His hand shook as he decided to stub the cigarette out. "The worst part was being sure we had done everything possible to make it look like a suicide, that we hadn't overlooked anything which might lead to a suspicion of murder. . . . Anyway, when we finished, we took Ben down to the next bathhouse, and while Matt kept watch—he's an excellent night watchman, he hears everything—Nugget and I hosed Ben down. He was covered in blood, but luckily he hadn't got his feet in it. I don't think we could have obliterated footprints. We burned his pajama pants. You were a pair short on your laundry count, do you remember?"

"How was Ben?" she asked.

"Very calm, and quite unrepentant. I think he still feels he was only doing his Christian duty. To him Luce wasn't a man, he was a demon from hell."

"So you shielded Benedict," she said coldly. "All of you shielded him."

"Yes, all of us. Even Michael. The minute you told him Luce was dead, he realized what must really have happened. I felt very sorry for Mike. You would have thought his own hand had done the deed, he was so upset, so choked with remorse. Kept saying he ought not to have been so self-centered, ought not to have stayed with you, that his duty was to stay with Benedict."

She didn't flinch; this too was a part of her share of the guilt. "He said that to me, too. That he ought not to have stayed with me, that he ought to have been with *him*. He . . . him! He never used a *name!* I thought he meant Luce." Her voice broke, she had to pause to compose herself before going on. "It never, never occurred to me that he meant Benedict! I assumed he meant Luce, and I assumed he was homosexually involved with Luce. All the things I said, all the things I did! How much I hurt him! And what a mess I made of it! I'm ill even remembering."

"If he didn't use a name, you made a natural mistake," Neil said. "His papers implied homosexuality."

"How do you know that?"

"From Luce, via Ben and Matt."

"You're a very clever man, Neil. You knew or guessed it all, didn't you? And you set out to compound the confusion, deliberately. How could you do that?"

"What else did you expect us to do?" he asked, using the collective rather than the singular. "We couldn't just hand Ben over to the authorities! Luce was no loss to the world, and Ben certainly doesn't deserve to be shut up in some civilian mental asylum for the rest of his life because he killed Luce! You forget! We're all inmates of ward X! We've had a tiny taste of what life must be like for mental patients."

"Yes, I understand all that," she said patiently. "But it doesn't negate the fact that you took the law into your own hands, that you deliberately elected to cover up a murder, and that you also elected to deprive me of any opportunity to rectify the matter. I would have had him committed on the spot had I known! He's dangerous, don't any of you understand that? Benedict belongs in a mental asylum! You were wrong, all of you, but you especially, Neil. You're an officer, you know the rules and you're supposed to abide by them. If you plead your own illness as an excuse, then you belong in an institution, too! Without obtaining my consent, you've made me a party to it, and had it not been for Michael, I would never have known. I have a lot to be grateful to Michael for, but above all, I'm grateful to him for telling me how Luce really died. Michael's thinking isn't the straightest, either, but he's one up on the rest of you! Thank God he told me!"

He threw his cigarette case down on the desk so violently that it bounced into the air and fell to the floor with a clatter, the catch springing open, cigarettes flying. Neither of them noticed; they were too intent upon each other.

"Michael, Michael, Michael!" he shouted, face convulsed, tears starting to his eyes. "Always, always Michael! For God's sake will you snap out of this—this *obsession* you have for Michael? Michael this, Michael that, Michael, Michael, Michael! I am so sick to death of that bloody name! Since the moment you set eyes on him you've had no time for anyone else! *What about the rest of us?*"

As in that scene with Luce, there was nowhere to go, nowhere to hide; she sat there filled with a dawning understanding of what Neil was crying from the heart about, her anger at him suddenly vanquished.

Rubbing his hand angrily across his eyes, he fought visibly for self-control, and when he spoke again he tried to make his voice sound calmer, more reasonable. Oh, Neil, she thought, how you've changed! You've grown. Two months ago you could never have managed that kind of self-discipline in the midst of such torment.

"Look," he said, "I know you love him. Even Matt, blind as he is, saw that a long time ago. So let's take it as read, and put it to one side as the prime consideration. Before Mike came you belonged to all of us, and we belonged to you. You *cared* about us! Everything you had, everything you were, was channeled to us—

toward healing us, if you like. But when you're sick you can't see it as objectively as that, it's completely, exclusively personal. You—you wrapped us in you! And it never occurred to any of us that you spent your heart anywhere but inside X, and on us. When Michael came, it stuck out like a sore thumb that there was nothing the matter with him. To us, that meant you shouldn't need to bother with him at all. Instead—you turned right away from us, you went toward him. You abandoned us! You betrayed us! And that's why Luce died. Luce *died* because you looked at what Michael was, all that sanity and—and strength of being, and you loved it. You loved him! How do you think that made the rest of us feel?"

She wanted to shriek, But I didn't stop caring about you! I didn't, I didn't! All I wanted was something for myself for a change! There's only so much you can go on giving without taking something for yourself, Neil! It didn't seem a very large something at the time. My tenure in X was ending. And I loved him. Oh, God, I'm so tired of giving, giving! Why couldn't you be generous enough to let me have something too?

But she couldn't say any of it. Instead, she leaped to her feet and headed for the door, anywhere to get away from him. He grasped at her wrist in passing, swung her round and held her hard, grinding the bones of both her hands cruelly until she ceased to struggle.

"You see?" he asked softly, his grip slackening, his fingers sliding up her arms. "I've just held you a lot harder than Ben probably had to hold Luce, and I don't think you'll have any bruises."

She looked up into his face, a long way further than Michael's would have been, for Neil was very tall. His expression was both serious and aloof, as if he knew well all that she was feeling, and didn't blame her. But as if, like a priest-king of old, he was fully prepared to endure anything in order to achieve the ultimate end.

Until this interview she had not even begun to understand what sort of man Neil was; how much passion and determination lay in him. Nor the depth of his feelings for her. Perhaps he had hidden his hurt too skillfully, perhaps, as he charged, her absorption in Michael had made it all too easy for her to assure herself Neil was not devastated by her defection. He had been devastated. Yet it had not prevented him from moving to contain the threat Michael presented. It had not stopped his functioning. Bravo, Neil!

"I'm very sorry," she said, sounding quite matter-of-fact. "I don't seem to have the strength left to wring my hands as I say it, or weep, or go down on my knees to you. But I *am* sorry. More than you'll ever know. I'm too sorry to try to justify myself. All I can say is that we, those who care for you, our patients, can be as blind and misguided as any patient who ever walked through the door of a ward X. You mustn't think of me as a goddess, some kind of infallible being. I'm not. None of us are!" Her eyes filled with tears. "But oh, Neil, you have no idea how I wish we were!"

He gave her a light hug, kissed her brow, and let her go. "Well, it's done, and you know the old saying—even the gods can't unscramble eggs. I feel better for speaking my piece. But I'm sorry too. It's no joy for me to find that I can hurt you, even though you don't love me."

"I wish I could love you," she said.

"But you can't. I know. It's inescapable. You saw me the way I was when I first came to X, and it put me under a liability to you I don't suppose I'd ever cancel, even if there had been no Michael. You fell for him because he started out as a man for you—a whole man. He never hid himself away, or blubbered with self-pity, or completely unmanned himself. You never had to change his pants or clean up his messes or listen for long boring hours at a time to a litany of his woes—the same woes you must have heard from two dozen men just like me."

"Oh, please!" she cried. "I have never, never thought of it—or you—like that!"

"It's how I think of myself, looking back. I *am* able to look back now. So it's probably a more accurate picture of me than you're prepared to admit. But I'm cured, you know. From where I'm standing now I can't even see why it ever happened to me in the first place."

"That's good," she said, walking to the door. "Neil, please, can we make this goodbye? Right now, I mean. And can you manage to take it for what it is, not a sign of dislike or neglect or lack of love? It's just been the sort of day I want desperately to see end. And I find I can't end it with you. I'd rather not see you again. Not for any other reason than it would be like holding a wake. Ward X is no more."

He accompanied her out into the corridor. "Then I shall hold my own wake. If you ever feel you'd like to see me, you'll find me in Melbourne. The address is in the phone book. Toorak. Parkinson, N.L.G. It took me a long time to find the right woman. I'm thirty-seven years old, so I'm not likely to change my mind in a hurry." He laughed. "How could I ever forget you? I've never kissed you."

"Then kiss me now," she said, almost loving him. Almost.

"No. You're right. Ward X is no more, but I'm still standing in its uncooled corpse. What you're offering is a favor, and I want no favors. Never any favors."

She held out her hand. "Goodbye, Neil. All the best of luck. But I'm sure you'll have it."

He took the offered hand, shook it warmly, then lifted it and kissed it lightly. "Goodbye, Honour. Don't ever forget—I'm in the Melbourne phone book."

The last trek from X across the compound; one never really thought it would come to that, even after one began to long for it. As if Base Fifteen represented a segment of life as huge as life itself. Now it was over. And it had ended with Neil, which was only fitting. That was quite a man. Yet she could see the truth in his saying he had started out with a big disadvantage. She *had* thought of him chiefly as a patient. And lumped him in with the rest. Poor, sad, frail . . . Now to find him none of those things was exhilarating. He implied his cure had come out of the situation in X during the last few weeks of its duration, but that wasn't true. His cure had come out of himself. The cure always did. So, in spite of the grief, the horror, and the pain, she commenced this last trek feeling as if ward X had existed for a purpose, a good purpose.

Neil hadn't even bothered to ask her whether she was going to try to exact the justice he felt was already done and she felt had been miscarried. Too late by far. Thank God Michael had told her! Knowing what they had done had freed her from a large measure of the guilt she might otherwise have preserved over her conduct toward them. If they thought she had betrayed them in turning to Michael, she knew they had betrayed her. For the rest of their lives they would have to live with Luce Daggett. So would she. Neil hadn't wanted her told because he feared her brand of intervention would liberate Michael, and because he genuinely wished to spare her a share of the guilt. Half good, half bad. Half self, half nonself. About normal, that was.

PART 7

1 When Honour Langtry got off the train in Yass there was no one to meet her, which didn't dismay her; she hadn't let her family know she was coming. Loving them was one thing, facing them quite another, and she preferred to face them in private. This was childhood she was coming back to, and it seemed so very far away. How would they see her now? What would they think? So she had put the moment of reunion off. Her father's property wasn't far out of town; someone would give her a lift.

Someone did, but he was no one she knew, which meant she could sit back and enjoy the fifteen-mile drive in peace. By the time she arrived home the family would know she was back, of course; the stationmaster had welcomed her with open arms, found her the lift, and undoubtedly telephoned ahead that she was on her way.

They were all gathered on the front verandah, waiting: her father growing stouter and balder; her mother looking exactly the same; her brother Ian a younger, slimmer edition of her father. There were hugs, kisses, much standing back to look, exclamations and sentences that never got finished because someone else interrupted.

It was only after a fatted-calf sort of dinner that some semblance of normality returned; Charlie Langtry and his son went to bed, for their days began at dawn, while Faith Langtry followed her daughter to her bedroom, there to sit and watch her unpack. And talk.

Honour's room was pleasant and unpretentious; however, it was large and had had money spent on it. No particular skill with color or line had been applied when the money had been spent, but the big bed looked comfortable, so did the chintz-covered easy chair in which Faith Langtry sat. There was a highly polished old table with a wooden carver chair to serve as a work area, a vast wardrobe, a full-length mirror on a stand, a small dressing table, and one more easy chair.

While Honour moved around between wardrobe, dressing table drawers and her suitcases on the bed, her mother sat fully absorbing her daughter's appearance for the first time since her arrival home. Of course there had been periods of leave during the years in the army, but their lack of permanence, their atmosphere of urgency, had permitted no real and lasting impressions. This was different; Faith Langtry could look her fill without applying half her mind to what had to be fitted in tomorrow, or how they were all going to get through the next period of duty for Honour when it was bound to be dangerous. Ian hadn't been able to go into the army, he was needed on the land. But when she was born, thought Faith Langtry, I never realized it would be my daughter I sent to war. My firstborn. Sex isn't as different or as important as it used to be.

Each time she had come home they had noticed changes, from the atabrine yellow in her skin to the little tics and habits which branded her an adult, her own woman. Six years. God knows exactly what those six years had contained, for Honour had never wanted to talk about the war when she came home, and if asked, parried the questions lightly. But whatever they might have contained, as Faith Langtry looked at Honour now she understood that her daughter had forever moved farther than the moon from the place which had been her home.

She was thin; that was to be expected, of course. There were lines in the face, though there was no sign of grey in her hair, thank God. She was stern without being hard, extraordinarily decisive in the way she moved, locked away without being withdrawn. And though she could never be a stranger, she was someone different.

How glad they had been when she chose to do

nursing rather than medicine! Thinking of the suffering that decision would spare their daughter. But had she done medicine she would have stayed at home, and looking at Honour now, Faith wondered if that might not have meant less suffering in the long run.

Her service medals came out, and her decorations—how bizarre to have a *daughter* who was a Member of the British Empire! And how proud Charlie and Ian would be!

"You never told me of your MBE," Faith said, a little reproachfully.

Honour looked up, surprised. "Didn't I? I must have just forgotten. Things were pretty busy around that time; I had to hurry through my letters. Anyway, it's only recently been confirmed."

"Have you any photos, darling?"

"Somewhere." Honour fished in the pocket of a case, and produced two envelopes, one much larger than the other. "Here we are." She came across to the second easy chair and sat down, reaching for her cigarettes.

"That's Sally and Teddy and Willa and me. . . . That's the Boss at Lae. . . . Me in Darwin, about to take off for I can't remember where. . . . Moresby. . . . The nursing staff on Moratai. . . . The outside of ward X. . . ."

"You look wonderful in a slouch hat, I must say."

"They're more comfortable than veils, probably because they have to come off the minute you walk inside."

"What's in the other envelope? More photos?"

Honour's hand hovered as if not sure whether to take both envelopes away without revealing the contents of the second, bigger one; after a slight hesitation she opened it. "No, not photos. Some drawings of some of my patients from ward X—my last command, if I can put it that way."

"They're marvelously well done," said Faith, looking at each face closely, but, Honour was relieved to see, passing over Michael as if he held no more significance for her than any of the others—but how could he? And how strange, that she had fully expected her mother to see what she had seen that first meeting in the corridor of ward X.

"Who did them?" asked Faith, putting them down.

"This chap," said Honour, riffling through them and putting Neil on the top of the sheaf. "Neil Parkinson. It's not very good; he failed miserably when it came to drawing himself."

"It's good enough for his face to remind me of someone, or else I've actually seen him somewhere. Where does he come from?"

"Melbourne. I gather his father's quite a tycoon."

"Longland Parkinson!" said Faith triumphantly. "I've met this chap, then. The Melbourne Cup in 1939. He was with his mother and father that year, in uniform. I've met Frances—his mother—several times in Melbourne at one do or another."

What had Michael said? That in her world she met men like Neil, not men like himself. How odd. She might indeed in the course of time have met Neil socially. Had there not been a war.

Faith leafed through the pile again, found the sketch she was looking for and laid it down on top of Neil. "Who *is* this, Honour? That face! The expression in his eyes!" She sounded almost spellbound. "I don't know whether I like him, but it's a fascinating face."

"Sergeant Lucius Daggett. Luce. He was—he committed suicide not long before Base Fifteen folded up." Oh, God! She had nearly said he was murdered.

"Poor chap. I wonder what could have led him to do that? He looks so—well, above that sort of thing." Faith gave her back the drawings. "I must say I like them much better than photos. Arms and legs don't tell you nearly as much about people as faces do, and I always find myself squinting at photos to try to see the faces, and all I ever do manage to see is blobs. Who was your personal favorite among the lot?"

The temptation was too great to resist; Honour

300

found Michael and held the drawing out to her mother. "That one. Sergeant Michael Wilson."

"Really?" asked Faith, looking at her daughter doubtfully. "Well, you knew them all in the flesh, of course. A fine chap, I can see that. . . . He looks like a station hand."

Bravo, Michael! thought Honour. There speaks the wealthy grazier's wife who meets Neil Parkinson at the races and knows her social strata instinctively, about as well as anyone can without being a snob. Because Mummy's not a snob.

"He's a dairy farmer," she said.

"Oh, that accounts for the look of the land." Faith sighed, stretched. "Are you tired, darling?"

"No, Mummy, not a bit." Honour put the drawings on the floor beside her chair and lit a cigarette.

"Still no sign of marriage?" Faith asked.

"No," said Honour, smiling.

"Oh, well, it's better to stay a spinster than to marry for the wrong reasons." This was said with a tongue-in-cheek demureness that made her daughter splutter into laughter.

"I quite agree, Mummy."

"I suppose that means you'll be going back to nursing?"

"Yes."

"Prince Alfred again?" Faith knew better than to ask if it was likely her daughter's choice would fall on little Yass—Honour had always liked high-powered places of work.

"No," said Honour, and paused, unwilling to go on.

"Well, where then?"

"I'm going to a place called Morisset to train as a mental nurse."

Faith Langtry gaped. "You're joking!"

"No, I'm not."

"But—but that's ridiculous! You're a senior sister! You can go anywhere after the sort of experience you've had! *Mental nursing?* Good God, Honour, you might as well have applied to become a prison wardress! The pays' better!"

Honour's mouth set; her mother suddenly saw the best display yet of the power and determination which were so alien to her concepts of her daughter.

"That's one of the reasons why I'm doing mental nursing," she said. "For the last year and a half I've nursed men who were emotionally disturbed, and I found I liked that sort of work better than any other branch of nursing. People like me are *needed*—because people like you become horrified at the thought of it, among other reasons! Mental nurses have so little status it's almost a stigma to be one, so if people like me don't get into it, it will never move with the times. When I rang up the Department of Public Health to get some information about training as a mental nurse and said who and what I was, they thought I was some sort of crank! It took two trips in person to convince them that I, a senior nursing sister, was genuinely interested in becoming a mental nurse. Even the Department of Public Health, which administers all mental hospitals, thinks of it as becoming a madmen's keeper!"

"That's exactly what you will be," said Faith.

"When a patient enters a mental hospital he enters a world he will probably never leave," Honour tried to explain, her voice full of feeling. "The men I nursed weren't as badly off as that, but there were still enough direct comparisons to make me see that people like me are needed."

"Honour, you sound as if you're doing penance, or preaching conversion to some religion! Surely whatever happened to you during the war can't have warped your judgment that much!"

"I suppose I do sound as if I'm all fired up with a sense of mission," Honour said thoughtfully, lighting another cigarette. "But it isn't so. Nor am I atoning for anything. But I *won't* concede that to want passionately to do my bit to help lessen the plight of mental patients is an indication of mental instability on my part!"

"All right, darling, all right," Faith soothed. "I was wrong to suggest anything of the kind. Now don't get hot under the collar if I ask you whether you're going to get anything concrete out of it, like another certificate?"

Honour laughed, her indignation dead. "I'm very much afraid I don't get a thing out of it, Mummy. There's no proper course of instruction, no certificate, no nothing. Even when I'm finished my training I won't be a sister again, I'll still be plain Nurse Langtry. However, when I'm put in charge of a ward I understand my title becomes Charge Nurse Langtry—'Charge' for short."

"How did you find all this out?"

"I went to see the Matron of Callan Park. That was where originally I thought I'd go, but after we'd talked for a while she said she strongly advised me to go to Morisset instead. The teaching's just as adequate, it seems, and the atmosphere's a lot better."

Faith got up and began to pace. "Morisset. That's near Newcastle, isn't it?"

"Yes, the Sydney side of Newcastle. About sixty miles from Sydney, which means I'll be able to pop off to Sydney when I need diversion, and I think I'm going to need all the diversion I can get. I'm not looking at this through rose-colored spectacles, you know. It's going to be very hard, especially being a probationer again. But do you know, Mummy, I'd rather be a probationer and learning something new than stuck at P.A. as a senior sister, bowing and scraping to everyone from Matron to the HMOs to the Super, and having to leap some sort of rules and regulations hurdle every five minutes. I just couldn't take the formality and the drivel after the sort of life I've led in the army."

Faith reached out for Honour's packet of cigarettes, took one and lit it.

"Mummy! You're smoking!" said Honour, shocked.

Faith laughed until the tears came. "Oh, well, it's comforting to know you still have some prejudices! I was starting to think I'd produced some sort of latter-day Sylvia Pankhurst. You smoke like a chimney. Why shouldn't I?"

Honour got up, went to hug her. "You're quite right. But do sit down and be comfortable about it! No matter how enlightened one thinks one is, one's parents are always godlike. No human failings, no human appetites. I apologize."

"Accepted. Charlie smokes, Ian smokes, you smoke. I just decided I was being left out in the cold. I've taken to drink as well. I join Charlie in a whisky every night before dinner, and it's very nice."

"Very civilized, too," said Honour, smiling.

"Well, I just hope it all turns out as you hope, darling," Faith said, puffing away. "Though I confess I do rather wish you had never been posted to a troppo ward."

Honour thought before she spoke, wanting her words to be telling. "Mummy, even to you I find I can't talk about the things that happened to me while I was nursing troppo men, and I don't think I ever will be able to talk about them. Not your fault, mine. But some things go too deep. They hurt too much. I'm not bottling them up, exactly. Just that no one could ever understand unless they knew the kind of world ward X was. And to try to explain with all the details I'd need to make you understand—I don't have that kind of strength. It would kill me. And yet, this much I can tell you. I don't know why I think so, but I do know that I'm not finished with ward X. There's more of it to come. And if I'm a mental nurse, I'll be better equipped to cope with what's still to come."

"What could possibly come?"

"I don't know. I have some ideas, perhaps, but I don't have any facts."

Faith stubbed out her cigarette, got to her feet, and bent to kiss her daughter tenderly. "I'll say good night, darling. It's so good to have you home! We worried a lot when we didn't know where you were exactly, or how close you were to the lines. After that sort of worry, mental nursing's a sinecure."

She went from Honour's bedroom to her own, ruthlessly switched on the bedside lamp and flooded her sleeping husband's face with light. He grimaced, grunted, and turned away from it. Leaving it on, she climbed into the bed and leaned heavily on Charlie's shoulder, patting his cheek with one hand and shaking him with the other.

"Charlie, if you don't wake up, I'll murder you!" she said.

Opening his eyes, he sat up, running his fingers through his almost nonexistent hair and yawning. "What's the matter?" he asked, knowing her too well to be annoyed. Faith didn't wake a man up for the fun of it.

"It's Honour," she said, her face crumpling. "Oh, Charlie, I didn't realize it until just now, when I was talking to her in her room!"

"Realize what?" His voice sounded wide awake.

But she couldn't tell him then, for the grief and the fear overcame her; she wept instead, long and bitterly.

"She's gone and she can never come back again," she said when she was able.

He stiffened. "She's gone? Where?"

"Not bodily. That's still in her room. I'm sorry, I didn't mean to frighten you. It's her soul I'm talking about, whatever it is keeps her going. Oh, God, Charlie, we're such *babies* compared to her! It's worse than having a nun for a daughter—at least if your daughter's a nun you know she's safe, the world hasn't touched her. But Honour's got the footprints of the world all over her. And yet she's somehow bigger than the world. I don't know what I'm saying, it isn't right, you'll have to talk to her and watch her for yourself to see what I mean. I took up smoking and drinking, but I think Honour took up all the cares of the world, and that's unbearable. You don't want your children to have to suffer like that."

"It's the war," said Charlie Langtry. "We oughtn't to have let her go."

"She never even asked us for permission, Charlie. Why should she? She was twenty-five when she joined up. A grown woman, I thought then, old enough to survive it. Yes, it's the war."

2 So Sister Langtry doffed her veil, donned a cap and became Nurse Langtry at the Morisset mental hospital. A huge rambling place of many buildings scattered over many acres, it lay in some of the loveliest country to be found any-where: sea lakes to form a part of its boundaries, wild mountains behind it smothered in rain forest, fertile placid flatlands, and the coastal surfing beaches not far away.

At first her situation was a little awkward, for no one at Morisset had ever heard of a general-trained sister giving up all that her career had gained for her to become a mental-nursing train-ee. Many of her fellow trainees were at least as old as she was, some had been in the armed services during the war even, since mental nurs-ing tended to attract women rather than girls, but her peculiar status set her apart. Everyone knew that Matron had told her she would be permitted to sit the charge nurses' examination at the end of two years instead of three, and everyone knew that Matron not only respected but esteemed her. Gossip said she had done arduous nursing during the war, for which she had been made an MBE, and gossip it remained, for Nurse Langtry made no reference to those years whatsoever.

It took her six months to show everyone she was not doing penance, was not snooping on behalf of some mysterious agency in Sydney, or was not a little mental herself. And at the end of those six months she knew she was very well liked by the charge nurses, for she worked hard and with superb efficiency, was never sick, and proved on countless occasions that her general nursing training could be a godsend in a place like Morisset, where the handful of doctors could not possibly keep an eye on every patient to detect the physical maladies which tended to compound the mental state. Nurse Langtry could spot an incipient pneumonia, knew how to treat it, and had a knack for transmitting her knowledge to others. She could spot herpes, tuberculosis, acute abdomens, inner and middle ear infections, tonsillitis and most of the other complaints which occasionally struck at the patients. She could also tell a sprain from a break, a cold from hay fever, a migraine from a tension headache. It made her very valuable.

The work was gruelling. There were two shifts only, day duty from 6:30 A.M. to 6:30 P.M., and night duty, which covered the other twelve hours. Most wards contained between sixty and a hundred and twenty patients, had no domestic staff whatsoever, and only three or four nurses including the charge nurse. Every patient had to be bathed daily, though most wards owned only one plunge bath and one shower. All cleaning duties from the washing of walls and light fixtures to the polishing of floors were the sole responsibility of the nursing staff. The hot water was supplied to each ward by a coke-fired boiler which the nurses had to stoke. The nurses cared for the patients' clothes, from laundering to mending. Though the food was cooked in a central kitchen, it was delivered to each ward in bulk, which meant it had to be reheated, then portioned or carved by the nurses, who often had to cook the dessert and the vegetables in the ward as well. All the dishes, cutlery, pots and pans were washed in the ward. Patients on special diets had their food prepared by the nurses on the ward, for there was no such thing as a diet kitchen, no dieticians either.

No matter how hard or how long they were prepared to work, three or four nurses without domestic help looking after a minimum of sixty patients, often double that number, could never have hoped to complete all that had to be done. So, as at Base Fifteen, the patients worked too. Jobs were highly prized, and the first thing a new nurse learned was not to interfere in any way with any patient's job. When trouble broke out it was usually because one patient had stolen another's job, or made the execution of a job intolerable. The jobs were done well, and there was a strict patient hierarchy which depended upon patient usefulness, and patient pride. The floors always shone like glass, the wards were spotless, the bathing facilities and kitchens sparkled.

Contrary to popular opinion about mental hospitals, and perhaps fairly peculiar to Morisset, there was a lot of love. Everything possible to create a homelike atmosphere was done, and the vast majority of nurses cared about their patients. The staff was a part of the same community as the patients; indeed, there were whole families—mother, father, grownup children—all employed and living at Morisset, so that to many of the staff the hospital was a genuine home, and meant what any genuine home means.

Social life was quite active, and of great interest to patients and staff alike. Pictures were screened in the hall every Monday night for patients and staff together; there were frequent concerts in which patients and staff participated as well as formed the enthusiastic audience; once a month a dance was held, followed by a lavish and delicious supper. At the dances the male patients sat along one wall, the female along the opposite wall, and when a dance was announced the males would dart across the floor to grab their favorite partners. The staff were expected to dance too, but only with patients.

All the wards were locked, and male patients were kept in separate buildings from females; before and after the social functions where the two sexes were permitted to mix, a careful count of patients was always performed. Female patients were nursed by female staff, male patients by males only.

Very few of the patients ever had visitors, very few had private incomes; some received a small remuneration for doing special jobs about the hospital or grounds. To all intents and purposes the inmates regarded the hospital as a permanent home; some remembered no other, some had forgotten any other, some died from pining after a remembered real home with loving parents or spouses. It was not uncommon to see an aged demented patient keeping company during the hours permitted with a spouse who though quite sane had committed himself or herself rather than part completely.

It was no paradise, but the attitude was a caring one, and most of the staff realized there was nothing to be gained but much to be lost by making it an unhappy place; the lot of the patients was unhappy enough to begin with. Of course there were bad wards, bad charges, bad nurses, but not in the large proportions myth and legend contended. Overly sadistic staff, at least in the female wards where Nurse Langtry worked, were not tolerated, nor were charges permitted to run their wards like independent empires.

At times it could be an unconsciously humorous, old-fashioned place. Some of the wards were so far removed by distance from the nurses' home that the nurses staffing them were fetched on and off duty and to and from meals by a male patient driving a horse-drawn covered buggy. Matron and the superintendent did daily rounds, commencing at nine o'clock in the morning. They travelled from ward to ward in a horse and sulky driven by a male patient, Matron sitting up regally in all the splendor of her full whites, a parasol held above her head in strong sunlight, an umbrella when it rained. At the height of summer the horse always wore a big straw hat with his ears poking out of two holes cut in it.

Nurse Langtry knew that the things which troubled her most were to be expected. It was difficult to go back to probationer status, not so much in the taking of orders as in the lack of privileges and comforts, though she suspected it would have gone far harder with her had she not gone through and survived the grind of wartime nursing. However, for a woman turned thirty who had already been a sister-in-charge, who had helped man a field ambulance under fire in battle conditions, who had worked in casualty clearing stations and a military general hospital, it came hard to have to turn out her room for Matron to inspect every Tuesday morning. Her mattress had to be rolled up so Matron could examine beneath her bed, her blankets and sheets folded in a stipulated manner and neatly arranged on top of the mattress. She tried not to mind, for at least she had not been asked to share a room with another nurse, a small concession to her age and professional status.

As her first year at Morisset drew to a close she began to get into stride; and her personality popped to the surface again at full strength. There had been no struggle to subdue it, for it had sunk to the bottom of its own accord, a protective mechanism engineered to cope with protioner status and a job which was not yet at her fingertips.

But truth will out, and the tartar in Honour Langtry was still very much present, considerably refreshed too from its enforced rest. Its reappearance did her no harm, for it had only ever lashed out at stupidity, incompetence or negligence, as it did again now.

She caught a nurse abusing a patient physically, and reported the incident to the charge nurse, who tended to think that Nurse Langtry was being hysterical in her interpretation of what had happened.

"Su-Su's an epileptic," said the charge, "and they can't be trusted."

"What rot!" said Nurse Langtry scornfully.

"Don't you try to tell me my job just because you've got your general!" snapped the charge. "If you doubt me, read your Red Book, it's there in black and white. Epileptics are not to be trusted. They're sly, deceitful and malicious."

"The Red Book is wrong," said Nurse Langtry. "I know Su-Su well, so do you, and she's completely trustworthy. Which is beside the point anyway. Even the Red Book doesn't advocate the beating of a patient."

311

The charge looked at her as if she had blasphemed, as in truth she had; the Red Book was a red-covered manual of notes for mental nurses, and represented the only written source of authority the nurses possessed. But it was out of date, hopelessly inaccurate and designed for students of degradingly low mentality. No matter what the illness, it seemed chiefly to recommend an enema as treatment. Nurse Langtry had given it one perusal which showed her so many glaring errors she largely abandoned it, preferring to go on her own abilities to learn about mental disorders, and to buy textbooks in psychiatry every time she visited Sydney. She was convinced that the reform in nursing techniques, when it came, would reflect what the latest textbooks of psychiatry were already saying.

The battle over Su-Su went all the way to Matron, but nothing could quieten Nurse Langtry, or make her back down. In the end the guilty nurse was disciplined and transferred to another ward, where she was watched carefully; the charge nurse was not disciplined, but got the message where Nurse Langtry was concerned: have your facts absolutely straight when you dealt with Langtry or you'd live to rue the day you crossed swords with her. She was not only intelligent, she was quite unawed by titular authority, and she had an extremely persuasive tongue.

When she went to Morisset, Honour Langtry was well aware that Michael's dairy farm was only about eighty miles away to the northwest, though its proximity was not the reason she chose to nurse there. In that she had allowed herself to be guided by the Matron of Callan Park, and knew after a year on the Morisset staff that she had been excellently advised.

During the times when she wasn't so physically spent that she simply slept and ate when she was off duty, she thought often about Michael. And about Benedict. One day she would venture over to Maitland instead of heading down to Sydney, she knew, but not yet. The wound still hurt, yes, but that was not the reason why she kept postponing the day of her visitation. She had to give Michael time to understand that what he was attempting to do with Ben couldn't succeed. If her first year at Morisset had taught her anything, it was that people like Benedict must not be thrust into the isolation of a farm, for instance, couldn't be allowed to limit themselves even further by limiting the company they kept to one other human soul, no matter how gentle and loving a keeper that one human soul was. In a situation like Michael's farm, Benedict could only grow worse. Which worried her, though she felt there would be no point in her interfering until enough time had elapsed to show Michael he was wrong and she was right.

Within the grounds of Morisset Hospital was a prison hospital for the criminally insane; the sight of it above the trees, tall red brick blocks barred and walled and under the rigid supervision of a separate staff, always had the power to chill her. In there would Benedict now be living, had events in the bathhouse taken a different turn. And it was not a good place to be. So how could she blame Michael for trying? All she could do was to hold herself ready for the day when he might appeal to her for help, or she gauged she could offer it.

3 When she was notified one evening that some-one was waiting to see her in the visitors' room, Nurse Langtry thought immediately of Michael. If he had had the patience to trace her, he must have need of her indeed—though it could also be Neil waiting, Neil who had the sophistication and the money to know how to go about tracing anyone. It would be like Neil too, the new and tempered Neil from whom she had parted eight-een long months ago, to grow tired of waiting for her to come to him, to decide it was time he insinuated himself into her life again. Also, she was aware that her mother and his could cross paths at any time, though nothing in a recent letter from her mother indicated it.

She walked to the visitors' room as sedately as she could, enacting the scene to come with every possible variation, and for two different men. For there was no doubt in her mind that she was going to be very glad to see either of them.

But the person in the chair, feet stretched out and shoeless, was Sister Sally Dawkin.

Nurse Langtry stopped as if she had been shot, both hands over her heart. Oh, God, *why* are women such fools? she wondered, finding a smile and sticking it in place for this first-ever visitor to find her at Morisset. We all live like this, focussed on some man. We can convince ourselves for months on end that it isn't so, but give us half a chance and there's the man again, right back in the middle of everything.

Sister Dawkin smiled broadly, but didn't get up. "I was here earlier, but I didn't like to drag you off your ward, so I had a bit of tea at the fish-and-chippery in Wyong, and came back again. How are you, Honour?"

Nurse Langtry sat down in the chair facing her, still smiling fixedly. "I'm very well. How are you?"

"Oh, a bit like one of those balls tied to a racquet with a long piece of elastic. I don't know which is going to give out first, me or the elastic."

"It won't ever be you," said Nurse Langtry. "You are the great imperishable."

"You tell that to my feet; I've given up trying. They might believe you," said Sister Dawkin, scowling down at them ferociously.

"You and your feet! Some things never change."

Sister Dawkin was wearing rather drab and badly put together mufti, as was the tendency of so many long-term nurses, used only to appearing awesome in all the starched severity of a uniform and veil.

"You look so different, Honour," said Sister Dawkin, staring. "Much younger and happier!"

And indeed she didn't look any older than the average trainee nurse anywhere, clad in the same sort of uniform she had worn while training at P.A. The variations were minor. At Morisset she wore a dress pinstriped in white and lilac, long-sleeved and high to the neck, with detachable celluloid cuffs and collar. And the apron was the same, a voluminous affair in white, stiff with starch, wrapping completely around the skirt of the dress, up over the chest in a bib, securing across the back with broad straps. Her waist looked neat and very tiny, confined by a wide stiff white belt. Both dress and apron were mid-calf in length. She wore black lace-up shoes with flat heels, and opaque black cotton stockings, just as she had at P.A. The Morisset cap was less attractive than the P.A. one, being a pudding-cloth design, white, secured at the nape of the neck with a drawstring and with a broad stiff band across its front, notched twice in Nurse Langtry's case to indicate that she was a second-year trainee.

"It's just the uniform," said Nurse Langtry. "You're used to seeing me without an apron and with a veil."

"Well, whatever you wear, you still look like a new pin."

"Did you get your deputy matronship at North Shore?"

Sister Dawkin looked suddenly very sad. "No. I couldn't stay in Sydney after all, worse luck. I'm back at Royal Newcastle because it's close enough to home to live at home. How's mental nursing?"

"I love it," said Nurse Langtry, her face glowing. "It's not like general nursing in the least, of course, though we do have our medical crises. I've never seen so many status epilepticus cases in all my life! We don't save them all, poor things. But as a mental nurse I feel more important, somehow, more wanted and needed. As a senior sister I'd lost all touch with real nursing, but here, no matter what, you *nurse*. The patients are like relatives, almost. You know they're going to be here as long as you are and longer, unless they die in status or of pneumonia—they're frailer than people whose brains are intact, I've found. And I'll tell you this much, Sally—if you think general nursing involves a commitment, you ought to try mental nursing." She sighed. "I wish I'd done a couple of years here before I had charge of X. I made a lot of mistakes on X through sheer ignorance. Still, better late than never, as the bishop said to the dancing girl."

Sister Dawkin grinned. "Now, now, that's my style of remark, not yours! If you don't watch out you'll end up just like me, a cross between a dragon and a court jester."

"I can think of worse fates," said Nurse Langtry, smiling in a sudden genuine rush of pleasure. "Oh, Sally dear, it's so nice to see you! I didn't know who might be waiting for me. This place is so far out in the sticks that I've never had a visitor before."

"It's nice to see you, too. You've been conspicuous by your absence at reunions and suchlike. Don't you even try to keep up with the old gang from Base Fifteen?"

"No. Funny, I always did loathe post-mortems," said

Nurse Langtry uneasily. "I think it's the way they take the face, grab it round the edges and yank it down—one should never have to see what's on the inside of a face."

"But that's mental nursing you're describing."

Nurse Langtry folded her arms across her stomach and leaned forward. "I never thought of it quite like that. But I still hate post-mortems."

"You're going dotty, is your trouble," said Sister Dawkin comfortably. "I knew you would, living and working in a place like this, pretty gardens and all."

"What made you ask about Base Fifteen, Sally?"

"Oh, nothing, really, except that before I left North Shore to go to Newcastle I had one of your men from X as a patient."

Nurse Langtry's skin prickled and shivered and twitched like a horse's. "Which one?" she asked, dry-mouthed.

"Matt Sawyer. His blindness was no hysteria."

"I knew that. What was it?"

"Walloping great tumor impinging on the optic tract. An olfactory groove meningioma. Sitting getting bigger all the time. Only it didn't cause his admission to North Shore. He had a subarachnoid bleed."

Nurse Langtry sighed. "So he's dead, of course."

"Came in comatose and passed away a week later in no pain. Shame about his family. Lovely little girls, nice little wife."

"Yes, it is a shame," said Nurse Langtry colorlessly.

A small silence fell, not unlike the silence of respect which is accorded to those of sufficiently worldly note who go to meet their Maker. Nurse Langtry occupied it by wondering how his wife had coped with Matt's blindness when she finally learned of it. What effect had it had on his children? And did his wife understand the magnitude of the stigma they had attached to him, the diagnosis of hysteria? Had his wife perhaps railed at a mind which obstinately refused to permit its eyes to see any more? Or had she been convinced something more malignant than mere mind was causing the blindness? Surely the last, if the photographer had truly captured the eyes of the real Mrs. Sawyer in that picture he used to keep on his locker. Well. Sleep easy, my dearest Matt, she thought tenderly. The long battle's over.

"What made you leave North Shore to go to Newcastle, Sally?" she asked, puzzled as to why when Sister Dawkin had dreamed so of that deputy matronship she had been willing to let it go.

"It's my old father, actually," said Sister Dawkin miserably. "Atherosclerosis, senile dementia, cortical atrophy—same difference. I had to commit him this morning."

"Oh, Sally! I am so sorry! Where is he? Here?"

"Yes, he's here. I just hated to have to do it, and I did try not to, believe me. I came home to Newcastle hoping I'd be able to manage, but Mum's well into her seventies, and she can't cope with Dad piddling his pants and taking it into his head to trot down to the grocer's without a stitch on. The only way I might have managed was to give up work entirely, but I'm the only one, there isn't that sort of money, and I'm an old maid into the bargain. No husband to bring home the Dawkin bacon, worse luck."

"Don't worry, he'll be all right," said Nurse Langtry, her voice strong with reassurance. "We're good to our oldies here, and we've got lots of them. I'll look in on him regularly. Is that how you found out I was here?"

"No. I thought you were at Callan Park, so I tried desperately to get Dad in there rather than here. I even went to see Matron at Callan Park—thank God I'm on the inside of the profession, it makes such a difference! —and I found out from her that you were here. She remembered your interview with her at once. It isn't often nurses with your kind of background front up to apply to train as mental nurses, I suppose. Well, as you can imagine, it was manna from heaven to find out you were here. I've been paddling around this place all day. Matron offered to call you off your ward to see me, but I didn't like to do that, and anyway, I'm an awful coward. Lord, I don't want to have to walk in tonight and face poor old Mum—" She stopped for a moment to compose herself. "So I put the nasty deed off for a few hours, and here I am to cry on your shoulder."

"Always, Sally, you know that. I've cried on yours."

Sister Dawkin brightened. "Yes, you certainly did, didn't you? That bloody little bitch Pedder!"

"I don't suppose you know what's happened to her?"

"No, and what's more, I don't care. Oh, by now she'll be married, I'd bet a year's pay on it. Pedder wasn't cut out to work for a living."

"Then let's hope whoever her husband is, he's comfortably off and sanguine by nature."

"Yes," said Sister Dawkin, but a little absently. She hesitated, drew a breath as if to embark upon something she found unpalatable, and spoke awkwardly. "Actually, Honour, there's another reason besides Dad why I wanted to see you. When Matron at Callan Park told me where you were, a few pennies dropped. Do you by any chance read the Newcastle papers?"

Nurse Langtry looked blank but wary. "No."

Sister Dawkin nodded. "Well, I knew you weren't a Hunter Valley girl, and I just had an idea when I found out where you were that you couldn't be reading anything out of Newcastle. Because if you did, I don't think you'd still be here."

Nurse Langtry flushed, but sat looking so proud and unapproachable that Sister Dawkin found it difficult to go on.

"Your fondness for Michael Wilson was fairly obvious to me in Base Fifteen days, and I must confess I rather expected you and him to make a go of it after the War. But when I read the story in the Newcastle paper I knew you hadn't made a go of it. Then when I found out you were here at Morisset, it looked to me as if you'd put yourself down somewhere close but not too close, maybe hoping to run into him, or planning to see him after the dust settled. . . . Honour, you don't have the foggiest idea what I'm talking about, do you?"

"No," whispered Nurse Langtry numbly.

Sister Dawkin didn't flinch; she had been dealing with situations akin to this for too many years to flinch, but she performed her duty with great kindness, understanding and directness. "My dear, Michael Wilson died over four months ago."

Nurse Langtry's face looked empty, featureless, lifeless.

"I'm not a gossip-monger, and I'm not telling you all this just to watch you suffer. But I thought if you didn't know, you ought to know. I was your age once, and I understand exactly what you're going through. Hope can be the cruelest thing in the world, and there are times when the very best thing one can do for someone is to kill a hopeless hope. I decided if I told you now, you might want to do something different with your life before it's too late, and you find yourself ingrained. Like me. And it's better that it should come from me than from some Maitland shopkeeper one nice sunny day."

"Benedict killed him," said Nurse Langtry tonelessly.

"No. He killed Benedict, and then he killed himself. It was all over a fool dog they owned that got in and played merry hell with another farmer bloke's chooks. The farmer bloke drove over to Michael's place hopping mad, and went for Michael. Then Benedict went for the farmer bloke, and if Michael hadn't managed to hold Benedict off, the farmer bloke might have died too. He went to the police instead, but by the time the police got out to Michael's place, it was all over. They were both dead. Michael had given Benedict an overdose of barbiturates, and then he shot himself. He didn't suffer at all. He knew too much about where to aim."

Nurse Langtry literally heaved her whole body away from Sister Dawkin, flopping, sagging limply, an old rag doll.

Oh Michael, my Michael! All the buried love and need and hunger leaped fully armed into consciousness. She ran with pain, she rocked with it, she smothered in it. *Oh, Michael!* Never, never, never to see him again, and she had missed him so miserably. All these months close enough to call in on him any off-duty day, and she had not. He was dead and she hadn't even known it, hadn't even felt it in the bones which missed him so much, so terribly.

The thing with Benedict had gone to its inevitable end. There was, she saw now, no other possible end for it. While he was there Benedict was safe; that was what he had to believe, for he had willingly shouldered the burden of caring for Benedict, and every duty must have its reward, in the knowledge of a job well done. So when he could no longer be sure, he had put Benedict down, quietly and kindly. After which he had no choice save to put himself down as well. No prison could hold Michael, even ward X, even Morisset. He was a bird, but the cage had to be one of his own making.

Oh, Michael, my Michael! A man is no more than he can be. Cut down like the grass.

She turned on Sister Dawkin fiercely. "Why didn't he come to me?" she demanded. "Why *didn't* he come to me?"

Was there a way to deliver the truth without hurting? Sister Dawkin doubted it, but she tried. "Maybe he just forgot you. They do forget us, you know," she said gently.

That was unbearable. "They have no right to forget us!" Nurse Langtry cried.

"But they do forget. It's their nature, Honour. It isn't that they don't love us. They move on! And we move on. None of us can afford to live in the past." Her hand swept, encompassing Morisset mental hospital. "If we did, we'd end up in here."

One by one Nurse Langtry picked up the pieces, old and cold and lonely. "Yes, I suppose we would," she said slowly. "Still, I'm already in here."

Sister Dawkin rose to her feet, slid into her shoes, held out her hand and pulled Nurse Langtry up out of the chair. "That's right, you are in here. But you're on the caring side of the fence. You've got to stay on the caring side, never forget that, no matter what you decide to do." She sighed. "I have to go. Mum's still waiting."

Oh, Sally, you're the one with real troubles! thought Nurse Langtry, walking with her friend through the foyer of the nurses' home. It was no way to end a life, too little money and aged parents and no hope of help. And eventual aloneness. All duty had bought for Sally Dawkin was more duty. Well, decided Nurse Langtry, I for one am fed up with duty. It has ruled my whole life. And it killed Michael.

They walked to where Sister Dawkin had left the car she had borrowed to move her father to Morisset; before she climbed into it Nurse Langtry reached out and hugged her briefly, tightly.

"Do take care of yourself, Sally, and don't worry about your father. In here he'll always be all right."

"I'll take care, don't worry. Today I'm down, but tomorrow, who knows? I might win the lottery. And Royal Newcastle's not such a pipsqueak of a place. I might get to be matron instead of just one of her deputies." She clambered into the car. "If you ever decide to head north to Newcastle, give me a ring, and we'll meet for a bite and a natter. It isn't good to lose all contact with people, Honour. Besides, every time I come to see Dad I'm going to force my company on you."

"I'd love that, but I don't think I'm going to be here very many days longer. There's someone in Melbourne I intend to remind that I still exist before it's too late," said Nurse Langtry.

Sister Dawkin beamed. "Good girl! You get on with your life the way you feel it ought to be lived." She let in the clutch, waved cheerfully, and kangaroo-hopped away.

Nurse Langtry stood watching for a moment, waving back, then turned to walk to the nurses' home, head bent to let her eyes follow the alternating black blurs of her feet in the night.

Neil had said he would wait for her. It wasn't very far to Melbourne if she flew. She could fly down on her next four days off. And if indeed he was still waiting, she need never come back to Morisset again. She was thirty-two years old, and what did she have to show for it? A few scraps of official paper, a few ribbons, a couple of medals. No husband, no babies, no life of her own. Just service to others, a memory, and a dead man. Nowhere near enough.

Her head lifted; she stared at the yellow squares of light all around her in this vast dumping ground for the hopeless and the destitute. When was she next due for four days off? She was on for three more days, had three days off, on for four days, then off for four days. About ten days away.

Oh, that worked out well! She wouldn't have to go to Melbourne until after the big concert. It was going to be their best effort yet, if only poor old Marg could manage to remember the two words she had to say. But she had wanted so badly to be in it no one had the heart to say no. Everyone prayed a lot, that was all. What luck charge had found out Annie could sing! She was quite a pretty little soul when she was all done up, and some of the male patients in basketry were going to make a great big wicker cage, and paint it gold, and Annie would sing "I'm Only a Bird in a Gilded Cage." The sketch about the cat and the mouse would bring the hugely uncritical house down, if only Su-Su could get through her part without falling over in a fit. . . .

Nurse Langtry halted as if a giant hand had suddenly chopped down to bar her way. What on earth am I thinking of? I can't abandon them! Who else have they got, if people like me go rushing off blindly chasing a dream? For it is a dream! A silly, immature girl's dream. This is what my life is all about. This is what I served my apprenticeship for. Michael knew. And Sally Dawkin is right. The truth is cruel, yet there's no escaping the truth forever, and if it hurts, one must simply bear the hurt. They forget us. Eighteen months without so much as a word from him. Neil too has quite forgotten. When I was the center of his universe he loved me and he needed me. What does he need me for now? And why should he love me now? I sent him on his way back to a different sort of life, bigger, more exciting, oh, yes, more exciting by far, and dewed with women. Why on earth should he remember a part of his life that gave him so much pain? More importantly, why do I expect him to remember? Michael was right. Michael knew. A strong bird needs lots of room to fly.

She had a duty here. How many people were equipped to do what she could do effortlessly? How many had the training, the knowledge, the inborn skill? For every mental nurse who had the stamina to last the three-year training period, ten didn't last. She had the stamina. And she had the *love*. This wasn't just a job—her heart was in it, fathoms deep in it! This was what she truly wanted. Her duty lay here among those the world had forgotten, or couldn't use, or sometimes just plain couldn't bear to look at.

Nurse Langtry began to walk again, briskly and without any fear, understanding herself at last. And understanding that duty, the most indecent of all obsessions, was only another name for love.

Beatific. When I was the center of his universe be

loved me and he loved me. What does he want in re

turn? And who should he love me now? I sent him an

he was back in a different sort of life, bigger, more

exciting, yes, more exciting by far, and more in tune with

anyone. What, he must ask himself, do I care about a girl of

the sort you are, just a small girl? More to the point,

why do I expect that to change? If I had, he was right

Michael spent a moment that made him feel sure of once.

So had she ... there. How many people had

experienced ... the ... a ... all ... attention ...

wanted some thing dreaming so that she ... the one in all

beginning ... there once upon ... space ... would ...